DEATH'S
FORGOTTEN REAPER

KEVIN M. BROADWAY

Table of Contents

Chapter 1: The End of Death's Reign

The air in Purgatory was unnaturally still. A world suspended between life and the afterlife, its endless gray expanse seemed to stretch into nothingness, where souls awaited judgment—many lost, some repentant, others damned. There, at the heart of this liminal world, resided Death, an ancient being whose time was nearing its end.

Death stood before his twelve reapers, his skeletal frame draped in robes of midnight black, his scythe resting heavily at his side. Behind the hollow sockets of his face, something ancient and knowing gleamed, a weight of eons that even the reapers could feel. This was not a meeting like any other—today was a turning point.

At the far end of the half-circle of reapers, Aeron's eyes on the figure of Death. Though the gravity of the moment hung in the air like a shroud, but he stood with his back straight, steady. He had always understood his purpose as a reaper, his duty to guide souls through the transition from life to death with compassion and care. But today was different. Today, the trials begin.

At Death's side stood Oblivion, the embodiment of nothingness and non-existence, a towering figure of swirling darkness without a face or discernible form. Its presence filled the room with an overwhelming pressure, a reminder of the delicate balance the Horsemen kept in the universe.

Death raised his hand, the skeletal fingers clicking together in the silence, and his voice, a hollow echo of time itself, broke the stillness. "It is time. My reign nears its end." His voice reverberated in each of the reapers' minds rather than in the air. "One of you will take my place as Death, the harbinger of souls and the keeper of the balance between life and the beyond."

Silence stretched as his words settled over them.

Merripen's eyes gleamed with barely concealed anticipation. Her gaze flickered to Aeron, the one reaper who had always stood out, the one who had earned their master's respect and that of the others with his balanced, merciful approach. Her lip curled in contempt. He didn't deserve this. She had always believed herself stronger, more deserving. After all, it was strength, not compassion, that defined a leader. She would prove that soon enough.

Aeron, standing across the hall, caught Merripen's glare but chose to ignore it, focusing instead on the swirling void in the center of the room. His heart thudded steadily, not from fear but from purpose. This is the moment I've been waiting for, he thought, his grip tightening on his scythe. For centuries, I've done my duty without question, learning what it truly means to guide a soul. Compassion, understanding, balance—these are the things that make us worthy of wielding the mantle of Death. Not arrogance, not pride.

He straightened his posture, humbled by the weight of the task but ready to face it. If I pass these trials, I can show them that strength isn't just about power. It's about knowing when to act and when to stay your hand. This is my calling, my chance to prove that mercy and resolve are what make Death eternal.

Death's voice pulled Merripen back from her thoughts. "There will be four trials. These will test more than your strength. They will test your judgment, your control, your understanding of what it means to be Death."

His gaze swept over them, his hollow sockets lingering on Aeron and Merripen longer than the others. Aeron met Death's empty stare and felt a sense of calm resolve wash over him. *I won't let him down.*

Then, without any further preamble, Death's arm rose, pointing a bony finger toward the swirling void in the center of the hall.

"The first trial begins now."

The room was replaced by a desolate plain under a sky tinged with twilight. A single soul stood before each reaper, translucent and flickering, as though caught between existence and oblivion. These were souls lost to indecision, lives full of both cruelty and kindness, beings who had not yet earned their place in any of the afterlife's realms.

Aeron blinked, the fog of the transition lifting from his mind. Before him was a woman, her hands clasped together, her eyes filled with fear. Her form shimmered, caught in the limbo between judgment and nothingness. Her life had been difficult—a child raised in violence, a woman shaped by hardship, but there had been moments of beauty, of redemption. Aeron felt them, like threads of light woven into the darker strands of her existence.

"Where am I?" the woman asked, her voice trembling as she looked around.

"You stand between life and the afterlife," Aeron said, his voice calm and full of understanding. "I am here to judge whether you peacefully move on or face oblivion."

Her eyes widened, panic flickering across her face. "Oblivion?"

Aeron hesitated, feeling the weight of her fear. He had been trained not to let emotions sway him, but this was never easy. He glanced at the others—Merripen, with her cold, calculating expression, was already moving toward her soul, her scythe held at the ready.

"I have to ask you something," Aeron said, turning his attention back to the woman. "What do you regret most?"

The woman blinked, her face tightening with confusion and shame. "I … I made mistakes. Hurt people. My children …" she trailed off, her voice thick with sorrow. "But I tried. I tried to make it right."

Aeron felt the weight of her guilt, the moments where she had fallen short, but also the light of her efforts, the genuine desire to atone. He closed his eyes briefly, feeling the balance of her life teetering before him.

"I understand," he whispered. He raised his scythe, not as a weapon, but as a tool of judgment. "Your time is finished, but your intentions were not lost. You will find peace."

The woman's eyes filled with tears of gratitude as her form began to fade, dissolving into light. She was gone. Aeron let out a quiet breath, feeling the rightness of his decision settle in his chest.

Across the plain, Merripen's voice sharply rang out. "Oblivion," she spat, condemning her soul without hesitation. Her eyes gleamed with satisfaction as the soul disintegrated into nothingness, her scythe held high in triumph. This is how you handle judgment, she thought, casting a sideways glance at Aeron, who she was certain had made the weaker choice.

When the trial ended, the twelve reapers reappeared in the hall. The transition was jarring, the silence heavy as Death surveyed his charges. His expression, as always, was unreadable, but there was something in the way his gaze lingered on Merripen and Aeron that suggested the weight of their decisions had not gone unnoticed.

Merripen stepped forward, her voice cutting through the stillness, "I made the only choice. The soul deserved oblivion. Only the strong should move on."

Death remained still, his voice a low murmur. "Your judgment was harsh, Merripen, but you performed as expected."

Merripen's chest swelled with pride, but before she could revel in it, Death's gaze shifted toward Aeron.

"And you, Aeron?"

Aeron's heart thudded in his chest, but his voice remained steady. "I judged the soul deserving of peace. There was light in her, despite her mistakes. It was not a decision made lightly."

Death slowly nodded, the silence stretching for what felt like an eternity. "You see the complexity of life, Aeron. That is what makes you different."

Merripen's eyes narrowed, the heat of jealousy sparking in her veins. Different? She clenched her fists, her mind racing with thoughts of how she would surpass him in the next trial. This wasn't over.

Death's voice filled the chamber once more, signaling the end of the first trial. "You will face three more tests. Prepare yourselves, for they will not be as simple as judgment."

As the reapers dispersed, Aeron saw Merripen glaring at him with a look filled with loathing and something more dangerous. Her ambition burned like a flame, and Aeron knew this was only the beginning.

But in his heart, he felt ready. The trials would reveal the truth about Merripen, about himself, and about what it truly meant to wield the power of Death.

And so the wheels of fate began to turn.

The reapers gathered in the antechamber of the Hall of Judgment, a vast, cold room with stone walls that stretched high into the endless gray sky of Purgatory. Between them, a heavy tension hung in the air, the gravity of what had transpired during the first trial weighing on everyone. It was rare for all twelve of them to be together in one place. Normally, they operated separately, each reaper focused on their duties across the many realms of the afterlife.

Aeron stood by himself near one of the tall, arched windows that looked out over the bleak landscape of Purgatory. His thoughts lingered on the soul he had judged. There had been no easy answers, no simple right or wrong. But that was the way of death, wasn't it? It was about balance, not just judgment.

Across the room, Kaelin—the brash, youngest reaper—piped up, breaking the silence. "I'm telling you, I did the right thing. That soul deserved oblivion." He paced, his eyes darting between the other reapers, searching for affirmation. "It was weak, corrupt … its entire life was wasted."

"Kaelin, you're an idiot," Torin, the cynical reaper, scoffed, leaning back against the stone wall and crossed his arms. "You condemned that soul because you didn't want to seem indecisive. It wasn't about right or wrong. It was about you proving something."

Kaelin's face twisted into a scowl, but before he could retort, Liora, calm and detached as always, interjected. "I chose peace," she said softly, her voice cool and distant. "There's no need to dwell on these things. Death is just a release, a transition. Why make it more painful than it has to be?"

Aeron remained silent, but his gaze drifted toward Merripen, who stood at the far end of the chamber, her expression hard, her fingers idly tracing the handle of her scythe. He could feel her resentment from across the room, the way her eyes followed him with a predatory sharpness. She had always been ambitious and ruthless. But now, there was something more in her gaze. Something dangerous.

As the reapers continued to murmur and discuss their decisions, Merripen slipped toward a dark corner of the chamber. She didn't care about the discussions of morality or balance. She was already preparing for the next trial, and for what she knew she would need to do.

Zorath, ever the silent figure, watched her move, his eyes cold and calculating. He had seen ambition like hers before. It never ended well.

Elira, mysterious and quiet, followed Merripen's movements with a curious gaze. She had always found Merripen's drive intriguing, if a little reckless. But there was more at play now, and

Elira could sense something dark brewing beneath the surface.

Merripen's eyes flickered toward Zorath, and she hesitated before moving even further into the shadowed corner of the room, away from the others. She stood with her back to the wall, her fingers drumming against her scythe.

"That was a mistake, wasn't it?" a voice whispered beside her.

Merripen turned her head to see Corvus, dark and ominous as ever, his grim face nearly concealed beneath the hood of his cloak.

"What?" Merripen asked, her voice low, filled with irritation.

"You think Aeron's decision was a mistake," Corvus said, his voice like a cold wind through a graveyard. "But you and I both know this isn't about who made the better choice. It's about power."

Merripen's eyes narrowed. She was never one to play coy, not with Corvus. "If Aeron is chosen to replace Death," she whispered harshly, her voice dripping with venom, "I will kill him."

Corvus tilted his head slightly, regarding her with that same detached grimness. "You know that's against all created law. Combat between reapers is forbidden."

Merripen let out a dark chuckle. "Laws are for the weak. If Aeron ascends, there will be no place for me. I've worked too hard to let him take what's mine. I don't care about the law. If I must, I will kill him when Death isn't watching."

Before Corvus could respond, the atmosphere in the room shifted. The air grew heavy, a dark presence swept through the antechamber. Merripen stiffened as she felt something approach, something powerful and ancient. She turned, her hand tightening around her scythe, and her breath caught in her throat.

Standing in the doorway was one of the Four Horsemen — Conquest.

The embodiment of domination and deceit, Conquest was a tall, imposing figure with golden armor that gleamed despite Purgatory's dim light. His eyes, sharp and calculating, scanned the room. When they settled on Merripen, a slow, knowing smile spread across his face. He walked toward her with a confidence that bordered on arrogance. A few reapers glanced his way, but when they noticed his attention wasn't on them, they continued their conversations.

"Merripen," Conquest said, his voice smooth and beguiling. "I overheard your little … dilemma."

Merripen tensed but didn't speak.

Conquest stepped closer, his voice lowering to a conspiratorial whisper. "You're right. To ascend to become Death … you must take it. No one will hand you such power on a silver platter."

She glanced around nervously, her eyes darting between Conquest and the other reapers, who seemed oblivious to the conversation.

Conquest chuckled. "They can't hear us. Death might be watching, but even he can't see everything."

Merripen's heart raced, her ambition and anger flaring even brighter. "If I kill Aeron, I break the law."

"The law," Conquest scoffed, "is made by those in power. If you want to become Death, you must take what is yours by force. Do you think the first Death rose to power by being compassionate? No, Merripen. Power is seized, not gifted. The others are too weak. If you wish to rise above them, you must prove you're stronger. More ruthless."

She hesitated for a moment, doubt flickering in her eyes, but Conquest leaned in closer, his voice wrapping around her like a serpent's coil.

"Think about it, Merripen," he whispered. "If you want to become Death, you must embody it. You must be willing to do what others cannot."

Merripen's jaw clenched, her mind racing. She had always known power wasn't something handed out based on worthiness or fairness. Conquest was right. If she wanted to ascend, she must take it by force.

"And if I kill Aeron?" she asked, in a whisper.

Conquest's smile widened. "Then the seat of Death will be yours."

He straightened, casting one last glance around the room. "Just remember, Merripen. In the end, the strong take what they want while the weak perish."

With that, Conquest turned, his golden armor gleaming as he strode out of the room, leaving Merripen standing in the shadows, her heart pounding, and her mind buzzing with the weight of what had just been offered.

Corvus, who had been watching in silence, finally spoke. "Are you really going to risk everything?"

Merripen's eyes hardened, her grip tightening around her scythe. "I'm not risking anything. Aeron won't stand in my way."

The room fell quiet again as the reapers sensed something shifting in the air. The second trial was about to begin.

But in Merripen's heart, a new determination had taken root—a willingness to do whatever it took to claim the power she believed was hers.

The Trial of Power

The Hall of Judgment was transformed once again. The vast stone walls of the antechamber dissolved into a desolate battlefield stretching endlessly under a dark, roiling sky. The Trial of Power had begun.

Each reaper stood alone in the barren wasteland, their tasks clear before them. Rogue spirits, wild and dangerous, had escaped from Purgatory, wreaking havoc on the realm. Their purpose was simple: subdue the spirits and return them to the underworld. But power was not the only measure of success. Control, balance, and the ability to rein in one's strength without letting it consume them were key.

Aeron stood at the edge of the battlefield, his eyes sweeping over the chaos as several rogue spirits darted across the sky, their forms twisting and turning in erratic patterns. He felt the pulse of Purgatory's imbalance, the spirits desperate to escape the order of the underworld. They were creatures of unrest, born of unfinished lives, and it was his task to guide them, not destroy them.

Across the battlefield, Merripen stood, her expression cold and determined, her scythe gleaming in her hand. She watched the spirits with a hunger that had nothing to do with balance or control. She would subdue them, yes, but she would do it with sheer force and enjoy it.

I'll show Death my strength, she thought. *I'll show him I'm the most deserving.*

With a single step forward, Merripen leaped into the fray, her scythe swinging in a deadly arc. The blade sliced through the air, and the spirits recoiled at the sheer power of her attack. She felt their panic, their fear, as she bore down on them with an intensity that burned in her chest. They scattered before her, but she hunted them with a vicious efficiency, her scythe cutting through their ranks, forcing them back toward the underworld.

Aeron moved more deliberately. His scythe wasn't a weapon, but a tool of guidance. He watched the spirits closely, his movements calculated. Instead of rushing forward with brute strength, he used his presence to corral them, guiding them back toward Purgatory's gate with patience and control. His strikes were precise, never more forceful than they needed to be. The spirits responded to his calm movements, his quiet authority.

One by one, they began to relent, drawn to the balance he presented. Aeron moved through the battlefield like a shadow, unseen but ever-present, and soon, the spirits that had been so wild and erratic began to slow, their resistance fading as they returned to the underworld.

Merripen, meanwhile, grew more aggressive, her scythe slashing through the air as she struck down spirit after spirit. She felt a surge of power with each blow, a thrill that made her heart race.

This is what it means to be Death, she thought. *This is what power feels like.*

But as she cut down yet another spirit, something shifted. The battlefield seemed to grow darker, the air heavier, and she froze as a familiar voice slithered into her mind.

"Merripen," Conquest's voice echoed in her thoughts, smooth and commanding. "You are doing well. But you could do better."

Her grip tightened on her scythe, her heart pounding in her chest.

What are you doing here? she thought, her mind racing.

"I'm here to help you," Conquest replied, his voice oozing with temptation. "I see your strength. I see your ambition. But you're holding back. You think following the rules will get you the power you crave? No, Merripen. To truly ascend, you must take what is yours. Death doesn't care about control. He cares about power."

Merripen's eyes flickered, doubt creeping into her mind. She had always believed sheer force was the answer. Strength was what Death sought. But now, Conquest's words twisted in her thoughts, planting a seed of uncertainty.

What if he's right? What if I'm wasting time trying to play by the rules?

"The trial isn't about control," Conquest continued, his voice a whisper in her ear. "It's about dominance. Show Death your true power, Merripen. Crush these spirits with all the force you have. Prove to him you're the strongest."

Merripen's heart pounded, her mind racing with the choice before her. She could feel the temptation pulling at her, the desire to unleash her full strength, to prove once and for all she was the most powerful reaper.

But something held her back. A voice—fainter, quieter—whispered in the back of her mind. Balance. Control. This is not just about strength.

She glanced across the battlefield, her eyes finding Aeron in the distance. He moved with calm, even steps, guiding the spirits with precision and care. He wasn't rushing in, wasn't overwhelming them with brute force. He was maintaining balance, showing the restraint that came with true power.

Merripen's jaw clenched. Aeron. He always seemed to make the right choice, always seemed to embody the balance that Death revered. And yet, Conquest's words echoed in her mind, filling her with doubt.

"You can't win by holding back," Conquest whispered again. "Take what's yours. Prove you're stronger than him. Prove you're stronger than them all."

Merripen's fingers tightened around her scythe, her mind at war with itself. She could feel the power surging through her, the temptation to let it loose, to dominate the battlefield with raw strength. But then a single thought cut through the haze: this isn't just about power. It's about becoming Death.

She looked again toward Aeron, who was now finishing his task, the spirits around him returning to the underworld with quiet submission. His scythe was lowered, his movements thoughtful and deliberate.

And in that moment, Merripen made her choice.

With a growl of frustration, she loosened her grip on her scythe and stepped back, her chest heaving. She would not listen to Conquest's voice. She wouldn't let her hunger for power consume her—at least, not yet. She would show Death she understood balance, even if it went against everything she had believed up until now.

As the last of the spirits were subdued, the battlefield began to fade. The sky cleared as the reapers were pulled back to the Hall of Judgment. The trial had ended.

The twelve reapers stood before Death once again, awaiting his judgment. The silence was heavy, each reaper feeling the weight of their actions during the trial.

Death's hollow voice echoed through the chamber. "You have faced the Trial of Power," he began, his tone unreadable. "And once again, you have shown me who you truly are."

His gaze swept over the reapers, lingering on each of them in turn. Kaelin fidgeted nervously, Bryn stood tall with arrogance, and Isolde's face was marred with guilt. But Death's gaze lingered longest on Merripen and Aeron.

"Two of you," Death continued, "understood the nature of this trial. Power is not just strength. It is control, balance, and the ability to wield it without letting it consume you."

Merripen held her breath, her mind still racing from her internal struggle.

"Aeron," Death said, his voice heavy with approval. "Once again, you have shown wisdom. You did not let power blind you. You guided the spirits back to Purgatory with balance and control."

Aeron bowed his head slightly, humbly accepting his judgment.

Death turned to Merripen, and her heart pounded in her chest.

"Merripen," he said, his voice softer but no less commanding. "You were tempted to let your power overwhelm you. But in the end, you made the right choice. You shown restraint. You chose balance."

Merripen's heart raced. She had done it. She was tied with Aeron now.

I am still in this.

But even as Death's approval washed over her, Conquest's words lingered in her mind. You can't win by holding back forever.

Death's gaze passed over the other reapers, the weight of his judgment settling on those who had failed to understand the trial's true nature.

"The next trial will begin soon," he said. "Prepare yourselves."

As the reapers dispersed, Merripen's mind was already spinning with thoughts of what was to come. She had made the right choice this time, but the hunger for power still burned within her. And Conquest's voice, though silent for now, lingered in the back of her mind.

She would not let Aeron win. Not now. Not ever.

And if it came down to it, she would take what was hers — by any means necessary.

The Trial of Resolve

The Hall of Judgment grew colder. The air thickened with anticipation as the reapers gathered once again. Each of them felt the weight of their choices from the previous trials. For most, the stakes were higher than ever; for Aeron and Merripen, they were personal.

Merripen stood with a look of restrained satisfaction. She had proven herself in the Trial of Power, and Death had acknowledged her restraint. She finally felt tied with Aeron. But in her heart, she knew it wasn't enough. *I'll surpass him. One way or another.*

Aeron, meanwhile, stood quiet and focused. His gaze was distant as he thought back to the previous trial. He didn't trust Merripen's sudden display of restraint. He saw the hunger in her eyes, the ambition that burned like a hidden flame. But he couldn't dwell on her motives. He needed to focus. There were more trials ahead, and he could feel the journey testing the very core of who he was.

Death raised a skeletal hand and the hall fell silent at once. His hollow gaze settled on each reaper, lingering on Aeron and Merripen, a faint spark of something ancient and unreadable flickering in his sockets.

"The third trial is upon you," Death intoned, his voice a deep echo that filled the vast hall. "This trial will test not your strength, nor your judgment, but your resolve."

A ripple of unease spread among the reapers. Resolve—true resolve—meant confronting their deepest fears, their weaknesses. Death was searching for something far deeper than mere skill or power.

He raised his bony hand, and the hall shimmered, dissolving into a landscape of darkness and shadow. Each reaper stood alone in a place of their own nightmares, a vision drawn from their inner fears and insecurities. It was a trial without weapons, without guidance. They would face their fears alone, and only those with unbreakable resolve would emerge.

Chapter 2: Aeron's Trial

Aeron found himself standing in a familiar landscape, a vast, desolate plain under a dark sky, silent and foreboding. But this time, he wasn't alone. Figures began to appear around him, souls he had once reaped. They wore faces of confusion, fear, and anger. Their hollow eyes fixed on him with a mix of accusation and sorrow.

One stepped forward, a young woman he remembered reaping not so long ago. She looked at him with tears in her eyes. "Why did you take me? I wasn't ready."

Aeron swallowed, his heart aching at the pain in her voice. "Your time had come," he replied softly. "It wasn't my choice to make."

More souls emerged, each one echoing similar sentiments. Lives had been cut short, dreams unfulfilled, families left behind. They surrounded him, voices rising in a chorus of despair and blame. Aeron felt the weight of their grief bearing down on him, an overwhelming wave of sorrow threatening to consume him.

He took a steadying breath. *This isn't real. They're echoes of past lives.* But as the voices grew louder, the doubt gnawed at him. *Was I too quick? Did I judge them fairly?*

One voice broke through the din, deeper and colder than the others. "You took their lives without a second thought," it sneered. "And now you think yourself worthy to become Death?"

Aeron's heart pounded, but he straightened, meeting the gaze of the accusing spirit. "Death is not about cruelty or mercy. It's about balance," he said firmly. "I'm not here to take for pleasure. I'm here to fulfill a purpose, to bring peace, even if it's misunderstood."

The voices grew silent, the shadows fading away. Aeron stood alone, his resolve unshaken. He knew each life he had taken had been done with care, with purpose. The pain, the grief—he would carry it, but he wouldn't let it break him.

Chapter 3: Merripen's Trial

Merripen found herself on a battlefield, strewn with the bodies of her fellow reapers, all fallen. Her scythe dripped with blood as she looked around, recognizing the faces of her comrades—Elira, Torin, Vareth—all dead by her hand. She felt a strange thrill at the sight, but then a voice whispered behind her.

"Is this what you want, Merripen? To destroy them all?"

She spun around, finding herself face to face with an apparition of Death, his hollow gaze fixed on her with cold disapproval.

"You think power is all that matters," Death said, low and cutting. "But what good is power if you wield it alone?"

Merripen's heart pounded. "They were weak. They deserved to fall. Only the strong survive."

Death's apparition moved closer, his skeletal form towering over her. "Then show me your strength, Merripen. Embrace your power. But know this—power alone will leave you empty."

The vision shifted, showing her a future where she had achieved her desire, becoming Death. She stood alone on a throne of bones, but there was no satisfaction, no fulfillment. Only a vast, empty void.

She clenched her fists, her breath heavy. *Is this truly what I want? To be feared and stand alone?*

The vision began to fade, and Merripen found herself back

on the battlefield, her scythe dripping with the blood of those she once called comrades.

For a moment, she hesitated, the loneliness creeping into her heart. But then she shook her head, steeling herself.

It doesn't matter. I'll take what's mine, no matter the cost.

The shadows dispersed, and Merriper stood alone, her resolve hardened, but a seed of doubt was taking root, one she would refuse to acknowledge.

Chapter 4: The Hall of Judgment

The reapers returned to the Hall of Judgment, each one bearing the weight of their own trial. Some looked shaken, others resolved. Death's gaze swept over them, lingering on Aeron and Merripen.

"Aeron," Death said, a faint trace of approval in his tone. "You confronted your own doubts, your own grief. Resolve lies not in denying fear, but in facing it."

Aeron nodded, acknowledging the trial's lesson. He had been tested, but his purpose was clear.

Death's gaze shifted to Merripen. "Merripen," he said, his voice softer, colder. "Your ambition blinds you. Be wary of a path where power alone drives your heart."

Merripen held her head high, her expression defiant. "I understand, Master," she replied, her voice steady. But in her heart, she felt only anger—a simmering rage at Death's subtle rebuke.

Death looked over the rest of the reapers, his expression unreadable. "The final trial lies ahead," he announced. "Prepare yourselves, for it will demand more than any of you have yet faced."

As the reapers dispersed, Merripen cast a lingering glare at Aeron, a dangerous glint in her eyes. She wouldn't lose. Not to him, not to anyone. But as she turned away, she could still feel the hollow, empty vision of herself sitting alone, the weight of her ambition pressing down on her.

Aeron, however, felt a renewed sense of purpose. He had faced his fears and doubts, and he understood the burden of what would come with becoming Death. He was prepared to carry it all, to be both the harbinger and the comforter of souls.

The stage was set. The final trial awaited them all.

The Hall of Judgment was quiet. Its cold, vast expanse filled with an oppressive stillness. Death lingered at the center, unmoving, his skeletal frame draped in shadows. Before him stood the other Horsemen: War, imposing and battle-hardened; Famine, gaunt and calculating; and Conquest, regal and ever-smirking. Each of them carried the weight of their roles, but none bore the burden of decision quite like Death.

The trials were nearing their end, and the time to choose a successor was closing in. Yet, Death's mind was clouded, the decision more difficult than he anticipated.

"The third trial is done, but still, you hesitate," War said, his voice deep and impatient. His armor clinked as he shifted, always prepared for action. "You've seen their strengths. What's left to decide?"

Death's hollow gaze swept over the other Horsemen. "This choice is not one I can make lightly," he said, his voice an ancient echo. "The balance of the universe hangs on my successor, and if I choose wrong ..."

Famine, his fingers steepled, spoke in a low voice, "You're thinking of the priestess, aren't you? The one you let live."

The mention of the priestess sent a shiver through the hall. Conquest's smirk widened, but his eyes darkened. "Ah, yes. The soul you spared. And because of your failure, the mirages were sent to fix your mistake."

War growled in frustration. "That was centuries ago. The mirages corrected the imbalance. Why are you still haunted by it?"

Death's grip on his scythe tightened. The memory of that moment lingered with him. The weight of his compassion for the priestess caused a ripple that nearly destroyed everything.

"The mirages may have corrected the balance," Death said, "but the universe was nearly torn apart. Oblivion had to intervene because I let my emotions cloud my duty. I failed to reap her, and the consequences were nearly catastrophic."

The other Horsemen fell quiet, remembering the legends of the time. The priestess had been a pivotal figure, her death a necessary step in the cosmic order. But Death had shown mercy where he shouldn't have. His compassion had delayed her reaping, and that delay had sent ripples through the fabric of the universe. The mirages — agents of Oblivion — had appeared, terrifying and unstoppable, to correct the imbalance.

"It's not just about who's strongest or wisest," Death continued, his voice somber. "It's about ensuring the same mistake isn't made again. If I choose the wrong successor, the balance could unravel, and next time the mirages may not be enough to save us."

Conquest folded his arms, his tone deceptively casual, "You're saying the next Death must be perfect. Flawless in judgment. Such perfection doesn't exist."

"No," Death admitted, his hollow eyes focused on the distant horizon of his thoughts. "But they must be close. Compassion, strength, and balance … All must be in harmony. If one outweighs the others, the consequences could be irreversible."

Famine's voice cut through the silence, sharp and brittle. "You fear your successor will repeat your mistake. But you've seen Aeron and Merripen. They are your two best options. Each has shown their strengths and weaknesses."

War's fiery eyes narrowed. "Merripen's ambition is dangerous, but it could also be her greatest asset. Aeron's compassion is much like yours."

Death turned his gaze to War. "And that's why I hesitate. Aeron's compassion is his strength, but it's also his greatest vulnerability. If he lets it guide him as I once did, the universe could again fall into an imbalance. Merripen's power and ambition could maintain the balance, but her heart is cold. She could bring about destruction without even realizing it."

Conquest's smirk returned, though his tone was serious. "So you're stuck between mercy and ambition. The compassionate reaper or the ruthless one. It's a delicate balance."

Death nodded. "Yes. And if I make the wrong decision, the universe may not survive another imbalance."

The other Horsemen were silent for a moment, each weighing Death's words. They had all witnessed the consequences of imbalance before. Though the mirages were now only a story, a legend of the past, the fear of their return was real. If the balance was disturbed again, Oblivion's intervention could tear the universe apart rather than repair it.

Finally, War spoke, his voice low but resolute, "The world still fears the legends of the mirages, but we know what's at stake. If you hesitate too long, the choice will be taken from you."

Conquest tilted his head, his voice softening as he added, "The trials have shown their resolve, their strengths, and their weaknesses. But there's one more test you can give them. One that will reveal who is truly worthy."

Death turned toward Conquest, his hollow gaze narrowing. "And what do you suggest?"

Conquest's smirk returned. "A test of mercy. The very thing that caused your failure in the past. Have them face it. Show them a situation where mercy must be weighed against duty. Only then will you know who is truly ready to take your place."

Death considered Conquest's words, the weight of them settling heavily in the silence. A test of mercy—a chance to see if Aeron or Merripen could face the same decision that had once brought the universe to the brink.

"Very well," Death said. "The final trial will be a test of mercy. And this time, the one who understands the balance between mercy and duty will be the one to ascend."

The other Horsemen nodded, understanding the gravity of the coming trial. The decision would not only determine the next Death, it would determine the future of the universe itself.

As the Horsemen faded into the shadows, leaving Death alone in the Hall of Judgment, the weight of his past failures pressed upon him. The final trial loomed, and the choice that lay before him would decide the fate of everything.

Chapter 5: The Test of Mercy

The air in the Hall of Judgment was heavy with anticipation. It felt thicker than it had before, the weight of the coming trial pressing down on every soul within the ancient chamber. Death stood at the center, his form towering and shadowed, his bony fingers gripping his scythe as he prepared to speak.

Before him, the twelve reapers stood, but only two of them held the room's full attention—Aeron and Merripen. They had survived the previous trials, proving their strength, their resolve, and their judgment. But now, the final test awaited them—a trial that would reveal their worth.

Death raised his skeletal hand, his hollow voice resonating through the chamber like a distant echo. "This is the final trial," he said. "A trial of mercy. Each of you will be faced with a single mortal soul. That soul's time has come, but the circumstances of their death are not simple. You must decide whether to show mercy or to reap the soul."

The silence deepened, and the tension between Aeron and Merripen was palpable. Merripen stood rigid, her eyes burning with fierce determination.

I'll prove I'm worthy, she thought. *I'll show him that I can balance mercy and duty.*

Aeron, on the other hand, felt a sense of quiet dread. He knew this test wouldn't be easy. The weight of the decision before him pressed heavily on his heart, but he also understood this wasn't just about mercy. It was about the delicate balance between compassion and duty. I must do what is right, even if it brings sorrow.

Death's skeletal hand swept through the air, and the chamber around them shifted, dissolving into a new scene. Each reaper now stood in isolation, faced with a mortal whose fate was in their hands.

Chapter 6: Merripen's Trial

Merripen found herself standing on the edge of a bustling city square, a bright, sunny day casting long shadows on the ground. Before her stood a woman, worn and weary, her hands trembling as she cradled a small child in her arms. The woman's life had been difficult. Years of hardship, poverty, and illness had taken their toll, but she had survived to care for her child.

Merripen could feel the pull of the woman's soul. Her time had come, but it was clear that if she died now, her child would be left alone in the world, without anyone to care for him. The thought gnawed at Merripen's mind. If I take her now, her child will suffer.

The woman looked up at Merripen, her eyes filled with quiet desperation. "Please," she whispered, "my son … He needs me. I can't leave him. Not yet."

Merripen's heart raced. *This is it. This is what Death wants to see — compassion, mercy.* She thought back to the previous trials, to the way Aeron had shown compassion and balance. *I must show mercy. That's what will prove I'm the right choice.*

Her fingers tightened around her scythe as she weighed the decision. The pull of the woman's soul was undeniable. Her time had come. But Merripen hesitated, her mind swirling with doubt.

If I show mercy here, if I let her live just a little longer, that will prove I understand mercy. That will prove I'm not heartless.

Taking a deep breath, Merripen lowered her scythe. "You may stay," she said, her voice steady but tense. "For now."

The woman's eyes widened with relief, tears streaming down her face. "Thank you," she whispered, clutching her child tightly.

But as Merripen stepped back, a cold realization crept into her heart. *Have I done the right thing?*

Chapter 7: Aeron's Trial

Aeron found himself standing in a quiet, sunlit garden, a peaceful scene that seemed almost dreamlike. Before him stood a man—old, with a gentle smile and tired eyes. The man's life had been long, filled with both joy and sorrow, but he had found peace in his final years. His family surrounded him—children, grandchildren, all of them laughing and smiling as they celebrated the simple moments of life together.

But Aeron could feel the pull of the man's soul. His time had come.

The man turned to Aeron, his eyes full of warmth and a quiet understanding. "I know it's my time," the man said softly. "I've lived a good life. But … my granddaughter … she's just learned how to walk. I'd love to see her take a few more steps."

Aeron's heart tightened. The scene before him was filled with happiness, and the man's request was so small, so simple. But Aeron knew this wasn't just about the man's desire to stay.

If I let him live, something greater may be lost.

He looked deeper into the fabric of the man's life, seeing the ripple effects of his existence. The man's death, though tragic, would allow something else to bloom. His passing would push his granddaughter to grow stronger, to bond with her family in ways that wouldn't happen if he stayed. His family's sorrow would eventually give way to a new joy—a joy that couldn't exist without his death.

Aeron knelt before the man, his eyes filled with sorrow. "I

wish you could stay longer," he said softly. "But your time has come. And though it may bring sorrow, know that your passing will create a happiness for your family you cannot yet see."

The man smiled gently, his eyes softening. "I understand," he said, a tear slipping down his cheek. "I take solace in that."

With a heavy heart, Aeron raised his scythe, and with one swift, gentle motion, he reaped the man's soul. As the man's body faded, Aeron felt the weight of his decision, but he knew it was the right one. Mercy is not always about prolonging life. Sometimes, it's about allowing life to move forward.

Chapter 8: The Hall of Judgment

The scene shifted again, and the reapers found themselves back in the Hall of Judgment. The weight of the final trial hung over them, heavier than before. Merripen's head held high, confident she'd proven her understanding of mercy. Aeron, meanwhile, stood quietly, his heart heavy but resolute.

Death stepped forward, his hollow gaze sweeping over the two reapers. His voice carrying the finality of millennia. "Merripen," Death began, "You overstepped. You were more merciful than you should have been. Mercy is not about prolonging life at any cost. You let your fear of appearing heartless cloud your judgment."

Merripen's expression faltered. "But … I thought—"

Death cut her off. "You overthought. You let your ambition to prove your worth interfere with your duty. Mercy is not just sparing a soul. It is understanding the balance between compassion and necessity."

Merripen's heart sank, the weight of her failure crashing down on her. She had miscalculated. She had failed.

Death turned to Aeron, his voice softer but no less powerful, "Aeron, you understood. You saw the sadness in the soul's passing, but you also saw the greater purpose. Mercy is not just about sparing life—it is about knowing when to let go, to allow something greater to flourish in its place."

Aeron bowed his head, accepting Death's judgment. The sorrow he felt for the reaped soul lingered, but there was also peace in knowing he had done what was right.

Death stepped back, his voice rising to fill the hall, "The trials are complete. The next Death has been chosen."

Merripen was frozen, her mind racing with disbelief. She had failed, and Aeron … Aeron had succeeded.

Aeron lifted his gaze, meeting Death's hollow eyes. There was a burden of becoming Death, but he understood now — compassion, strength, and balance. These were not separate qualities, but a harmony that must be maintained.

Death nodded solemnly. "Aeron, you will take my place."

The Hall of Judgment fell silent, and the universe itself seemed to hold its breath.

Chapter 9: The Final Night

Merripen stormed through the shadowed corridors of the Hall of Judgment, her fists clenched and her heart pounding with rage. The cold stone walls felt like they were closing in on her, mocking her with their silence. She had failed. After everything—her ambition, her strength, her resolve—Death had chosen Aeron. Aeron, of all people.

Her mind swirled with disbelief and fury. She had done everything right, hadn't she? She had shown mercy, just as she thought Death had wanted, yet it had been Aeron who succeeded. Aeron had understood something she couldn't grasp.

She slammed the door to her chambers behind her, the boom from the force echoing through the halls. Pacing like a caged animal, Merripen's mind raced.

It should have been me. I'm stronger than him. I deserve this. But even as the thoughts overwhelmed her, doubt crept in. *What if Aeron truly is the right choice?*

Before she could wrestle with her thoughts any further, a low voice interrupted the silence.

"You've been wronged, Merripen."

She froze, her heart leaping into her throat. Slowly, she turned toward the voice. Standing in the shadowed corner of her chambers, was Conquest. His golden armor gleamed faintly in the dim light, and his eyes burned with a sinister intensity.

Merripen's breath caught. "What are you doing here?"

Conquest stepped forward, his voice soft and insidious. "I'm here because I see the truth, Merripen. You've been robbed. You're the strongest of the reapers, the one most fit to wield the mantle of Death. And yet, that fool chose Aeron."

Merripen's anger flared again, hot and sharp. "He's weak. He lets emotions cloud his judgment, and now he's going to carry that weakness into the mantle of Death."

Conquest's smirk widened, his eyes gleaming with malice. "Exactly. And that weakness will be the end of us all. You know the consequences of a leader ruled by compassion, don't you? The universe nearly unraveled once because of Death's mistake. Do you think Aeron will be any different?"

Merripen's hands clenched into fists. She had always known Aeron's compassion was his greatest flaw, but now, standing before Conquest, the weight of that truth hit her with brutal force. Aeron will destroy everything.

"I should have been chosen," she growled, pacing again. "I wouldn't let the universe fall apart because of some misplaced sentimentality."

Conquest stepped closer, his voice like the soft hiss of a serpent, "Then take what's yours, Merripen. Before the mantle passes to him."

Merripen stopped, her heart racing. The thought had crossed her mind, but now, hearing Conquest say it out loud, it felt possible. "What are you saying?"

Conquest's eyes narrowed. "Tomorrow he will take the mantle of Death. You still have time. Tonight, before the ritual, you can stop him. You can kill him and take the mantle for yourself."

Merripen's breath quickened. "It's forbidden," she said, though the words felt hollow. Reapers weren't meant to fight one another—certainly not kill. It was against all law. Against everything they stood for.

But Conquest pressed on, relentless, "Laws are made by those who wield power. If Aeron takes the mantle, all will be lost. He'll tear the universe apart with his weakness. You're the only one strong enough to stop it. You're the only one who can save us."

The rage in Merripen's heart surged, fueled by Conquest's words. The heat of it burned in her chest, urging her forward. Aeron didn't deserve to be Death. If she didn't act, the entire universe would crumble under his flawed leadership.

"I'll do it," she whispered, her voice trembling. "I'll kill him before he takes the mantle."

Conquest's smile widened, satisfied. "Good. Don't hesitate, Merripen. Tonight is your only chance. Take what is yours."

As Conquest faded into the shadows, leaving her alone in her chambers, Merripen's mind whirled with anger and determination. She knew what she had to do. Aeron would never make it to the ritual.

In the heart of the Hall of Judgment, Death and Aeron stood together, the ancient scythe resting heavily in Death's skeletal hand. The room felt colder than before, the gravity of what was about to take place chilling Aeron.

Aeron looked at Death, his heart weighed down with the knowledge of what was to come. "How does the mantle pass?" he asked, his voice quiet.

"The mantle of Death is not simply given," Death said, his voice a low echo. "It must be taken, and with it, the responsibility that has burdened me for ten thousand years."

Aeron swallowed hard. "What must I do?"

Death's bony fingers tightened around his scythe. "You must reap me."

Aeron's heart skipped a beat. He hadn't expected this. "Reap you?"

Death nodded slowly. "I am not eternal, Aeron. I have a lifespan, just like the souls I've reaped. My lifespan is far longer than any mortal's—ten thousand years. But my time has come. For the mantle to pass, you must release me."

Aeron felt the weight of the scythe in his hand, heavier than ever before. The thought of reaping Death himself filled him with an overwhelming sense of responsibility—and sorrow.

"Where will you go?" Aeron asked, his voice barely above a whisper.

Death was silent for a moment, his hollow eyes staring out into the vastness beyond the Hall. "To where all gods and cosmic beings go when their time is done. A place beyond the veil, beyond existence as we know it. I will become one with the fabric of the universe."

Aeron's grip tightened on the scythe. The reality of what was to come settled over him like a heavy cloak, and in the stillness, the full weight of his future role pressed upon his shoulders.

Chapter 10: The Passing of the Mantle

The Hall of Judgment had never felt so heavy. The air itself seemed to hum with tension as the reapers gathered, their forms solemn, each understanding the gravity of what was about to take place. Death stood at the center, his skeletal figure looming over them all. The other Horsemen—War, Famine, and Conquest—stood nearby, their expressions unreadable.

This was the moment. The passing of the mantle of Death.

Aeron firmly gripped his scythe, his heart heavy. The weight of his duty pressed down on him. He knew what was coming.

Merripen, standing a few paces away, seethed inwardly. Her eyes never left Aeron, burning with a mixture of hatred and envy.

Death raised his skeletal hand, commanding silence. His voice, hollow and ancient, echoed through the hall. "The time has come," he began. "For ten thousand years, I have carried the mantle of Death, reaping souls, guiding the balance of the universe. But now, my time has ended."

The reapers stood still, their eyes fixed on Death.

"For the mantle to pass," Death intoned, his voice deeper, "it must be taken. The reaper who is chosen must reap Death, himself. Only then will the mantle pass."

A murmur rippled through the gathered reapers. Aeron nodded, understanding his role. *I must reap Death to take his place*, he thought. It was an immense responsibility, but one he had accepted.

As Death's announcement filled the hall, a voice slithered into Merripen's mind, smooth and familiar.

"See, Merripen? The mantle can be yours," Conquest whispered, his voice only audible to her. "All you have to do is kill Aeron. And then, before anyone can react, reap Death. You'll inherit the mantle."

Merripen's heart raced. Kill Aeron, then reap Death … It was such a simple plan, and yet so brilliant. She could feel the anger burning in her chest, the rage at being passed over, at being told she wasn't worthy.

I deserve this.

As Death stepped aside, gesturing for Aeron to come forward, Merripen made her decision.

Aeron took a deep breath and began walking toward Death, his scythe raised. The air in the room was thick with anticipation. But before Aeron could reach Death, Merripen lunged.

With a feral cry, Merripen swung her scythe toward Aeron, the blade glinting in the dim light. The attack came without warning, a vicious strike meant to end him.

Aeron barely had time to react. He knew combat between reapers was forbidden. He couldn't fight back, but instinct took over. He moved with incredible grace, dodging her attack with fluid, practiced motions. He ducked and spun, evading each of her strikes without raising his weapon to counter.

"Merripen!" Death's voice rang out, sharp and disapproving. "Stop this at once!"

But before Death could say more, War and Famine stepped forward, their expressions dark and cold.

"Let it play out," War growled, crossing his arms. "This is as much a test as the trials were."

Famine nodded in agreement. "Let them show who is truly worthy."

Death hesitated, his hollow eyes narrowing, but he fell silent, watching with a heavy heart.

Merripen's strikes grew more frantic, her anger pushing her to attack faster, harder. Aeron remained calm, dodging each blow with precision. His movements were effortless, as though he anticipated every swing of her scythe.

Her fury deepened. *Why won't he fight back?* she thought, her frustration boiling over. Every time her blade missed, her hatred for him grew. She needed to kill him, to prove she was stronger. This was her moment, her destiny.

Then, in a moment of desperation, Merripen saw her chance. She twisted her scythe in a deceptive maneuver, aiming to catch Aeron off guard. She swung, her scythe arcing toward him with deadly precision.

Aeron, calm as ever, raised his scythe to block hers.

The instant the two scythes made contact, the air around them shifted. A shockwave of energy exploded outward from the point of impact, shaking the very foundations of the Hall of Judgment. The Horsemen and the other reapers were thrown back, the force of the implosion so powerful it shattered the stillness of the room. Dust and debris filled the air, and for a moment, everything went dark.

When the dust finally began to settle, the reapers scrambled back, their eyes searching for the two combatants. But Aeron was nowhere to be found.

Merripen stood alone, breathing heavily, her eyes wide with shock. But then, as the realization dawned on her, a slow, wicked grin spread across her face. *He's gone.* Aeron had disappeared, and now, nothing stood in her way.

With the other reapers still recovering from the blast, Merripen turned toward Death, her eyes gleaming with cold determination. Without a word, she raised her scythe and swung it with all her might.

Death, too weak to stop her, looked at her with a mixture of sadness and resignation.

Before he could speak, Merripen's blade sliced through him,

reaping his soul with a brutal finality.

As Death's form dissolved into nothingness, Merripen felt the power surge through her as the mantle of Death passed to her. The weight of the universe settled on her shoulders, and she reveled in it.

It's mine. All of it is mine.

The Hall of Judgment fell deathly silent as Merripen stood victorious, her scythe gleaming in the dim light.

But the others knew—this was only the beginning of something far darker.

Chapter 11: Awakening in a New Life

The room was dim, lit only by the soft glow of daylight filtering through a small window. The air smelled faintly of herbs and linen. The walls were lined with wooden shelves stocked with vials and simple medical tools. Roland's eyes fluttered open, his vision blurred and unfocused. A dull ache throbbed at the back of his skull, and as he tried to move, his limbs felt sluggish, as though he'd been asleep for days—maybe longer.

The sound of soft footsteps reached his ears, followed by the quiet rustling of fabric. He blinked, slowly turning his head, and saw a woman across the room, her back to him as she folded linens. Her long hair cascaded down her back, and though he didn't know her, there was a familiarity that sent a faint shiver through him.

Where am I?

He tried to sit up, but his muscles protested, and a wave of dizziness crashed over him. His movement must have been louder than he realized, because the woman suddenly turned around, her eyes widening.

"Oh!" she gasped, dropping the linens. "You're awake!"

Roland struggled to find his voice, his throat dry. "Where …?" The word came out as a barely audible rasp. He tried to swallow, his mind sluggish and blank.

The woman crossed the room, her expression a mixture of relief and disbelief. "You've been unconscious for nearly two weeks," she said softly. "We … we didn't think you'd wake up."

Roland frowned, his mind grasping for some thread of memory, something to hold on to. But there was nothing. His name, his life—everything was a blank. "I … I don't remember."

The woman's brow furrowed, her concern deepening. She pulled a stool closer and sat beside the bed. "You were in an accident at your beat farm," she explained as she lifted a cup of water to his lips. "Your horse and plow caught a boulder in the field, and when the leather hitch snapped, the strap and buckle struck you in the head. The milk delivery boy found you and brought you in."

Roland stared at her, the words washing over him like distant echoes. A farming accident? A leather strap? None of it made sense, but there was something deeper, something far more unsettling gnawing at him.

She hesitated for a moment before continuing. Her voice softened as she added, "I'm Seraphina, Roland. I work here under Doctor Hallis, learning from him."

"Roland …" The name felt foreign on his tongue, as though it didn't belong to him. He shook his head slowly. "I don't … I don't know who that is."

Seraphina blinked, her eyes widening slightly. "You don't remember anything? Not even your name?"

Roland ran a hand through his hair, wincing as his fingers grazed the back of his head where the pain was most intense. "No," he whispered, frustration creeping into his voice. "I don't know who I am, where I am. None of this feels right."

Seraphina glanced at the door, as if considering whether she should call for the doctor. But instead, she stayed seated, her hands clasped in her lap. "You've been unconscious for so long. I guess memory loss isn't surprising after a head injury like yours. But to forget everything …"

Roland closed his eyes, trying to push through the fog in his mind. Flashes of darkness, swirling shadows, fleeting glimpses of something far beyond this small room. He couldn't hold on to any of it. It all slipped away as soon as it appeared. *Why can't I remember anything?*

After a long silence, Seraphina stood up. "I should get Doctor Hallis," she said softly. "He'll want to know you're awake. He might be able to help figure out what's going on with your memory."

Roland nodded weakly, unsure of what else to do. His thoughts swirled with confusion and doubt. The name "Roland" felt like a lie. The man Seraphina described—middle-aged, a beet farmer—none of it fit with the flashes of something far more important, far darker, that lingered just beyond the edges of his awareness.

As Seraphina left the room, Roland stared up at the ceiling, feeling a strange emptiness settle over him. *Who am I?*

Chapter 12: The Doctor's Visit

Roland's thoughts were interrupted by soft, approaching footsteps. Seraphina returned with an older man with a weathered face and keen eyes—Doctor Hallis. He carried himself with an air of authority tempered by years of experience, his movements steady and practiced.

Doctor Hallis approached the bed, his eyes carefully assessing Roland. "So you've finally decided to rejoin us," he said, his tone brisk but warm. He pulled up a stool beside Roland, his expression serious as he studied him.

"Seraphina tells me you're having trouble with your memory," he said, folding his hands in his lap. "Can you tell me what you remember?"

Roland shook his head, frustration flickering in his gaze. "Nothing. I don't know my name, where I am … everything feels like a blank slate."

Doctor Hallis nodded, seemingly unfazed. "Memory loss can be a tricky thing," he explained. "After a blow like yours, sometimes memories take time to come back, in pieces, or sometimes not at all. Other times, certain triggers—sounds, smells, dreams—can bring them back. There's no guarantee, though."

Roland looked down at his hands, flexing his fingers. He felt physically connected, grounded in his body, but his mind was a blank. "So … this could be permanent?"

"Possibly," the doctor replied with a kind but honest tone. "But it's just as likely your memories will return over time. It's best to pay attention to dreams or moments that feel familiar. They could guide you back to your past."

Doctor Hallis gave him a reassuring nod before rising and placing a hand on Seraphina's shoulder. "For now, just take it slow. Your body needs time to heal." With a final look at Roland, he turned and left the room.

Once they were alone, Seraphina sat beside the bed, studying him with a thoughtful expression. She clasped her hands in her lap, a question lingering in her eyes.

"If you don't remember who you are, where you're from … what do you know?" she asked gently. "What's on your mind?"

Roland thought for a moment, searching for any fragments of clarity. "I know … I know basic things," he began slowly. "I know what language is, how to speak, what everyday items are. It's as if I remember the essentials of living, but …"

He trailed off, and she nodded, encouraging him to continue.

"But there's no connection to anyone or anything," he finished. "It's like … I have the framework, the knowledge of the world, but nothing personal to fill it."

Seraphina tilted her head, her curiosity softening into understanding. "So, you know what things are but don't remember where they fit or who you are."

"Yes." Roland frowned, frustration and confusion clouding his expression. "I know that this is a bed," he gestured to the cot he lay on, "and I know how to describe what I see and feel. But this place … this room, the village, even myself. It's all like trying to read a book with blank pages."

She smiled faintly, a look of sympathy in her eyes. "Well, maybe I can help fill in some of those pages. We're in a village in the Kingdom of Dawn," she explained. "This place is home to many families, mostly farmers and traders. It's a quiet life here, one close to the land. We're surrounded by farms and fields, with a river not far off and mountains to the west."

Roland nodded, trying to picture it. "So this is … all there is?"

"Not quite," she said, smiling as if amused by the simplicity of his question. "The Kingdom of Dawn stretches far beyond here, connecting us to other lands and kingdoms. Great Oaks is to the south, with forests as old as the earth itself, and Tideheaven, a kingdom of islands, is scattered like jewels in the sea. And to the north ..." she trailed off, her eyes shifting as though the memory of that place brought a chill.

"The north?" Roland prompted, feeling an odd pull of curiosity.

"A cold, harsh kingdom," she said after a moment, "where many are sent but few return." She glanced back at him, her tone softening. "But it's a long way from here. Most people in this village never leave. They don't have much reason to. This world might seem small to you, but for most here, it's everything."

He listened, absorbing her words, beginning to form an outline of the place he found himself in. It was a quiet world, a grounded one. Not the blank, gray space he could vaguely sense lingering in his mind, but something solid and real, connected to the earth.

"Thank you," he said softly, his eyes drifting to the window where the faint silhouette of fields stretched into the distance, the rooftops of houses beyond. "This ... helps."

Seraphina gave him a warm smile. "There's no rush. Take your time, and let it come as it will."

He nodded, his thoughts churning with a mix of confusion and calm. This place was new, strange, but somehow, he felt a quiet pull toward it. *It's not where I'm from... but maybe it's where I belong. For now.*

With a gentle pat on his shoulder, Seraphina rose to leave. She glanced back at him, her expression kind. "And, Roland—" she hesitated, then offered an apologetic smile. "Or ... whatever name you choose to go by. Don't be afraid to ask questions. Memories sometimes come back when you least expect."

Roland watched her go, feeling an odd weight lift from his chest. She was right. He didn't know who he was, or where he'd come from. But he knew the essentials, knew the framework of the world, and that was a start.

He stared out the window, watching the wheat in the fields sway under the gentle wind, and felt a strange sense of anticipation. This world might not be where he was from, but it was his reality now. And somehow, he knew he was meant to understand it.

Chapter 13: The Storm and the Dream

The night was restless, with rain hammering against the small window beside Roland's bed. Thunder rumbled in the distance, rolling through the sky like giants in battle. Roland tossed fitfully in his sleep, trapped in a dream that felt both foreign and familiar.

In his mind, he saw flashes of lightning illuminating a dark mountainside, fierce and jagged. Shadows writhed in the darkness, figures reaching out to him, their mouths open in silent screams. A blade shimmered through the darkness, its form unmistakable—a scythe, ancient and gleaming, resting at the peak of the mountain. The sight filled him with a mixture of awe and dread, a sense of purpose he couldn't name.

A blinding flash of lightning and a scream startled him awake. He sat up, gasping for breath, his heart racing. The storm outside roared in rhythm with his pounding heart, each crash of thunder echoing the terror he couldn't shake.

The door to his room flew open, and Seraphina rushed in, her face pale with worry. She crossed to his bed, her hand finding his shoulder, offering warmth and comfort.

"Are you alright?" she asked, her voice soft but urgent. "I heard you calling out. It sounded like a nightmare."

Roland swallowed, still shaking. "I … I saw things. Lightning, shadows … There was screaming." He took a shaky breath, searching for the right words. "And a scythe, on a mountain. It was so vivid. I don't know why, but it felt … real."

Seraphina nodded, her hand resting lightly on his. "Sometimes, dreams reflect fragments of what we can't remember. A scythe … well, that could just be your imagination, or even memories of your tools back at the farm."

Roland frowned, trying to make sense of it. "But this wasn't like a tool. It felt different, like it had a purpose." He trailed off, still trying to grasp the meaning of it all.

Seraphina offered a comforting smile. "Maybe you're disoriented. A scythe can mean many things, especially if it's something familiar from your life. Once you're back at your farm, things might become clearer."

He nodded, the fear beginning to ebb, though the image of the scythe lingered in his mind, sharp and vivid. "Back at the farm. Maybe you're right. It might help me remember."

She gave his hand a gentle squeeze. "In a few days, when you've regained your strength, I'll help you get settled back at home. For now, try to rest. You've been through a lot."

Roland took a deep breath, letting her words ground him. The storm raged outside, but her presence brought him a sense of calm. He lay back down, the haunting image of the scythe slightly fading, replaced by the steady rhythm of the storm.

As he drifted off to sleep, the mystery of his dreams hung in the back of his mind, unanswered and waiting.

Chapter 14: A New Start

Morning sunlight filtered into the room, casting a warm glow across the worn wooden floor. Roland sat up, still adjusting to the idea of returning to his supposed life on the farm. He looked up when he heard the door creak open. Seraphina held a bundle of simple, well-worn clothes in her arms, a playful smile tugging at her lips.

"Well," she said, placing the clothes on the edge of the bed, "looks like it's time for you to reclaim your farm. You've had quite the extended vacation."

Roland chuckled, appreciating her lighthearted tone. "Extended vacation? Feels more like I've been in hiding."

Seraphina raised an eyebrow, amusement dancing in her eyes. "Hiding from what? Weeds? Chickens? It's a beet farm, not some enchanted castle."

They both laughed, easing some of the tension Roland felt about returning to this unfamiliar life. But before they could continue, Doctor Hallis entered, his expression a mix of professional seriousness and warmth.

"Now, Roland," he began, slipping easily into the name everyone knew him by, "take it easy out there. You're still healing. I don't want you to lift anything heavy or working in the fields until you've fully regained your strength. Patience is key."

Roland nodded, smiling gratefully. "Understood, Doctor. No beet-lifting competitions for a while."

Doctor Hallis chuckled, clapping him on the shoulder.

"Good man. And if you feel any dizziness or pain, come straight back. No heroics, alright?"

With that, Roland thanked the doctor, and he and Seraphina made their way out of the doctor's house, stepping into the crisp morning air.

The village stretched before them. People were starting their daily routines, children running down the dirt paths, and merchants setting up stalls. Roland took it all in as they began their walk, trying to find some connection to the place that was supposedly his home.

After a few moments of silence, Roland turned to Seraphina, curiosity getting the better of him. "So ... what about you?" he asked. "How did you end up as the doctor's assistant?"

She looked at him with a hint of surprise in her expression. "Oh, me? Well, I suppose it just ... happened. My family had the means, but I wanted to do something different, something useful. So I volunteered to work with Doctor Hallis, and eventually, he started teaching me more about medicine." She smiled, sheepishly. "It wasn't what I planned, but I enjoy it."

Roland nodded. "What did you plan on doing, if not this?"

She glanced away, a wistful smile crossing her face. "I suppose I always thought I'd travel, see the world beyond this little village. But that's easier said than done. Things here ... they're familiar, and they matter. People here need someone to take care of them."

Roland couldn't help but feel a hint of admiration. She was grounded, yet there was something in her—a quiet strength, a longing for more—that resonated with him in a way he couldn't quite explain.

"You must be good at it," he said softly. "It takes a special kind of person to care for others."

Seraphina glanced at him, and he saw a hint of surprise in her expression. "Thank you," she murmured, looking away with a faint blush. "And what about you?" she asked, trying to deflect the attention. "Any grand plans for when you're settled back on the farm?"

Roland chuckled, running a hand through his hair as he considered the question. "Honestly? I'm not sure yet. I think I'll just take it one day at a time." He glanced over at her, a flicker of warmth in his gaze. "But I think this village has its own kind of charm."

Their eyes met for a moment, an unspoken understanding passing between them. There was something about her—her kindness, her humor, the way she seemed to find a balance between strength and gentleness—that made him feel at ease. She was beautiful, too, in a way that went beyond appearances.

As they walked together, the village unfolding around them, Roland realized that perhaps this place, with all its simplicity, held more mystery and depth than he'd first thought. And maybe, just maybe, Seraphina was at the heart of it.

Chapter 15: The Farm and the Stranger

Roland and Seraphina walked up the path to the farmhouse. The land stretched out around them in neat, well-kept rows of beets and vegetables. The air smelled fresh, tinged with earth and the faint scent of hay. As they approached the house, Roland noticed a tall, broad-shouldered man slouched on the porch, his shirt partially untucked. He wore fine clothes, though they were a bit rumpled, and his grin was both welcoming and mischievous.

"Well, well," the man said as he straightened, flashing a grin at Roland. There was a hint of drink on his breath, despite the early hour. "So, the dead has risen." He chuckled, leaning back against the porch railing. "You had us worried there, Roland. I had my workers tending the place, thinking if you didn't wake up, I might have to take over the whole farm myself." He gave a playful wink, though there was an edge to his tone that suggested he'd been half-serious.

Roland forced a smile, unsure how to respond. The man seemed friendly enough, but he had no memory of him—or anyone, for that matter. He glanced at Seraphina for reassurance, and she gave him an encouraging nod.

The man tilted his head, looking Roland up and down with a curious gleam in his eye. "But here you are, all healthy and hale." He gave Roland a slap on the back, nearly sending him stumbling. "Though you look a bit … lost."

Roland took a breath. "I don't remember anything," he admitted, his voice steady but uncertain. "Not you, not the farm — nothing."

The man raised an eyebrow, looking at him with a mixture of amusement and curiosity. "Ah, amnesia, is it?" He chuckled. "Well, that could be your lucky break! Sell me the farm, Roland, and go start yourself a new life, free as a bird." He grinned, clearly enjoying the idea. "Leave the beets to me and find out what's beyond this patch of dirt!"

Roland forced a polite laugh, though the man's words stirred an odd sense of both possibility and discomfort. "I'll think about it."

The man chuckled again, leaning against the porch. "Well, I'd say give it a good think." His expression grew more serious, his eyes darkening slightly. "But in all seriousness, the world's a bit trickier these days. Things aren't as quiet as they used to be."

Roland looked at him, curious. "What do you mean?"

The man scratched his chin, a shadow crossing his face. "Ever since that earthquake a few weeks back, the day you, well, 'dropped off the map,' so to speak, there have been strange things happening around here. Dark beings, attacks on nearby villages." He paused, his expression grim. "Small towns getting raided by things that don't belong in our world."

Roland's pulse quickened. Something about the man's words struck a familiar, uneasy chord within him. "What kinds of things?"

The man let out a low whistle, as though searching for the right words. "Creatures, shadows ... like animals but wrong. One of my workers was attacked by a shadowy, goo-like dog. Big as a wolf, but black as pitch. The poor lad struck it with his shovel, and the thing just disintegrated into dust. A black cloud that disappeared as soon as it touched the air." He shook his head, a dark look in his eyes. "No normal beast behaves like that."

Roland glanced at Seraphina, who looked equally unsettled. "These attacks … are they happening often?"

The man nodded. "Not just here. Word's been spreading from all over. Small attacks, nothing too organized, but enough to scare folks. People say they can't kill these things, not in the usual way. They turn to dust, like they were never really here. And every temple, elder priest, and religious group around is scurrying through old texts and archives, trying to figure out what's going on."

Seraphina nodded, adding, "The largest temples in the cities are just as baffled. They're searching for anything that might explain the attacks. But as far as I've heard, no one seems to know what's causing it."

The man nodded. "Aye, exactly. These things don't seem real, and yet here they are. They've got everyone scared—priests, villagers, even the toughest soldiers."

Roland's mind whirled, piecing together the fragments of this new world. The earthquake, his sudden awakening, these strange attacks. None of it felt coincidental. A faint sense of dread settled over him, mingling with a lingering curiosity. The world he'd woken up in was far from peaceful.

"Well," the man said, shaking off his grim expression with a forced grin. "Enough dark talk for now. I'll be on my way, but remember my offer, Roland. If you ever want to sell this place, you know where to find me." He started down the steps, then paused, smirking as he looked back over his shoulder. "Well, wait … no, you don't, since you've lost your mind and all." He held out a hand. "Name's Thad."

Roland took the hand, feeling its rough strength, and nodded. "Good to meet you … I think."

Thad laughed, gave him a final nod, and headed back toward the village, his figure swaying slightly as he disappeared down the path.

Roland stood on the porch, watching him go, his mind full of questions. He felt Seraphina's hand rest lightly on his arm, grounding him.

"We'll get you settled," she said softly, though her expression was thoughtful. "If you remember anything, or if you need anything, I'll be around."

Roland nodded, looking out over the farm. This was supposed to be his life, his home, but it didn't feel even remotely familiar. The strange events, and the world's growing unease felt tied to him in a way he couldn't understand. As he looked at the fields stretching out before him, he knew this quiet life wouldn't stay quiet for long.

Chapter 16: The Dream and the Encounter

A few days passed, and Roland found himself slowly settling into the rhythms of farm life. He moved through the rows of beets, his hands working with a familiarity he couldn't explain, as if his body remembered what his mind couldn't. He was preparing the harvest to take to market, filling the back of his cart with bundles of beets when he heard approaching footsteps.

He looked up to see Seraphina, a warm smile lighting her face. She held a basket in one hand, and waved to him with the other as she walked over.

"Thought you might be ready for a break," she said, holding up the basket.

Roland's face softened, and he wiped his hands on his trousers. "A break sounds good."

They walked down to a stream that cut through the middle of the farm, the gentle flow of water reflecting the sunlight. They sat on the grass, and Seraphina began unpacking the basket—a loaf of fresh bread, some cheese, and a few ripe apples. Roland leaned back, enjoying the simplicity of the moment, though the faint memory of his recurring dreams lingered in his mind.

They ate in companionable silence for a while, but as they finished, Seraphina noticed his distant expression. "You look troubled," she said gently. "Is something bothering you?"

Roland hesitated, then decided to share what had been

haunting him. "I've been having this dream," he admitted. "The same dream, every time. There's a mountain—tall and bleak, with a plateau at the top. And on that plateau, there's … something. A blade, or maybe a scythe, lying in a heap of rubble."

Seraphina's brows knitted in thought. "That's an odd image. A scythe on a mountain. When you told me about it at the hospital, I thought it might have been your memory coming back. Do you recognize it?"

He shook his head, frustration edging into his voice. "No, but it feels like something I need to find. Like it's important."

She was quiet for a moment, then spoke thoughtfully. "From what you're describing, it sounds like Mount Limbo. It's north, overlooking the Frozen Kingdom of BrokenScale. There's nothing there but the main town and the prison. But it's strange that you'd know about it. As far as anyone knows, you've never left town."

Roland frowned, mulling over her words. Mount Limbo. The name stirred something faint within him, but it was just out of reach, like a half-remembered song. "Mount Limbo …" he murmured, letting the name settle over him.

Seraphina glanced at him, her curiosity clear. "It's just strange, that's all. Dreams are odd things, but they don't usually show you places you've never been."

Before they could delve any further, a rustling sound in the nearby thicket caught their attention. Roland turned, his gaze narrowing as the bushes shifted and parted. In an instant, a large wild boar burst from the brush, charging directly toward them.

But this was no ordinary boar. Its hide was black as pitch, seemingly dripping with a dark, viscous goo that left slick patches on the grass. Its eyes gleamed with a strange, eerie light, and it moved with an unsettling purpose.

"Get back!" Roland shouted, instinctively shoving Seraphina to the side, out of harm's way. He scrambled to his feet, his eyes darting around for anything he could use as a weapon. Nearby, propped against his cart, was a hoe.

He grabbed it, gripping the wooden handle tightly,, and turned to face the creature. The boar circled him, snarling, thick black drool seeping from its tusks. In the back of his mind, he remembered Thad's warning about the dark, unnatural creatures that had been appearing since the earthquake.

As the boar charged, Roland swung the hoe, but the creature was faster than he anticipated. The hoe missed, and he felt the sharp pain of its tusk slashing across his calf. He stumbled back, gritting his teeth, but the wound wasn't deep. He could still fight.

The boar turned, preparing to charge again. This time, Roland steadied himself, closely watching the creature's movements. As it rushed toward him, he tightened his grip on the hoe and swung with all his might. The metal struck true, connecting with the boar's head.

Instantly, the creature froze, its form trembling as though struggling to hold itself together. With a sickening hiss, it disintegrated, dissolving into a cloud of black dust that scattered into the air.

Roland lowered the hoe, breathing hard as he stared at the empty space where the boar had been. The sight left him shaken; this wasn't just a strange animal. It was something far darker. Something that didn't belong.

Seraphina scrambled to her feet, rushing to his side. "Are you alright?" she asked, her voice thick with worry.

Roland nodded, though his mind was still reeling. "I'm fine. It barely grazed me."

She looked around, her eyes wide with unease. "That … that wasn't natural."

"No," Roland agreed, a chill creeping up his spine. "It wasn't."

They stood together in the stillness, the residue of the dark creature's dust floating in the air. Roland knew this encounter was no mere coincidence. Whatever these beings were, they had come for a reason. And somehow, he felt certain that his past—whatever it was—held the key to understanding it all.

As the eerie black dust drifted away on the breeze, Roland and Seraphina stood by the stream, catching their breath. The unexpected confrontation left an electric tension hanging between them. Seraphina glanced at Roland, her brows furrowed.

"You just threw me out of the way without a second thought," she said, half-serious and half-amused. "Usually, people at least hesitate before tossing a lady aside."

Roland met her gaze, the faintest hint of a smile on his lips. "Guess I'm not 'most people.' Besides, it seemed like the right thing to do. To keep you safe."

She tilted her head, a teasing glint in her eye. "Aren't you supposed to be the injured farmer? Yet you fought like you've been doing it your whole life."

His expression shifted, a flicker of uncertainty crossing his face. "I can't explain it. I just reacted." He paused, looking down at his hands. "But it was more than instinct, wasn't it? That creature ... it seemed like it was coming after me."

Seraphina's eyes narrowed thoughtfully. "You're right. It didn't even look at me. And the way it moved—it was almost like it knew who to target. As if it was sent."

Roland nodded, a dark sense of dread forming in his stomach. "But who, or what, would send something like that after me?"

Silence stretched between them, broken only by the soft murmuring of the stream. Seraphina wrapped her arms around herself, glancing back at the spot where the creature had disintegrated. "I think we need more answers than either of us have right now."

Roland looked at her, waiting as she seemed to weigh her words carefully.

"There's one person in this town who might have some insight." She turned back to him, her gaze resolute. "The priest. He's a little odd, but he knows a lot about the old beliefs and strange happenings. If there's anyone who can shed light on this, it's him."

He gave her a small, grateful nod, his face softening. "Thanks, Seraphina. For everything."

She raised an eyebrow, a slight smile curving her lips. "For everything? You mean saving your hide from a goo-like boar?"

Roland chuckled, the tension lifting a little. "And for being thrown across the grass. Though if that's what it takes to keep you safe, I'd do it again without hesitation."

Seraphina shook her head, laughing. "Well, let's hope next time you're not quite so reckless. But thank you. I do feel a little safer knowing you're around."

Their eyes met, and for a moment, there was a deeper warmth between them, unspoken but undeniable.

"Well," she said, breaking the silence and looking toward the village. "Shall we go see this priest?"

Roland nodded, and they began gathering their things, readying themselves for the walk to town.

Roland and Seraphina left the farm, the lingering memory of the creature casting a shadow over them. As they neared the edge of the village, they spotted one of the townsfolk, an older man named Joss, leaning against his cart stacked with bundles of hay.

"Ah, afternoon you two," Joss called, eyeing them curiously. "Heard a ruckus from the farm. Everything alright out there?"

"We managed," Roland replied, exchanging a glance with Seraphina. "Actually, we're headed to see Reverend Ted. You haven't seen him around, have you?"

The old man chuckled, a knowing smile spreading across his face. "Our Reverend? Last I saw, he was wrangling with a wedding sermon for the Mayor's daughter. Poor fella's been locked up in the temple half the day. Seems he forgot how to tie his own robes."

Seraphina stifled a laugh, and Roland's lips twitched in amusement.

"Sounds like he's working hard," Roland replied.

"Oh, that he is," Joss said, nodding sagely. "Hard as ever. Real pillar of wisdom, our Reverend Ted."

"Thanks, Joss," Seraphina said with a grin. "We'll go relieve him from his studies."

The two continued into town, sharing a quiet laugh as they walked up the winding path to the temple. The building was modest, worn with age but well-kept. A small bell above the door swayed gently in the breeze. As the two stepped into the temple, the scent of aged wood and incense drifted over them. Inside, Reverend Ted was hunched over a desk, furiously scribbling on parchment, his robes slightly askew. At the sound of footsteps, he looked up, eyes widening as he recognized Seraphina.

"Ah, Seraphina! And Roland, of course!" he greeted, quickly gathering himself and standing, attempting a look of dignity that came off a bit awkward. "To what do I owe the pleasure of this most ... divine visit?"

Roland and Seraphina exchanged a glance, both holding back smiles.

Seraphina stepped forward, clasping her hands with a polite smile. "Reverend Ted, we were hoping you might be able to help us with something ... unusual that happened on the farm."

Ted's eyebrows shot up, and he attempted to soften his features to a more serious expression. "Oh, unusual, you say? Well, I'm quite familiar with unusual things," he said with a wave of his hand. "What kind of unusual are we talking about?"

Roland cleared his throat. "We were attacked by some kind of creature," he began. "A black, goo-like boar that disintegrated when I struck it. Seraphina and I have never seen anything like it."

Ted's eyes grew wide, and he stared at Roland, mouth slightly open, before composing himself. "Ah, yes, well ... that does sound ... profoundly unusual." He shifted, glancing down at his papers as though searching for something. "You see, creatures like that, Ted, it's, uh, rare. Very rare indeed."

Seraphina leaned in, trying to catch his eye. "Ted, do you know anything at all about these creatures? Or perhaps if anyone else has seen anything similar?"

The reverend scratched the back of his neck, clearly floundering. "Well, to be honest, creatures of that sort are, uh ... a bit out of my expertise. I mostly handle, you know, weddings and funerals. Important matters," he added quickly, a touch defensively.

Roland exchanged a sidelong glance with Seraphina. "Do you know anyone who might know more?"

Ted's face brightened with relief. "Ah! Now *that* I can help with! I've got a friend, a fellow priest, in a larger town to the west," he said, tapping his forehead as though pulling the thought from the air. "Reverend Gregory. Now, he's the smart one, knows all sorts of things. Keeps his nose in old books and records. He's been sending me letters about strange attacks cropping up in his town, even more than here. Says it's been happening two, maybe three times a day." He nodded, as if impressed by his own answer. "Likely has something to do with their population, but, well, that's just my theory."

Seraphina gave Ted a warm smile. "Thank you, Reverend. It sounds like Reverend Gregory might be just the person we need to speak to."

Ted puffed up, pleased with himself. "Glad I could be of help! I always knew I'd come in handy someday For more than weddings and funerals." He coughed, straightening his robes with an air of importance. "If you do go to see him, please give him my regards. Tell him I sent you, so he'll know you're … reputable."

Roland stifled a chuckle. "We'll be sure to mention it."

He and Seraphina shared a glance, both of them suppressing smiles as they turned to leave, the sound of Reverend Ted shuffling his papers filling the quiet temple.

As they walked back through town, Roland noticed the subtle tension in Seraphina's expression as she considered the task ahead. The soft afternoon light gave the village a warm glow, but there was an undercurrent of anticipation between them.

"So, heading west?" Roland prompted, giving her a sidelong glance.

A slight smile tugged on her lips. "It won't be a simple trip. I've never actually left the village before. Not for this long. The journey alone could take up to a week. Maybe more, depending on the weather and how the roads are."

Roland nodded thoughtfully. "Guess it's a first for both of us. I can't remember ever traveling before, but I suppose that's not surprising."

His tone was light, but there was a hint of frustration beneath it, and Seraphina caught it.

"Hey, it's a fresh start, right?" She nudged him playfully, her smile widening. "Besides, you handled that creature today easier than I expected from a beet farmer. Who knows? Maybe you're a natural traveler, too."

He chuckled. "I'll take your word for it."

They walked in comfortable silence for a few minutes, passing fields and cottages until the path veered back toward the edge of the village where his farm sat. As they neared the house, Seraphina took a deep breath and turned to face him.

"I'll need to go home and prepare a few things," she said, her voice soft. "If we're really going to do this, I want to make sure we're ready. Clothes, food, bandages … everything we might need on the road."

Roland nodded, feeling a strange blend of excitement and trepidation. "Makes sense. I guess I'll pack up whatever I have that might be useful."

She hesitated, her gaze lingering on him. "I'll meet you at sunrise tomorrow, here at the farm," she said. "This ... this is a big step for me. For both of us."

He nodded, his gaze steady. "Then we'll take it together."

She gave him a small, appreciative smile, then turned to leave. Roland watched her go, feeling the weight of the journey ahead settling over him, mingling with the sense that this was just the beginning of something larger than either of them had anticipated.

As the sun dipped lower in the sky, Roland found himself alone on the farm again, the quiet sounds of animals shuffling in their pens and the gentle rustling of leaves his only company. He paced the familiar grounds, casting his eyes over the fields with an odd sense of detachment. Though memories of this place had begun to resurface, they felt distant, like someone else's life.

He lingered by the fence, watching his mule, Koko, chew contentedly at a patch of grass. The loyal creature lifted his head, sensing his gaze, and gave a small bray in acknowledgment. Roland smiled faintly. Koko was the one part of this farm he actually felt connected to. Steady and reliable, he had been his companion through all the chores and routines, day in and day out.

Roland thought about the rows of crops, the sturdy little farmhouse, and the stretch of fields. There was something hollow in it all, something that made him realize leaving wouldn't be as difficult as he'd imagined. This life, this farm — he could let it go.

With a slow exhale, he made a decision. He'd take up Thad's offer to buy the farm. He didn't need much, just Koko and a few essentials. Everything else would be better off in the hands of someone who actually wanted to be here.

As twilight settled, he made his way across town to the other man's property. The man, a burly figure with a jovial grin and slightly too much ale in his breath, met him on the front porch.

"Well, if it isn't Roland!" the man said with surprise. "Didn't expect you'd be coming 'round this soon."

Roland offered a faint smile. "I've been thinking about your offer Thad. I'd like to take you up on it. I'm leaving tomorrow, so the farm could be yours, if we can agree on a fair price."

The man's eyes brightened, but he tried to play it cool, rubbing his chin thoughtfully. "Ah, well, you know, Roland, that farm of yours is a bit run down. It'll take some real work to get it back up to snuff."

Roland suppressed a sigh, understanding the game. "The land's solid, and the crop yield was strong last year. It's worth a fair price, especially since I'm leaving most of the livestock and equipment." He actually wasn't sure if the crop was strong last year.

The man hummed, eyeing Roland for a moment before finally relenting. "Alright, alright. How about this?" He made an offer, which Roland countered until they finally settled on a price that would give Roland enough coin for his journey without completely emptying the man's pockets.

As they shook hands on it, Roland's eye caught something glinting in the corner of the room—a sword with a worn leather scabbard, hung carefully on a hook. The blade looked old but well-cared for, its hilt adorned with a simple yet elegant cross guard.

"What about the sword?" Roland asked, gesturing at it.

The man raised an eyebrow, his grin growing wider. "Ah, that beauty? That's a family heirloom," he said, his voice taking on an almost reverent tone. "Belonged to some great knight in the family, they say. Not that I've much use for it, being more of a plow-and-pitchfork man, myself."

Roland met his gaze steadily. "Throw it in with the price we agreed on, and I'll take it off your hands."

The man hesitated, visibly weighing his attachment to the sword against the lure of easy coin. After a moment, he gave a resigned chuckle. "Alright, Roland, you drive a hard bargain. She's yours. But keep in mind, that's no ordinary sword. She's got history in her."

Roland accepted the sword and the handful of gold coins the man pressed into his hand. The sword felt good. The weight was both familiar and foreign, as if his hand had known the feel of a sword long before he'd ever been a farmer.

"Thank you," Roland said, fastening it at his side.

The man nodded, giving him a rough slap on the shoulder. "Safe travels, Roland. And give ol'Koko a good pat for me. He's a gem, that one."

Roland nodded, feeling a sense of resolution settle over him as he walked back toward his farm. Tomorrow, he would leave behind this life and step into the unknown, armed with only the essentials, Koko, and the curiosity that had led him this far.

As Roland approached the farm, he had the distinct feeling something was off. The usual quiet stillness was broken by an absence he couldn't quite place. Koko, his faithful mule, was no-where to be seen, not standing in his usual spot near the gate. Roland's brow furrowed as he scanned the field, a prickling sense of dread settling over him.

Suddenly, a series of sharp, panicked brays echoed from the far end of the pasture. He turned just in time to see Koko gallop-ing erratically, nostrils flaring and eyes widening with terror. But it was what followed him that sent a jolt through Roland's spine. A hulking, bear-shaped creature covered in thick, inky black goo, its form shifting and writhing like molten tar.

Without thinking, Roland vaulted over the fence, his boots hitting the ground with a thud. At that exact moment, the dark bear, which had been closing in on Koko, froze in its tracks. Its head snapped up, fixing Roland with a soulless stare. It was as if an invisible force had pulled the creature's attention directly to him, and Koko, momentarily freed from the pursuit, bolted toward the edge of the pasture, away from the threat.

The bear's dark, empty gaze locked onto Roland, and then it charged. Adrenaline rushed as he sprinted toward the stalls, the creature's pounding footsteps growing louder with each second. Roland jumped over a line of square hay bales, his heart racing as he heard the bear closing the distance. But as he turned, his boot caught on an old bucket he'd carelessly left by the stall door.

He crashed to the ground with a "Umph," the breath knocked out of him. He instinctively reached down, feeling the cold metal of the sword at his side. He barely had time to register what he was doing; his body acted reflexively, pulling the blade free as he rolled onto his back.

With a low, guttural snarl, the dark bear leapt over the hay bales, its massive, gooey form casting a shadow over him. Roland had no time to stand or swing. He raised the sword, pointing it upward as the creature descended.

The bear hit the blade full-force, its dark body seeming to melt around the sword's edge. It let out a distorted, human-like wail as its form dissipated into thin air, leaving only a faint residue of black dust that quickly vanished into nothing.

Roland lay there, breathing hard, his eyes fixed on the now-empty space where the creature had been. He glanced down at the sword, still gripped tightly in his hand, its blade gleaming in the fading light.

For the second time that day, Roland felt that strange sense of familiarity—the sword, the way he'd instinctively used it, felt like pieces of a puzzle that hadn't quite clicked together yet.

Roland lay on his back, catching his breath as the shock of the encounter settled into a strange calm. Just as he began to gather his thoughts, he felt warm breath on his forehead. He opened his eyes to find Koko, nostrils flaring, staring down at him. The mule let out a snort, his ears flicking back and forth before giving Roland an affectionate, slightly slobbery lick across the cheek.

Roland chuckled, gently pushing Koko's face away. "You've got impeccable timing, you know that? And here I thought you'd be the brave one."

Koko snorted again, his big eyes blinking as if he were trying to follow along. Roland shook his head with a smile. "So much for survival skills, huh?" he muttered, giving the mule an affectionate pat. "But thanks for coming back. Brave soul, that's what you are … in your own way."

He pulled himself to his feet, still a bit shaken but grateful for the odd comfort Koko's presence brought. As he brushed himself off, he glanced toward his farmhouse, knowing he still had preparations to make for tomorrow's journey.

Inside, he set about gathering what he'd need—food, a sturdy cloak, a small bedroll, and a pouch for the coins he'd acquired. He lingered on the sword, running his fingers along the hilt, feeling the weight of it as he secured it at his side. With Koko waiting, he stowed the supplies in a pack, the night's silence filling the small house as he mentally prepared himself for the journey ahead.

Once everything was ready, Roland lay down on the bed, exhaustion pulling at him. But his mind continued to race, lingering on the day's events, the strange creature, and the inexplicable instincts that had guided him. Slowly, his eyes grew heavy, and he drifted off to sleep.

In his dream, Roland was no longer in the farmhouse, but standing on a barren mountain plateau, the wind whipping around him. At the far edge of the cliff, illuminated by a dim, ghostly light, lay a scythe, its dark, ornate handle reaching up like a hand, a shadow against the sky.

A deep, resonant voice echoed through the air, as if coming

from the very mountain itself. The voice was powerful, commanding, yet strangely familiar.

"Aeron ..."

The name echoed, a comforting presence that seeped into his bones, warming him. The sound of it felt like a key slipping into a lock, fitting into a place deep within him that he hadn't known was there.

"You are chosen ..."

The words blurred, slipping away like sand through his fingers. But the name—Aeron—remained, repeating with a warmth that felt like home. He clung to it, letting the sound wash over him, grounding him in a way he couldn't understand. It felt right, true, as though he were discovering himself for the first time.

Then the dream began to fade, and the mountain and the scythe disappeared into darkness.

Roland woke with a start, his heart pounding. He lay in the stillness of the farmhouse, staring into the dimness of early morning. He whispered the name aloud, tasting it, feeling its strange familiarity settle over him.

"Aeron ..."

It didn't make sense, and yet ... it felt more real than anything he could remember. Roland was a name, a memory, but Aeron—that felt like truth. He sat up, the weight of the revelation lingering as he prepared to face the day, the name echoing softly in his mind.

The first light of dawn painted the sky in soft hues of pink and gold as Seraphina made her way down the dirt path to Roland's farm. The air was cool, filled with the scent of morning dew and the quiet song of birds waking up with the sun. As she approached, her eyes fell on Koko, who stood patiently near the gate, saddled down with packs and supplies. The mule seemed to shift restlessly, his eyes bright and alert, as if he already sensed an adventure on the horizon.

But it wasn't just Koko that caught her attention. Roland—or rather, the man she thought of as Roland—was waiting as well, his figure silhouetted against the morning light. He looked different, dressed in sturdy traveling clothes that hinted at the journey ahead, but her eyes landed on the sword strapped to his back. It was unexpected, so out of place with everything she knew about the mild-mannered farmer.

She approached, raising a hand in greeting. "Good morning, Roland. Or should I say, warrior?"

Aeron—though he still hadn't fully settled into the name—turned at the sound of her voice, a grin breaking across his face. "Morning, Seraphina."

She took in the sight of him, her gaze drifting to the sword. "Alright, explain this new addition. I never took you for a swordsman."

He chuckled, reaching back to tap the hilt. "A lot has changed since we last spoke," he said. "I sold the farm last night to that other farmer. Figured I wouldn't need it anymore. Not with everything going on. Got this sword thrown in the deal as well, so it seemed like fate, you know?"

Seraphina raised an eyebrow, clearly intrigued. "And just like that, you're ready to be an adventurer?"

"Well," he replied, his smile fading slightly, "last night, after I made the deal, I came back here, and there was another one of those creatures. A bear this time, black and covered in that strange goo. It went after Koko, but when I jumped the fence, it changed its mind and came after me instead."

Her eyes widened in alarm, and she took a step closer. "Another attack? Are you alright?"

"Yeah," he nodded, still feeling the faint adrenaline of the encounter. "It went down, like the last one. I used the sword, which, honestly, was pure luck. I tripped and ended up pointing the blade just in time for the thing to ... well, disappear."

Seraphina looked at him with a mix of concern and admiration. "So you've sold the farm, faced down two dark creatures, and now you're heading out with a sword and supplies. You really are creating a new life for yourself."

Aeron paused, glancing down at the ground before meeting her gaze. "That's actually something else I wanted to tell you." He hesitated. "After the bear attack, I had a dream. It wasn't like the others. It wasn't just a vision. I heard a voice … calling me by a name. Aeron." The name hung in the air between them, feeling strange yet right on his tongue. "And I realized, I've never felt connected to 'Roland.' But this name, Aeron, feels like mine."

She looked at him, surprised but slowly nodded as she absorbed his words. "Aeron … well, I can't explain it, but it does suit you."

He laughed softly, rubbing the back of his neck. "Guess it's about time I let go of Roland. Besides," he added, with a hint of a grin, "considering the bears are coming for the beets, I think I made a smart decision."

Seraphina laughed, shaking her head. "Well, I suppose if it means one less bear attack, I'll call you whatever you want. Aeron it is, then." She gestured toward Koko, giving the mule an affectionate pat. "Seems like he's ready to go, too."

Aeron smiled, feeling a surge of confidence settle over him. "Then let's not keep the road waiting. Aeron and Koko are ready for whatever lies ahead."

With a final glance around, Aeron tightened his pack, nodding to Seraphina as they set off toward the western road, the beginning of a journey that would lead them to answers, and perhaps even more questions.

Chapter 17: The Road to Fort Gray-stone

The morning sun was still climbing as Aeron and Seraphina set off, Koko dutifully plodding along beside them with his packs securely fastened. The road was calm, the kind of peaceful that let them almost forget the strange creatures that had haunted Aeron's farm over the past few days. They walked in companionable silence, with the faint chirping of birds and rustling of leaves filling the gaps.

As they passed a stretch of woods, however, the peace was shattered. A flash of movement came from the shadows, and a small, dark figure darted into their path. Aeron barely had time to react before the creature—a wolf-like shadow, though smaller than the one he'd fought back at the farm—leapt toward him.

Aeron's sword was out in a flash, meeting the creature head-on. The wolf lunged as Aeron raised the sword, but the creature immediately changed course. Unable to stop, the wolf went low, knocking Aeron off his feet. They both struggled to their feet, and as the wolf moved to snap at Aeron, he swung the sword, and the dark creature dissipated into a swirl of black dust.

Breathing hard, he lowered his sword. Seraphina, wide-eyed but steady, stepped forward. "Well, that was an exciting start to the trip. They really seem determined to get to you."

Aeron nodded, wiping sweat from his brow. "Seems like they're tracking us. I don't know how, but it's like they're following something."

They exchanged a look, unspoken worry hovering between them, then resumed their journey.

That Evening: The Tent Realization

As the day wound down, they found a quiet spot by a grove to set up camp. Aeron knelt to unpack his gear, pulling out the tent he'd packed without much thought. As he unfolded it, a realization dawned over him.

He glanced at Seraphina with a sheepish grin. "I only brought one tent."

She paused, raising an eyebrow. "One tent? What were you planning, Aeron? Cozy quarters?"

He shrugged, chuckling lightly. "Guess I didn't think that far ahead. But hey, it'll be cozy. We'll stay warm, right?"

Seraphina shook her head, smirking. "Just make sure you leave me some room." She rolled her eyes but couldn't hide a faint smile as they set up the tent, both of them adjusting to the idea of sharing.

Inside, as they tried to make themselves comfortable, Aeron muttered, "At least if another one of those creatures shows up, we're both within reach of protection."

She nudged him playfully. "Just don't hog the blanket, 'Aeron.' Or should I say, 'beet farmer turned warrior'?"

They shared a quiet laugh, the tension of the day easing as they settled into the shared space. Despite everything, the moment left them both feeling more comfortable—an unspoken trust growing between them.

Second Day: The Squirrel Attack

As they moved through a denser part of the forest, a faint

rustling from above caught Aeron's attention. He paused, scanning the trees. "Did you hear that?"

Before Seraphina could respond, a small, dark creature darted down from the branches. A squirrel-shaped mass of black ooze, eyes glinting with a wild intensity moved fast, lunging directly at Aeron and sank its teeth into his forearm before he could react.

Aeron let out a sharp gasp, flinging his arm in an attempt to shake it off. Seraphina, caught off-guard, stumbled backward, catching a scrape as she reached for her own defense.

The creature leapt again, swift and relentless, and Aeron finally managed a solid swipe with his sword, causing it to dissolve into wisps of black dust. He looked down at his arm, where faint punctures marked where the creature had bitten.

Seraphina approached, examining his arm with a concerned frown. "Even the smallest of them are getting more aggressive."

Aeron gave a dry chuckle, rubbing his sore arm. "So much for starting small, huh?"

Her expression remained tense. "We'll need to stay sharp if we're running into these things every day."

They both shared a determined look, ready to press on, despite the escalating challenges. The journey was proving harder than expected, but each new test only seemed to bring them closer together.

After defeating the swift, squirrel-like creature, Aeron and Seraphina continued down the winding forest path. The bite marks on Aeron's arm stung, but he ignored it, determined not to show discomfort. As the hours passed, they found a rhythm, the day's quiet was broken only by Koko's steady steps and the occasional breeze rustling through the leaves.

By the time dusk fell, they were nearing the end of their strength, grateful to find a small clearing to make camp. Seraphina gathered kindling, and soon a modest fire crackled between them, casting a warm glow over the campsite. She prepared a simple meal, stirring together a mix of wild herbs, dried meat, and vegetables they'd packed. The savory scent filled the air, and Aeron's stomach rumbled.

"Never thought I'd be this grateful for a hot meal," he said, accepting a bowl from her.

Seraphina gave him a half-smile, sitting back. "Let's just hope it's enough to keep us going. We've still got a long way to go."

The warmth of the fire and the food eased the tension of the day. But just as they were beginning to relax, a low growl broke the quiet. A small, dark creature, cat-like in shape but with that same unsettling black ooze, slinked into the firelight.

Aeron sighed, setting his bowl aside and reaching for his sword. "I don't suppose we'll get a night off from these things?"

Seraphina shook her head, standing and stepping back to give him space. "Doesn't seem like it."

The creature lunged, quick and agile, but Aeron had grown accustomed to their movements by now. With a few swift strikes, he managed to land a blow that sent it dissolving into black dust, the eerie particles vanishing into the night.

After ensuring it was truly gone, Aeron sheathed his sword, settling back down beside the fire with a weary look. "I'd say they're getting bolder, but maybe it's just our luck."

Seraphina shook her head, a soft laugh escaping her. "If this is your luck, I hope mine's better."

They shared a chuckle, and Seraphina finally settled back down, pulling her cloak around her shoulders as they relaxed by the fading firelight. After finishing their meal, they prepared their modest camp for the night, each sinking into their own thoughts as the exhaustion of the day caught up with them.

The first light of dawn filtered softly through the tent, casting a gentle glow over Seraphina's sleeping form. Aeron lay awake, his gaze drifting over her, drawn by the peaceful rise and fall of her breath. In the quiet of the morning, he found himself noticing details he hadn't before—the delicate curve of her lips, the way her hair framed her face, the relaxed beauty that seemed so different from her usual lively energy.

His thoughts wandered, admiration mixing with curiosity about the woman who had chosen to join him on such a journey. There was a strength in her he respected, but also a warmth he hadn't realized he missed.

Lost in thought, he didn't notice her eyelids flutter open. She caught him staring, a slow smile spreading across her face.

"Enjoying the view, Aeron?" she murmured, a hint of amusement in her sleepy tone.

Aeron blinked, caught off guard, and quickly looked away, a faint blush coloring his cheeks. "Just waiting for you to wake. Long day ahead," he muttered, failing to mask his embarrassment.

"Oh, I bet," she replied, propping herself up on one elbow. "But if you're going to be watching me while I sleep, I might need to start charging for the privilege."

He chuckled, the tension easing. "Well, consider it payment for saving you from that terrifying squirrel yesterday."

She rolled her eyes, laughing softly. "Ah, yes, our first great battle together. Just don't tell the villagers. It'll ruin your reputation as a fierce swordsman."

Aeron grinned, feeling lighter as they shared the joke. They stretched, the awkwardness fading as they prepared to break camp, the bond between them feeling just a bit stronger as they packed up to face another day on the road.

The towering stone walls of Fort Graystone loomed ahead, the worn but sturdy gates marking the town's quiet authority. Aeron and Seraphina exchanged a look of relief, feeling the weight of their journey begin to lift as they neared the fortified city.

But the respite was short-lived. A low growl echoed from the tree line just to their left, and Aeron instinctively reached for his sword. Emerging from the shadows was a dark creature, larger than any they'd faced yet. Its sleek, cougar-like body crouched low, muscles coiled as it prepared to strike.

The creature lunged, and Aeron met it with a swift swing of his blade. This creature was faster, dodging and circling back to swipe with its sharp claws. Aeron spun and swung the sword again, landing a strike, the swinging again and landing another, but the creature was resilient, and each hit dispersed only a fraction of the oily darkness. Suddenly, it pounced, its jaws finding the same spot on Aeron's arm that the squirrel had bitten days before. He gritted his teeth, stifling a cry of pain as it tore through the already tender flesh.

Seraphina shouted, searching for something to throw or knock it back with, but her attention shifted as a distant voice called out. From the gates, a guard had spotted the struggle. With a smooth, practiced motion, he drew his longbow, aimed, and let an arrow fly. The shot struck true, landing squarely in the creature's shoulder, causing it to release Aeron's arm with a guttural hiss. Another shot, and the creature finally dissipated into black dust, scattering on the wind.

The guard jogged over, his face showing both concern and relief. "Are you both alright?" he asked, glancing at Aeron's injured arm.

Aeron nodded, though his voice was strained, "Thanks to you."

"Let's get you inside. We've had a few of these strange attacks on the outskirts, but it's rare to see one this close to the gate. You're lucky I was patrolling."

He gestured for them to follow, escorting them past the fortified gate and into the heart of Fort Graystone. Aeron and Seraphina took in the town, nestled within thick stone walls, its age softened by a quaint elegance.

The guard led them along winding cobblestone paths, pointing out notable spots as they went. "To your left, you'll find the hot springs. Many travelers come here for their healing properties," he explained with a smile. "Just up ahead is the inn. They'll have rooms and some basic medical supplies to help with that arm."

Aeron nodded gratefully, feeling the sting in his arm pulse with every step. As they reached the inn, the guard stopped and gestured toward the door. "The healer here is no expert, but she's patched up plenty of folks in her time. If you need anything else, just ask around. Fort Graystone is known for its hospitality."

"Thank you," Seraphina said, giving the guard a warm smile. "You saved us out there."

The guard tipped his head modestly. "All in a day's work. Safe travels to you both. Be careful out there. These creatures seem to be getting bolder."

With a nod, he turned and walked back toward the gate, leaving Aeron and Seraphina standing at the entrance of the inn.

Aeron and Seraphina stepped into the cozy, dimly lit inn, the scent of roasted meat and fresh bread welcoming them. No sooner had they entered than a man with a well-worn medical satchel hanging from his shoulder approached, his eyes immediately locking onto Aeron's injured arm.

"You there—let's get that arm sorted," he said in a brisk but kind tone, guiding Aeron to a seat near the fire. "Name's Dr. Faulkner. Looks like you've had a bit of a run-in out there."

Seraphina watched as the doctor began cleaning and bandaging Aeron's arm, using quick, efficient care with a practiced hand. She used the opportunity to arrange for their room, and leaned over the counter to speak with the innkeeper about stabling Koko.

"Good sturdy mule you've got," the innkeeper noted with an approving nod. "The stable's around back. We'll make sure he's well looked after."

With Koko's accommodations arranged, she returned to the doctor's side just as he was finishing bandaging Aeron's arm. "That should do the trick," Dr. Faulkner said, pulling the wrap tight. "You're lucky. No real damage, just a few deep bites. Those things out there are getting nastier."

"Thank you," Aeron replied, testing his arm with a wince, but giving him a grateful nod.

The innkeeper, a large man with a friendly smile, handed Seraphina a key and motioned them over to a nearby table. "Let me get you both something to eat. It's on the house. Travelers like you look like you've earned it."

They settled in, and after a few moments, the innkeeper returned with hearty bowls of stew and thick slices of bread. He lingered, a curious glint in his eye. "So, what brings the two of you to Fort Graystone?"

Seraphina exchanged a glance with Aeron before explaining, "We're looking for answers about those dark creatures. We were told there might be someone here who could help."

The innkeeper nodded thoughtfully, wiping his hands on his apron. "Ah, you're here to see Reverend Douglas then. Priest in charge of the temple here. Bit on the young side, but he's knowledgeable. Temple's right at the heart of town. Just follow the main road until you see the large oak doors."

Aeron and Seraphina thanked him, grateful for the lead. After settling their affairs and enjoying their meal, they gathered their things, leaving Koko safe and well-fed in the stable. As they stepped out onto the cobblestone streets, they followed the main road toward the center of Fort Graystone, the temple's tall spire visible above the rooftops.

At last, they stood before the temple's large oak doors, and with a shared glance, Aeron pushed them open, stepping into the quiet, reverent space to seek the counsel of Reverend Douglas.

Aeron and Seraphina entered the cool, echoing space of the temple, taking in the quiet grandeur of the vaulted ceiling and the soft glow of candles lining the walls. Near the front, a middle-aged man in simple robes adjusted an altar cloth with a careful, practiced hand. When he noticed them, he turned, his expression calm and attentive.

"Welcome," he greeted, his voice gentle and steady. "I'm Priest Douglas. What brings you to the temple today?"

Seraphina broke into a wry smile. "Well, Father Douglas, we came to Fort Graystone looking for answers about some dark creatures we encountered on the road. We first went to Reverend Ted."

Aeron chimed in with a grin. "Let's just say the 'great Reverend Ted' couldn't help us. But he was kind enough to send us to you."

Douglas chuckled, shaking his head. "Ted's a good man, though perhaps not the most scholarly. I take it he felt this was more within my realm?"

Seraphina nodded. "Yes, he thought you might have some knowledge of these creatures. They've been attacking us almost daily. We thought they might have been an isolated threat, but it's starting to feel like something more."

Douglas's brow furrowed, and he gestured for them to follow him to a quieter corner of the temple, lined with ancient shelves of books and scrolls. He took a seat and motioned for them to do the same.

"These creatures you describe ... I don't know much," he admitted, "but there's an old story, mentioned only in fragments. There's rumor of an ancient, secret order who guards records of times when such creatures appeared before. Some believe these creatures were summoned long ago to correct a disturbance in the natural order. Specifically, when Death failed to carry out its duty."

Aeron listened intently. The mention of Death had triggered

a strange, irreplaceable sense of familiarity. "So this order—do they still exist?"

Douglas leaned forward, a look of caution in his eyes. "If they do, they would be well hidden. Many priests believe it's just a legend. But if they're real, they would operate within the Great Oaks—the largest temple in the realm. Its library is the size of a small town. It's a place for scholars, a center for learning, located in the heart of the world. The journey there would be long, and finding the answers you seek might be even more difficult."

Seraphina took a breath and let it out slowly. "Thank you, Father Douglas. It seems like our next step is clear."

Douglas gave a small, thoughtful nod. "Fort Graystone is a peaceful place, but there are dangers beyond these walls. I urge you to travel with care and be prepared for the worst. The path to truth is seldom easy."

With a final thanks, Aeron and Seraphina left the temple, the road ahead growing clearer as they returned to the quiet bustle of Fort Graystone's streets.

Aeron and Seraphina made their way to the center of Fort Graystone, where the famed hot springs lay nestled in a quiet garden surrounded by stone paths and flowering trees. Steam rose from the mineral-rich pools, carrying with it a gentle warmth that melted the tension of their journey.

As they approached, they exchanged a look, each realizing the allure of a few moments of relaxation.

"Well," Seraphina said with a grin, "we've earned a bit of a break, don't you think?"

Aeron chuckled. "I'd say so."

They moved to the side to change, each slipping into their modest bathing clothes, though Aeron couldn't help but glance over as Seraphina adjusted her clothing. She caught him staring and her lips quirked up into a smirk.

"You know, Aeron," she teased, giving him a playful look, "I don't think those creatures we've been fighting are the only things standing at attention."

Aeron's face reddened as he quickly looked away, clearing his throat. "I-it's the warm air," he stammered, trying to play it off. "Relaxing, that's all."

She laughed softly, settling into the warm water. "Relaxing, huh? Well, in that case, let's both relax." She patted the spot next to her, and Aeron, still slightly flushed, slipped in beside her. The warmth of the water enveloped them, and the stress of travel began to ease.

They soaked in silence for a few minutes, the gentle bubbling of the spring lulling them into a peaceful quiet. Finally, Aeron broke the silence, glancing over at her. "You know, I still don't quite understand why you decided to leave everything behind and join me on this journey. I mean, it's not exactly the safest life. And you seemed content working with the doctor."

Seraphina looked thoughtful, leaning back against the edge of the pool. "I suppose it's because there wasn't much for me back there. And before you ask," she added, "no, I wasn't with anyone romantically."

Aeron leaned in with a half-smile. "So, you're telling me all this time, no one has caught your attention?"

She shook her head. "No one who made me feel like I'd be missing out if I left. Life there was comfortable, but a little dull. I've always wanted something more." She looked over at him, her gaze steady. "And you're interesting, Aeron. More interesting than anyone I've ever met."

The warmth in her eyes made his pulse quicken. "Well, I'm glad you're here. It's strange, but I feel like I couldn't do this without you."

They shared a quiet smile, a moment of understanding passing between them through the soothing waters, letting the burdens of their journey drift away, if only for a short while.

But the comforting warmth of the hot springs ended when a sudden, harsh clang shattered the tranquil air. Bells rang out from the edge of town, warning chimes echoing urgently through the quiet streets. Shouts rose in response. The muffled sound of commands barked and the unmistakable *thunk* of arrows loosed into the distance.

Aeron and Seraphina's heads snapped up; their relaxation forgotten in an instant. They exchanged a tense glance before scrambling out of the water and pulling on their clothing. Without another word, they bolted toward the source of the commotion, following the rising shouts and the sound of arrows piercing the air.

As they reached the wall surrounding Fort Graystone, they clambered up the stone steps to join the guards stationed along the ramparts. The guard who had helped them at the gate, was there, his expression grim as he focused on the chaos below.

Outside the wall, a swarm of dark creatures covered the open ground—a twisted, writhing mass of shifting shadows in countless shapes, all moving as one unnatural force toward the town. Some appeared as wolves, others hulking bears. Smaller, quicker shapes darted through the herd, each creature marked by the same dark, oily mass that seemed to pulse with malevolence.

The guard turned as Aeron and Seraphina joined him, recognition flickering across his face.

"You two! I don't know if you're cursed or just unlucky, but I've never seen anything like this. They're attacking in numbers we've never seen before."

Aeron scanned the creatures, feeling a chill run down his spine. "They've been following us since we left our village. Attacking us every day. But never like this."

The guard shook his head, nocking another arrow. "We've dealt with a creature or two, sure, but ... this many? They're working together, like they're answering some call." He loosed his arrow, the shot finding its mark in one of the creatures, which dissolved into dark mist. It was immediately replaced by others surging forward.

Seraphina's eyes were wide as she took in the swarm. "This … this isn't normal, is it?"

"No," the guard replied, his voice tense. "Normally, they come as one or two, scattered across the outskirts. But this feels like a coordinated attack. If they breach the walls, we're going to need every blade we can find."

Aeron tightened his grip on his sword, a surge of determination rising within him. "Let us help."

The guard nodded, looking both grateful and wary. "We're grateful for any help we can get. But be prepared — this is unlike anything we've faced before."

As the horde of dark creatures advanced, the guards braced themselves, Aeron and Seraphina among them, ready to defend Fort Graystone from a threat beyond anything they had yet encountered.

Aeron and Seraphina grabbed bows from a nearby stand, joining the line of guards sending arrows down into the approaching creatures. Aeron pulled back on the bowstring, aimed at the writhing mass below, and let his first arrow fly. It soared well above the intended target, disappearing somewhere in the distance. He tried again, but his aim was no better. Every arrow seemed to have a mind of its own, missing wildly.

Beside him, Seraphina took to the task with a bit more success. She wasn't perfect, but her arrows at least occasionally found their mark, each one landing with more confidence than the last.

The guard from earlier watched Aeron's failed attempts, shaking his head with a smirk. "You know, friend, you might do better just handing arrows over to her," he said, nodding toward Seraphina.

Aeron grunted, letting another arrow loose that veered off course, not even close to the swarm. "Apparently, I'm better with things up close."

Seraphina stifled a chuckle, nudging him with her elbow. "Stick with the sword, Aeron the Archer."

As the battle continued, the creatures began to thin, their numbers dwindling with each passing moment. The guards, now more relaxed, took careful shots as the remaining few were picked off one by one. Finally, the last creature dissolved into black mist, leaving an eerie silence in its wake.

A collective sigh of relief swept over the guards, and each one lowered their bow. Aeron let out a breath he hadn't realized he'd been holding, glancing at Seraphina, who wore a tired but triumphant grin.

The guard beside them gave Aeron a light clap on the shoulder. "Well, let's hope you don't have to rely on that bow anytime soon. Though, at least you've got her to cover for you."

Aeron chuckled, shaking his head. "Guess I'll leave the archery to her next time."

With the threat finally passed, they returned their borrowed bows and made their way toward the inn. Exhausted from the battle and the long day, they found their way to their room, grateful for a moment's peace. As they settled in for the night, the sound of distant, hushed conversations and faint cheers from relieved townsfolk echoed through the inn, a celebration of yet another night defended.

Aeron lay asleep in the quiet of the room, the fatigue of the day settling heavily over him. But as he drifted off to sleep, a familiar scene unfolded before him. A vast mountain plateau shrouded in mist, Mount Limbo, rose ominously in the distance. In the center of the plateau lay the scythe, its dark, shadowed form radiating an otherworldly pull, as if calling his name.

He moved toward it, the ground beneath him almost insubstantial. The scythe's handle seemed to pulse with life, each beat drawing him closer. The air around it crackled, whispering words he couldn't fully understand, but the tone was clear. It was calling him.

Just as his fingers brushed the cold metal, a furious, piercing scream tore through the silence. "The mantle is mine!" a female voice shrieked, laced with venom and rage. "I deserve it!"

The sound reverberated around him, filled with dark, twisted energy. The ground beneath him trembled, and the scythe seemed to recoil, slipping just out of reach. A thunderous crash echoed, sending a violent shockwave through the dream. The force was so intense it hurled him backward, the dark figure of the woman screaming with fury as his vision blurred.

Aeron jolted awake, heart pounding, the echo of the woman's shriek lingering in his mind. He sat up, breathing hard, as if he could still feel the power of the final crash. The faint glow of dawn seeped through the window, casting long shadows across the room. His gaze drifted to his hand, still tingling as though he'd touched something far beyond his understanding.

The scythe and that voice. Whoever she was, she was holding on to the mantle with a desperation that unsettled him.

Aeron eventually drifted back to sleep, the lingering tension of his dream slowly ebbing away as he succumbed to exhaustion. When he woke the next morning, it wasn't the sunlight that stirred him but a gentle, unexpected warmth—a soft, lingering kiss on his forehead. Blinking his eyes open, he found Seraphina leaning over him, a gentle smile on her face.

"Morning," she said, slightly pulling back. "I heard you wake up in the middle of the night but didn't want to pry. You looked shaken."

Aeron rubbed his eyes, the memory of the dream still vivid in his mind. He sat up, stretching slightly as he collected his thoughts. "I was ... I had another dream. It was about the mountain again. Mount Limbo." His voice grew quieter as he recalled the details. "The scythe was there, calling to me. I reached for it, but there was this voice. A woman's voice, angry, shouting that the mantle was hers, that she deserved it."

Seraphina frowned, her usual playful demeanor replaced by genuine concern. "That sounds intense. And it felt real to you?"

Aeron nodded, running a hand over his face. "More real than any dream I've had. I think it's telling me something, urging me toward that mountain."

She placed a reassuring hand on his arm. "Then we'll find it. Whatever it is, it seems important." She paused, then added with a wry smile, "Though I don't mind saying, we should be a bit better prepared before we tackle a mysterious mountain. Maybe we get you a freshly sharpened sword, and I could use a bow of my own, just in case."

He chuckled, the warmth of her encouragement easing the remnants of his unease. "Agreed. Let's head over to the blacksmith before we set out. Maybe he'll have something stronger. These creatures seem to be getting tougher."

Fort Graystone's morning bustle greeted them as they left the inn, ready to seek out the blacksmith who might provide the edge they needed.

Aeron and Seraphina stepped into the blacksmith's shop, a mixture of heat and the rich scent of metal filling the air. The forge glowed bright in the corner, and tools of all shapes and sizes were scattered around with an organized chaos that only a seasoned blacksmith could navigate.

Seraphina's attention was immediately drawn to a bow displayed on a nearby rack. The limbs were crafted from a dark, polished wood, but the grip in the center was made of clear, sturdy glass—a beautiful and rare design.

Her eyes lit up as she picked it up, admiring the craftsmanship. "This is stunning," she breathed.

The blacksmith, a tall, no-nonsense woman with a braid of dark hair thrown over her shoulder, turned from her work at the forge and grinned. "Ah, you have a good eye," she said, wiping her hands on a cloth. "That piece is special—strong and light. It'll serve you well for aiming true."

After some back-and-forth haggling over the price, Seraphina secured the bow, her excitement palpable as she tested the string's tension.

As the transaction wrapped up, the blacksmith's gaze fell on Aeron's sword. She raised an eyebrow, studying it with a critical eye. "That sword of yours has seen better days, I'd wager."

Aeron glanced down at his weapon, nodding. "It's held up, but I could probably do with something a little sharper."

She took the blade, turning it over in her hands. "It's a well-crafted piece, got that old-world touch. But I've made something more efficient, something sharper and more lightweight." She placed a newer sword on the counter, the blade glinting with a deadly edge, its design sleek and balanced. "I'll trade you for it, if you're interested."

Aeron admired the craftsmanship of the new sword, feeling the weight of it in his hand. It felt natural, balanced. It would serve him better in the fights ahead. "Deal."

Once the trade was made, Aeron hesitated before asking, "What do you think about those creatures we've been hearing about? The ones attacking the town?"

The blacksmith's face grew serious. "I've heard plenty of stories lately. People fighting those creatures in twos and threes on the outskirts. If they're getting bolder, it's only a matter of time before they're a real problem for the whole town." She paused, eyeing Aeron's new sword. "If you're looking for something stronger, though, something to give you an edge, you might want to find someone who crafts weapons for more than just defense."

Seraphina raised an eyebrow. "Where would we find a person like that?"

The blacksmith leaned closer, her voice lowering. "There's a bladesmith in Tideheaven, a former assassin and swordsman. He's known for crafting some of the sharpest blades and the most specialized weapons in the realm. Rumor is, his skills are unmatched, but he doesn't take just anyone as a customer."

Aeron exchanged a look with Seraphina, intrigued. "And how would we reach Tideheaven?"

The blacksmith gestured toward the harbor. "You're in luck. A ship is leaving for Tideheaven today. It's about a two-week journey, but if you want to meet this bladesmith, that's your best bet."

Aeron nodded, grateful for the lead, and thanked the blacksmith before he and Seraphina left the shop, their next destination set.

The salty breeze swept through the harbor as Aeron and Seraphina approached the docked vessel, its sails furled but ready. The captain, a broad man with a grizzled beard and a single gold earring, watched them approach with a wary, yet curious, gaze. He extended a hand, grinning slyly.

"Captain Treble," he introduced himself, his voice as rough as the sea he sailed. "What brings two land-dwellers to my trade ship?"

"We're looking to buy passage to Tideheaven," Seraphina said. "There's someone there we need to meet. A master swordsman, Miya Ashi. We're hoping he can help us with better weapons."

Treble raised an eyebrow. "Ashi, eh? Heard tales of him. Never met the man, though. He keeps to himself. Dangerous fellow, if half the stories are true."

Aeron felt a weight settle over him. This journey to Tideheaven was one step closer to confronting the darkness that had been plaguing them.

Captain Treble scratched his chin thoughtfully. "Well, I'll take you there, but know this—Tideheaven isn't a quick jaunt. You'll be at sea for a while. But if you're keen on learning to handle that blade better," he gestured toward Aeron's sword, "I'll set you up with my first mate, Xavier. Retired military, knows his way around a fight. He can train you in some simple combat.

Might make this trip more productive."

Aeron exchanged a look with Seraphina, who nodded encouragingly. "We'll take those terms, Captain. When do we leave?"

"Dawn," Treble replied.

As he was turning away, Aeron cleared his throat. "One more thing. We'll be bringing a mule along. His name's Koko."

The captain's eyes widened in surprise. "A mule? Well, that's a first." He let out a hearty laugh before fixing them with an amused look. "But a deal's a deal. You can bring your mule, but it'll cost extra."

Aeron chuckled, shaking the captain's hand. "We wouldn't dream of leaving him behind."

With that settled, the captain tipped his hat. "Get your things in order, pay up for the mule, and welcome aboard."

As the sun dipped below the horizon, Aeron and Seraphina headed off to make their preparations, ready for days of training, rest, and the promise of what lay ahead.

As dawn broke over the harbor, Aeron and Seraphina made their way back to the docks, their belongings packed and ready. The sea stretched out before them, calm and shimmering in the early light. Captain Treble's trade vessel swayed gently, its sails unfurled and ready to catch the morning breeze.

Captain Treble stood at the gangplank, arms crossed, a satisfied look on his face as he watched them approach. "Right on time," he said in greeting, casting a quick glance behind Aeron. "I trust you have the mule ready to board?"

Aeron grinned, pulling on Koko's reins as she trotted dutifully beside them. "We couldn't leave him behind."

Treble let out a chuckle, motioning them forward. "Welcome aboard, then. It's not often I have such eager passengers—and even rarer I'm carrying a mule to Tideheaven!"

Aeron and Seraphina stepped onto the ship, Koko trailing behind them, his hooves clattering against the wooden deck.

They settled in, stowing their packs and finding places for themselves near the rail as the crew moved with swift precision, preparing the vessel for departure.

The first mate, Xavier, approached, giving Aeron a short nod. He looked every bit the seasoned soldier the captain said he was, with a few gray streaks in his hair and a no-nonsense gaze. "Captain says you're looking to train during our journey," he said, voice deep but friendly. "We'll get you started soon enough."

Aeron nodded, feeling a rush of anticipation. The journey ahead would be no idle voyage. He would hone his skills, readying himself for the dangers that awaited.

With a booming call from Treble, the ship's ropes were cast off, and the crew sprang into action, setting the sails to catch the morning wind. Slowly, the ship pulled away from the dock, leaving the harbor behind as they set course for Tideheaven.

Aeron leaned against the rail, watching the coastline recede. Beside him, Seraphina smiled, the glint of adventure bright in her eyes. Together, they set their sights on the distant horizon, prepared for whatever challenges lay ahead.

As the vessel sliced through the waves, their journey truly began.

Chapter 18: The Veil of Tideheaven

During their journey, Aeron has spent hours each day training under the first mate, Xavier, who, despite his gruff manner, taught him about hand-to-hand combat and wielding a blade with precision. Xavier was impressed by Aeron's resilience and focus, though he sensed there was something unusual in the way Aeron picked up skills that would typically take years to learn. Seraphina watched some of the sessions from the sidelines, amused at Aeron's efforts and proud of his rapid progress. She was even convinced Xavier to let her try a few moves, surprising the crew with her natural agility and perceptiveness.

The evenings brought a different rhythm, with Aeron and Seraphina sharing stories with the crew over simple meals. Seraphina, ever observant, asked the crew about Tideheaven, absorbing every detail to prepare for what awaited them. Captain Treble often joined in, spinning tales of his adventures and revealing the undercurrents of danger in Tideheaven's dark alleys and hidden coves.

In quieter moments, Aeron reflected on the strange memories that surfaced in his dreams—visions of a mountain, the gleam of the scythe, and shadowy figures he couldn't quite place. Seraphina noticed his distracted moments, occasionally coaxing him to share, though he offered only fragments, unsure of what those images mean. They fell into a steady rhythm, strengthening their bond as both allies and tentative friends.

On the final evening of their journey, Tideheaven's jagged

silhouette appeared on the horizon, glowing faintly under a starlit sky. The sight of it sent a chill through Aeron. The city exuded an air of mystery and danger, a fitting gateway for what awaited them.

The docks of Tideheaven exuded a sense of barely-contained chaos, and as Aeron and Seraphina stepped off the gangplank, they were swept up in the bustling energy of the city. Captain Treble gave them a knowing nod. "Watch yourselves. Tideheaven's got its own rules, and outsiders are rarely found in favor."

They set out through the winding streets, leading Koko to a stable where Seraphina insisted on paying extra for his care. The city's rough edges showed even more clearly as they made their way to the local temple—a small, worn stone building tucked between two towering inns. Inside, the cool, smoky air carried a scent of incense and sea salt.

They were greeted by the unexpected sight of a tough-looking priestess with an eye patch and a wooden leg. With a crooked grin, she sized them up. "Visitors, eh? Don't get many of those in here. Name's Talia. So, what'll it be—a blessing, a confession, or both?"

Seraphina smiled, immediately warming to Talia. "Actually, we're looking for a blacksmith. A man named Ashi. We were told he might be able to help us."

Talia's one good eye narrowed slightly, but she kept her voice casual, "Ashi, hmm? Can't say I know much about any Ashi," she said, turning toward the altar as if suddenly fascinated. "But plenty of blacksmiths in Tideheaven. Just be sure to keep your coins close and your trust closer. Both are in short supply around here."

Aeron and Seraphina exchanged glances, understanding Talia's reluctance. Sensing the conversation has reached its end, they thanked her for her advice and left the temple, stepping back into the lively streets.

"She knew something," Aeron muttered as they weaved through the marketplace, passing vendors who shouted out their wares and offered dubious deals.

"Absolutely," Seraphina agreed, glancing toward the temple. "But she's not the type to give information to strangers. We'll need to find another way."

Their day stretched on as they moved through Tideheaven, questioning people who responded with shrugs, laughter, or suspicious glares. It was nearly nightfall when they returned to the pub, weary and frustrated. Seraphina ordered a meal, and they settled in a corner, trying to process what little they learned.

As they ate, a loud group of young thieves stumbled into the pub. One of them, a man with a mess of curly hair and a wild grin, was showing off a finely-crafted dagger with a gleaming edge. "Fresh off Ashi's forge!" he bragged, swaying slightly, clearly enjoying the attention.

Aeron leaned over to Seraphina. "This might be it." He stood and approached the group slowly, nodding toward the dagger. "That's a fine blade. Where'd you get it?"

The thief sneered, looking Aeron up and down. "Ashi doesn't work for just anyone, farm boy. Only for those in The Eye."

His friends snickered, and one of them muttered, "Only way you're getting a blade like that is if you've got skills."

Aeron held his ground, standing up straighter. "Maybe I'm interested in joining The Eye, then."

One of the thieves with shoulder-length hair flowing like two rivers from his scalp and a deep fascination with the many knives strapped across his body, chuckled, his hand toying with a blade. "Oh, you want to join, do you?" He stepped forward, eyeing Aeron with interest. "My name's Pinder. The Eye doesn't take just anyone." His voice held a mocking tone. "You don't look like a thief, and you don't move like an assassin. Why don't you head back to your farm?"

Aeron ignored the dig, pulling out a few coins. "I'm not here to waste anyone's time. Maybe this will help me earn some consideration."

Pinder took the coins, weighing them thoughtfully but ultimately shook his head. "Coin's one thing, farm boy, but it doesn't prove anything." He tilted his head, sizing Aeron up with a mischievous gleam. "Tell you what. You want a shot at information? Prove yourself." He gestured to the street outside. "Hand-to-hand. You take me on. Show me you've got something to offer."

Aeron glanced at Seraphina, who gave him a small nod. Turning back to Pinder, he said, "Fine. You've got a deal."

A crowd gathered in the street as Aeron and Pinder faced off, with Pinder's many knives glinting in the lamplight as he unstrapped them and handed them to a friend, a knowing grin playing on his lips. "Farm boy against the blade lover. This'll be a show."

The fight began, and Aeron quickly realized Pinder was both quick and ruthless. Every strike felt like it was delivered with precision, and while Aeron blocked and countered each one, Pinder's attacks are relentless. The crowd jeered and cheered, the noise and lights creating an intense, disorienting atmosphere.

Just as Aeron felt his stamina waning, a deep growl reverberated through the street. A chilling figure emerged from the shadows—a massive humanoid form, covered in black, viscous goo that seemed to absorb all light around it. It was like a nightmare made of flesh, towering at least nine feet tall with eyes that glimmered eerily in the dark.

Chaos erupted as bystanders scattered, some shrieking while others dove for cover. Only Aeron and Pinder remained, both rooted to the spot, wide-eyed but unwilling to show fear.

"What ... what is that?" Pinder whispered, his confidence shaken.

Aeron stepped forward, bracing himself.

Pinder gritted his teeth and joined him, muttering, "Let's see what you're made of, farm boy."

Seraphina, from the sidelines, shouted, "Aeron, catch!" and threw his sword toward him. He caught it in mid-air, brandishing it as he advanced on the creature, his stance steady. Pinder grabbed a dagger, his face a mix of fear and determination.

The creature lunged at them, its goo-covered limbs swinging with terrifying force. Aeron and Pinder dodged and struck, their attacks barely making a dent at first. Pinder landed a quick jab to the creature's side, only for the goo to reassemble.

"This thing doesn't want to go down!" he hissed, sweat dripping down his face.

Aeron, focusing on the creature's movements, noticed a slight hesitation in its stride, and a plan formed. "Aim low! Go for the legs!" he shouted to Pinder. They moved in unison, Pinder's dagger flashing as Aeron swung his sword, their combined efforts finally causing the creature to stagger.

With one last coordinated effort, Aeron slashed at the creature's Achilles' tendon, and with a guttural roar, it collapsed, dissolving into a thick, dark mist that dissipated in the night air.

As the street quieted, Pinder stared at Aeron, breathing heavily, eyes wide with a mixture of respect and shock. "Well, farm boy … maybe you've got more guts than I thought." He clapped Aeron on the shoulder, giving him a crooked smile. But then his expression shifted to something more serious, his brows knitting together. "What the hell was that thing?"

Aeron exhaled, lowering his sword and glancing at the mist lingering in the street. "Honestly, I wish I knew. These things have been popping up lately—strange, dark creatures that don't seem to belong in this world." He sheathed his sword, meeting Pinder's questioning gaze. "We've seen them in different shapes and sizes. Sometimes they're like animals, other times, well, whatever that was."

Pinder raised an eyebrow, intrigued. "Different shapes, you

say? So, that's not the first one?"

Aeron shook his head. "Not by a long shot. On the way here, we had one that looked like a seagull attack us. Thought it was just a bird looking for scraps, but the thing had black goo dripping off it. Went straight for us, too. Caused quite a scene on the ship." He chuckled, though there's a weariness in his eyes. "Never thought I'd have to fight off a possessed bird."

Pinder let out a surprised laugh, shaking his head. "A goo-covered seagull attacking a farm boy and his girl on a boat to Tideheaven. Sounds like a story right out of a tavern tale."

"Would be funnier if it weren't true," Aeron replied, managing a small grin. "We've seen others. Smaller, like mice and squirrels. Then some larger, like a boar that attacked us outside a village. But this one ..." He glanced back toward where the creature had stood. "This one was different. Bigger, stronger. They seem to be getting worse."

Pinder crossed his arms, looking thoughtful. "So, what do you plan to do about it? Because I don't know about you, but I'd rather not be tangling with those things every night."

"That's why I'm here," Aeron said, his tone resolute. "I need a stronger weapon. The fights are getting more intense, and whatever's going on isn't stopping. If I'm going to survive these attacks, I need something that can keep up."

Pinder's eyes narrowed as he studied Aeron. "So, you're after Ashi to get yourself a blade that can go toe-to-toe with whatever these things are?"

Aeron nodded. "That's the hope. I've heard he's the best, and if anyone can make a weapon that'll hold its own against these creatures, it's him."

Pinder was quiet for a moment, looking like he was weighing his options. Finally, he clapped Aeron on the shoulder again. "Well, farm boy, you've got more grit than I expected. Tomorrow night, I'll take you to Ashi. But remember, he's not the type to take kindly to demands. You'll have to prove yourself to him, too."

Aeron met Pinder's gaze, determination in his eyes. "I'm ready for that."

The next morning, Aeron and Seraphina woke to find the pub nearly empty, with no sign of Pinder or any of the thieves from the night before. After a quick breakfast, they decided to try their luck exploring the town once more, hoping to cross paths with someone who might know where Pinder and his crew were hiding.

As they wandered through the winding streets, they pass the small temple where they'd met Talia, the one-legged priestess. As if on cue, Talia appeared at the entrance, her crutch tapping against the stone as she beckoned them over with a sly grin.

"Well, well," she said, her eye twinkling. "I heard you two made quite the scene last night. A strange, black goo-covered giant? Not your average scuffle."

Aeron chuckled, scratching the back of his neck. "Word travels fast."

"Especially when it's something unusual," she replied, stepping closer, lowering her voice as her gaze sharpened. "And I'd wager a creature like that's got the locals more than a little spooked. Pinder, though … I heard he handled himself well. He's not one to make friends easily, mind you." She glanced between Aeron and Seraphina, thoughtfully considering them. "If Pinder trusts you, then I suppose I can, too."

With a glance around to make sure no one was watching, she motioned for them to follow. Leading them inside the temple, she approached the altar and, with a practiced hand, moved aside a concealed stone panel, revealing a narrow passageway that spiraled down beneath the temple. "This way. I think it's time you see The Veil."

They descended the stone steps, the air growing cooler and damp with each step. The passage opened into a massive underground chamber—a hidden lair nestled beneath Tideheaven. A vast, circular room stretched far beyond what they expected, with a central chimney rising from a roaring fire, its smoke trailing up into what must connect with the temple's chimney above, blending seamlessly with the smoke of incense.

Tents were set up around the perimeter, each one bustling with activity: vendors displaying a range of weapons, purveyors of oddities, and merchants fencing stolen goods to interested buyers. Laughter, bartering, and the occasional clash of metal filled the air. The fire in the middle cast a warm glow, illuminating the area with a sense of mysterious camaraderie and intrigue.

"This," Talia said, gesturing to the sprawling hideout, "is The Veil, the hidden heart of The Eye in Tideheaven. It's where Pinder and his lot run their trade and keep the city's secrets." She leaned in with a conspiratorial smile. "That's how we keep things discreet. The smoke mixes with the temple's incense, masking any ... less-than-holy activities."

Seraphina's eyes widened, taking in the sprawling network of tents and activity around them. "This place is incredible. And it's been here the whole time?"

Talia nodded, clearly proud of the secret she'd shared. "Centuries old, built over what used to be burial chambers. But the dead don't mind a little company, so long as we respect the rules." She smirked. "And if you head this way, Pinder will be somewhere near the vendors, no doubt flaunting his latest collection of knives."

Aeron took it all in, amazed at the scale of the operation. The Veil was more than a den. It was a thriving, secretive society of thieves, merchants, and misfits, all hidden beneath the temple. He exchanged a glance with Seraphina, who looked equally impressed, though her brow furrowed slightly with tension as they stepped further into the depths of The Veil.

Talia gave them a pat on the shoulder, her grin widening.

"Welcome to Tideheaven's underworld. Just remember, every-one here's got a purpose, and you're welcome as long as you don't get in anyone's way. Good luck finding Pinder." With that, she turned and started up the spiral stairs, leaving them to navigate the bustling world of The Veil on their own.

Aeron and Seraphina wandered deeper into The Veil, passing vendors selling everything from intricate weapons to strange potions and oddities that glinted in the firelight. Seraphina pointed out a finely carved figurine of a wolf, its surface inlaid with delicate silver. Aeron paused to admire an unusual compass, its needle spinning erratically, while a vendor described it as a "finder of hidden fortunes."

The vibrant, lawless market had a magnetic energy, unlike anything they'd seen.

As they neared the heart of the market, they heard a familiar voice rising above the chatter. Pinder stood atop a crate, gesturing wildly as he wove a tale for a small crowd gathered around him.

"Fifteen feet tall, this thing was!" he bellowed, arms spread wide, eyes glinting with the thrill of his story. "Covered in a thick, black sludge that swallowed the light whole! It came at us with fists the size of boulders. One hit could've taken down an ox! But did I flinch? Not a chance!" He puffed out his chest, clearly savoring the attention.

Aeron and Seraphina exchanged a look, amused at Pinder's embellishments. They stepped closer, watching as he carried on, completely absorbed in his narrative.

"But then," he said, lowering his voice dramatically, "just when it looked like all was lost, out of nowhere comes this farmer, of all people, with balls of steel and a cheap one-handed blade! We fought side by side, until we took the beast down. And let me tell you ..." he paused, locking eyes with Aeron and, grinning broadly, "this farmer didn't just hold his own—he led the charge!"

The crowd murmured with a mix of amazement and laughter, casting curious glances at Aeron as they realized he was the one Pinder had been talking about. Gradually, they dispersed, the thrill of the tale lingering as they moved on to the next attraction.

Pinder hopped down from the crate, his grin widening as he approached Aeron. "Didn't expect to see you two up and about so early. How's it feel to be a hero?" he asked with a wink, giving Aeron a hearty slap on the back.

Aeron smirked. "Fifteen feet tall, huh? And here I thought you were a man of facts."

Pinder laughed, unbothered. "The truth is for priests, my friend. Stories are for the rest of us. Besides, it's the spirit of it that counts, right?" His expression turned thoughtful as he glanced around, making sure no one was listening too closely. "Last night ... that was something else. Can't say I've ever seen a creature like that before, and I've seen my fair share of things."

"Neither have we," Aeron admitted. "And that was the first time it's been that big or strong."

Pinder nodded, looking lost in thought for a moment before snapping back to his usual self. "Well, whatever it was, you didn't back down. That counted for something." He reached into his belt and pulled out a small dagger, offering it to Aeron. The blade was simple but well-crafted, with a symbol etched into the hilt. A mark of The Eye.

"Look, I promised I'd introduce you to Ashi, and I always keep my word," Pinder said. "But I also want to give you this. If you ever run into anyone from The Eye, show them this. It's a symbol that you've done a service for us. They'll know we owe you a debt of gratitude."

Aeron accepted the dagger, studying the symbol on the hilt before nodding gratefully. "Thank you, Pinder. I'll keep it close."

"Good man." Pinder clapped him on the shoulder. "Now,

let's get you to Ashi's tent. He's got a sharp tongue and an even sharper blade, so be ready." With a mischievous grin, he motioned for them to follow, leading them through the winding paths of The Veil toward the blacksmith's domain.

Inside the tent, the air was thick with the scent of heated metal and charred wood. Ashi stood at his workbench, entirely absorbed in his craft as he meticulously adjusted the hilt of a battle ax. The weapon wasn't ordinary. It had intricate grooves along the handle, reinforced edges, and small mechanical features that suggested hidden functions.

Pinder watched, his gaze sharpening as he studied the ax. "Another one of Tarin's designs, huh?" he asked with a grin, clearly familiar with the weapon's unique details.

Ashi set down his tools, glancing up with a nod. "It is. The man may be insufferable at times, but I'll admit, his ideas are solid." He picked up the ax, admiring his work. "Tarin's tactical sense is unmatched, especially when it comes to weaponry. These upgrades are designed to be efficient, adaptable. The kind of thing you'd want in close combat."

Pinder chuckled, crossing his arms. "Seems the Eye's got quite a few people who swear by his designs."

Ashi let out a dry laugh. "Not everyone, but enough to keep me busy. I don't mind the challenge. Keeps the work interesting." He set the ax down, finally turning his attention to Aeron and Seraphina, sizing them up with a curious gleam in his eye. "Who are these newcomers you've brought into my tent, Pinder?"

Pinder glanced at Aeron and Seraphina with a faint smirk, as if he'd been waiting for this moment.

Pinder gestured toward Aeron and Seraphina, his smirk growing wider. "This is Aeron, the farm boy with more guts than sense. And this," he said, nodding to Seraphina, "is his equally bold companion. They're looking for something special. Something that'll stand up to ... well, let's say, unusual foes."

Ashi raised an eyebrow, glancing between them. "Unusual foes?" His tone was skeptical but intrigued. "Farm boys don't typically seek out weapon masters, let alone show up in The Veil. What kind of trouble have you brought to my door?"

Aeron stepped forward, meeting Ashi's sharp gaze. "I've encountered creatures… things I can't explain. Dark, monstrous figures that keep appearing out of nowhere. Each time they're stronger. It's like they're drawn to me."

Seraphina chimed in, "We've seen them in different shapes — a boar, a bird, even a giant. They seem to grow more powerful every time. Last night was the worst one yet."

"Pinder and I barely got out of it in one piece."

Ashi considered their words, a flicker of surprise crossing his face before he could mask it with a stoic expression. "Sounds like a cursed lot, if you ask me," he said. He picked up the battle ax he'd been working on, running a hand along its handle with a faint glimmer of pride. "You think a blade will fix this?"

Aeron nodded. "It's not just any weapon I'm after. Whatever these things are, they don't go down easy. I need something exceptional. And I was told you're the best."

Ashi studied Aeron carefully, his expression unreadable. "Flattery isn't payment, farm boy. Nor is it reason enough for me to take a custom order." He paused, weighing his options. "But if Pinder's vouching for you, maybe there's more to this than I see."

He set down the ax and leans in slightly, a sharp glint in his eye. "If I'm going to make you a weapon, I need to understand what I'm up against. Tell me everything you know about these creatures."

Aeron took a steadying breath, recalling each encounter. "The first of these creatures appeared near my farm. They were covered in this thick, black goo. They weren't normal animals, even though they looked like it. They came at me like it was their purpose, but they were easy enough to bring down with one hit." He glanced at Seraphina before continuing. "Then, as we traveled west, one came at us again. This time, it was smaller, looked like a squirrel, but it moved fast. It was harder to handle." He paused, his gaze darkening. "Then last night … it was no animal. It was massive, twisted, and shaped like a human but covered in that same black substance, and it was relentless. I don't know what it is, but every time they show up, they're stronger. And it's like they're coming after me."

Ashi listened, his expression growing more severe with every word. "Strange creatures, covered in black goo, coming after one person?" He shook his head. "I've crafted weapons all my life—swords, hammers, axes meant to take down beasts and men alike. But what you're describing … these aren't beasts nor men." He lifted his chin, looking straight at Aeron. "So, what do you want me to make? A hammer, a blade, an ax?"

Aeron hesitated, his gaze distant as he though. "Honestly, I don't know exactly. But I keep having these dreams …"

Ashi raised an eyebrow, intrigued. "Dreams?"

Aeron nodded, his voice steady as he described it. "I keep seeing this mountain plateau. At the top, there's a scythe. Not like a farmer's tool. It's meant for battle. The handle looks like bone, and the blade is dark, almost black, with a faint purple hue. It's so sharp I can feel it even in my dreams."

As Aeron described it, Ashi's eyes widened, and with a sudden clatter, he dropped the tool he was holding. A spark of both fear and excitement lit his face, as if Aeron has just handed him the missing piece to an ancient puzzle.

Ashi took a slow breath, his gaze shifting between Aeron and the half-finished battle ax on his workbench. After a moment, he muttered, almost to himself, "I've never told a soul about this. Thought I'd keep it quiet, figure it out on my own. Maybe even take it for myself."

Aeron and Seraphina exchanged a look. What he was about to reveal was important.

"Months ago," Ashi began, his voice low and steady, "I was up on Mount Limbo, mining for ore. That mountain's known for its strength, the kind of minerals that can forge weapons like nothing else. Of course, everyone here says it's haunted, cursed. Folklore says it's the closest place in the human world to Purgatory." He paused, his eyes distant as he recalled the scene. "While I was working, there was this sudden earthquake. Light flashed through the air like lightning, and rubble flew everywhere. I should've taken it as a sign to get out of there, but I was curious. I started clearing the rocks, following a path that had just been revealed, as if something had carved it into the mountain itself."

Ashi leaned in, his voice barely above a whisper, "At the end of the path, there was a plateau. And in the middle, on this black, glass-like altar, was the scythe you just described. Long handle, almost like bone. Blade dark as night, with a faint, unnatural hue, like tempered steel dipped in shadows."

Aeron's heart raced as Ashi described the blade from his dream.

"I thought, well, maybe this was it. Maybe this was my prize. I reached out to grab it, but as soon as I got close, something stopped me. It was like a strange, electrical field. Something that made the hair on my hand stand up. My fingers couldn't even reach the handle. It was as if an invisible wall kept me inches away."

He shook his head, a mix of frustration and fascination in his eyes. "I figured I'd come back. Try to think of a way to bring it down without touching it. But I couldn't come up with any solid ideas. So, I covered the path back up, made sure no one would stumble on it. I figured if I couldn't have it, no one could."

Just then, Pinder let out an exaggerated gasp, breaking the tension in the room. "Wait, wait—you've been hiding a mystical blade from me?" He gave Ashi an accusing look, crossing his arms with a grin. "And here I thought we were friends!"

Ashi smirked. "Some things are better left unmentioned, especially when it comes to people like you, Pinder."

Pinder laughed, shaking his head. "A mystical, untouchable scythe, hidden on a mountain plateau … this just keeps getting better." He clapped Aeron on the shoulder, looking thoroughly entertained.

Pinder shook his head, chuckling as he looked at Aeron with a newfound respect. "Well, I'll be damned. You're not just a farm boy after all. Guess you're a fortune teller, too." His grin widened as he crossed his arms, clearly enjoying the moment.

Aeron, slightly taken aback, glanced between Pinder, Ashi, and Seraphina, feeling the weight of what they'd just discussed settling over him. Seraphina, sensing the growing gravity, said quietly, "There's no other explanation, is there? There's no way Aeron could have known about this scythe, down to the last detail, unless … unless he's somehow connected to it."

Ashi gave a slow nod, his eyes still locked on Aeron, as if reevaluating him. "It seems that way. Whatever's drawing those creatures, and whatever's giving you these visions must be tied to this scythe. It's like you're meant to find it."

Pinder, leaning back against the edge of a table, watched the exchange with a glint of excitement in his eyes. "So what you're saying is, our boy Aeron here is destined to go on some grand quest to a haunted mountain to find a weapon that nobody else can even touch. Now that sounds like a story worth telling."

Aeron gave a faint smile, but his gaze remained serious. "This isn't just a story to me. If this scythe is the only thing that can stop these creatures, I have to get to it. But I have no idea what I'm walking into."

Pinder shrugged, clearly unbothered by the uncertainty. "Then it's a good thing you've got a few friends here, isn't it?" He straightened, patting the daggers at his belt with a grin. "Things have gotten a bit stale here in Tideheaven. And a quest to find a mythical scythe on a haunted mountain sounds like just the thing to shake up my life. Count me in."

Aeron raised an eyebrow, surprised. "You'd really come along?"

Pinder's grin widened. "I wouldn't miss it for the world. Besides, if it's a weapon of legend we're after, I'd say you could use a knife man at your side." He glanced at Ashi. "What do you say Ashi?"

Ashi considered them both, a spark of interest in his gaze. He crossed his arms, eyeing Aeron with a calculating look. "Now, before you get too excited, understand that the location I'm about to share isn't exactly a free handout. That scythe isn't the only thing I want from Mount Limbo."

Aeron glanced at him, curious. "What else is there?"

"There's a rare type of glass up there," Ashi explained, his eyes glinting with ambition. "Most people call it ghost glass. It's a translucent, black material, hard as steel but with a strange flexibility. I've only seen small shards brought down the mountain, but if you could bring me back a large enough crate, enough to actually work with …" He trailed off, clearly envisioning the possibilities. "Let's just say I'd be able to craft weapons unlike anything this world's ever seen."

Seraphina raised an eyebrow. "You want us to haul a crate of ghost glass down from a haunted mountain?"

Ashi smirked. "If you can manage it. Consider it the price for my knowledge of the path to the scythe. Otherwise, you'll be searching blind up there."

Aeron nodded, determination in his eyes. "If we find ghost glass, we'll bring it back. You have my word."

Ashi gave him a satisfied nod. "Good. Then I'll tell you everything I know. But be prepared—Mount Limbo's not a place for the faint of heart. You'll need every bit of that resolve you just showed."

Ashi spread out a worn, hand-drawn map on the workbench, pointing to a faint trail that snaked up the side of Mount Limbo.

The mountain loomed ominously on the parchment, with jagged peaks and countless switchbacks marked along the way.

"This here," he began, tapping a spot near the base, "is where you'll start. There's a massive rope bridge nearby that travelers use to cross to the upper trails, but it's barely stable as it is, and anything heavier than a person won't make it across. So, you'll need to take this path here," he traces the line on the map, "which winds along the mountain's base. Not many people dare use it. It's narrow, treacherous, and steep—definitely not for the weak."

Aeron and Seraphina exchanged glances, both understanding the challenge ahead.

Ashi continued, "It'll take you about two days to reach the peak once there. The higher you get, the thinner the air, so pace yourselves. And the temperature drops fast at night. Now, when you reach the summit, look for a massive boulder. One so big, it practically blends into the mountainside. Behind it is a crack in the rock, almost invisible if you don't know where to look."

He glanced up, making sure they were paying attention. "That crack leads to the plateau where I saw the scythe. It's narrow, so you'll have to go single file. Nothing bigger than a person can fit through, which means you'll be carrying that ghost glass back by hand, piece by piece, until you get to the entrance."

Pinder leaned over the map, studying the path with keen interest. "So, not only do we have to climb a haunted mountain, but we have to haul crates of glass back down by hand through a death trap. This just keeps getting better."

Ashi chuckled, folding up the map and handing it to Aeron. "Consider this part of the trial, if you will. If you're after a weapon of legend, you're going to have to work for it. And remember, the mountain doesn't take kindly to visitors. There's a reason people say it's haunted."

Aeron tucked the map into his bag, nodding with resolve.

"We'll make it work."

"Good." Ashi gave him a final, approving look. "Then you've got everything you need. May fortune favor you, though I suspect you'll need more than luck up there."

Pinder clapped Aeron on the back with a gleeful grin. "Alright, farm boy," he said, eyeing the crowded market of The Veil. "Before we go climbing that mountain of death, I say we stock up on supplies. And tonight we'll celebrate properly." His grin turned mischievous. "I know just the place. A little tavern off the main alley. They've got the best ale this side of the realm and some bath wenches that'd make a man forget all about haunted mountains."

Aeron raised an eyebrow. "I think I'll leave the drinking and wenches to you, Pinder."

Seraphina crossed her arms, giving Pinder a mockingly stern look. "Yes, do enjoy your 'celebrations.' But I think I'll pass on drunken shenanigans tonight."

Pinder winked, unfazed. "Suit yourselves. But don't blame me if you two regretting your dull evening while I'm making Tideheaven history."

As they made their way through The Veil, Pinder stopped at various vendor tents, enthusiastically grabbing supplies and occasionally haggling with the merchants for a better deal. He picked up a sturdy rope, a grappling hook, some dried meats, and a flask of something strong and unidentifiable that he insisted would "keep them warm" on the mountain.

Aeron and Seraphina gathered their own supplies, finding a tent that sold thick cloaks and insulated bedrolls to ward off the mountain's cold nights. Seraphina also picked up a small pouch of herbs for minor injuries, while Aeron grabbed an extra set of straps to secure their gear onto Koko.

As they finalized their purchases, Pinder swung by, holding a bottle in each hand, grinning from ear to ear. "Tomorrow, we brave the unknown. But tonight?" He raised one bottle in a toast, already in high spirits. "Tonight, I'll drink to our quest. Don't wait up!"

Aeron chuckled, shaking his head. "Go easy on the ale, Pinder. We'll need you sharp for the mountain."

Pinder waved him off with a laugh. "Please, this is standard preparation. Keeps the nerves steady." He raised an eyebrow at them. "You sure you won't join me for a bit of fun?"

Seraphina shook her head, smiling. "I think we'll stick to a quiet evening at the inn. Early start tomorrow, remember?"

Pinder rolled his eyes dramatically. "You two are going to regret it, you know. But fine, enjoy your rest. I'll see you both at the stables in the morning. Bright and early." He winked and sauntered off through the crowd, already humming a tune as he disappeared.

Aeron and Seraphina exchanged a look, both stifling a laugh.

"Well," Aeron said, "I think we made the right choice."

After a final check of their supplies, they headed back to the inn, ready to unwind and prepare for the long journey ahead. The quiet evening settled over them as they enjoyed a simple meal, resting in the calm before the challenge awaiting them on Mount Limbo.

As Aeron and Seraphina settled into the cozy warmth of their small room, the quiet wrapped around them, a comforting contrast to the wild energy of Tideheaven. The candlelight flickered gently, casting soft, golden hues across the room, highlighting the peacefulness of the evening.

Seraphina sat on the edge of the bed, smoothing her fingers over the worn quilt as she looked around the room. "It's simple," she said softly, a small smile playing on her lips. "But … it's nice. After all that noise and commotion, it feels good to have a bit of quiet."

Aeron nodded, leaning against the wall, arms folded. He watched her, his gaze softening as he took in the way the candlelight danced over her face, illuminating the subtle sparkle in her eyes. "I think I needed it, too. Just a moment to breathe." He moved closer, almost as if drawn by some quiet pull, and lowered himself down beside her.

Seraphina let out a soft sigh, her eyes meeting his. "It's strange, you know?" she whispered, her fingers brushing against his arm. "In just a short time, we've gone from strangers to … well, here. Sharing quiet moments, preparing for a journey we know so little about."

Aeron's hand found hers and their fingers gently intertwined. "I think we've both needed someone to understand … to stand beside us, even if everything else is uncertain." His voice was soft, earnest, and he gave her hand a slight squeeze, his thumb brushing over her knuckles.

They sat in silence for a moment, the quiet between them deep and tense. Seraphina turned slightly, her gaze lingering on his, her breath catching as the space between them narrowed. "I think we have more in common than I realized," she said softly, her voice barely above a whisper.

Aeron's eyes searched hers, his heart quickening at the warmth of her hand against his. He leaned in close enough to feel the faint brush of her breath. "Maybe that's why it feels so … easy," he said, his lips just a whisper away from hers.

Seraphina's hand rose to his face, her fingers carefully tracing along his jaw, pulling him in gently as her lips meet his. The kiss was soft at first, hesitant, as they savored the electricity that had been building between them since the start of the journey. But it deepened, the world around them fading as they gave in to the pull.

Their kisses grew more fervent, hands exploring one another as they lost themselves in each other, their worries and the coming journey forgotten for the moment. The quiet room filled with the warmth of their shared passion, their laughter and whispers mixing softly with the sound of their hearts racing in the flickering candlelight.

As the night unfolded, their passion grew, filling the small room with warmth and tenderness. They explored each other with a mix of curiosity and intensity, letting down the walls they'd each built, savoring every touch, every shared breath. Eventually, wrapped in each other's arms, they drifted into a peaceful sleep, lost in the quiet comfort of each other's presence.

The morning light filtered through the small window, gently waking them. Seraphina stirred first, a playful smile tugging at her lips as she stretched. She glanced at Aeron as he began to wake.

She smirked, giving him a nudge. "Good morning, hero. I think we're going to have to work on your stamina before we start up the mountain. That was … quick." Her eyes sparkled with humor, a mischievous grin spreading across her face.

Aeron chuckled, running a hand through his hair, his cheeks tinged with embarrassment and amusement. "I'll have you know that was merely the warm-up," he replied, leaning in to kiss her as she laughed.

They lingered a moment longer, sharing quiet smiles and gentle touches, but soon, the reality of the day ahead set in. They gathered their things, packing up their supplies, and preparing to meet Pinder and Koko at the stable. With one last glance around the room, they stepped out into the morning light, ready to face whatever Mount Limbo had in store for them.

Aeron and Seraphina arrived at the stable just as the sun was casting a golden glow over Tideheaven. Pinder was already there, looking remarkably well despite what was likely a rowdy night. Koko, however, was the real star of the morning—ears perked, eyes bright, almost as if he sensed the adventure ahead and couldn't wait to get started.

"Look at you, Koko," Seraphina said, patting his side. "You're more excited than all of us combined."

Koko let out a satisfied snort, stomping a hoof as if to confirm.

They packed the sturdy mule's saddle with provisions—bed-rolls, ropes, extra cloaks, and the food they gathered the day before. Pinder insisted on carefully balancing his collection of bottles, muttering about "keeping morale high," earning an amused eye roll from Seraphina. Aeron double-checked the map Ashi had given them, tucking it securely in his satchel.

Once everything was packed, they made one last stop at the temple to say farewell to Talia. The priestess stood the doorway, her crutch balanced in one hand, looking both curious and proud as they approached.

"So, off to find that haunted mountain, eh?" Talia said, eyeing their supplies and Koko's packed saddle. "I'd say you've got everything except good sense."

Pinder grinned. "Good sense would've kept us back in Tideheaven. Besides, where's the fun in that?"

Aeron stepped forward, extending his hand to shake hers, gratefully. "Thank you for all your help, Talia. We're going to bring back something worthwhile."

She nodded, her expression turning more serious. "Mount Limbo is no joke, you know. People have been lost up there for less. But something tells me you've got what it takes." Her gaze lingered on Aeron a moment before shifting to Seraphina. "Look after each other. And take care of that mule. He looks like the only one here with any real sense." She pat Koko on the side, chuckling as he let out another enthusiastic snort.

With a final wave, they left the temple and made their way past the south harbor, following a winding path that led north, out of the city. The noise and bustling life of Tideheaven faded behind them as they pressed onward, the shadows of the distant mountains looming on the horizon, their journey to Mount Limbo just beginning.

Chapter 19: Echoes on Mount Limbo

The bustling life of Tideheaven faded behind them as Aeron, Seraphina, Pinder, and Koko moved steadily along the winding path northward. Mount Limbo loomed larger with each step, its jagged peaks casting long shadows that stretched across the landscape. The journey to the base of the mountain was marked by silence, each of them keenly aware of the daunting task ahead.

As they reached the base, they encountered a massive rope bridge swaying in the breeze. Though wide enough for travelers, it was clearly unstable and unsuitable for a loaded mule. They consulted Ashi's map, which showed a narrower, hidden path that wound around the base, bypassing the bridge and following a steep, twisting route up the mountainside. Aeron guided them onward, and Koko, as steady as ever, followed closely behind.

The path grew more rugged as they climbed. Loose rocks and steep slopes tested their endurance and balance, but with Koko's supplies and steady presence, they managed. As night fell, the wind turned colder, and they set up a small camp on a ledge, huddling close around a small fire.

Seraphina glanced up at the towering peaks above them, her voice soft. "Do you really think that scythe is up there, Aeron? What if Ashi was lying?"

Aeron stared into the flames, his expression serious. "I don't know for sure. But it feels right. Like it's been calling to me."

Pinder stretched out beside them, his gaze flickering between the mountain and the fire. "Ashi wouldn't have lied. And haunted or not, if there's something worth finding, we'll get it. Though, I wouldn't mind a little less climbing."

The night passed in restless sleep, each of them jolting awake at every strange echo or sound carried by the wind. By dawn, they were packing and continuing their climb. The path narrowed further, clinging to the edge of the mountain, forcing them to move cautiously with Koko trailing behind.

Hours pass, each step taking them higher. Just as midday approached, Aeron froze, raising a hand in warning. From a nearby ledge, a dark, twisted figure emerged—a Mountain Goat, its form half-animal, half-shadow, covered in the familiar black goo. It lunged forward, forcing them into a quick, intense battle. Aeron dodged and struck with precision, while Seraphina's arrows pierced its form. The creature finally collapsed, disintegrating into dark mist.

They exchanged tense looks, realizing this was only the beginning. As they pressed onward, they faced two more goo covered creatures—smaller but equally vicious, testing their endurance and resolve.

The trio and Koko reached the summit, exhaustion and tension filling the air. The steep, rocky path leveled out, revealing a seemingly endless array of rocks and crevices—yet no sign of the hidden crack leading to the plateau. They began their search, scanning the rocks with furrowed brows, each growing increasingly frustrated.

Pinder sighed dramatically, hands on his hips. "I swear, if this crack's as invisible as Ashi's sense of humor, we're going to be up here all day."

Seraphina rolled her eyes, patting Koko's neck as he sniffed the ground, his ears flicking toward one specific area.

Koko let out an indignant snort and nudged Pinder's shoulder as if trying to guide him, but Pinder brushed it off. "Keep your enthusiasm to yourself, Koko. This is real search-and-discover work, not just grazing for hay."

Aeron chuckled, shaking his head. "Well, Ashi did say it's practically hidden in plain sight. Maybe we're looking too hard."

Koko, seemingly fed up, planted himself firmly in front of a boulder, swishing his tail and flicking his ears toward a narrow crevice that was mostly obscured by shadows. He let out a loud, purposeful bray.

Pinder rolled his eyes. As he strode toward the boulder, Koko shifted slightly and gave Pinder a solid nudge with his nose. The push sent Pinder stumbling forward, right into the hidden crack. He let out a surprised yelp, his hand landing on the entrance's edge.

"Found it!" Pinder shouted triumphantly, dusting himself off and turning to the others with a proud grin. "See? Just took a little expert intuition, is all."

Aeron and Seraphina exchanged amused glances, but they humored him, stepping over to inspect the narrow passage. "Well done, Pinder," Seraphina said, a smile tugging at her lips. "Definitely couldn't have done it without you."

"Of course you couldn't," Pinder boasted, oblivious to Koko's role in his "discovery."

With the crack now located, Aeron crouched down beside Koko, patting his nose. "Alright, Koko. This is where we'll have to part for a bit. Wait here, keep an eye out. And if any trouble comes, run. Don't wait for us."

Koko gave an understanding bray, nodding his head as if in agreement.

Pinder leaned down, giving Koko a conspiratorial pat. "Just hold down the fort, you heroic mule, you. We'll be back soon, hopefully with a legendary scythe and no new bruises."

With one last pat, they turned toward the narrow path, leaving Koko with a watchful look, standing guard at the entrance.

The three of them squeezed through the narrow, jagged path, the walls pressing close on either side as they inched forward, carefully avoiding the uneven stone beneath their feet. Pinder muttered complaints under his breath about the tight space, but they kept moving, pushing through the dark corridor for what felt like an eternity. After what must have been at least three hundred yards, the pathway opened abruptly, and they stepped out onto a plateau that looked like no place they'd seen before.

The air was strangely still, yet thick with an eerie energy. The sky above was a swirling canvas of deep purples and blues, unlike any earthly sky. Wisps of clouds drifted low, their edges faintly glowing, as if they were lit from within. Shadows clung to the edges of the plateau, and a heavy silence filled the space, occasionally broken by a faint, echoing sound, like the distant wail of souls. Aeron shivered, instinctively brushing it off as the wind.

"Alright," Pinder said, his voice a bit too loud as he glanced around, rubbing his arms as if to keep warm. "This… this is something, alright. Really not at all like the stories." He laughed awkwardly, though it came out a little shaky. "You know, haunted mountains sound a lot less terrifying when you're swapping tales over a drink."

Seraphina gave him a gentle nudge. "What's wrong, Pinder? Ready to turn back?"

He cleared his throat, straightening. "Maybe we don't stay too long, eh?"

Aeron nodded, though his eyes remained fixed on the plateau. Strange shards of ghost glass were embedded in the rocks around them, catching the unnatural light in a mesmerizing way. "Look at this," he murmured, kneeling down to inspect a piece of glass. It was sharp and glossy, its color shifting between shadowy black and translucent gray. "Ashi wasn't exaggerating. There's enough ghost glass here to keep him busy for a lifetime."

Seraphina ran her fingers along one of the shards, her expression thoughtful. "This place doesn't feel natural. It's like it's part of somewhere else entirely."

As they took in the strange landscape, a new sound reached their ears—a faint hum that seemed to rise from the very ground beneath them, winding through the air like a whisper. They exchanged uneasy glances, brushing it off as just another oddity of the mountain.

Then, at the far edge of the plateau, Aeron's eyes narrowed. His breath caught as he spotted it.

The scythe.

Resting on a dark, glass-like altar, its long handle seemed almost like bone, and the blade—a tempered black with a faint purple sheen—gleamed even in the low light. It was exactly as Aeron saw in his dreams, an otherworldly presence radiating both beauty and danger.

The three of them stood in silent awe, knowing what they'd come for was right before them, yet feeling the weight of its power and mystery bearing down on them.

A crack of lightning split the sky, so sudden and loud that Pinder yelped, staggering back, his eyes wide as he struggled to compose himself. "Bloody hell!" he shouted, looking around as if everyone else missed the sheer force of it.

He pointed at the weapon and said a bit too loudly, "Hey, there it is! The scythe!"

Without a second thought, Pinder strode over to the altar, reaching toward the weapon. Just as his hand got close, a sharp, invisible force repelled it, a crackling sensation racing up his arm like static electricity. He pulled his hand back, wincing, but undeterred, he tried again—only for the same invisible charge to repel him once more. This time, his fingers tingled, and he stumbled back, frowning.

"Alright, farm boy," he said, glancing over his shoulder at Aeron with a wry smile, "looks like it's all yours. I'll, uh, handle the glass." With a shrug, he turned to start gathering ghost glass into a crate, casting wary glances at the scythe every now and then.

Seraphina stayed close, watching intently as Aeron stepped forward. Her gaze flickered with concern and curiosity, sensing the connection he felt with the weapon. Aeron's eyes never left the scythe. It was as if everything he'd experienced so far had led him to this very moment. There was a pull, a sense of something calling him home, a familiarity he couldn't quite place but felt in every inch of his being.

He reached out slowly, anticipation tightening his breath, his fingers stretching toward the scythe. But before he could even make contact, the scythe suddenly rose from the altar, moving through the air as though guided by unseen hands. It flew straight into his grip, a perfect fit, as if it had been meant for him.

Another crack of lightning flashed across the sky, illuminating the plateau in an eerie glow.

Aeron's grip tightened around the scythe's handle, the weight of it feeling natural, powerful—alive.

A sudden, overwhelming rush of energy flooded his veins—a sensation like the pure passion he shared with Seraphina, but amplified a thousand times. His heart raced, every nerve alive with an intense power he'd never felt before. The weight of the scythe felt almost nonexistent in his hands, as if it were an extension of his very self.

Without conscious thought, he spun the scythe, each movement fluid and precise, a natural grace guiding his hands. He sliced through the air, testing its weight—or lack thereof—and marveled at how effortlessly it glided. It was as though his body remembered every technique, every maneuver, even though his mind couldn't place the memory. Each spin and slice was as effortless as breathing—natural, second nature.

Pinder, watching with narrowed eyes, huffed, a hint of envy in his voice when he said, "Quick ... think fast, farm boy!" With a smirk, he hurled a chunk of ghost glass straight at Aeron.

Aeron's instincts reacted before his mind could even process. In an instant, he sidestepped with blinding speed, raising the scythe and slicing cleanly through the glass, which split in two and fell to the ground without a sound. The movement was so swift, so seamless, that it took Seraphina and Pinder a moment to even register what happened.

They exchanged a look, stunned. Aeron stood calm and composed, the scythe resting in his grip as if he were born wielding it.

Before Pinder or Seraphina could question Aeron's new-found agility, the ground beneath them shook violently. A deep, guttural rumble filled the air as a massive shadow loomed overhead. With a sudden crash, a towering, twenty-foot cyclops landed before them, its grotesque frame dripping with thick, black goo. In one massive hand, it wielded a tree trunk like a crude maul, splintered and jagged at the ends.

The creature let out a chilling roar that reverberated across the plateau. Its single, glaring eye locked onto Aeron, and, despite its enormous size, it lunged forward, the tree raised high to strike. Aeron froze, and Pinder and Seraphina watched in horror as the cyclops brought the tree crashing down on him with a force that shook the ground, sending up a cloud of dust.

"Aeron!" Seraphina cried out, her voice laced with panic.

But as the dust began to clear, they heard a calm voice from the other side of the massive tree, just a few feet beyond the cyclops's reach.

"What?"

They turn, wide-eyed, to see Aeron standing just beside the fallen tree, his expression focused but relaxed. He'd moved a few feet to the side, just enough to evade the crushing blow by a hair, showing impressive speed.

The cyclops let out a confused growl, its eye darting around as it processed that its target wasn't where it expected. Aeron nodded to Seraphina and Pinder with a small, reassuring smile, then turned back to face the cyclops, gripping the scythe firmly as he prepared for the real fight.

The cyclops swung its massive tree maul with brutal force, each strike barely missing Aeron as he dodged with nimble precision. He stepped in after every swing, finding openings and landing precise cuts with the scythe. Each slice was measured, deliberate, yet left deep, dark gashes in the creature's goo-covered skin.

Seraphina stood a few paces back, her eyes focused as she loosed arrow after arrow, each one finding a different mark on the cyclops's massive frame. The creature roared in frustration, swinging wildly, but Aeron's movements were too quick and calculated. He sidestepped every strike with hairbreadth precision, the scythe flashing as he carved through the creature's limbs.

Seraphina drew her bow taut, aiming carefully before releasing a final arrow. It struck the cyclops directly in its single eye. The creature recoiled, letting out a bellow of agony and clutching at its face as dark goo oozed from the wound. Its roar echoed across the plateau, raw and furious, yet it remained standing, refusing to dissipate.

Taking advantage of the distraction, Pinder slipped in close, circling behind the cyclops. With quick, calculated strikes, he sliced into the back of its massive Achilles tendon, his blade cutting through goo and flesh. The cyclops let out another howl, stumbling as its leg buckled beneath it. With a shuddering groan, it dropped to its knees, its massive form shaking the ground.

Aeron seized the opportunity. With a determined look, he gripped the scythe, took a running start, and leaped, rising to the kneeling cyclops head height. In a single, swift motion, he swung the scythe with deadly precision, decapitating the creature in one clean strike.

As the head fell, the cyclops's body shuddered, dissolving into dark mist before it even hit the ground. Aeron landed lightly beside Pinder, barely disturbing the dust on the ground. They exchanged a brief nod, both breathing heavily but triumphant, while Seraphina lowered her bow, a proud smile spreading across her face.

The plateau fell silent again, the remains of the creature dissipating in the air like shadows fading with the dawn.

As the last wisps of the cyclops's dark form faded into the breeze, Aeron stood, his chest rising and falling steadily, the scythe resting comfortably in his grip as though it had been his weapon all his life. Pinder and Seraphina stared, the sheer skill and ease with which Aeron handled the scythe leaving them both in silent awe.

Pinder was the first to break the silence, shaking his head with a bewildered grin. "Alright, farm boy, what in the world happened back there? Leaping around, swinging that scythe like it's a feather ... you're telling me you didn't train with this thing for a thousand years?"

Aeron laughed, looking at the scythe in his hand as if he, too, could hardly believe it. "Honestly? It feels ... familiar, but I can't explain it. It's like my body knows exactly what to do, even if my mind doesn't."

Seraphina crossed her arms, a curious smile on her lips. "Familiar? So, what else can you do now, Aeron?" Her gaze was half-teasing, half-encouraging, as if eager to see just how far his newfound abilities go.

Pinder raised an eyebrow, rubbing his chin with a smirk. "Only one way to find out. Let's test it!" Without warning, he reached down, grabbing another piece of ghost glass and tossing it straight at Aeron.

Aeron's body reacted instinctively. He shifted smoothly to the side, letting the glass sail past him, his eyes met Pinder's with a grin. "That all you've got?"

"Oh, we're just getting started." Pinder grabbed another piece, tossing it at him from a different angle.

Aeron stepped back effortlessly, slicing the shard mid-air with a quick flick of the scythe, each movement smooth and precise. The pieces clatter harmlessly to the ground, Pinder and Seraphina exchanging impressed looks.

Pinder chuckled, clearly amused. "Alright, let's see how high you can jump, hero." He pointed to a rocky ledge about fifteen feet above them, his eyebrows raised. "Think you can get up there?"

Aeron eyed the ledge, feeling a strange sense of confidence. He bent his knees, focused, and sprung upward, clearing the distance in a single leap, landing lightly on the ledge as if it were second nature. He looked down at them, a mix of surprise and exhilaration in his expression. "I ... I didn't know I could do that."

Seraphina laughed, shading her eyes to look up at him. "Neither did we! This is incredible."

Aeron hopped back down, landing gently beside them, his movements fluid. He was still marveling at his newfound abilities when Pinder decided to test him one last time. He sidled up close, pretending to be lost in conversation with Seraphina, then suddenly swung a fist toward Aeron, hoping to catch him off guard.

But Aeron's reflexes were too sharp. He stepped back in the blink of an eye, catching Pinder's wrist before his punch could even land. He let out a laugh, shaking his head. "Nice try, Pinder."

Pinder, now genuinely laughing, threw his hands up. "Alright, alright, you win! Whatever's going on, you're faster and stronger than I've ever seen." He glanced at the scythe, a hint of awe in his gaze. "This thing is turning you into something else."

Aeron looked down at the scythe, turning it thoughtfully in his hand. "Maybe it's helping me remember who I am," he said softly, the weight of the words settling over all of them as they contemplated the mysterious powers that were undeniably a part of him. With the thrill of discovery still lingering, Pinder clapped his hands together, glancing around the eerie plateau. "Alright, fun's over," he said, rubbing his arms against a sudden chill. "Let's get off this haunted rock before we're dealing with more surprises. The sooner we're back in Tideheaven, the better."

They began gathering as much ghost glass as they could carry, each shard glinting with a strange, shadowy sheen. Pinder's eyes narrowed thoughtfully as he watched Aeron. "Hey, Aeron, what do you say you carve us some bigger pieces from that altar? You're slicing through things like butter. Bet you could give us a nice stackable set."

Aeron nodded, stepping toward the altar, the scythe humming with an odd sense of readiness in his hands. He surveyed the dark glass-like surface, then, with four precise movements, made two horizontal and two vertical slices. The scythe glided through the altar effortlessly, the stone separating into even, manageable chunks. They each grabbed a piece, admiring how perfectly stackable they were.

Pinder chuckled, shaking his head in amazement. "Ashi's going to love this. These'll keep him busy for years."

They gathered the larger chunks and piled them together, emptying their bags of smaller shards to make room for the solid pieces. With a final glance at the plateau, they turned and retraced their steps down the narrow path, rejoining Koko, who greeted them with a soft bray, as if impatient to leave.

Aeron and Seraphina loaded down Koko carefully, balancing the pieces on his saddle as Pinder tied them off securely. With their haul packed, they set off down the mountain, feeling a sense of accomplishment—and perhaps a little relief—as they left the strange, otherworldly plateau behind them.

As dusk fell, rain began to patter down on the rocky slope of

Mount Limbo, growing heavier with each passing minute. The trio found a wide ledge on the pathway—a rare, sheltered spot with a narrow crevice nearby just big enough for Koko to take cover. They set up camp as best they could, though with no way to start a fire in the wet conditions, they settled in for a cold, damp evening.

Pinder dug around in his pack, pulling out a small stash of rabbit jerky. "Well, it's not exactly a feast," he said, handing out the pieces. "But it'll do."

They munched quietly for a few moments, the steady rain creating a soft, rhythmic background. Pinder glanced around, squinting through the dim light, and suddenly raised an eyebrow. "Wait a minute … did we only bring two tents?"

Aeron cast a glance at Seraphina. "What can I say? Perks of traveling with good company," he said, nudging her.

Seraphina grinned back, raising an eyebrow at Pinder. "Maybe you should've brought one of your bar wenches along, Pinder. They could've kept you warm through this cold, rainy night."

Pinder laughed, rolling his eyes. "Very funny. As if anyone could survive the climb with me just to freeze their tail off up here. I'll stick with my trusty bedroll, thank you very much."

They shared a few more laughs, the camaraderie easing the chill of the rain. As night settled in, each of them drifted off to sleep, bundled tightly in their bedrolls, with Koko dozing peacefully nearby, shielded from the rain.

The next morning, the trio awoke to a gray sky and a lingering drizzle as they quickly broke down camp, rolling up their damp bedrolls and securing their packs. Koko shook the morning dew from his coat as they began their descent, picking their way carefully down the remaining stretch of Mount Limbo.

As they neared the base, a rustling from a nearby bush caught their attention. A dark, goo-covered humanoid figure suddenly lunged, its eyes fixed on Aeron. Without a thought,

Aeron's hand moved instinctively, slicing clean through the creature in a single, fluid motion. The creature barely had time to react before it dissipated into a wisp of dark mist, scattering in the air.

Pinder raised an eyebrow, crossing his arms with a smirk. "Alright, I'll take the next one, then. Can't let you hog all the fun."

Aeron chuckled, shrugging. "Be my guest. Somehow, I think we'll have plenty of chances."

The three of them shared a knowing glance, fully expecting the next couple of days to be filled with relentless, dark creatures. But surprisingly, the rest of their journey was calm, with only the occasional eerie silence reminding them of the mountain's strange energy.

As they approached Tideheaven on the evening of the second day, they were met with a final challenge. A massive bear-like figure, easily twice the size of any they'd encountered before but smaller than the cyclops, emerged from the tree line, its body dripping with thick, black goo. Its deep growl echoed across the path as it fixed its gaze on them, charging forward with a guttural roar.

Pinder grinned, stepping forward. "Alright, my turn," he said, twirling his dagger and giving Aeron a playful wink. "Watch and learn, farm boy."

Aeron and Seraphina exchanged amused glances as they step back, watching as Pinder danced around the bear's heavy, lumbering swipes. He darted in and out, landing small cuts along its sides and shoulders, each slice drawing the creature's attention and gradually slowing it down. His movements were quick and precise, and he seemed to enjoy the challenge, a cocky grin never leaving his face.

But after a few minutes, Seraphina sighed, crossing her arms. "This is taking forever," she muttered, pulling an arrow from her quiver and nocking it. She took aim, steadying her breath, and released. The arrow flew straight and true, striking the bear directly in the heart. With a pained groan, the creature stumbled, its body dissipating into dark mist.

Pinder spun around, his mouth open in mock outrage as Seraphina laughed, lowering her bow. "See? One cut, one death," she said, grinning.

Pinder huffed, pretending to be offended. "You're just jealous of my technique."

"Sure," Seraphina replied with a wink. "But some of us prefer efficiency."

With laughter lightening their spirits, they turned toward Tideheaven, knowing they'd finally reached the end of their journey.

The group, with Koko proudly leading the way, made their way into the village. They headed toward the stables, where Pinder dug into his coin pouch, handing the stable keeper a handsome sum. "Make sure Koko gets a feast fit for a king— fruits, vegetables, whatever he wants," Pinder said, patting Koko's neck.

The stable keeper nodded, eyeing the mule with newfound respect. "A feast it is. You've earned it, haven't you, lad?"

Koko gave a contented bray, as if fully understanding the treat awaiting him.

With Koko settled, they unloaded the large, stackable chunks of ghost glass, each piece glinting with an eerie, shadowy hue as they shouldered the weight of their haul and made their way toward the temple. They were greeted by Talia, the one-legged priestess, who watched them with a spark of curiosity in her eyes.

"Well, well," she said, her tone half-amused, half-suspicious. "Seems you brought back more than ghost stories this time."

Pinder grinned, gesturing for her to follow. "Come, come— no need for temple talk. Let's go down to the bar near the center of The Veil. The whole crew's going to want to hear this tale."

Talia raised an eyebrow, intrigued, before nodding and falling in step beside them as they descended into the hidden world below the temple. They walked down the winding paths of The Veil, their presence quickly drawing attention. Word spread quickly, and by the time they reached the bar tucked in the heart of the thieves' den, a small crowd had gathered.

Around them, familiar faces appeared—the band of small-time thieves and assassins, their expressions ranging from skeptical to curious. Ashi, arms crossed, watched them intently; and Talia, who settled herself at the edge of the bar with an expectant look.

Pinder stepped forward, gesturing for silence, a smirk on his face as he prepared to share the tale of their journey up Mount Limbo. The bar was thick with anticipation, the entire den hanging onto his every word, waiting to hear what treasures and tales they'd brought back from the haunted mountain.

Pinder hopped up onto a crate near the bar, his face lighting up with a mischievous grin as he surveyed the gathered crowd. He cleared his throat, spreading his arms wide. "Ladies, gents, rogues, and ne'er-do-wells of Tideheaven! Lend me your ears, for I have a tale to tell. Atale of bravery, of battle, of horrors and treasures the likes of which you can only dream!"

The crowd leaned in, intrigued, as Pinder dove in, his voice rising theatrically. "We climbed up Mount Limbo, that treacherous beast of a mountain, in rain that felt like it could drown the gods themselves! The wind howled like a banshee, the cliffs ready to crumble beneath our feet at any moment! And did we flinch? Not a chance! We had our mighty mule, Koko, who could have wrestled a bear if we'd asked!"

The room chuckled, and a few raise their mugs in tribute to Koko, who would now be enjoying his well-deserved feast in the stables.

"But that was only the beginning," Pinder continued, eyes glinting. "As we climbed higher, we encountered creatures of shadow, each one stranger than the last! A Mountain goat, a heard of wolves, a bear—all twisted, dripping with dark goo, hurling themselves at us with the fury of a hundred storms! Aeron here," he said, pointing dramatically at Aeron, "cut through them like a hot knife through butter, not even breaking a sweat!"

Aeron shook his head slightly at Pinder's over-the-top retelling, while Seraphina rolled her eyes, amused.

"Oh, but it got worse," Pinder said, lowering his voice, his face going somber as he leaned forward. "We reached a plateau at the mountain's peak. A cursed place, where the very air was thick with magic. The clouds? Purple as bruises! The ground? Shattered glass everywhere, sharp as daggers and black as midnight!"

The room fell silent, everyone hanging onto his words as he paused for dramatic effect.

"And there it was ... the scythe," he whispered, eyes widening. "Not just any scythe, mind you. No, this was a weapon straight from legend, its blade blacker than night, sharper than the devil's grin. Aeron grabbed hold of it like it was made just for him, and suddenly, he was unstoppable! The ground shook beneath his feet! He moved faster than any man alive!"

At this, Ashi raised an eyebrow, a hint of skepticism in his gaze, but he said nothing, simply folding his arms and listening.

Pinder's voice rose, his face breaking into a grin. "Just when we thought we'd seen it all, we faced the biggest creature of them all. A cyclops, towering twenty feet tall, carrying a tree trunk like it was a toothpick!" He waved his arms around for emphasis, nearly knocking over a nearby mug. "This thing was covered in dark goo, with an eye like a full moon, furious and red. It charged us, roaring like thunder, and if you think I'm exaggerating, well—" he leaned closer to the crowd "—you'd be right!"

The crowd erupted into laughter, and even Talia cracked a

smile.

"But I'm telling you, I took on that beast with my own two hands," Pinder said, putting his fists on his hips. "And Aeron took it down in one swift motion, like slicing through silk!" He turned to Ashi, pointing with a flourish. "And as if all that wasn't enough, we've brought you back something special, my friend."

The crowd leaned in, intrigued, as Pinder gestured to the crate stacked with chunks of ghost glass. "We didn't just bring back any old rock, no. We brought back some of the rarest, most valuable material ever known: Mount Limbo's ghost glass! Enough to keep you crafting for years, Ashi!"

The gathered crowd burst into cheers and applause, mugs raised, laughter echoing through the Veil as Pinder took a dramatic bow. Ashi nodded approvingly, a faint grin on his usually stoic face as he stepped forward to examine the glass, the rare material gleaming under the dim lights of the bar.

Pinder hopped down, accepting claps on the back and a fresh drink, his grin as wide as ever as the tale settled in, the Veil buzzing with excitement at their adventure.

As the night wound down and the laughter faded, the crowd dispersed, leaving only Ashi, Talia, and the trio of adventurers. Pinder and Aeron were still basking in the thrill of their storytelling, while Seraphina stretched, grateful for the break from climbing mountains and battling monsters.

Talia stood off to the side, her face marked with a thoughtful frown. After a moment, she turned toward them, her brow furrowed. "You mentioned the creatures you faced were covered in black goo?"

Aeron nodded, and Seraphina answered with a reassuring but puzzled look, "Yes, they all were. We first noticed it with smaller animals—a boar and a bear near the farm, then a squirrel, and eventually ... well, that cyclops on the mountain. They all had the same dark ooze."

Talia's expression shifted from confusion to sudden realization. "Follow me. Quickly."

Without waiting for them to respond, she headed back toward the temple. The group hurried after her, climbing the winding stone steps. She led them into a small, tucked-away room, filled with dusty tomes and scattered stacks of parchment. A tiny library. She pulled an old scroll from a shelf, the parchment worn and fraying at the edges, barely held together.

"This," she said, unrolling it carefully on a small table, "is something I bought off a fence a few months ago. I thought it was just another scrap of junk at first, but when I looked closer … well, it's clearly ancient. Damaged, too, and barely readable."

Aeron, Seraphina, and Pinder leaned in, their eyes scanning the faded, crumbling text. Much of it was written in an undecipherable script, but here and there were inked drawings: crude depictions of humanoid figures covered in thick, dark goo. Sketches showed creatures that resembled bears and other animals, all marked by the same shadowy coating.

Talia ran a finger along the edge of the scroll. "I don't know enough of the language to translate it all, but I've managed to piece together fragments. From what I can tell, it describes the same kinds of creatures you've been encountering." She paused, her eyes narrowing as she studied the scroll. "Here's the interesting part—I believe this scroll was stolen from the Great Oaks Temple, home of the largest library. They have entire rooms dedicated to ancient languages and texts."

Aeron glanced up from the scroll. "You think they might have more like this? Maybe answers about where these creatures are coming from?"

Talia nodded and said in a low voice,. "I'd bet on it. There's talk of a secret order within the temple. They're rumored to deal with the … stranger, darker side of knowledge. Things that aren't meant for the general public. If anyone would know about these creatures, it's them."

Pinder let out a low whistle. "Well, looks like our next stop is Great Oaks, then."

Talia rolled up the scroll, carefully handing it to Aeron. "Take this with you. Maybe they can translate it, or at least help you figure out what we're dealing with."

Aeron accepted the scroll with a determined nod. Their journey now led to Great Oaks, where more answers, and likely, more dangers, awaited in the vast library of the temple.

As dawn broke over Tideheaven, the streets fell quiet, casting long shadows across the worn cobblestones. The team gathered their belongings, securing everything they would need for the journey ahead. For the first time, there was an air of finality. They weren't simply preparing for another adventure. This time they were getting answers.

Pinder lingered near the entrance of The Veil, saying his goodbyes to the familiar faces he's come to call his friends. His old crew stood around him, a mix of curiosity and melancholy on their faces. Pinder, grinning, spread his arms wide. "Well, you sorry lot, looks like I'm off for real this time. But trust me, I'll be back with stories you won't believe, and blades even finer than what I've got now." He tapped the hilt of one of his many knives, his smirk full of mischief.

One of his crew clapped him on the back. "You'd better, Pinder. I don't care how far you go; no one can tell tales quite like you."

Pinder winked before rejoining Aeron and Seraphina, who were waiting just outside the temple.

Inside, Talia met them with a solemn nod. "I know you're all set on Great Oaks," she said, glancing between the three of them. "If the scroll's origin is there, as I believe, then there may be answers waiting for you. And if the rumors of the secret group are true, this hidden order could help. Or, at the very least, they'll know something."

Aeron nodded. "We'll be careful. If they're as secretive as you say, we'll need to approach them wisely."

Talia opened her mouth to respond but Ashi strode in, interrupting the conversation with a serious expression.

"One piece of advice, all of you," he began, his gaze steady. "The only way to Great Oaks from Tideheaven is through the Great Expanse."

Seraphina tilted her head. "The Great Expanse?"

Ashi nodded, his voice low. "A barren desert. Empty of all life. No water, no shelter, just miles upon miles of sand and ruins from a civilization long gone. You're looking at a two-day journey, if you make good time. But you'll need to stay sharp and ready. There's nothing out there, and I mean nothing."

Pinder raised an eyebrow. "Sounds charming."

Ashi cracked a faint smile. "You'll find it anything but charm. Make sure you pack enough supplies to last. I won't be there to hand you a flask when the water runs out."

They each gave Ashi a nod, words of gratitude passing between them before they head out of the temple, making their way back to the marketplace for last-minute preparations. They gathered extra waterskins, dried rations, and sturdy, weather-worn cloaks to guard against the desert winds.

With everything packed, they stood at the eastern edge of Tideheaven, the Great Expanse stretching out before them, endless and unyielding. With a final look back at the city, they stepped forward, heading east into the unknown.

Chapter 20: "The Watchful Eye"

The relentless sun beat down on them as they stepped into the Great Expanse, the desert stretching out before them like a vast, empty sea. Sand and fragments of stone spread as far as the eye could see, interrupted only by the occasional ruin — remnants of some long-forgotten civilization. The heat settled heavily on their shoulders, and they shielded their eyes against the intense glare of the sun.

Aeron and Seraphina walked in comfortable silence, but Pinder, for once, looked more thoughtful than mischievous. After a while, he glanced over at Aeron, clearing his throat. "You know, I realize I haven't really told either of you much about myself," he said, his tone soft.

Aeron looked over, surprised. "I'd say you've told us plenty, with all those wild stories."

Pinder grinned faintly, but his usual spark was missing. "Yeah, well, those are different. Stories are easy." He stared at the sand for a long moment, the barren land stretching around them in every direction. "But the real stuff? That's harder. But I figure, you two have shown me I can trust you."

He paused, the warmth in his grin giving way to something more vulnerable. "I was born in Tideheaven, or as far as I know, I was. I never knew my parents. Never had a family. I'd like to think they were pirates or adventurers or something exciting like that, but honestly? I have no idea. I was left at the docks one day, and that was that."

Seraphina glanced over at him with a soft expression, sympathy in her eyes. "You grew up alone?"

Pinder shrugged, kicking at a loose stone. "Alone, yeah. Tideheaven's not exactly an easy place for a kid. I had to learn quick. You either figure out how to survive, or you don't last long. I was a little street urchin, scrounging for scraps, picking pockets when I could manage it. Not exactly the sort of thing you hear in the stories, is it?"

Aeron's face softened, listening intently. "So that's how you learned to handle yourself on the streets?"

Pinder nodded, a small, wistful smile crossing his face. "Yeah. I'd watch the sailors and the merchants, mimic how they moved, how they talked. Over time, I got pretty good at blending in. People started to notice me, and not as some street rat, but as someone they could talk to. That's when I figured it out." He looked up, his eyes glinting with that familiar spark. "People like a good story. They'd gather around, just to listen. I'd make things up, spin wild tales, and they'd laugh. For the first time, I felt like someone. Like I mattered."

He fell silent, his gaze fixed on the horizon. "So I kept at it. Built myself up, one story at a time. It was like armor, in a way. The stories made me more than just some kid who didn't have a family. I could be anything. An adventurer, a pirate, a hero."

Aeron slowly nodded, understanding. "You found a way to belong."

"Yeah," Pinder said softly, almost to himself. "I did. And maybe that's why I wanted to come along with you two." He rubbed the back of his neck. "Guess I was hoping for a real story, one that didn't need any embellishing."

They walked in silence for a while, Pinder's words lingering between them like the heat of the desert sun. Seraphina broke the silence, her voice gentle. "You know, Pinder, you're not just a character in a story to us. You're family now."

Pinder's expression softened, caught off guard. He chuckled, glancing away as if to hide his embarrassment as his cheeks pinked. "Well, thanks for that. But don't go getting too sentimental on me. I've got a reputation to uphold."

Aeron chuckled, clapping a hand on his shoulder. "Don't worry. We'll keep your street-rat image intact."

The conversation drifted back to lighter topics, but a new sense of closeness lingered. Pinder's story had drawn them in, revealing a depth to him they hadn't fully seen before. The barren landscape felt a little less desolate, softened by their shared memories and growing bond.

But as the day wore on and the sun began to sink lower, a faint feeling of unease settled over them. Seraphina glanced back occasionally, feeling as if they were being watched. But each time she looked, there was only the emptiness of the desert stretching behind them.

As the sun dipped lower in the sky, casting warm hues across the vast sands of the Great Expanse, Aeron and Seraphina drifted a few paces behind Koko and Pinder. The two in front were engrossed in animated conversation, Pinder's laughter carrying back on the desert wind to Aeron and Seraphina.

Aeron glanced over at Seraphina, a small smile tugging at the corners of his mouth. "You know, it's funny ... I've been through a lot since waking up in that little village, barely knowing who I was. But I never expected to feel this way." His eyes met hers, an unmistakable warmth in his gaze.

Seraphina gave him a playful nudge, her eyes sparkling. "What way?"

Aeron rubbed the back of his neck as he searched for the words. "That night we spent together ... it was more than just passion. It was like I'd finally found something worth holding onto." He hesitated, his voice quieting, "And maybe it's more than that. Maybe it's you."

Seraphina's face softened, her usual quick wit tempered by something gentler. "You know, Aeron, I've felt that way too.

When I agreed to go on this journey with you, I thought it was just adventure calling, something exciting to shake up my life. But being with you feels different." She paused, a small smile playing on her lips. "It feels like I finally found a place where I belong."

They walked in silence for a moment, the unspoken feelings settling comfortably between them.

Aeron reached for her hand, his fingers intertwining with hers as they continued along the path.

Seraphina let out a soft laugh, breaking the quiet. "Imagine going back to that little village with the not-so-brilliant priest, Ted. We could have him marry us on the spot. The ceremony might not be exactly traditional, but I'm sure he'd put on a great show." She met his eye, then looked away, her cheeks turning pink.

Aeron laughed, shaking his head. "He'd probably forget half the vows, or mix up our names halfway through." He squeezed her hand. "But I'd do it. Every word. Whether he remembered them or not." The idea of marrying Seraphina made him feel at peace.

They shared a warm, lingering look, each knowing that their journey had brought them not only closer to their destination but closer to each other. With a renewed sense of purpose, they walked on, side by side, ready to face whatever the Expanse held for them.

The sun continued its slow descent, casting a warm glow over the desert, when Pinder suddenly glanced back and caught sight of Aeron and Seraphina walking hand in hand. He stopped dead in his tracks, a broad grin spreading across his face as he raised an eyebrow, clearly unable to resist the opportunity.

"Well, well, well," he said, loud enough to make sure they heard him. "Look at this. Hand-holding now, eh? I knew the two of you were sharing a tent and likely bumpin' uglies, but this here?" He gestured dramatically, as if he caught them red-handed in the middle of a grand scandal. "This looks like something a little more … real."

Seraphina chuckled, rolling her eyes but not letting go of Aeron's hand. "Always the romantic, Pinder."

Aeron gave Pinder a playful glare, shaking his head. "Maybe it is real, Pinder. Some things don't need embellishing, you know."

Pinder smirked, crossing his arms and leaning in as if he was ready to hear all the details. "So, you're telling me that once we've taken care of these goo-covered horrors and saved the world from whatever darkness is coming, you two are going to go settle down in some sleepy village?"

Aeron and Seraphina exchanged a look, the warmth between them unmistakable. Aeron nodded. "We were thinking of going back to that little village I woke up in, where Seraphina's from. After all of this is over, we want something peaceful. Something simple."

Seraphina squeezed Aeron's hand, grinning at Pinder. "And you know what? You'd better be there. We're counting on you to be the best man at our wedding."

Pinder's eyes widened in mock surprise. "Me? The best man? At a real wedding?" He put a hand over his heart, feigning emotion. "I never thought I'd live to see the day. You two getting all settled and respectable, and me, the proud, upstanding best man."

Seraphina laughed, raising an eyebrow. "You'd better behave, Pinder. Or I'll make you wear a suit."

Pinder winced as if the very thought was torture, but a hint of genuine warmth slipped into his expression. "Fine, fine. If I can get a decent story out of it, maybe even a few drinks on the house, I'll suffer through it. For the two of you." He glanced away, a rare softness in his voice. "Besides, I think maybe it'd be nice to be part of something real."

Aeron reached out, clapping him on the shoulder. "Then it's

settled. When all this is over, we'll go home together. And you'll be right there with us."

Pinder's grin returned, full of his usual mischief. "I'll even give a speech. Just wait. Everyone will be in tears, calling it the best wedding they've ever seen."

With shared laughter and a new sense of hope between them, the trio, with Koko plodding steadily ahead, continued their journey into the Expanse. For the first time, their minds were filled with thoughts of a future beyond the dangers they faced. A future where they'd each have a place to belong.

As twilight advanced, the group found a perfect spot to set up camp—a small ruin perched atop a hillcrest, overlooking the sprawling desert. The remnants of broken stone walls offered a bit of shelter from the wind, and the cool night air settled comfortably around them. They shared a simple meal, passing around dried fruits and meats, while Koko enjoyed a bucket of water drawn from their precious supply of skins.

They laid out their bedrolls on the ground, choosing to forgo the tents for once. The stars were breathtakingly clear, scattered across the sky in a brilliant array. The desert night seemed almost magical, with the cool breeze and the soft, silvery light bathing everything in a gentle glow.

As they settled in, Seraphina looked over at Pinder, an expectant smile on her face. "So, Pinder," she said, pulling her bedroll closer. "Since we're all here under the stars, and it's a night as beautiful as this, care to tell us one of those legendary tales from your days in Tideheaven?"

Aeron leaned back, his gaze on Pinder. "Yeah, something on the cheerful side for once. Like that first big score that got you started."

Pinder laughed, running a hand through his hair. "Alright, alright. I'll tell you about the day I landed my first real score. The one that made me more than just some street rat and let me start moving up in the world." He leaned back, eyes glinting with nostalgia. "So, I was maybe twelve at the time, still a scrappy little thing. Barely even knew what I was doing most of the time, just picking pockets here and there to get by. But one day, word went around that a merchant ship was coming in. One loaded with silk and spices, all sorts of rare goods. And I thought, well, wouldn't it be nice to get my hands on something like that?"

Aeron and Seraphina chuckled, already drawn into the story.

Pinder continued, his grin widening. "I knew I'd need a plan, though. So I spent all night watching the docks, getting the timing down. I knew exactly when the guards changed shifts, when the merchants unloaded, everything. And when the time was right, I snuck in—quiet as a cat, mind you—and managed to get my hands on this little carved ivory box, filled with coins." He paused, his eyes gleaming. "That box was worth more than I'd ever seen in my life. Enough to buy food, clothes, even some new blades. It set me up for weeks. More than that, it got me noticed by the right people. Before I knew it, I was working with a proper group, learning the tricks of the trade from some of the best in Tideheaven. That score didn't just buy me food, it bought me a future."

Seraphina smiled, her eyes warm. "Sounds like you were made for it. I'm surprised you didn't end up leading the whole crew."

Pinder chuckled, scratching his head. "Who knows, maybe someday I will. But for now, I'm glad I've got a different crew." He glanced at Aeron and Seraphina, his gaze lingering with an unspoken gratitude.

As his story faded into the quiet night, he noticed that Aeron and Seraphina had both drifted off, their breathing steady and peaceful. He gazed up at the stars for a while, reflecting on how, for the first time in a long time, he felt like he'd truly found something meaningful. A real family.

With a contented sigh, he settled back onto his bedroll, a soft smile on his face as he, too, drifted off into sleep beneath the vast, star-strewn sky.

In the dead of night, a piercing, frantic neigh split the silence, jolting Aeron, Seraphina, and Pinder from their sleep. Koko stomped and brayed wildly, his eyes wide with terror, his ears pinned back and pointed to the darkness behind them.

Aeron was on his feet in an instant, heart pounding. Pinder frantically rubbed the sleep from his eyes, taking in the scene.

"Koko… what's got him so spooked?" Aeron asked, his voice thick with confusion. The ground beneath them trembled, a slow, steady thrum building into a shaking that reverberated through the sand and stone.

"An earthquake?" Seraphina asked, panic rising in her voice.

But Pinder, wide-eyed, pointed behind them. "No … no, look!"

The team turns, and there it was—a nightmarish sight surging over the horizon, silhouetted against the pale moonlight. An army of countless figures, dark and twisted, stampeded toward them with a relentless hunger. Goo-covered humanoids, wolves with dripping jaws, hulking bears, and creatures they couldn't even name surged forward, an endless wave of darkness.

Aeron's voice was barely a whisper. "There's… there's too many of them."

Pinder snapped into action, grabbing what supplies he could. "No chance in a fight, not against that!" He tossed their gear onto Koko, giving the mule a reassuring pat even as his own hands trembled.

"We have to run—now!"

The group scrambled, grabbing what they could in the frantic chaos, each of them thrown into motion by sheer survival instinct. They broke into a sprint, heading for the ruins, hoping to use the broken walls and scattered stones as obstacles. But as they weaved in and out of the crumbling structures, their hearts sank. The army barely slowed, the creatures moving at an unnatural, terrifying speed.

Each step, each turn, each desperate glance over their shoulders revealed the same horrifying sight: the creatures pressing in, their eyes gleaming with dark intent. Seraphina knocked over a crumbling pillar, but nothing seemed to slow the advancing horde.

They ran, breath coming in gasps, feet pounding against the warm sand, weaving through the dark, moonlit desert. Every instinct screamed at them to keep going, keep running, as the monstrous army charged after them, an unstoppable tide of darkness and death devouring the ground behind them.

In the silent, haunting light of the moon, they ran for their lives, the desert stretching endlessly before them.

As they sprinted through the desert, Pinder suddenly stumbled, pulling to a halt. "Wait!" he shouted, breathless, pointing ahead. "Look!"

Aeron and Seraphina skidded to a stop beside him, and their hearts sank. Looming just ahead, a massive cliff wall rose over seventy feet high, its sheer face stretching wide on either side, disappearing into the darkness. The moonlight glint off its stone surface, smooth and impossible to climb. They were trapped.

"It's too wide to go around," Seraphina said, her voice laced with dread. "We've been herded here."

Realization dawned as Aeron's gaze snapped back to the horde closing in behind them. "It's a trap," he whispered. "They've been pushing us here the whole time."

The three of them pressed their backs to the cold stone, weapons raised, breaths heavy. A silent understanding passed between them, a mix of determination and the quiet acceptance of what might be their last moments together.

Pinder forced a shaky grin, trying to keep things light. "Well, if this is it, at least I got to share a drink with you two."

Seraphina's eyes shone, even in the darkness, as she reached over to grip Pinder's shoulder.

"You're more than just a drinking buddy, Pinder. You're family. And we'll go out fighting together."

Aeron nodded, raising his scythe as the horde came within a few hundred feet from them. "For every step we take back, they'll pay for it."

Just then, a voice rang out from above, echoing down the cliff face. "Go left! That way. There's a hidden stairway!"

The three of them looked up, startled, and saw a figure perched at the top of the cliff. The stranger was cloaked, their hood pulled low to hide their face, but before they could question him, the figure hurled something down—a clay jar blazing with flames. It smashed into the ground just in front of them, and a wall of fire roared to life, spreading across the sand and forming a barrier between them and the oncoming horde.

The creatures screeched, hesitating just outside the flames, their dark forms shimmering in the heat.

"Move!" Aeron yelled, spotting a narrow opening to the left.

They grabbed Koko's reins, guiding him to the hidden stairway, barely wide enough for him to squeeze through. The mule didn't hesitate, scrambling up the zigzagging stone steps and away from the flames, his hooves clattering against the rough stone as he ascended. Seraphina, Pinder, and Aeron follow, pressing close to the walls as they climb.

Behind them, the hooded figure threw another flaming jar that smashes at the base of the stairs, igniting the entrance. The fire surged, creating an impenetrable blaze that cut off the creatures' path, their enraged screeches muffled by the roar of the flames.

The group didn't stop until they reached the top, breathless and shaken, each of them casting a grateful glance toward their mysterious savior. They made it to the summit, hearts pounding, the terror of the chase finally behind them. For now.

The group collapsed onto the rocky ground, breaths coming

in gasps, each of them feeling the weight of their frantic escape. The desert sprawled out below, quiet once more, with only a faint line of smoke marking where the fires continued to burn. They sat in silence for a moment, letting the adrenaline ebb, grateful for the reprieve.

The hooded figure, who had been watching them intently, stepped forward. With a graceful, calculated motion, he pulled back his hood, revealing a sharp-eyed, thoughtful face with an expression of intense focus. His frame was slight, almost delicate, but there was a nimble energy about him, as though he'd spent more time in libraries and on the road than in combat.

"I've been tracking those creatures for months," he said, his voice calm, measured, and precise. "All over the world, they've been cropping up—small appearances at first, minor sightings here and there. It seemed random at first, like an unfortunate pestilence. But these latest reports ..." he paused, glancing down at the smoldering desert below. "None of it makes any sense."

Aeron, still catching his breath, looked up at him, a mixture of gratitude and curiosity in his expression. "Who... who are you?"

The man straightened, a faint smile flickering across his face. "Ah, yes, proper introductions. Forgive me. I'm Tate. Some people call me Spud, though I imagine that's of little relevance." He extended a hand with a refined gesture, then narrowed his eyes as though deep in thought. "Researcher, academic, collector of anomalous data. My interest, however, is far from casual. These creatures, these entities, have been an ever-expanding curiosity for me."

Pinder, who was recovered enough to lean on his knees, raised an eyebrow. "Ever-expanding curiosity, huh? And what are you planning to do about it?"

Tate's eyes glinted with a mix of frustration and fascination.

"Oh, if only it were that simple. You see, I can't operate on guess-work or 'feelings.' I require observable patterns, repeatable phenomena, verifiable data." He gestured toward the desert. "The recent appearance of this swarm, for instance—far larger and more organized than any I've seen—is a deviation. An aberration."

Seraphina tilted her head. "So you don't know what's causing it?"

Tate pursed his lips. "Precisely. Which is why I continue to study them. To discern a method, an underlying structure, if you will, behind this chaos. Until then, all we have are fragments of data and, of course, a few rudimentary solutions," he added, gesturing to the remnants of the fire jar at the base of the stairs. "One of my own concoctions. Crude, perhaps, but quite effective."

Aeron nodded, taking in Tate's words, feeling both a sense of relief and a growing curiosity about this strange new ally.

As the group settled, Aeron reached into his pack, pulling out the old, tattered scroll they'd received from Talia. He unfolded it carefully, spreading the fragile parchment across a flat rock. The faded ink and worn edges made it almost unreadable, but the drawings were unmistakable: crude depictions of creatures with dark, swirling shapes encasing them in shadowy, goo-like forms.

Tate's eyes lit up as he leaned closer, studying the scroll with an almost reverent fascination. "This… this is extraordinary." He examined the drawings, his finger tracing over the inked lines. "These figures are unlike anything I've seen recorded before." His brow furrowed, and he squinted at the words scrawled beneath the images. "Unfortunately, the script is largely unfamiliar. I can't decipher most of it. But here," he pointed, his finger tapping a single word under one of the sketches. "Mirage."

Aeron nodded. "That's all we know about them so far. We

found this scroll with the help of a friend, who believes it was stolen from the Great Oaks Temple library. If it really came from there, someone in the temple must have more information."

Tate's expression shifted from cautious excitement to a full-fledged eagerness, his mind clearly racing. He stood, pacing as he spoke, his words spilling out in a torrent of thoughts. "The Great Oaks Temple, with its vast archives... this could be it! This could be the breakthrough I've been hoping for. If their library holds texts on these creatures—mirages as they seem to be called—we may finally have access to firsthand accounts, research, and ancient lore that might shed light on their origin, their purpose, the reason for their coordinated behavior."

He paused, eyes gleaming. "Think about the possibilities! Perhaps these mirages serve as a warning or as some manifestation of an ancient curse. Or maybe they're being summoned, deliberately unleashed by some hidden hand." His gaze sharpened, his mind racing down every path. "If we could find records on similar events from the past, we'd be closer to understanding their patterns. Knowledge isn't just power here. It's survival."

He caught himself, glancing at the group, his voice softening as he said, "But this attack ... the way they organized, pursued you so relentlessly—it's unprecedented. There's nothing in their behavior that would suggest intelligence, let alone strategy. It's almost as if ..." He trailed off, his face shadowed with doubt. "As if something—or someone—was guiding them."

An ominous silence fell, heavy and contemplative, as each of them considered the implications.

Pinder cleared his throat. "Listen," he said, shrugging, "all I need to know is two things: how to kill these creatures, and how to make sure they don't come back. Don't care if they're mirages or monsters or cursed shadows from some ancient scroll. If they're after us, we need to get rid of 'em, plain and simple."

Tate let out a quiet, almost exasperated sigh, turning his head to fix Pinder with a pointed look. "That's the issue with such an approach," he began, his tone a blend of irritation and conviction.

"You see, understanding every detail about a subject—the origins, the anatomy, the motivations—allows you to navigate that subject with a glorious efficiency."

Pinder raised an eyebrow, but Tate wasn't finished. He gestured to the crumbling ruins around them.

"Efficiency, Pinder, is the difference between thriving and being left behind, like these stones. If we're to survive, we need to know more than just how to fight them off. We need to know how they think, why they exist, how they operate. Every piece of knowledge is a potential advantage over our enemy."

Pinder smirked, crossing his arms, but there was a glint of interest in his eyes. "So you're saying if we know them well enough, we'll know exactly how to kill them and stop them from coming back?"

"Precisely," Tate replied, a gleam of satisfaction in his eyes. "Only by comprehending the entirety of the problem can we hope to eliminate it fully. Anything less, and we're just reacting to the next wave, never staying ahead of it." He let his gaze settle on Pinder. "And in a world that's constantly moving forward, those who can't navigate it are simply left behind."

Pinder chuckled, shaking his head. "Sounds like you've got your work cut out for you, Spud. But if it keeps these things off our backs, I'm all ears. "Seraphina chuckled, nudging Pinder with her elbow. "Good thing we've got you, huh? Just point you in the right direction and let brute force do the rest."

Pinder snorted, feigning offense. "Brute force? I'll have you know my technique is refined, thank you very much. I'm an artist with these blades."

Aeron smiled, then turned to Tate, his expression a mix of curiosity and amusement. "So, you're coming with us to Great Oaks, then?" he asked casually, but there was a hint of sincerity behind the question.

Tate let out a dry, almost incredulous scoff, crossing his arms. "You think I'd let a group of adventurers run off with the only promising lead I've come across in ages?" He shook his head, giving Aeron a bemused look. "No, no, I have to see this through myself. You three may be perfectly fine blundering your way through, but I require precision. If Great Oaks holds answers, I intend to be there when they're uncovered."

Pinder chuckled. "Looks like we've got ourselves a new teammate, whether we asked for one or not."

Tate raised an eyebrow. "Think of it less as teamwork and more as a collaboration." He glanced at each of them, his eyes softening. "Of course, if you'll have me."

Aeron and Seraphina shared a look, each giving a slight nod of agreement. Their paths were now entwined, bound by the same mystery and the quiet sense that, somehow, they were stronger together.

As dawn broke over the desert, the first rays of sunlight casted a soft, golden light across the summit, illuminating the ancient stone ruins around them. The group sat in a quiet stillness, each of them catching their breath and letting the warmth seep into their bones. The events of the night hung heavy, and though they were all exhausted, there was an unspoken agreement. They'd had enough of the summit.

Aeron stretched, glancing at the others. "We've got light now. Might as well make use of it."

Pinder yawned, rubbing his eyes as he stood, shaking the stiffness from his legs. "More sleep would've been nice, but I'd rather keep moving than sit here waiting for the next attack."

Seraphina nodded, adjusting her pack. "Agreed. And I don't think it's wise to linger any longer than necessary."

Tate was already on his feet, his small bag secured over his shoulder, his expression focused.

"Quite right. There's little benefit to remaining at such a conspicuous location. Let's get moving."

They set out from the summit, navigating the narrow path that wound down the cliffside. The desert stretched before them, still and quiet, but as they descended, there was a subtle, unsettling feeling that clung to them, as if the echoes of the horde were still watching, waiting.

Aeron glanced over his shoulder, unable to shake the prickling sensation on the back of his neck. He caught Seraphina's eye, and her wary expression told him she felt it too.

"Does anyone else feel like we're being followed?"

Pinder rolled his shoulders, his hand instinctively hovering near his blade. "If something's out there, let's hope they're smart enough to keep their distance this time."

Tate pursed his lips, scanning the horizon as he walked. "An army of creatures does not vanish without a trace. If they have intelligence—guidance—then they would certainly be tracking our movements. In fact, I'd venture to say we're their primary focus."

They walked in tense silence, each of them hyper-aware, eyes darting over the landscape. The vast emptiness of the desert offered little cover, but every shadow seemed to loom a bit darker, every whisper of the wind a bit sharper. Though they were moving away from the ruins, that eerie sense of pursuit never quite faded, hanging over them like a shadow they couldn't outrun.

As they continued down the path, Tate's keen eyes settled on Aeron's scythe, his gaze lingering with obvious curiosity. After a moment, he cleared his throat. "I must say, Aeron, that scythe is a rather unique choice of weapon. There's something almost … otherworldly about it." He tilted his head. "And forgive my bluntness, but you three are an odd ensemble of adventurers. What exactly is it you're all doing? With scrolls, strange creatures? This is no ordinary quest, I gather."

Aeron glanced at Tate, considering how much to share. Finally, he took a breath, gripping the scythe a little tighter as he spoke. "It's complicated. I didn't start out looking for trouble. In fact, I didn't start out looking for anything. My first memory is waking up in a small village with no idea of who I was or where I came from."

Tate raised an eyebrow, interest sparking in his eye. "No memory? Intriguing."

Aeron nodded, the memories stirring as he continued. "I was told I'd been in a farming accident, that I was lucky to be alive. But I started having these dreams—visions, really. I'd see a mountain, and at the summit, a scythe. Not just any scythe," he said, lifting it for emphasis, "this one. I felt drawn to it, like it was part of me. So, with Seraphina, and later Pinder, by my side, I set out to find it."

Tate listened intently, his face a mix of fascination and concentration.

"When we reached the mountain," Aeron continued, "I found this scythe at a plateau, resting on what felt like an altar. And as soon as I touched it ..." he trailed off, searching for the words. "Something changed in me. I felt stronger, faster, like I knew exactly how to wield it. Almost as if I'd been waiting for it all my life."

Tate's gaze narrowed, his eyes gleamed with intrigue. "So, you believe this scythe is tied to you somehow ... spiritually, perhaps? Fascinating. And I take it that's when these creatures— the goo-covered mirages—began pursuing you?"

Aeron nodded. "That's when it got worse. We were attacked a few times before I found the scythe, but they were scattered, only one every so often. After I took the scythe, though, it's been different. The attacks seem to be focused on me now, almost like they're drawn to either the scythe... or to me personally. They haven't let up."

Tate stroked his chin, absorbing every detail. "And this

scroll," he said, gesturing to the pack. "A map of sorts, perhaps, or a record? It seems likely these entities have roots in something older—something ancient and largely forgotten."

"That's what we hope to uncover in Great Oaks," Aeron said, glancing back at the horizon. "If the answers are anywhere, they're in that library."

Tate nodded, a faint smile crossing his face. "Well, I must admit, you three have taken on a mystery of considerable depth. I may have misjudged you. You're not just adventurers, are you? There's a greater purpose at play. Something fated."

Aeron shrugged, sharing a quick with Seraphina and Pinder. "We don't know much about fate. We're just doing our best to figure this out and survive."

Tate's eyes lingered on the scythe, his curiosity evidently piqued. "Then perhaps … you're not as lost as you think. In any case, consider my interest thoroughly captured."

The desert stretched endlessly ahead, each of them carrying a piece of the puzzle, a silent commitment to uncovering what binds them to this strange, perilous path.

As they pressed through the endless stretch of desert, Tate fell slightly behind, his mind racing as he watched Aeron from a distance. The scythe glinted in the early light, a weapon that, to Tate's trained eye, wasn't merely a tool. It was something ancient, something carrying a weight beyond even Aeron's understanding.

This is no ordinary quest, Tate thought, his gaze narrowing as he considered the details. *And Aeron is no ordinary man.*

The attacks, the strange and relentless creatures—they defied all logic, all natural order. Tate had seen monsters, curses, and anomalies in his travels, but nothing with this level of coordinated intensity. The creatures' singular focus on Aeron spoke of something greater, something intentional.

They're being drawn to him, or perhaps even directed.

A cold realization settled over him. Aeron, with his strange amnesia, his unnatural connection to this scythe. It was more than a coincidence. Tate suspected there was a design at work here, something woven into the very fabric of Aeron's existence. And if Aeron was tied to it, then so were the answers Tate sought.

Tate, you fool, he thought with a hint of frustration, *this is exactly why you need to stay close. If he's at the center of this enigma, he may be the key to unraveling it all.*

A quiet resolve filled him as he watched Aeron lead the way, unaware of the theories forming in Tate's mind.

Whatever this mystery is, it's connected to him in ways he doesn't even realize. And until Tate had those answers, he would follow, observe, and uncover every piece of this puzzle, no matter where it led.

As they crossed the center of the dry, cracked basin, Pinder's voice echoed across the empty landscape, filling the air with another one of his wild stories, "So, there I was, trapped by three dock guards," he said, a mischievous grin lighting up his face, "armed with nothing but a broken dagger and a mind sharp as any blade. They thought they had me cornered, but I knew better."

Seraphina rolled her eyes, but there was a smile tugging at her lips. "Let me guess. You talked your way out of it?"

"Oh, did I ever," Pinder said. "I spun them a tale about a chest I'd 'accidentally' stashed nearby. I had them convinced it was filled with jewels and silver, a 'real treasure,' if they could only keep it hush-hush. So, what do they do? They rush right over and pry the thing open. And what do they find?" He paused, a laugh in his voice. "A box of rat bones — collected from some street kid who thought they were priceless relics!"

Aeron let out a chuckle. "I bet they were furious."

Pinder snorted. "Oh, they nearly tossed me into the harbor. But the look on their faces was worth every ounce of trouble."

Laughter rose between them as they walked, enjoying the

break in tension. But as they neared the basin's center, the ground beneath them felt brittle and uneasy, as if something far below was stirring.

A low, distant vibration suddenly hummed through the ground, cutting through their laughter. They paused, the humor fading as a familiar sense of dread settled over them.

"Do you feel that?" Aeron's voice was low, cautious.

The vibration intensified, becoming a rumble that reverberated through the basin, different this time. There was an odd, deep resonance, like the sound of something massive shifting beneath the sand.

Seraphina's eyes widened. "Is it … the horde?"

But before anyone could answer, the ground erupted, a massive shape bursting through the sand in an explosion of grit and dust. They staggered back, shielding their eyes as something towered above them—thirty feet of thick, coiled muscle, dark as midnight and covered in a familiar slick of black goo.

A massive cobra, as wide as an elephant and stretching high above them, reared up, its hood spreading like the sail of a ship. Its eyes gleamed with a malevolent intelligence as it swayed, its body shimmering with the black ooze.

The rumbling grew louder as the creature let out a deep, guttural hiss, a sound that seemed to vibrate through their bones. It stared down at them, massive and deadly, a powerful mirage in the form of a monstrous cobra.

They froze, breath caught in their throats, as the creature prepared to strike. The cobra's hood flared wide as it fixated on Aeron, eyes narrowed, its deadly focus directed at him. It coiled and twisted, its massive, goo-covered form undulating in the sand with each movement. The ground trembled beneath its weight, cracks forming in the dried basin floor as it reared back and lunged forward, striking at Aeron with terrifying speed.

Aeron moved swiftly, barely dodging the cobra's fanged maw that slammed into the ground, missing him by inches. He rolled to the side, jumping to his feet in an instant and leaping out of range. His movements were quick, precise, each jump more confident, each dodge more fluid. The scythe glinted in the sunlight, its blade seemingly guiding his every move.

From a distance, Seraphina and Pinder watched with tense focus, their eyes darting between Aeron and the cobra. "That thing is relentless," Seraphina muttered as it struck at him again, her hands tightened on her bow. She nocked an arrow, her gaze sharp as she tracked the cobra's movements, looking for a weak spot.

"Relentless doesn't even begin to cover it," Pinder muttered, gripping his blade. He darted forward, attempting a strike from the side, only to be swatted away by the cobra's tail as it coiled tighter, its attention never straying from Aeron. Pinder stumbled back, teeth clenched, frustration in his eyes. "I can barely get close to that thing!"

Seraphina let an arrow fly, aiming for the creature's hood. The arrow struck, lodging into the goo-covered skin, but the cobra didn't flinch. "Pinder," she said softly, "we're going to have to keep it distracted and give Aeron room to work. Keep your distance. Strike when you can."

Pinder nodded, circling wide and watching for any opening, but the cobra's focus on Aeron was unyielding. It lunged again, its jaws snapping shut inches from Aeron as he twisted out of the way, his movements impossibly fast. With every dodge, he landed lightly, barely touching the ground before springing up again, bounding from one spot to the next with a newfound agility that left the cobra a fraction of a second behind.

Tate stood back with Koko, watching with keen, calculating eyes. He noted every movement, every strike of the cobra's fangs, every slice of Aeron's scythe. The dance of danger and speed left Tate's mind racing, piecing together patterns in the creature's relentless attacks.

The cobra reared back, hissing, its body coiling tighter as it prepared for another strike. Aeron, breathing hard and fast, eyed its movements, ready to evade. But this time, the cobra was quicker. It struck downward with blinding speed, jaws wide as it slammed into the ground where Aeron stood.

The earth shook with the force of the impact, sand flying into the air in a dense cloud.

Seraphina gasped, her heart lurching as the dust settled and Aeron was nowhere to be seen.

"Oh no …" she whispered, eyes wide, gripping her bow tighter. Pinder's face paled, his hands clenched around his blade, staring at the spot where Aeron had disappeared.

The cobra rose, towering above them, its hood spread wide, letting out a triumphant hiss that reverberated across the basin. It coiled its body in satisfaction, black goo dripping from its mouth, its gaze fixed on the rest of the group as if daring them to challenge it.

But as the silence settled, a glint of silver sliced through the air, and the cobra's expression shifted from triumph to shock. A line split down its hood, from jaw to crest, and in a brutal flash, Aeron's scythe burst from within, tearing through the creature from the inside.

With a shuddering hiss, the cobra's head separated from its body, both parts dissolving in a mass of black goo that dissipated into the air, leaving only a faint, sickly mist in its wake, leaving Aeron, covered in thick, dripping cobra guts, breathing heavily.

The group stared in stunned silence as the remains of the cobra vanished around him. Aeron lowered his scythe, his face streaked with remnants of the battle, and met their gazes with a faint, exhausted grin, dripping with the remnants of the cobra's innards.

As the last of the dust settled, Tate stepped forward, a faint smirk pulling at the corners of his mouth and said dryly, "You're smarter than you look, Aeron."

The team turned to Tate with a mix of confusion and curiosity, still reeling from the intensity of the fight.

Aeron, wiping some of the goo from his face, shrugged. "The scales were too tough to break from the outside. Figured if I let it swallow me, I'd have a better shot at taking it down from within."

Pinder stared at him for a moment before bursting into laughter, stumbling backward until he fell over, clutching his sides as he laughed. "You're telling me you let yourself get eaten! That's brilliant, and completely insane!"

But Seraphina, still shaking from the ordeal, rounded on Aeron with an incredulous look. "You absolute idiot! You had me worried to death. I thought I'd lost you!" Her voice trembled, caught between relief and frustration, and she punched him lightly on the shoulder.

Aeron chuckled, a bit sheepish. "Hey, it worked, didn't it?"

She glared at him but couldn't hold back a smile. "Next time, just try not to get eaten. It's less stressful for all of us."

Tate's eyes gleamed with approval and intrigue. "Well, reckless or not, it was undeniably effective." He shook his head, almost as if recalculating his opinion of Aeron. "You've surprised me, Aeron.."

Aeron shrugged, giving his team a grateful look as he let out a weary sigh. They survived, and somehow, in their shared relief, they felt stronger, more united.

As they regrouped, catching their breath after the chaos of the battle, Tate surveyed Aeron with a thoughtful, almost troubled expression. After a long moment, he stepped closer, his gaze sharp, as if trying to puzzle out an unsolvable mystery.

"You know, Aeron," Tate began, his tone uncharacteristically hesitant, "I can't help but notice something curious. The way you moved out there, the speed, the power—frankly, it's beyond what any human should be capable of."

Aeron looked at him, surprised. "What are you saying,

Tate?"

Tate let out a small sigh, clearly conflicted. "I don't know, honestly. It doesn't make any sense. I've spent my life studying the boundaries of what's possible, mapping the limits of the human body, and you're defying those limits without even realizing." He crossed his arms, his expression a mixture of fascination and doubt. "It's as if you've tapped into something otherworldly. Like you're drawing from a well of strength that shouldn't exist."

Aeron glanced down at the scythe in his hand, its dark, bonelike hilt somehow familiar and foreign at the same time. "Ever since I found this scythe, I've felt ... different," he admitted, searching for the right words. "It's like I know what to do before I do it, and everything just feels lighter."

Tate's eyes narrowed, baffled. "But that's exactly the problem. It shouldn't be possible. This scythe, whatever it is, shouldn't grant you abilities that defy the very nature of what we know. Human strength has limits, and you're exceeding them with ease. It's almost as if ..." He trailed off, visibly struggling with his own conclusions.

"As if what?" Aeron pressed, both curious and unsettled.

Tate let out a frustrated sigh, looking away as he gathered his thoughts. "As if you aren't bound by the same limitations as the rest of us. As if you're something else. But that can't be, can it?" He met Aeron's gaze, conflicted. "It's maddening, honestly. My research is based on facts, data, observable limits, yet here you are, defying every rule without explanation."

Aeron's expression was unreadable. "I don't have answers for you, Tate. All I know is that something changed the day I found this scythe. And since then, I feel like I'm just trying to catch up with it."

Tate shook his head, both baffled and captivated. "Well, whatever the case, you're a living anomaly, Aeron. And that only deepens the mystery of who—or what—you truly are."

As the day began to wane, casting long shadows across the desert, the team caught sight of something remarkable on the horizon: a vast, dark-green line rising up against the amber sky. They stopped, staring in awe.

"Could that actually be ...?" Seraphina whispered.

"Great Oaks," Aeron breathed, eyes wide.

The forest was massive, even from a distance, towering trees stretching as far as they could see. They were still miles away, but the sight filled them with a renewed energy, a destination finally within reach.

But dusk had settled, and with night approaching, they decided to make camp one last time. As they sat around the fire, Pinder couldn't help himself. He nudged Aeron. "So, let's talk about the cobra," he said, looking around at everyone for effect. "I mean, did you all see this man?" He gestured dramatically, hands mimicking the snake's hood. "Not only does he let himself get eaten—eaten—but the next thing we know, he's gutting that beast from the inside out! It's like something out of a children's tale!" He chuckled, raising an eyebrow. "I mean, here we are, freaking out, thinking that's it, Aeron's snake food. And then—bam!—the guy slices right out of its belly! If that doesn't make for a story worth telling, I don't know what does."

Tate was still processing the event in his own analytical way, but even he couldn't suppress a small smile. "As reckless as it was, there is an undeniable poetry in the maneuver."

Seraphina rolled her eyes, but a smile pulled at her lips. "And here we thought you only had one way of telling stories, Pinder. I didn't know you could make even near-death encounters sound so entertaining."

"Oh, trust me," Pinder said, leaning back with satisfaction, "by the time I'm done with it, people will think Aeron slayed a dragon."

Laughter died down as the fire crackled, and slowly the team began to settle for the night. Seraphina lingered by the fire, her eyes following Aeron as he stepped away from the group, finding a quiet spot under the stars. After a moment, she followed, quietly taking a seat beside him, her face softened with something between sadness and relief.

A long silence stretched between them before Seraphina finally spoke, her voice barely a whisper, "I thought I lost you."

Aeron looked at her, the weight of her words settling over him, and a gentle quietness surrounded them, the distant forest casting its shadow on the camp as night fully embraced the desert.

Aeron turned to Seraphina, the flickering firelight reflecting in his eyes as he studied her face, his gaze softened with something deeper than before. He reached for her hand, holding it gently.

"Seraphina," he began, his voice low and filled with a quiet intensity. "I've been through things I can't even begin to understand, and this … what's happening with me, with the scythe. I don't have answers. But I do know one thing—my love for you is real, more real than anything else in this world." He squeezed her hand, his thumb tracing gentle circles over her skin. "When we're fighting, it's like everything slows down. Almost like time just … stops." He paused, struggling to explain what's happening inside him. "These ideas, these moves—they flash in my mind as I'm doing them, like my body already knows what to do, and my mind is just trying to keep up. It's peaceful … and terrifying. Kind of like how loving you feels," he said softly. "I feel like I'd do anything to protect you, but the thought of losing you scares me more than anything else."

Seraphina's face softened, her eyes shining with unshed tears. "I don't want you risking yourself like that, Aeron. Not if I can help it."

He leaned in, his voice a whisper. "I promise, I won't do anything that puts either of us at risk like that again. We're in this together, and I'll be by your side, always."

They shared a long, lingering look, each feeling the depth of their bond. Slowly, Aeron cupped her face, and they closed the distance, sharing a deep, passionate kiss that said everything their words couldn't.

A familiar, teasing voice cut through the night. "Oi! You two lovebirds need to get a room and call it a night," Pinder called. "We've got a lot to do tomorrow, you know."

Aeron and Seraphina broke apart, laughing softly, sharing a knowing glance before heading back to camp, hand in hand.

As dawn broke, casting the first rays of sunlight over the horizon, the team stirred from their bedrolls. They shared a quick, quiet breakfast, the excitement in the air palpable as they gathered their belongings, ready to finish their journey.

By mid-morning, the vast forest of Great Oaks loomed ahead of them, its ancient trees towering in dense rows, and beyond it, the city itself—an impressive sprawl of towering stone structures and winding streets, bustling with life even at this distance. High, fortified walls encircled the city, and beyond the gates, buildings rose in tiers, each level filled with houses, shops, and busy market stalls.

Aeron and Seraphina exchanged a glance, both of them awestruck. They'd traveled to towns and small villages, but this … this was something entirely new. Pinder let out a low whistle, his eyes wide as he took it all in, the sheer size of the city unlike anything he'd seen. The streets were lined with rows of merchants selling colorful goods, the hum of city life buzzing in the air, creating a pulsing energy that filled every corner.

"This place is massive," Aeron muttered, taking in the intricate stonework of the gate, the detailed carvings along its arch, and the thick iron doors that stood open, welcoming travelers in.

Tate, observing their reactions, couldn't help a slight smile. "Great Oaks is one of the largest cities in this part of the world. People come from everywhere, and it shows." His tone was calm, almost amused. "Don't get too distracted. Inside is just stone and streets, like any other city."

They approached the main gate, where guards stood at attention, and the noise of the city rose in a chorus of voices, carts, and hoofbeats. The air was thick with the scent of spices and the distant, savory aroma of street food cooking in the marketplace.

The team shared a final look, a mixture of anticipation and awe, before stepping through the gate and into the bustling heart of Great Oaks. Their journey had brought them to one of the most vibrant, lively places they'd ever seen, and as they passed beneath the gate's arch, they knew their search for answers was just beginning.

Chapter 21: The Great Oak's Feast

As they stepped through the gates of Great Oaks, the city's sheer size and bustling energy hit them. The towering buildings, layered balconies, and bustling streets created a maze of activity that stretched far into the city. People of every sort—traders, travelers, scholars—moved through the streets, filling the air with vibrant conversation and the hum of daily life.

Pinder let out a low whistle. "Now this is a city. Looks like our best stories are about to begin."

Aeron and Seraphina took it all in, wide-eyed. Tate, however, moved with a calm familiarity, navigating the crowded streets with the precision of someone who had done so before.

They made their way toward the heart of the city, where the towering spires of the Great Oaks Temple loomed above, a beacon of knowledge and mystery. The temple, grand and imposing, was a masterwork of carved stone and intricate architecture. Inside, they were met by solemn silence and a dim, candlelit atmosphere.

As they stepped into the vast hall of the Great Oaks Temple library, the quiet reverence seemed to settle over them like a shroud. Towering shelves stretched toward vaulted ceilings, lined with countless volumes, scrolls, and tomes, each promising secrets and stories from ages past. A priest, cloaked in muted robes and bearing an air of scholarly pride, approached them.

He studied the group with a calm, discerning gaze, and finally asked, "What brings you to the magnificent library of

Great Oaks? What knowledge do you seek?"

Before anyone else could respond, Tate stepped forward, his demeanor was respectful yet unmistakably sharp. "We are in search of records detailing the unusual, recent occurrences," he began, choosing his words with the precision of a practiced scholar. "Particularly accounts of dark, unnatural creatures — entities coated in a substance like black ooze, appearing in various forms and regions with seemingly growing frequency. These creatures defy the natural order, and their presence suggests some type of agenda".

The priest's expression shifted slightly, a hint of unease shadowing his face as Tate's words sank in. "Such knowledge is not typically sought by travelers," the priest said carefully. "There are indeed records in the restricted archives, though they are guarded."

Seraphina and Pinder exchanged a glance, both sensing the subtle resistance in his tone.

Tate, not missing a beat, pressed on. "Then surely, within a place as vast and revered as this library, there exists someone with the knowledge to discuss such matters. A more ... specialized group, perhaps?"

The priest's gaze hardened slightly, and he looked away, as though trying to find the words. "You speak of the Aethera Mortem. They are the keepers of knowledge not meant for ordinary eyes. Their purpose is to guard such matters closely, and I am afraid the answers you seek are beyond what I can grant."

Tate nodded, though his eyes flickered with frustration. "Of course. Thank you for your guidance." He stepped back, and the priest left them, casting a final cautious glance before disappearing deeper into the temple.

Outside, as they reconvene, Pinder's eyes gleamed with excitement. "Looks like we've been officially shut out," he said. "I suggest we get a bit ... creative."

Tate smirked knowingly. "I have a feeling you were waiting

for such an opportunity."

"Oh, you have no idea," Pinder replied, rubbing his hands together. "Now, here's what I'm thinking—"

As they stepped out of the temple, Pinder was already in the middle of outlining his plan, eyes gleaming with excitement. "We wait till nightfall. I'll get us access to the side gate. Nothing fancy, just a quick in-and-out. Once we're in, we'll make our way to the lower levels of the library. There'll be guards, sure, but with a bit of distraction, I figure we can slip past them. From there, we find the archives and get a look at whatever it is they're hiding."

Seraphina crossed her arms, her brow raised. "And if we're caught? This isn't some small-town tavern, Pinder. It's a temple full of scholars and priests. They might not take kindly to us ransacking their archives."

Pinder waved her off. "A small risk, sure, but nothing we can't handle. Besides, the Fang soldiers are the ones on the look-out for brawlers, not scholars sneaking into dusty old rooms."

Tate, who'd been listening thoughtfully, spoke up. "Breaking into a temple of scholars dedicated to guarding knowledge might not be the best approach to gaining their trust," he said dryly. "If the secret priests have the information we seek, it would be far more effective to access it through means other than theft. The order we're dealing with here is selective. Perhaps deliberately so."

As they debated, an amused chuckle interrupted their conversation. The group turned to see a hooded priest, much older and gray-bearded, quietly watering a patch of plants outside the temple. The priest glanced at them, his eyes twinkling with a keen, almost mischievous wisdom.

"Planning to break into our archives, are you?" he said, chuckling. "A bold move, if not entirely sensible."
Pinder's face flushed, but he quickly recovered with a smirk. "Depends on who you ask, old-timer."

The priest only laughed again. "If you truly wish to access the Aethera Mortem's knowledge, you don't need to sneak around. All you need is to make yourselves valuable enough for them to take notice."

Aeron stepped forward, intrigued. "Valuable? What do you mean?"

The priest set down his watering can, studying them with a sharp gaze. "The Aethera Mortem concern themselves with ancient knowledge, with truths and facts of great significance. They have no interest in trivial matters or day-to-day affairs. But if you can present something to them that piques their curiosity and advances their understanding of ancient mysteries or brings them closer to lost knowledge, they may find you worthy enough to grant access to their archives."

Seraphina leaned in, intrigued. "So, it's about trading knowledge?"

The priest nodded. "Precisely. Bring them something they cannot easily find, or prove yourself as someone who can advance their purpose. Whether that's information they seek or a skill they cannot replicate, they will only share their knowledge with those who hold value to their preservation."

Tate's eyes narrowed thoughtfully. "So, it's not just about what they know, but what they don't know—and what they desperately want to."

The old priest nodded, a faint smile tugging at his lips. "Precisely, young scholar. You must make them see you not as intruders but as allies in their pursuit of understanding."

The group exchanged a look, the gears already turning in each of their minds as they considered what they could offer.

Just as they processed the priest's words, a sudden, piercing scream split the air, followed by a cacophony of shouts and the clash of weapons echoing from the city walls. The group whipped around, tense, and saw townsfolk running toward the center of the city, panic etched on their faces.

Without hesitation, Aeron, Seraphina, Pinder, and Tate raced toward one of the main gates. The heavy thud of boots and the distant roars grew louder as they approached, and the sound of metal striking against unnatural flesh filled the air. They arrived to see soldiers of the Fang, the city's guard force, lined along the walls, hurling arrows and holding off countless dark, shifting figures—creatures cloaked in the familiar, thick black goo that marked the mirages.

Aeron spotted a commander barking orders, a hardened soldier with a grim expression. The team approached, and Aeron called out over the chaos, "What's happening? Are we under attack?"

The commander turned, his face drenched in sweat and battle-worn but fiercely focused. "It's worse than an attack," he said, voice strained. "The entire city is surrounded—north, south, east, and west. We're holding them at the gates, but I've never seen anything like this." He gestured to the horde, his jaw clenched. "These creatures just keep coming, as if drawn by something."

Tate narrowed his eyes, glancing at Aeron with a knowing look. "This isn't a random attack. They're here for a reason."

The commander shook his head, clearly outmatched. "Reason or not, if we don't find a way to stop them, this city will be overrun." He pointed toward the eastern gate, where the Fang soldiers pushed back another wave. "We're stretched thin, and every time we cut one down, another takes its place."

Seraphina unslung her bow, her face set in determination. "Then let's not waste any time." She readied an arrow, her gaze scanning the walls as she prepared to defend alongside the Fang.

Aeron nodded, his expression fierce. "Whatever's drawing them here, we'll find a way to stop it." He gripped his scythe, feeling the strange power within him surge as he readied himself to face the oncoming horde.

As the commander moved to rally his men, the team steeled themselves, knowing the battle was unlike anything they'd faced before.

As the team braced themselves, weapons at the ready, the commander's voice rang out in alarm. "Hold the line! Wait … Retreat! Fall back! We're about to lose the gate!" His voice wavered as he stared, eyes wide, at a massive figure emerging from the horde. A towering giant, nearly three stories high, its body dripping with the same dark ooze, gripped a shadowy great ax in its enormous hands.

The Fang soldiers stumbled back, and the commander turned to his men, desperation in his voice.

"We can't hold against that! Fall back!"

Aeron looked to Seraphina, seeking her gaze. She met his eyes, her expression unwavering, and gave him a nod, her confidence in him clear. With a steadying breath, Aeron stepped forward, his grip tightening on his scythe. In a powerful leap, he cleared the twenty-foot wall in a single bound, landing effortlessly on the other side.

Seraphina, Pinder, Tate, and the commander rushed to the edge of the wall, watching in awe as Aeron carved his way through the smaller creatures, each swing of his scythe sliced cleanly through the mirages as he moved closer to the giant. His pace was relentless, his movements a blur of precision and power, the black ooze dissipating with each strike.

At last, he stood toe to toe with the giant. The beast let out a deafening roar, swinging its colossal great ax down toward Aeron with a force that shook the ground. Aeron sidestepped, his scythe meeting the ax mid-swing, deflecting it with an explosion of sparks. The crowd on the wall gasped as Aeron deftly ducked under the next swing, the ax narrowly missing him as it carved a deep trench in the ground.

Aeron moved with fluid precision, slipping around the giant's attacks, every dodge calculated, every strike intentional.

He landed a series of critical hits—slashes across the giant's knees, a deep cut to its side—all the while dodging each deadly blow with an instinct that felt almost otherworldly. The giant roared in pain, each injury causing it to stumble, yet it continued to lash out, each swing as powerful as the last.

The fight reached a fever pitch as Aeron, sensing an opening, leaps high, his scythe flashing in the dim light. He brought it down with all his strength, the blade slicing through the giant's neck. In a single, decisive strike, the giant's head fell, its massive body staggering before collapsing to the ground.

As the giant's form hit the earth, the entire horde paused, a moment of eerie silence settling over the battlefield. Then, one by one, the mirages began to dissipate, their forms melting into wisps of black mist, vanishing as if they were never there. The giant, it seemed, was the heart of the horde, and with its defeat, the threat was instantly extinguished.

From the wall, the Fang soldiers cheered, their voices echoing through the city as the people of Great Oaks erupted in applause. Seraphina, Pinder, Tate, and the commander look down in awe and relief as Aeron stood amidst the dissipating shadows, breathing heavily, his scythe lowered in victory.

As the last wisps of the horde vanished, Aeron turned to see the commander making his way down from the wall, flanked by a few of his officers. The commander's expression was a mixture of respect, disbelief, and curiosity. He approached Aeron, extending a hand.

"Son, I've seen many battles, but I've never witnessed anything like that," the commander said, shaking Aeron's hand firmly. "You just saved this city from a massacre. I'll be recommending you for a medal, maybe even an honorary position within the Fang, should you want it."

Aeron nodded gratefully, trying to maintain a humble expression. "Thank you, Commander. I'm honored."

The commander narrowed his eyes, studying Aeron with

genuine curiosity. "But I have to ask. How in the hell are you so fast? So powerful? The way you moved … it's almost not real. I've seen some well-trained men in my time, but nothing comes close to what I just saw out there."

Aeron glanced away for a moment, then gave a modest shrug. "I've trained my whole life. Spent a lot of time learning how to handle myself in a fight," he lied, keeping his tone light. "Sometimes it pays off."

The commander raised an eyebrow, clearly not fully convinced but respectful enough not to press further. "Well, whatever training you've had, it's more than paid off tonight. The city owes you a great debt." He turned to his officers. "Make sure the citizens know what this man has done for us. And prepare his recommendation for a medal."

Aeron gave a respectful nod, saying nothing more as the commander and his officers exchanged murmurs of admiration. He stood quietly, his gaze distant, hoping his words had put their suspicions to rest.

The commander, visibly moved by the crowd's energy and Aeron's humble demeanor, turned to his officers. "Someone, get word to the mayor!" he called out, his voice carrying over the crowd. "We need a feast tonight, to honor this man and all he's done for Great Oaks!"

At his words, the crowd erupted into cheers, townsfolk clapping and raising their voices in gratitude and celebration. Children weaved through the crowd, mimicking Aeron's leaps and strikes, while adults shook hands and exchanged excited murmurs about the night's upcoming festivities.

As Aeron and his friends made their way back toward the city gates, one of the Fang guards hurried over, a broad grin on his face. "I just spoke with the innkeeper. He's heard of your heroics and insists on offering you and your friends free rooms and hot baths! You'll have the best of everything he can offer."

Aeron glanced back at Seraphina, Pinder, and Tate, each of

them grinning with a mixture of pride and relief.

"The feast will begin at nightfall," the guard added. "The whole city will be there to celebrate."

With one last wave to the crowd, Aeron and his friends headed back into town, anticipation and gratitude filling the air as they prepared to savor the respite they'd so rightfully earned.

As the group made their way into the inn, they were greeted by the warm glow of a roaring fire and the comforting scent of fresh linens and herbs. The innkeeper, a jovial man with a wide grin, waved them in. "Rooms for heroes!" he announced, beaming at them. "I've set aside our finest quarters, and hot baths are waiting. I reckon you've all earned a bit of peace tonight."

Pinder groaned in delight, practically bouncing on his feet. "You have no idea how much I need a hot bath," he said, stretching. "Feels like the last time I was this dirty, I was in a pigpen on a job gone wrong."

Seraphina chuckled, nudging him. "A little dirt builds character, but I think even I've hit my limit."

She glanced at Aeron, her smile softening. "We've all earned some rest."

Aeron nodded, his expression a mixture of exhaustion and gratitude. "A night of peace sounds perfect," he said, his eyes drifting toward the staircase leading to their rooms.

Just then, the stable master appeared in the doorway, smiling as he addressed them. "Don't you worry about that mule of yours. Koko, right? He's in good hands. I gave him a proper scrub myself," he said with a wink. "You'll have a gleaming mule come morning."

Pinder snorted, shaking his head. "Koko, treated like royalty. That mule deserves it after all he's put up with."

They all shared a laugh as the innkeeper directed them to their rooms, each separate, quiet, and lined with fresh linens. A steaming bath awaited each of them—a much-needed luxury after the trials they'd endured. As they each sank into the warmth, muscles relaxing for the first time in days, a rare sense of calm settled over them.

Tomorrow, the mysteries and battles would return, but tonight, they would savor the simple comfort of peace.

The group reconvened in the inn's dining hall, each looking refreshed and more relaxed than they had in days. Their clothes were clean, their faces glowing with the warmth of the baths, and there was a shared look of anticipation as they made their way outside.

As they stepped into the street, they were greeted by a vibrant scene. The city had transformed.

Colorful banners hung from every corner, music floated through the air, and laughter filled the streets. Children darted through the crowds, weaving in and out as they played games and waved ribbons. Stalls lined the streets, piled high with steaming plates of food: roasted meats, spiced breads, and tables overflowing with fruits and sweet treats.

Everywhere they looked, townsfolk were dancing, clapping, and singing along with musicians playing upbeat tunes. The sound of flutes and drums filled the square, and vendors called out to passersby, offering pastries and handcrafted trinkets. The air was thick with the scent of warm bread, roasted nuts, and the rich aroma of spiced cider.

In the center of it all stood a raised stage, adorned with colorful drapes and banners, marking the heart of the celebration. Atop it was the mayor, a stately figure dressed in formal robes, his face beaming as he surveyed the festivities. Spotting Aeron and the group, he raised a hand, calling for attention.

As the crowd quieted, the mayor gestured for Aeron to join him on the stage. Pinder gave Aeron an encouraging nudge, and Seraphina smiled reassuringly. With a deep breath, Aeron stepped forward, making his way up to the stage, the cheers of the crowd growing louder. A wave of applause and excited shouts filled the square.

The mayor stepped forward, placing a proud hand on Aeron's shoulder as he addressed the crowd. "People of Great Oaks!" the mayor called, his voice carrying across the square. "Tonight, we gather to celebrate not only our city, but this brave soul who fought valiantly to defend us. When the darkness of that terrible horde bore down upon our gates, it was Aeron who stood at the forefront, risking his life to protect ours."

The crowd erupted in another round of applause, and Aeron, a bit taken aback by the attention, gave an awkward nod of acknowledgment.

The mayor turned to Aeron, his expression serious. "Aeron, on behalf of every citizen here, I want to express our deepest gratitude. You not only defended our walls but gave us hope when we feared all was lost." He gestured toward a medallion glinting in his hands, the symbol of the Fang emblazoned on its surface. "This is a symbol of honor in Great Oaks—a mark given only to those who have gone above and beyond in service to this city. It is rare that we bestow it upon someone outside the Fang."

The crowd fell silent, watching as the mayor pinned the medallion onto Aeron's tunic. Aeron, feeling the weight of the honor, met the mayor's gaze, nodding in appreciation.

"Thank you, Mayor. I'm deeply honored," Aeron said, his voice steady but humble. "But I didn't do this alone. I had my friends by my side. And I wouldn't be here without them."

The mayor nodded, glancing over at Seraphina, Pinder, and Tate, who stood near the front of the crowd, watching with pride.

"Yes, we owe our gratitude to the entire group," the mayor said, motioning them forward. "Each of you played a role in today's victory. And, of course, Aeron, I must ask ... How is it you possess such skill, such strength? There are trained men in our ranks who would be hard-pressed to match you in battle."

A murmur of curiosity swept through the crowd as all eyes turned to Aeron. He paused, searching for the right words.

"I've trained hard," he said, his tone even, choosing his words carefully. "I've spent my life learning to handle myself, to be prepared for whatever might come. It's just... something that became part of me."

Pinder stifled a laugh, muttering just loud enough for those around to hear, "Prepared is putting it mildly."

The mayor chuckled, looking from Aeron to Pinder with an amused glint in his eye. "I'd say that's an understatement! But you're humble—an admirable quality. Tonight, we celebrate your strength, but also your humility and bravery." He turned back to the crowd, raising his hands. "Let the feast begin!"

At his signal, musicians struck up a lively tune, and the square filled once more with laughter and movement as people made their way to the food stalls and join the dancing. The mayor turned to Aeron, his voice softer, meant just for him. "You may be modest, Aeron, but we see something extraordinary in you. I hope you understand the significance of your actions here tonight."

Aeron nodded, his expression thoughtful as he watched the crowd. "Thank you, Mayor. I'll remember this."

The mayor gave him a warm smile before stepping back to join the others, leaving Aeron and his friends in the glow of the celebration.

The group found a table near the center of the square, where plates and platters of food were piled high, an array of dishes from roasted meats to fresh bread and vibrant fruits. The scent of seasoned meats and spiced cider filled the air, and they eagerly settled in, helping themselves as the festivities continue around them.

Pinder picked up a roasted leg of meat, holding it aloft with a grin. "This is what we should get every time we save a city! None of those hard rations or stale bread. Just imagine, feasting like this after every battle!"

Seraphina rolled her eyes but laughed. "If that were the case,

I think you'd save cities just for the food, Pinder."

"Well, you're not wrong," Pinder said, chuckling and biting into the meat. "But a man's got to enjoy life, doesn't he?"

Just as he was laughing, his eyes caught on someone across the square. A strikingly tall woman with strong shoulders and a confident stance, her hair pulled back in a thick braid, her arms well-defined beneath rolled sleeves, moved with an air of calm authority. She was clearly no stranger to hard work, perhaps a smith or guard by trade. As if sensing his stare, she glanced over and met his eyes, raising a brow in amused acknowledgment.

Pinder, caught a bit off-guard, quickly recovered and nudged Aeron. "Well, look at that," he muttered, grinning. "I think I've found someone who could probably toss me out of a bar if I ever got too rowdy."

Aeron smirked. "Better watch yourself, Pinder. She doesn't look like someone who'd be impressed by tall tales."

Undeterred, Pinder straightened, putting on his most charming smile as the woman approached. "Evening, ma'am," he said, offering a slight bow. "Didn't expect to see a warrior at a feast. Or maybe I should say, the feast is lucky to have you."

The woman crossed her arms. "A warrior, huh?" Her voice was steady, strong, with a hint of amusement. "I'd say the same to you. You're the storyteller, aren't you?"

Pinder raised an eyebrow, feigning surprise. "Guilty as charged. The stories are as good as true, though," he added with a wink.

She chuckled, clearly unconvinced. "Well, 'storyteller,' I'm Brynja. Blacksmith by trade. I've heard your tales. Including that one about the snake. I'm still trying to decide if I believe a man could gut a beast from the inside."

Pinder grinned wider. "Well, if it means getting to tell you the story myself, I'd be happy to convince you over a drink."

Brynja laughed, the sound warm and genuine. "You're bold, I'll give you that. Alright, storyteller — prove it. I'll listen to your tales, and if you can make me believe even half of it, I might let you buy me a drink."

Pinder glanced back at Aeron, Seraphina, and Tate, giving them a triumphant look before turning back to Brynja. "Deal. But I warn you, my stories have a way of sweeping people off their feet."

Brynja leaned in, her smirk confident. "I don't get swept off my feet easily, storyteller. You'll have to work for it."

As they settled into conversation, the others chuckled at Pinder's antics, the night growing richer with laughter and food as the celebration filled the air.

As the evening unfolded, Aeron, Seraphina, and Tate found themselves sampling a platter of delicate pastries and sweets, savoring the taste of something far removed from their usual provisions. They watched as a group of children, all dressed in vibrant colors, danced through the square, twirling banners and flags that fluttered in the night air. The children laughed and shouted, weaving through the crowd, their joy infectious.

Seraphina smiled, nudging Aeron. "Feels good, doesn't it? Seeing people like this, celebrating instead of hiding in fear."

Aeron nodded, a peaceful expression crossing his face. "It does. It's moments like these that remind us what we're fighting for."

Tate, observing the scene thoughtfully, added, "This city, its people ... there's a beauty in knowing they're safe, if only for a while. And perhaps, some answers lie ahead for us as well."

As they enjoyed the moment, a figure stepped quietly up beside them. Turning, they recognized the same elderly priest who had been outside the temple garden, the one who'd suggested they make themselves valuable to the Aethera Mortem.

He watched them with an unreadable expression, his gaze settling on Aeron in particular. After a moment, he cleared his throat, a slight smile tugging at his lips. "Well," he said, his voice soft but carrying a weight of reverence, "when I said you would need to prove yourselves valuable, I must admit, I didn't imagine you'd go as far as to save the city itself."

The trio glanced at each other, a bit surprised by the priest's approach.

The priest looked at Aeron, his eyes sharp with a quiet intensity. "But more than that, Aeron," he continued, "it wasn't just that you fought. It was how you fought. The strength, the speed … no ordinary human moves as you did tonight." He searched Aeron's face as if trying to unravel a mystery. "You've caught the attention of those who watch for something beyond the ordinary."

Aeron shifted slightly, uneasy. "I only did what I had to do. This city needed defending."

The priest's eyes narrowed slightly, a hint of intrigue sparking within them. "Indeed," he replied. "But the Aethera Mortem rarely take note of 'just anyone.' Tonight, however, you have earned their interest. You and your companions have been granted an audience with the highest priest of the Aethera Mortem. A rare honor. One that does not come lightly."

Tate's eyes widened, and he leaned in, his excitement barely contained. "So, they're willing to meet us, then? To share their knowledge?"

The old priest nodded slowly. "You've become more than mere travelers in their eyes. You've shown something extraordinary. A potential the Aethera Mortem cannot ignore. When the time is right, you will meet the highest among them, and perhaps, gain answers to questions you didn't even know to ask."

Seraphina glanced at Aeron, her eyes a mix of pride and concern. She took his hand under the table, a silent show of support.

"Thank you," Aeron says, his voice steady, though a flicker of uncertainty crossed his face. "We'll be there."

The priest inclined his head, a faint smile hinting at secrets untold. "Then may wisdom and patience be with you. You will need both." With that, he turned, blending into the crowd as quietly as he arrived, leaving the trio to process the unexpected turn of events.

As the music and laughter continued to fill the square, Tate glanced around, his face thoughtful. He stood, brushing off his tunic, and looked at Aeron and Seraphina. "I think I'll call it a night," he said, his voice calm but with a subtle intensity. "We have a big day tomorrow, and if we're to meet the leaders of the Aethera Mortem, I'd like to be at my sharpest."

Aeron nodded, understanding. "Probably a wise choice, Tate. Rest well."

Tate gave them a small, knowing smile. "You both enjoy the rest of the festivities. I'll meet you in the dining hall come morning, and we'll sort out our approach with the temple leaders."

Seraphina nodded, watching him go with a sense of respect. "Goodnight, Tate."

With a polite nod, Tate disappeared into the crowd, heading back toward the inn. Aeron and Seraphina remained at the table, watching the celebration continue around them, the promise of tomorrow's mysteries lingering in their thoughts.

The commander made his way through the bustling square, weaving past laughing townsfolk and tipsy soldiers, until he spotted Aeron and Seraphina at their table. He grinned, a little unsteady on his feet but in good spirits, and settled down beside Aeron, leaning in close. His tone, though slurred, carried a note of sharp curiosity.

"Now, Aeron," he began, his eyes gleaming with a mixture of intrigue and admiration, "you've got everyone here convinced you're some kind of hero, and believe me, they're not wrong. But a man doesn't fight like you did tonight from 'just training.'" He tapped his chest, then gestured broadly to himself. "I've trained my whole life, put everything I've got into it, and I've never seen anything like that."

Aeron shifted slightly, glancing at Seraphina before turning back to the commander. "I appreciate the compliment, Commander, but I'm really just a man trying to do what's right."

The commander snorted, leaning in even closer. "Oh, you're a man all right," he said with a low chuckle, "but there's more to it, isn't there? The speed, the strength ..." He squinted at Aeron as if trying to see something hidden. "You leaped over that wall like it was nothing. You moved faster than a man has any right to. And you took down that giant without breaking a sweat!"

He watched Aeron's reaction carefully. "So, what is it? Some kind of magic? A blessing? Something the rest of us can't see?"

Aeron took a breath, keeping his expression as steady as possible. "Commander, I promise you, I don't know of any magic or blessing. I'm just ... I don't know, maybe it's luck or something I picked up over the years." He forced a small, humble smile, hoping it might be enough to turn the conversation.

But the commander shook his head, undeterred. "I don't buy it," he said, though his tone remained more curious than accusatory. "A fighter like you, Aeron. There's something different. Maybe you don't know it yourself, but mark my words, there's a mystery here." He raised a finger, grinning slyly. "And one day, I'll find out."

Aeron held the commander's gaze, nodding slightly, trying to match the man's humor without revealing too much. "Perhaps, Commander, but until then, I'm just a man with a good scythe and good friends. That's all I need to be."

The commander chuckled, shaking his head as he leaned back, accepting the answer for now but still clearly unconvinced. "Well, Aeron, whether you're a simple man or something more, tonight, you're a hero. So, let's leave it at that." He raised an imaginary toast, then, satisfied with his probing, gave them a final nod and wandered off, leaving Aeron and Seraphina to share a knowing, relieved look as the night continued.

Aeron leaned back in his chair, a satisfied smile on his face as he watched Pinder across the square. Their friend was visibly flustered, stumbling slightly as the tall, sturdy woman—Brynja, the blacksmith—took him firmly by the arm and began leading him away with a determined grin. Pinder looked back over his shoulder, wide-eyed, as if silently pleading for rescue, but Aeron simply chuckled.

"Well," Aeron muttered, nudging Seraphina with a grin, "I don't think Pinder's in for his usual night with a bar wench. I hope he can handle all that. Looks like she's about to take him for all he's got."

Seraphina laughed, covering her mouth to muffle the sound as they both watch Pinder disappear into the crowd, helpless and resigned to his fate. "Oh, he's in for a memorable evening, that's for sure."

They shared a quiet laugh, the warmth of the celebration still hanging around them as the night began to wind down. Seraphina turned to Aeron, her eyes glinting with mischief. She leaned in, lowering her voice to a playful whisper. "Well, Mr. Hero," she said, a teasing lilt in her tone, "after a night like this, I can't say I feel very safe sleeping alone."

Aeron raised an eyebrow, his smile widening. "You don't, huh?"

She shook her head, a coy smile on her lips. "Not at all," she murmured. "I might need someone to keep me company. You know, just to be sure there aren't any stray mirages lurking about."

Aeron chuckled, standing and offering her his hand. "Well, if the lady insists, who am I to refuse?"

Seraphina took his hand, laughing softly as he led her back to the inn, their laughter mingling with the fading sounds of the feast outside as they slipped away for a night shared just between the two of them.

The morning sun streamed through the inn's windows as

Aeron, Seraphina, and Tate gathered around a large table in the dining hall, helping themselves to warm bread, fresh fruits, and steaming cups of tea. They looked a little more refreshed after the night's celebrations, the air filled with a comfortable camaraderie.

As they settled into their breakfast, the door creaked open, and in walked Pinder, a slight limp in his step. He was trying to appear nonchalant, but his wince with each step was unmistakable. Aeron and Seraphina exchanged a look, barely holding back their laughter.

"Good morning, Pinder," Seraphina greeted him, her tone dripping with mock innocence. "You're looking … well-loved this morning. Tell me, who took control last night? You, or Brynja?"

Pinder groaned, sliding into a chair with a dramatic sigh. "Let's just say I wasn't exactly in the driver's seat," he muttered, grabbing a piece of bread and biting into it with a grumble. "She left me in an empty bed, used up like yesterday's firewood."

Seraphina burst into laughter. "Oh, Pinder, the mighty storyteller reduced to a mere piece of meat?"

Pinder raised an eyebrow, looking her way with a smirk. "Laugh all you want. You wouldn't be laughing if you'd faced that blacksmith last night. I swear, she's got the strength of ten men. And the stamina to match." He sighed, shaking his head with a rueful grin. "I think I'm in love. She's the first woman I've met who can toss me around like that and leave me wanting more."

Aeron chuckled, raising his cup in a toast. "To Pinder, the warrior who finally met his match."

Pinder lifted his cup, winking. "To Brynja … and here's to hoping my bruises heal before tonight."

They all laughed, sharing a relaxed moment together, the previous day's battles now just a memory as they enjoyed the warmth of friendship and the simple pleasures of the morning.

As the laughter settled and they continued their breakfast, Aeron turned to Pinder, a hint of seriousness breaking through his grin. "There's something you should know about today. While you were … occupied," he said, trying to suppress a smirk, "we had an unexpected visit from the priest last night. He's arranged an audience for us with the head of the Aethera Mortem — the secret group within the temple."

Pinder raised an eyebrow, interest piqued. "The same secret group we were going to try and sneak into?" He chuckled, leaning back. "Guess that's what you call moving up in the world."

Aeron nods, his expression resolute. "Exactly. But this isn't a casual meeting. If we're going to get any answers about these mirages and, well, maybe even about me, we need to make an impression. That means no tall tales, no antics." He paused, giving Pinder a pointed look. "I need you on your best behavior." Pinder sighed, feigning wounded pride. "Best behavior? You're taking all the fun out of this, Aeron. But fine, for you and the mysterious knowledge-keepers, I'll keep it respectable."

Seraphina nudged him. "Think you can survive one morning without trying to charm anyone?"

Pinder rolled his eyes but grinned. "For answers, I'll do what it takes. But don't say I didn't warn you if they fall for my charm anyway."

The group finished their breakfast, gathering their things and readying themselves to head to the temple, anticipation filling the air as they prepared to finally uncover some of the mysteries that have haunted them since the beginning of their journey.

The morning sun cast a warm glow over the town square as the team gathered outside the inn, their packs ready, and spirits surprisingly high. As they look around, they spotted Koko near the stable, trotting around with an almost comical sense of pride, his coat gleaming from a thorough brushing. Someone had adorned him with a bright ribbon tied to his halter. He seemed to know he was being admired.

Pinder grinned, nodding toward the mule. "Look at that. Our noble steed, Koko, the true hero of this tale, prancing around like he owns the place. Can't say I blame him."

Seraphina chuckled, folding her arms. "He deserves it. Koko's carried us through a lot. Remember that mountain path he barely fit through? Or when we were dodging a horde of mirages, and he didn't flinch?"

Aeron smiled, resting a hand on Koko's side as the mule leaned in contentedly. "We've all come a long way," he said quietly, his gaze drifting over his friends. "From that first day … waking up in that little town with no memory. It's hard to believe we've made it this far."

Tate, leaning thoughtfully against a post, nodded. "Not just distance," he added, his tone reflective. "I'm sure you've each changed in ways I'm not sure you'd even recognize if we saw ourselves from the start. I joined you late, hoping to find answers in some dusty book or ancient scroll, and now I'm part of something I never expected."

Pinder raised an eyebrow, his usual grin softened by something more genuine. "The biggest surprise to me was sticking around. I'm not exactly the 'team player' type." He glanced at each of them, his expression warm. "But I guess you lot grew on me."

Seraphina smirked. "You make it sound like we're some kind of fungus."

He laughed. "Well, it wasn't always pretty, was it? Fighting monsters, nearly falling off cliffs, and dealing with that terrifying blacksmith …" He cleared his throat. "But you know, I wouldn't trade any of it. I think I'm a better man for having gone through all of this with you."

Aeron nodded, his gaze thoughtful. "I don't think I ever knew what friendship really was until now. I may not remember everything, but this …" He gestured to the group, then placed a hand on his chest. "This feels real. Like something worth holding onto."

There was a pause as they each took in his words, a comfortable silence settling over them.

Seraphina broke the silence, her voice soft but resolute. "Whatever lies ahead, we've proven we can face it. Together."

The team shared a look of understanding, a bond forged through trials and triumphs, now stronger than ever as they stood on the edge of what might be their greatest discovery yet.

The morning sun rose higher as the team moved from the inn into the heart of the town, Great Oaks coming alive around them in a bustling, rhythmic dance. The streets were paved with stone, worn smooth by the countless steps of travelers and townsfolk over the years, giving them a soft, almost polished gleam in the light. Small wisps of mist still clung to the edges of alleyways, slowly dissipating as the warmth of the day settled in.

Vendors were setting up their stalls, each brightly colored and decorated with trinkets or flags that fluttered gently in the morning breeze. The smell of fresh bread wafted from a nearby bakery, mixing with the earthy scent of herbs from the apothecary just across the street. A woman with silver-streaked hair arranged baskets of fruits and vegetables, the bright reds of apples and deep purples of plums contrasting against the greens of leafy vegetables.

Children dashed through the square, their laughter ringing out as they chased each other, weaving around townsfolk with the easy grace of those familiar with every corner of the city. One boy held a wooden sword, swinging it with enthusiasm as his friends cheered him on. An older gentleman, leaning against a cart stacked with woven blankets, watched them with a chuckle, shaking his head in fond amusement.

The group passed by a row of artisans showcasing their crafts. The clang of metal rang out as a blacksmith hammered a glowing blade, sparks flying into the air with each strike. Next to him, a potter smoothed the rim of a clay vase, her hands moving with steady precision, shaping the piece with an almost meditative focus.

As they moved farther into town, Aeron glanced around, taking in the life that pulsed through every corner of Great Oaks. The energy there felt different—purposeful, alive. Townsfolk greeted each other with nods and smiles, a sense of community evident in every exchanged glance. A young woman in a faded blue dress tended to a flower box outside her window, carefully pinching off wilted petals, while a nearby street musician strummed a gentle tune on a lute, his voice warm and inviting.

They approached the center of town, where the temple loomed ahead. The temple's tall spires reached skyward, crafted from ancient stone that held a sense of both history and mystery. The walls were intricately carved with symbols that wound their way upward like vines, each one telling a story in shapes and lines that seemed to hold secrets of the past. Stained glass windows lined the sides, catching the sunlight and casting soft, colored patterns across the cobblestone path leading up to the entrance. Reds, blues, and greens danced across the stone, painting the team in vibrant hues.

A small gathering of townsfolk stood near the temple entrance, whispering amongst themselves as they eyed the building with a mixture of awe and reverence. An older woman clasped her hands together, murmuring a quiet prayer before stepping forward to place a small offering of flowers on a stone pedestal at the temple steps.

As Aeron and his companions approached, the townsfolk parted, giving them space, yet watching them with a sense of curiosity and respect. Seraphina's gaze drifted over the temple's doors, which were heavy and dark, made of thick wood, reinforced with iron bands. Each hinge was intricately crafted, the metal shaped into the form of feathers and leaves, giving the doors a sense of both strength and elegance.

They paused at the base of the steps, each taking in the sight of the temple. There was a heaviness to the moment, a sense of anticipation settling over them as they prepared to step forward and cross the threshold into a place of secrets and ancient knowledge.

With one last glance at each other, they took a collective breath and approached the doors, feeling the history and power of the temple almost hum in the air around them, as though it, too, was waiting for whatever was to come.

Chapter 22: Fury Born of Loss

As Aeron, Seraphina, Pinder, and Tate stepped into the temple, the cool air and dim, candlelit atmosphere welcomed them. Shadows danced across the stone walls, their flickering shapes casting a sense of solemnity and mystery over the hall. A young priest in simple robes, no more than twenty, approached them with a polite but focused expression.

"We've been expecting you," he said, inclining his head respectfully. "The Order of Aethera Mortem was informed of your arrival last night. You're to be taken directly to the archives."

The group exchanged a glance.

Pinder leaned over to Seraphina with a smirk. "Guess we're a big deal now," he muttered under his breath, earning a quick elbow from her.

The priest gestured for them to follow, leading them down a series of long, echoing corridors lined with faded murals depicting scenes of the ancient world. Images of scholars in deep study, battles between forces of light and dark, and temples rising from barren landscapes. Each step deeper into the temple felt as though they were being drawn further back in time.

As they approached a set of heavy oak doors reinforced with iron bands, the young priest stopped and turned to them, his face solemn. "Beyond these doors are the archives of Aethera Mortem, where only a select few are allowed. The head priest will meet you inside and guide you through what you seek. Please ... respect the sanctity of this place."

Aeron nodded, feeling the priest's words resonate within him. "We understand. Thank you."

The priest pushed open the doors, and they stepped into the archives, a vast chamber lined with towering shelves filled with ancient tomes and scrolls. Dust motes drifted in the beams of light that filtered down from the high windows, giving the room a timeless, ethereal quality.

At the far end of the chamber, a tall, robed figure with a silver-threaded sash marking his rank, stood with his hands clasped. His face was weathered with age, his gaze sharp and penetrating. As they approached, he nodded in greeting. "Welcome. I am Head Priest Aldric of the Aethera Mortem. You bring with you abilities and questions that have piqued the interest of our order." His voice carried a gravitas that filled the room.

Tate stepped forward, holding the scroll carefully in his hands. "This scroll was found in Tideheaven. We believe it may be related to the creatures we've encountered. Creatures covered in a dark, viscous goo, appearing across the land with a ferocity and intent we haven't been able to understand."

Aldric's eyes narrowed slightly as he accepted the scroll, unrolling it carefully. His gaze intensified as he scanned the symbols, his fingers tracing them reverently. "This isn't just any scroll," he murmured, as if speaking to himself. "This is the missing half of a scroll we once held here, thought to be lost forever."

Aeron, curiosity piqued, exchanged a glance with Seraphina. "So, the scroll was already here?" he asked

Aldric nodded, his eyes still fixed on the scroll as if lost in its mysteries. "The first half has resided in these archives for generations. It tells a fragmented story of a time long past when strange creatures, similar to those you describe, overtook a town. They were relentless, as if seeking something."

Pinder shifted uneasily. "So, what happened? Did they get what they wanted?"

The head priest sighed, rolling the scroll with care. "From what we've been able to decipher over the years, it seems the creatures eventually overtook the town and then, mysteriously, stopped. Whether they found their goal or merely went dormant, we could not say."

Seraphina frowned. "But they've returned, after all this time. Could this scroll hold the key to understanding why?"

Aldric looked up, studying each of them in turn. "Perhaps. With this second half, we may finally be able to make sense of the language. It is an ancient tongue, one that resembles fragments of other languages we know but still remain largely unknown." He motioned to a nearby table. "We must examine the scrolls together to see what it reveals in full. Please, sit."

They gathered around as Aldric unrolled both halves of the scroll side by side. His eyes flickered with excitement, tempered by years of practice as a scholar. "These symbols here," he pointed, "bear a striking resemblance to certain words in the old tongue of the Scholars of Grace. And here ..." He gestured to another section, his brow furrowing. "Words that mean 'void,' 'balance,' and—" his finger stilled on a symbol that seemed almost alive with meaning, "'Death.'"

The group tensed, their gazes shifting to Aeron, who shifted uncomfortably under the scrutiny.

Tate cleared his throat, leaning forward. "I've encountered references to death before, though only in religious tales. But the way these creatures appear ... it's as if they are drawn to Aeron. They're hunting him specifically."

Aldric's expression darkened. "According to some of our oldest records, reapers were said to be Death's servants, carrying out his will to maintain the balance of life and death. Their speed, agility, and weaponry were unmatched, but a reaper would not inhabit a human body. It would be impossible. The lore explicitly states that reapers belong to the realm beyond."

Aeron, feeling Aldric's gaze, spoke up, his voice steady, "I don't know who or what I am. But I can't deny that ever since I found this scythe, I've been able to do things no one else can. Things I can't fully explain."

Aldric nodded slowly, his expression a mixture of fascination and skepticism. "It is curious, to say the least. But if this scroll speaks of a reaper, then perhaps there are pieces to this mystery that even we have yet to uncover." He looked at Aeron thoughtfully. "For now, with your permission, we will study this scroll in depth. If it can reveal more of your nature, or the origin of these creatures, we will let you know."

Seraphina, her voice soft but resolute, asked, "How long do you think it will take?"

Aldric met her gaze. "A few days, at most. We have scholars who can assist, and with both halves, we may finally have the full picture." He paused, a shadow of unease passing over his face. "Though, I must warn you. Whatever answers we uncover, they may raise more questions than they resolve."

With that, he carefully gathered the scrolls, tucking them safely away. "For now, rest. This mystery will soon reveal itself."

As the meeting drew to a close, Aldric gestured toward the tall shelves and dim, winding corridors that stretched through the vast archives. "You are welcome to access the archives as our guests," he said, his voice carrying the weight of reverence for the space around them. "Feel free to conduct any research you find necessary while we work on deciphering the scroll."

Tate's eyes lit up, an almost childlike excitement breaking through his scholarly demeanor. Without a moment's hesitation, he nodded to the others. "I'll take full advantage of that offer," he said, practically disappearing down the nearest aisle, his fingers already brushing the spines of ancient texts.

Seraphina watched him go with a smirk, shaking her head. "Somehow, I think we've lost him for the rest of the day."

Aeron chuckled, glancing down the rows of towering shelves

stretching deep into the archive's shadows. "I don't blame him. This place has everything, doesn't it?"

The archives seemed to breathe with a life of their own, a sense of history and mystery embedded in every stone wall, every aged leather spine. The shelves reached so high they vanished into the dim rafters, where narrow beams of sunlight slipped through cracks in the ceiling, casting faint, golden lines across the ancient tomes. Small ladders and movable platforms were scattered along the aisles, allowing scholars to reach the highest shelves with ease.

A quiet hum filled the room, not from voices but from the essence of knowledge collected over centuries. In the faint, dusty light, they could make out symbols on the shelves, indicating sections by era and subject. Here, it wasn't just history; it was lore, legend, and knowledge from a world they barely understood, preserved with meticulous care.

As they walked down the aisles, the scent of old parchment, ink, and leather hung in the air—a fragrance both calming and powerful, steeped in the weight of wisdom. Books of all sizes lined the shelves, their covers embossed with strange symbols, faded titles, and occasional notes in forgotten languages scrawled along the bindings. Scrolls were stored in neatly arranged cubbies, sealed with wax stamps bearing insignias of orders and kingdoms long since vanished.

Aeron paused, running his fingers along one row. The texture of the rough leather and worn paper felt oddly grounding, as if he was touching history itself. "It's hard to believe all of this knowledge has been hidden away for so long," he said.

Seraphina nodded, her gaze drifting over the shelves. "It feels sacred. Like every book, every scroll holds secrets that could change the world if only we could understand them."

Tate, already several rows deep into the archives, could be heard muttering to himself, his fingers flipping through pages as he dove into his research with fervor. His voice carried a hint of awe, tinged with the excitement of discovery. "Incredible," he murmured, pausing to examine a particularly thick tome with worn edges. "This is an account from the first era—nearly lost to time! And here, a study on early magical theory from the Kingdom of Dawn. Unbelievable."

Aeron and Seraphina exchanged an amused look, their friend's enthusiasm adding a warmth to the solemnity of the place. They followed the faint echoes of his voice, finding him surrounded by piles of old texts, his attention darting from one tome to another as he took hurried notes.

He glanced up briefly, his eyes shining with excitement. "You wouldn't believe the information they have here. Half of these texts are myths that historians claim never existed. Yet here they are, as real as you and me!" He dived back into his notes, already lost in another passage.

Seraphina raised an eyebrow, leaning over to Aeron. "He's going to be in here all night, isn't he?"

Aeron laughed softly, nodding. "Wouldn't expect anything less." A sense of reverence washed over him again as he took in the endless shelves. "Let him have his adventure. Something tells me he's waited his whole life for a place like this."

The soft rustle of parchment and the distant murmurs of other scholars surrounded them as Aeron and Seraphina wandered further down the aisles, leaving Tate to his research.

As they continued walking through the endless shelves, Seraphina glanced at Aeron, a pensive look in her eyes. "Aeron, did you notice how the head priest talked about Death. Almost like it's a person, not just an end to things?"

Aeron nodded, his gaze drifting over the worn leather tomes and aged scrolls around them. "I did. He mentioned Death almost like it has its own will, its own intentions. Like it's aware, somehow."

She frowned, crossing her arms. "It's unsettling. If Death is more than a concept, what does that mean for everything else?

And then there are these mirages. They feel connected to it somehow. How would they even be tied to Death?"

Aeron ran a hand over the spine of a nearby book, thoughtful. "Maybe it's like Tate said. They're trying to tell us something, or they're bound to some kind of role. But the way they keep coming after us, especially after we found the scythe, makes me wonder if they're not here to help."

Seraphina sighed, glancing down an aisle filled with tightly packed shelves of scrolls. "It's hard to say. I mean, if Death is like a person, would it have … helpers? Or, I don't know, guards? And if it does, maybe these mirages are acting out some part of that, like messengers, or something else."

Aeron gave a small laugh, though there was a tinge of unease behind it. "It's strange to think of Death having 'helpers,' isn't it? I don't think anyone's ever thought of it that way. The reaper they talked about sounded almost mythical, but if these mirages are real, then who knows what else might be?"

Seraphina nodded, her expression thoughtful. "It feels like we're barely scratching the surface. There's probably so much more to life and death than we've ever considered. And yet, somehow, here we are, caught up in the middle of it."

They shared a glance, each trying to make sense of the mysteries they were only beginning to uncover. Whatever the truth may be, it was clear there was a depth to this world they never anticipated, one that might take them further than they expected to go.

A muffled laugh came from the other side of the archive. They exchanged a look and followed the sound to find Pinder sitting on the floor, a large leather-bound book propped open on his lap, his shoulders shaking with laughter. He looked up as they approached, a mischievous grin spreading across his face.

"You two," he said, holding the book up with an exaggerated flourish, "are going to love this. I've found a whole book on the founding of the Eye." He tapped the cover with a smug look.

"Turns out the great, noble origin of my dear thieving family is far more inventive than I knew."

Seraphina raised an eyebrow, taking a seat across from him. "Oh, this I have to hear. What did you find?"

Pinder cleared his throat dramatically and read, "It all began, apparently, with a daring scoundrel named Roderic the Clever. Now, this man wasn't just a thief; he was the thief of his time. I'm talking breaking into royal treasuries, emptying vaults of gold, stealing pearls from the king's very crown. He even nabbed a whole pig from a nobleman's banquet. Right off the table."

Aeron chuckled. "So, what, the Eye started because some guy was hungry?"

Pinder's eyes gleamed. "Not quite. Roderic wasn't just good at stealing things; he was good at getting away with it. He managed to wriggle out of every guard's grip, slip away from every locked cell. It got to the point where nobles were hiring entire battalions just to keep him out of their homes."

He leaned forward, his voice dropping to a conspiratorial whisper, "So, here's the kicker: Roderic had this idea. 'What if,' he thought, 'instead of being just one thief with all these guards after me, I got myself a little network? People on the inside, all working together to confuse the poor saps trying to catch us.'"

Seraphina laughed, shaking her head. "And let me guess. That's when he founded the Eye?"

"Exactly!" Pinder said with a proud grin, thumping the book. "So he recruited a few friends, a couple of shady types from the market, even a couple of ex-guards who were tired of being on the other side of the law. And they formed this network, see? Roderic's 'Eye.' Watching everything, stealing everything, getting away with it all."

Aeron raised an eyebrow, clearly amused. "So the Eye wasn't some grand plan to undermine the kingdom or topple corrupt leaders?"

Pinder shook his head. "Oh, no. The Eye was founded on the principle of taking what you could, keeping out of sight, and, here's the best part, making sure the guards looked as foolish as possible." He flipped to another page and read aloud, "'If we can rob a noble blind and have him laugh about it in the end, then we've done our job well.'"

"Sounds like Roderic had a sense of humor." Seraphina smirked.

Pinder nodded. "Absolutely. He even had this tradition. Every time they completed a big job, they'd leave a single gold coin behind, placed somewhere only the guard would find. Like a calling card. A sort of, 'We were here, and you were too late.'"

"So it was all about pride and a bit of fun?" Aeron asked.

Pinder's face lit up with a mischievous glint. "Precisely! The Eye wasn't built to be some sinister organization. It was meant to be a game. A big, elaborate game that kept everyone on their toes. The thieves saw themselves as artists, performers even, and they wanted their heists to have flair, style."

Seraphina raised her eyebrow, a hint of admiration in her expression. "Well, I have to admit, I like the sound of that more than the usual cutthroat guilds. So what happened to this Roderic?"

Pinder sighed, flipping to another page. "Turns out he got a bit too clever for his own good. He staged this heist. Legend says it was his masterpiece, a caper so complex he planned it for three years. And the prize? A jeweled crown, made of pure emeralds, said to be the most beautiful artifact in the kingdom."

"Did he pull it off?" Aeron leaned in, intrigued.

"Oh, he pulled it off, alright," Pinder said, snickering. "But not exactly in the way he planned. Apparently, he got the crown, slipped out of the treasury, but he made one fatal error. He'd left a trail of pig tracks behind him, from boots he'd worn to throw off the guards."

Seraphina stifled a laugh. "Pig tracks?"

"Pig tracks," Pinder confirmed with a grin. "Thinking he was clever, he planned to blame it on some 'masked farm thief.' But the guards figured it out, chased him down, and cornered him in a pigsty. And thus, the grand master Roderic the Clever was caught, all because he outsmarted himself."

Aeron couldn't help but laugh, clapping Pinder on the shoulder. "And that's the man who inspired your precious Eye? A thief who lost himself in a pigsty?"

Pinder held up his hands defensively. "Hey, everyone's got their flaws. Besides, he may have been caught, but his legacy lived on. Every thief in the Eye honors Roderic's memory by bringing humor and style to the game. To this day, we play by his rules: a heist isn't worth pulling unless it leaves a mark." He sighed, glancing fondly at the pages before snapping the book shut. "That's why I joined the Eye. It wasn't just about taking things. It was about the thrill, the art of it all. It's the one thing I'd never change."

Seraphina patted him on the back, laughing softly. "Here's hoping you're a bit more careful than Roderic, Pinder. I'd hate to see you end up in a pigsty."

Pinder grinned. "Well, lucky for you, I'm just a bit cleverer than Roderic was. Though I can't promise I won't end up in trouble."

As the group gathered around the temple's main hall, Head Priest Aldric approached them with a look of tempered resignation. "I fear the translation is more complex than anticipated," he admitted. "This language is deeply rooted in ancient dialects, many of which are only partially understood. It will take longer than I initially believed."

Aeron glanced at the others, seeing a mix of relief and restlessness. Tate, however, looked thoughtful, his gaze fixed on the tall stacks of scrolls and books within the temple.

"If it's all right with you, Aldric," Tate said, stepping forward, "I'd like to stay here and assist. I've studied a variety of ancient languages, and perhaps I can help expedite the process."

Aldric nodded approvingly, sensing Tate's genuine interest. "Your assistance would indeed be welcome. We can use every hand and mind available to unlock these mysteries."

Seraphina nudged Aeron. "Looks like we've lost him to his books again. Not that I'm surprised."

Pinder shook his head. "No shock there. Let him have his dusty scrolls and ancient dialects. We'll be fine out there, won't we, Aeron?"

Aeron smiled, casting Tate a quick look. "Don't get too lost, Tate. We need you in one piece."

Tate rolled his eyes, giving a dismissive wave. "Go enjoy yourselves. I'll be here in the quiet, where real progress happens." He grinned at them, then turned to follow Aldric deeper into the archives, his fingers already itching to dive into the next scroll.

As they exited the temple and stepped into the sunlight, Seraphina stretched her arms wide, taking a deep breath. "Feels like ages since we've been out in a city during the day. Why don't we take advantage of it? See what this place has to offer?"

Pinder's eyes lit up, an eager grin spread across his face. "Now you're talking my language. I bet there's some prime food and drink here. If we're going to wait, we might as well do it in style."

Aeron glanced around at the bustling streets. "Sounds like a plan. We've been in dark corridors and temples for long enough. Maybe a day to breathe wouldn't be so bad."

Seraphina nodded, gesturing toward the lively market district down the road. "Alright then. Let's explore! Who knows? We might find something useful, or at least entertaining."

With a sense of excitement and lightness, the group set off, leaving the temple and its mysteries behind, if only for a little while, ready to immerse themselves in the vibrant city life around them.

As they made their way down the temple steps and into the bustling city, the sounds and scents of Great Oaks greeted them. Market vendors called out their wares, the aroma of freshly baked bread mingled with the spiciness of roasting meats, and colorful fabric banners fluttered overhead, creating a lively canopy along the streets.

Pinder sighed contentedly, casting his gaze around like a man who had finally returned to his element. "Ah, freedom at last! No dusty scrolls or quiet halls, just food, drink, and excitement around every corner." He patted Aeron on the back. "Now, my friend, what's the first order of business? A strong drink or something to eat?"

Aeron chuckled, glancing at Seraphina, who rolled her eyes with an affectionate smile.

"Maybe we start with food, Pinder. Don't want you passing out before the day's even begun."

Pinder placed a hand over his heart, feigning offense. "I'll have you know I can handle far more than a few drinks!" He paused, sniffing the air. "But food sounds tempting. Let's find something worthy of the Great Oaks' reputation, eh?"

Seraphina held up her arm, motioning for him to go first. "Lead the way, oh fearless one. But no strange meats or mystery stews this time. I'd like to know what I'm eating for once."

They wandered down a lane lined with stalls, each vendor more eager than the last to draw their attention. A plump woman held up a skewer of golden-brown roasted meat, calling out to them. "Fresh venison, seasoned with rare herbs from the western forests! Best in the city!"

Pinder's eyes lit up as he grabbed a skewer, handing a few coins to the woman. He took a hearty bite, his eyes widening in delight. "Now this. This is living!"

Aeron and Seraphina followed suit, grabbing skewers and sampling the food around them.

As they strolled through the market, Aeron glanced over at

Seraphina. "It's been a while since we've had a moment to just relax."

Seraphina smiled softly, a hint of something wistful in her eyes. "Feels strange, doesn't it? Like we've forgotten how to enjoy the small things." Her gaze drifted over the stalls filled with trinkets, spices, and baubles. "Sometimes I wonder if all of this will be worth it in the end."

Aeron tilted his head. "What do you mean?"

She shrugged, looking down at the skewer in her hand. "I guess I wonder if we'll ever get back to just ... living. Not fighting, not chasing answers, just living. A quiet life." She glanced up at him with a shy smile. "A life together."

Pinder, overhearing, smirked and nudged Aeron. "You're a lucky man."

Aeron blushed slightly, but he laughed, nudging Pinder back. "Better watch it, or I'll be planning a future with you, too."

They laughed together, a warmth settling over the group as they wandered through the market. Suddenly, they passed a stall filled with shiny trinkets and jewelry, and Pinder's eyes locked onto a delicate silver pendant engraved with intricate symbols.

He picked it up, inspecting it with a practiced eye. "Look at this. Reminds me of something the old-timers back in Tideheaven would wear. It's almost nostalgic."

"Nostalgic? Don't tell me you're getting sentimental on us now, Pinder," Seraphina said.

He slipped the pendant back onto the stand. "Sentimental? Maybe. But there's nothing wrong with remembering where you came from, right? Even if it's just some dusty streets and a bunch of cutthroats."

Aeron's expression softened as he watched Pinder. "You know, you joke about it, but you do have a heart under all that bravado."

Pinder winked, patting Aeron on the shoulder. "Careful, or

I'll make you pay for that drink I promised."

Seraphina laughed, shaking her head. "You two are hopeless."

Just then, a street performer caught their attention—a juggler balancing a stack of knives with remarkable precision. A small crowd gathered, clapping and cheering as he flipped the knives effortlessly through the air. Pinder watched, entranced, as the juggler tossed a knife high, catching it on the tip of his finger, and sending it spinning again.

"Think you could do that, Pinder?" Aeron teased, nudging him.

Pinder grinned. "Please. I'd be twice as good with half the knives." He stepped forward, raising his voice so the juggler could hear. "Bet you couldn't handle a real challenge!"

The juggler spotted Pinder's grin and raised an eyebrow. "Care to test that theory, friend?"

Before Pinder could respond, Seraphina grabbed his arm, laughing. "No way. We're not bailing you out of trouble in the middle of the city."

Pinder sighed dramatically, but he allowed himself to be pulled back. "Fine, fine. But only because I wouldn't want to show up this poor fellow."

They continued down the road, the energy of the market buzzing around them. When they passed a vendor selling small trinkets and good luck charms, Seraphina picked up a small, carved figure of a horse. She held it up, smiling. "Looks like Koko, doesn't it?"

Aeron grinned. "It does. Maybe we should get it for him, as a reminder of the day he was treated like royalty."

Pinder snorted. "Oh, I'm sure he'll appreciate that. Just don't tell him, or he'll expect a tribute every time we pass a market."

They laughed, pocketing the small trinket before making their way toward a quiet corner of the market, where a street musician played a soft tune on a lute, the melody lilting and haunting. They stopped to listen, each of them falling silent as the music filled the space around them.

After a moment, Seraphina spoke up, her voice barely above a whisper, "It's nice to be reminded that there's still beauty in the world, even when everything feels uncertain."

Aeron nodded, his gaze fixed on the musician. "Yeah. Sometimes I wonder if we'll find the answers we're looking for, or if it's all just a path we're meant to walk without knowing where it leads."

Pinder raised an eyebrow, his usual grin replaced with a rare look of sincerity. "For what it's worth, I'm glad to be on this path with you two. Life was a lot simpler before all this, but it's better now. More real."

They fell into a comfortable silence, the weight of their journey momentarily lifted by the music, the laughter around them, and the sense of belonging they found in each other's company.

They strolled down the narrow path leading toward the stables, each carrying a handful of freshly picked apples from the market. As they neared the stalls, they spotted Koko leaning his head over the fence, ears twitching as he caught sight of them. His eyes lit up as he recognized the apples, and he let out a welcoming bray, almost as if he'd been waiting for them all day.

"There he is," Aeron said, smiling warmly. He approached Koko, reaching out to scratch behind the mule's ears, a spot he knew Koko loved. "Hey, buddy. Look what we brought you."

Koko sniffed the air, his nostrils flaring as he stretched his neck, eyes fixed on the apples in Aeron's hand. He nudged Aeron's shoulder impatiently, letting out a soft snort.

"Alright, alright," Aeron laughed, holding up the first apple. "No need to rush. There's plenty for you."

He placed the apple on his open palm, and Koko leaned down, gently taking it with his lips before chomping down with a loud crunch. Aeron grinned, rubbing Koko's neck as the mule happily munched on his treat.

Pinder held his own apple out with a grin. "Look at him go. This mule eats better than most of us, you know that?"

Koko's ears perked up, and he turned toward Pinder, his large, expressive eyes seemingly judging him for the comment. Pinder laughed, holding up his hands in surrender. "Alright, alright, don't give me that look. Here, take your apple."

Koko accepted it eagerly, chomping it down just as quickly as the first. As he chewed, he leans his head against Pinder's shoulder, almost as if thanking him. Pinder chuckled, patting Koko on the neck. "You know, for a mule, you've got a lot of charm. Not many animals get under my skin, but you ... you're alright."

Seraphina approached next, holding up her apple, a soft smile on her face. "He's more than alright. He's gotten us through some of the toughest places and never complains. Right, Koko?" She stroke his mane gently, and Koko leaned into her touch, his eyes half-closed in contentment.

She held the apple just out of his reach, grinning as he tried to stretch his neck further. "Not so fast," she teased, moving the apple side to side. "You have to work for this one." Koko let out a huff, giving her a look that seemed almost pleading. Finally, she relented, laughing softly as she handed it over. "Alright, fine. You've earned it."

As Koko devoured the final apple, Aeron reached over, rubbing his hand along the mule's back. "You know, I don't think we'd have made it this far without him. He's not just a mule. He's family."

Pinder snorted, though his expression softened. "Funny, I never thought I'd grow attached to a mule of all things. But look at him. He's like the heart of this whole operation. Keeps us going, even when the rest of us are falling apart."

Seraphina nodded, scratching behind Koko's ear. "I don't think he even realizes it, but he does. He's kept us all grounded. Through every chase, every close call, he's been right there with us."

Koko let out a soft, contented bray, almost as if he understood every word they were saying. He nudged Aeron's arm, then Seraphina's, his eyes full of warmth and trust. Aeron looked down, feeling an unexpected tightness in his chest. "Thank you, Koko. For everything."

The three of them fell silent, enjoying the quiet moment with Koko, each one realizing just how much he meant to them. For Aeron, it was a bond he felt in his very core, as if Koko's strength and patience had somehow transferred to him, guiding him through every trial.

Pinder reached over, giving Koko a final pat. "Well, buddy, don't go getting too attached to the good life here. We'll be moving out soon enough, and you're still going to be carrying half our stuff."

Koko nudged Pinder, almost as if challenging him, and they all laughed. It was a simple moment, a quiet break in their long journey, but one that solidified Koko's place in their hearts. He wasn't just their mule—he was their companion, their steady constant, and, in so many ways, their reminder of what they were fighting for.

As Aeron, Seraphina, and Pinder finished up with Koko, the atmosphere around them calmed, with only the gentle rustling of leaves and distant sounds of the city filtering through the otherwise quiet. Koko nudged Aeron's hand, content after a handful of apples and a good brushing.

Just as they were about to gather their belongings and head into town, a guard hurried toward them, his expression serious.

"Excuse me," the guard called, stopping to catch his breath. "I apologize for the interruption, but Mayor Godfrey has requested your presence."

Seraphina raised an eyebrow. "Is something wrong?"

The guard shook his head, though there was a tension in his voice, "I don't know the details. Only that it's important. The mayor and some of the top brass of The Fang are waiting, and they urgently need to speak with you."

Aeron nodded. "Alright. Lead the way."

They left Koko behind, casting one last glance at the mule, who watched them with mild curiosity. With each step, the mood grew heavier, a subtle undercurrent of anticipation weaving through their thoughts. Whatever awaited them with Mayor Godfrey, they sensed it was more than just a typical meeting.

The guard led Aeron, Seraphina, and Pinder through winding streets, and soon they reached Mayor Godfrey's manor. Unlike the bustling town outside, the manor loomed quietly, a stately building of dark stone with narrow, stained-glass windows casting muted colors over the entryway. As they passed through the doors, an air of solemnity settled around them, an unspoken acknowledgment of the gravity of their summons.

They moved through corridors lined with tapestries depicting scenes from the city's past—foundations laid, battles fought, victories hard-won. Candle sconces flickered along the walls, casting soft, wavering shadows that played against the stone, adding to the manor's hushed atmosphere.

At last, they arrived at a set of heavy double doors, guarded by two soldiers who gave the group a cursory glance before opening the doors. The room beyond was cavernous and dim, illuminated only by a large chandelier hanging from the vaulted ceiling. In the center stood a massive table, carved from a single piece of oak, its surface scarred with the marks of past plans and battles discussed upon it.

Spread across the table were maps, meticulously detailed with inked symbols and notes scrawled in various hands. There were charts showing the city's walls, neighboring villages, and lines tracing routes of supply and trade. Heavy iron candelabras had been set at each corner of the table, their candles tall and half-melted, casting a warm but restrained light over the faces of those already gathered.

Around the room, shelves stacked with rolled-up maps and documents stretched from floor to ceiling. Weapons hung on the walls—swords, shields, and spears from past battles—each carrying its own history, now mere decoration in the mayor's war room. The air was thick with the faint smell of wax and old paper, mingling with a hint of steel and leather.

A large fireplace along the far wall crackled softly, casting an orange glow that flickered against the polished armor of the Fang commanders gathered around the table. They conversed quietly amongst themselves, their expressions serious, eyes occasionally darting to the maps before them. These were men and women marked by years of service, their armor worn and their faces bearing lines of experience and fatigue.

Aeron, Seraphina, and Pinder stood just inside the door, absorbing the gravity of the room. There was a tangible sense of history and decision-making, as if the very stones of the manor bore witness to the discussions held within these walls. For a moment, they were almost hesitant to break the quiet.

They remained unnoticed, observing the council in hushed reverence as the room pulsed with anticipation, as if the shadows themselves awaited the turning of fate.

The room stirred as Mayor Godfrey finally noticed the group by the door. With a gesture, he brought the quiet conversations to an end, and a hush fells over the commanders. He stepped forward, his gaze steady and serious as he acknowledged them.

"Aeron, Seraphina, Pinder," Godfrey greeted, his voice carrying a heaviness that matched the energy in the room. "Thank you for coming on such short notice." He glanced around, gathering the attention of everyone in the room before focusing on Aeron. "We're facing some troubling questions, and I hope you might be able to provide us with answers."

Godfrey folded his hands behind his back, his brow furrowed as he continued. "We've had small incidents before, sporadic attacks from these creatures, but nothing close to the scale of what we saw yesterday. It was as if—"

"They're called mirages," Aeron interjected, his tone steady, though the weight of the room pressed heavily on him.

Godfrey's eyes narrowed. "Mirages," he repeated, letting the word settle over the room. "That's exactly why I summoned you. We need as much information as you can give us. Our priests have locked themselves away in a meeting, and they refuse to share any information. They claim they're as baffled as we are, or at least that's what they want us to believe." The mayor's voice dropped, a flicker of frustration breaking through. "And then yesterday, they just vanished. A whole army, gone as if they'd never been here. Scouts have scoured the area and found nothing. No tracks leading away, no bodies left behind. It's as if they were pulled from existence itself."

The room was silent, every eye on Aeron as Godfrey took a step closer, his gaze imploring. "Please, Aeron. If you know anything, anything at all, we need it now."

Aeron cleared his throat, glancing briefly at Seraphina and Pinder before addressing Mayor Godfrey and the commanders. "We found ... well, a tattered scroll," he began, his voice even but cautious. "The priests at the temple have taken it to try and decipher the contents. I assume that's what they're likely locked away doing now."

Godfrey raised an eyebrow, the hint of frustration still evident, but he waited as Aeron continued.

"They need time to decipher it," Aeron explained, "but from what little we've managed to gather, these creatures are called mirages. That's about all we've confirmed." He looked around the room, meeting the serious eyes of each Fang commander. "When we face them in battle, they seem real enough, but once defeated, they vanish, as if they never existed in this world to begin with. No bodies, no traces left behind."

One of the commanders leaned forward, curiosity and concern evident on her face. "So, they're just ... illusions?"

Aeron shook his head. "They feel real when they're attacking, believe me. I've seen them up close, and we've fought against them more than once. In each fight, they disappear as soon as they fall. It's like they're drawn back to whatever brought them here in the first place." He paused, recalling previous encounters. "We've fought several of these creatures along the way, each time seeing the same outcome. They're relentless and dangerous, but they don't seem bound to this world the same way we are."

The commanders exchanged uneasy glances, murmuring amongst themselves. Mayor Godfrey listened intently, his expression thoughtful, but the concern lingered in his gaze.

"As soon as the priests manage to crack that scroll, I'm sure we'll all know more," Aeron concluded. "There's someone there with them. A researcher named Tate. He's been deeply involved in figuring this out, and I trust he'll check back with me as soon as they uncover anything significant."

The room settled into a heavy silence as Aeron's words sank in, the uncertainty thick in the air.

Mayor Godfrey nodded at Aeron, a small measure of relief flickering in his eyes. "Thank you, Aeron. Even knowing there's a step forward in understanding these creatures … well, it's a start. At least there's a chance the priests will find something useful from that scroll. It's more than we had."

The commanders around the table murmured in agreement, the tension in the room easing slightly. Godfrey gestured to a scout standing nearby, who stepped forward to relay a report.

"Our scouts have seen no further sign of mirages around the city," he stated. "No traces, no disturbances. As far as we can tell, it's quiet."

Godfrey nodded, then the scout continued, his voice tinged with a hint of skepticism. "However, word came in with some traders about a strange incident near Tideheaven. According to their report, a trade ship was attacked by a, well, a goo-covered giant octopus."

The room fell silent for a moment, the absurdity of the report hanging in the air. Pinder's lips curled into a smirk, and he raised his hand smacking his face. "Damn," he said, trying to keep a straight face. "Why didn't I think of that?"

The room erupted in a low chuckle, the tension easing as the commanders shared an amused glance. Even Godfrey allowed himself a small, weary smile.

With a nod, the mayor addressed them once more. "Thank you for your time. I'm sure you all need some rest. Goodnight, Aeron, Seraphina, Pinder. And again, thank you for your patience and your willingness to share what you know."

They bid him farewell, leaving the manor and stepping into the cool evening air. As they walked toward the inn, the quiet streets of the city felt peaceful, almost unnaturally so after the conversation they had just left behind. They paused outside the inn, standing together in silence for a moment, each lost in thought about what lay ahead. The cool night air was refreshing after the intensity of the meeting.

Seraphina stretched her arms above her head, letting out a yawn. "Well, I suppose we won't be waiting up for Tate tonight. He's probably elbow-deep in lore by now, more excited by scrolls than sleep."

Aeron chuckled. "Knowing him, he's already deciphered half the temple library."

Pinder glanced over his shoulder in the direction of the blacksmith's workshop. "I won't be at the inn tonight. I have a date with a certain blacksmith." He smirked, winking dramatically before prancing off, hands in his pockets, whistling a jaunty tune as he headed down the street.

Aeron and Seraphina shared a laugh, watching Pinder disappear around a corner.

"Well," Seraphina said, her laughter softening as she turned back to Aeron, "I think it's time we call it a night, too."

Aeron nodded, a warm smile tugging at his lips. They headed into the inn, each quietly grateful for the few peaceful moments they'd shared amid the mysteries and battles.

The weight of the day finally gave way to rest as Aeron and Seraphina slept soundly in their rooms. The city outside lay in a rare stillness, an almost unnatural lull.

Aeron jolted awake, heart pounding, as a blood-curdling scream shatters the night. The agonizing wails of people reached his ears. He sat up, instinctively grabbing his weapon. The horrifying sounds grew louder—a mix of desperate screams, panicked shouts, and the unmistakable clamor of guards shouting orders, their voices barely audible over the chaos erupting outside.

Across the hall, Seraphina was already awake, her face pale as she rushed out of her room and met Aeron in the corridor. The inn's walls trembled as the sounds of terror flooded through every crack and crevice.

"What ... what's happening?" Seraphina stammered, her voice tinged with shock as they exchanged a tense glance.

Aeron's jaw tightened, and he steeled himself. "I don't know, but it sounds like something we can't ignore."

They hurried down the stairs, the horrifying noise of the city growing louder with each step. The moment they stepped outside, they were met with a scene of pandemonium. People were running, guards were shouting, and the air was thick with fear.

The night that had once seemed so still had erupted into a nightmare, and neither Aeron nor Seraphina knew what awaited them in the darkness.

The night air carried an overpowering, metallic scent that was thick and unsettling, laced with something sharp and almost rancid, unmistakably the smell of blood. But it was more than that. There was an unnatural taint to it, a sickly undertone that clung to the back of Aeron's throat, unlike anything he'd experienced before. It felt wrong, as if death itself had taken root in the air, lingering like a poison.

All around them, people rushed frantically from the lower parts of the city, eyes wide with terror, clutching loved ones and carrying whatever possessions they could grab in their haste. Their faces were pale, etched with fear and disbelief, as they fled from the horrors unseen, yet all too present. Some stumbled in their panic, calling out for family members, their voices drowned in the cacophony of screams and cries that filled the streets.

In the opposite direction, packs of guards stormed past, armored footsteps pounding against the cobblestone. Their expressions were grim, hardened, as they gripped their weapons tightly, heading toward the lower city where the sounds of chaos echoed like a distant battle—clashes of metal, inhuman roars, and the terrible, haunting cries of those caught in the onslaught.

It was as if the city itself had become a war zone, and Aeron's gut twisted with an instinctive dread.

Aeron barely had a moment to absorb the chaos around him when a guard rushed past, his face ashen and eyes wide with a look of pure, unfiltered horror. He skidded to a halt, noticing Aeron, and stumbled over his words, desperation in his voice.

"Quick—you have to come, now!" the guard gasped, his voice raw and shaky. "They… they breached the gate. It's… it's horrible. A giant… a three-headed dog. It just tore through the gates like they were nothing."

He paused, swallowing hard as if the words were too terrible to utter. "It came so fast… the guards didn't even have time to sound the alarm. It's tearing the lower city apart… there are… there are so many bodies. So many people…"

The guard's face was a mask of trauma, eyes haunted, unfocused, as if he was trapped somewhere between the memory of what he'd seen and the nightmare unfolding around him. His breaths came in ragged, shallow gasps, and his hands trembled as he clutched his sword—still unsheathed, though he was long past any notion of fighting.

Aeron's chest tightened, a chill settling over him as the guard's words hung in the air, the sounds of destruction and despair echoing in the distance.

Aeron and Seraphina sprinted through the streets, weaving past fleeing civilians and fallen debris. The stench of blood grew stronger, mingling with smoke and the acrid scent of splintered wood. As they rounded a corner, they skidded to a halt, eyes widening at the scene before them.

Towering in the center of the street, illuminated by flickering torchlight and the glow of nearby fires, was a monstrous, three-headed dog—a massive mirage that seemed more nightmare than reality. Each of its heads snarled and snapped, jaws dripping with dark ooze as it thrashed, tearing through guards who attempted to hold the line. Its claws scraped against the cobblestones, leaving deep gouges as it trampled over anything in its path, including the remains of shattered trade carts now crushed beneath its weight.

Behind the creature lay a trail of utter devastation. Broken beams, shattered glass, and scattered belongings littered the streets. But it was the stables, or what was left of them, that seized Aeron's gaze, freezing him in place.

The structure lay in ruins, its walls torn open, roof collapsed, and stalls crushed beyond recognition. Dark patches stained the ground where animals had once been, their bodies now little more than scattered remnants. Bits of tack and shattered boards laid strewn about, mixed with the blood-soaked earth.

Aeron stared, the horror of the sight sinking in as he took in the gruesome remains of what was once a place of warmth and safety, now reduced to nothing but a scene of brutality and carnage. The night felt heavier, and Aeron's heart pounded with a mixture of fury and grief as he stared at the devastation left in the beast's wake.

Everything slowed. The screams, the distant clash of metal, the monstrous snarls—all of it faded into silence as Aeron's gaze landed on a familiar shape amid the rubble.

Koko.

Time seemed to freeze, every heartbeat stretching into eternity as Aeron's mind registered the scene before him. His faithful companion laid half-buried beneath broken beams and shattered stones, his brown coat matted with blood, his small frame crushed under the weight of the debris. The once-bright eyes that had always watched Aeron with trust and warmth now gazed dully, flickering with the barest spark of life.

In an instant, Aeron was beside him, moving with a speed he'd never known. The world blurred as he dropped to his knees, reaching out to gently cradle Koko's head in his arms. His hands trembled as they touched the coarse fur, and he felt the feeble rise and fall of Koko's shallow breaths—a fragile rhythm slipping away.

Koko's eyes flickered open, just barely, and a soft light filled them. Despite the pain that must be consuming him, a faint, familiar warmth shone in his gaze as he recognized Aeron. There was no fear, no agony, only a gentle happiness—a comfort in these final moments, a solace found in the presence of his master.

Aeron's throat tightened, his voice catching as he whispered, "I'm here, Koko. I'm right here." His hands stroke the mule's head gently, his touch as tender as if Koko were made of glass, something precious and fragile he could still protect.

Koko's breaths came slower, each one fainter than the last. His body shuddered, weakened and worn, yet his gaze never left Aeron's face. He nuzzled weakly against Aeron's hand, his eyes softening, and for a single, fleeting moment, Aeron saw a spark of joy—pure and untainted—reflecting back at him.

Then, with one last, gentle breath, Koko's eyes closed, the light within fading like the last ember of a dying fire. His body went still, his head growing heavier in Aeron's arms, yet there was a peace there—a quietness that settled over him in his final rest.

Aeron felt the world collapse around him, his grief so profound it seemed to echo in the silence. He clutched Koko's lifeless body, the pain twisting deep within him, an ache that cut through his soul like the edge of a blade. The world around him shattered, but in that moment, all that existed was the stillness—the weight of Koko in his arms, and the hollow silence left in his wake.

Aeron knelt beside Koko's lifeless body, the reality of his loss sinking in with a force that felt like a physical blow, tearing through his chest and hollowing him from the inside out. Grief surged up in a wave so powerful it threatened to consume him, a raw, primal anguish that burned hotter with each second. His fingers tightened around Koko, trembling as his heart shattered, leaving nothing but pain in its place.

Then, something snapped.

A pulse of force burst outward from Aeron, sending chunks of rubble and shattered wood flying from his body in every direction, scattering across the ground like leaves caught in a storm. At the center of the maelstrom, Koko's body remained untouched, cradled carefully in Aeron's lap, undisturbed amidst the chaos.

Seraphina stumbled back at the first shockwave, her eyes widening in horror and disbelief. She collapsed to her knees, hands clasped over her mouth as she watched the impossible unfold before her. Her gaze was transfixed on Aeron, barely recognizing the figure she saw. There was something otherworldly about him, an energy radiating from his very being, warping the air around him as if reality itself bent in response to his sorrow and rage.

Another pulse ripped outward, then another, each one growing faster, the space around Aeron distorting with every burst.

With each surge of power, faint, flickering bursts of purple light pulsed from his body, illuminating the destruction around him. His grief escaped him in a gut-wrenching scream that echoed through the streets, reverberating with a sound not entirely human, filled with an agony so profound it seemed to shake the earth.

Aeron's body began to rise, slowly levitating above the ground as pulses of energy emanated from him faster and faster, the bursts of purple light intensifying with each second. His cries transformed into roars, each one filled with a terrible wrath and pain that resonated through the city like thunder. The air grew heavy, oppressive, as if the very essence of his despair was pressing down on everything around him.

The final burst was blinding, an explosion of violet light that engulfed everything, forcing Seraphina to shield her eyes as a wave blasted outward, rattling windows, shaking the earth, and casting everything in a shadowed, unnatural glow.

And then, silence.

When the light faded, a figure stood where Aeron once knelt. Dark, ominous, and cloaked in an aura of absolute power. Aeron was unrecognizable, transformed into an armored dark figure. His armor resembled bones, though it wasn't bone. It is something far darker, otherworldly metal forged in a way that defied human craftsmanship. The armor clung to him, intricately carved to resemble the skeletal form beneath, yet radiating a blackened gleam, giving him an aura of haunting, unyielding strength.

A hood shrouded his face in darkness, hiding his features completely, leaving only the faint impression of something terrible lurking in the shadows behind it. A torn, ethereal cape flowed down his back, moving in an unseen wind, as if bound to his very soul. In his hand, a scythe materialized, its blade sharp and cruel, glowing with a fierce, otherworldly purple aura that pulsed like a heartbeat—a power never seen before, ancient and unknown.

His hands and feet were encased in bone-like gloves and boots, almost skeletal in appearance, yet seamless with the dark armor that consumed him. He stood motionless, a dark silhouette against the ruin and wreckage surrounding him.

Seraphina stared with wide eyes, heart pounding, struggling to comprehend what she was witnessing. The man she knew was gone, replaced by this being of shadow and vengeance, his very presence radiating an unearthly power that chilled her to the core.

Aeron was something far darker than the man he once was, a figure reborn from fury and loss. His gaze fixed on the path of destruction ahead, his heart now as silent and cold as the grave.

Chapter 23: Fury Unleashed

The city laid in stunned silence, as if holding its breath in the wake of Aeron's transformation.

Smoke rose from the ruins of the lower district, swirling in ghostly tendrils through the night air. The acrid scent of burning wood and blood lingered, mixing with a strange, metallic tang. The force radiating from Aeron seemed to thicken the air with every pulse.

Aeron stood motionless, cloaked in dark, bone-like armor, his figure barely recognizable. His scythe glowed with an intense violet aura, casting an eerie, pulsating light across the ground, illuminating the broken cobblestones and scattered debris littering his path. His every breath vibrated with unrestrained fury, sending ripples through the space around him and filling the air with a sense of unyielding menace.

Seraphina knelt a short distance away, her expression frozen between horror and awe as she tried to comprehend the scene before her. She's seen him fight countless times, but this was something else. Her heart pounded as she stared at Aeron's transformed figure, feeling the weight of his grief and rage pressing down on her like a tangible force.

A group of guards approached cautiously, weapons drawn, though their hands shook as they took in the dark, armored figure towering over the carnage. They hesitated, whispering amongst themselves.

"What… what is he?" one of them breathed, his voice barely

audible.

Another guard, wide-eyed and pale, whispered, "I don't know. Something beyond us."

A low hum filled the air, growing louder with each heart-beat—a resonant, otherworldly sound that seemed to emanate from Aeron himself, as if his very presence was bending reality. His scythe glowed brighter with each pulse, the violet light pulsing in rhythm with his steady, measured breaths.

Aeron's gaze shifted, fixing on the source of the destruction. The massive three-headed dog was still wreaking havoc in the ruined lower city. The creature's eyes glowed a sickly yellow as it crushed everything in its path, each of its heads snapping and snarling, jaws dripping with black ooze that sizzles against the ground. Its massive claws left deep gouges in the cobblestone, the ground shuddering beneath its relentless assault.

Slowly, Aeron lifted his head, his eyes narrowing as he locked onto the monstrous beast before him. His voice, cold and unrecognizable, cut through the night. "You've taken enough."

The air around him seemed to tense, filled with the energy building within him as he gripped his scythe, his stance bracing, ready. His gaze sharpened, fixed entirely on the three-headed creature in a silence heavy with anticipation.

The air crackled as Aeron's cold gaze locked onto the monstrous three-headed dog standing amidst the rubble. The creature loomed, each head snapping and snarling, eyes glowing a sickly yellow that cut through the smoke-filled night. It was a beast of nightmares—massive and wild, its dark, matted fur bristling, oozing dark sludge from its mouths that hissed when it splattered against the ground, leaving scorch marks.

Finally, Aeron moved.

In a blur of speed, his figure almost disappeared, leaving only the faint trace of violet light and the lingering echo of his breath in the wake of his charge. He was faster than anything the city had seen, faster than any human could dream. His scythe arced through the air, a streak of purple trailing its deadly edge as he closed the distance in a heartbeat.

The first head lunged, jaws wide, razor-sharp teeth dripping with the same corrosive ooze. But Aeron was already gone, a shadow flickering past, untouchable. He reappeared in an instant, beside the beast, his scythe slicing down in a single, fluid motion. The blade cleaved through the air, and with a sickening thud, the first head was severed, dark ooze spilling from the neck as it collapsed to the ground.

But before Aeron's scythe has even left its arc, the head regenerated, as if woven back together by the shadows themselves. The three-headed beast snarled again, its once-missing head now glaring with fresh fury, its movements savage, untamed.

Unfazed, Aeron launched forward once more, his form an uncatchable phantom against the beast's snapping jaws. The second head struck at him, a flash of yellowed fangs snapping at his side, but Aeron twisted in midair, his movements a dance of deadly precision. He sidestepped effortlessly, his dark armor catching the faintest glint of torchlight, and in the same breath, he brought his scythe down, cleaving the second head from its body in another swift motion.

A brief pause, and then, impossibly, the head reappeared, knitting itself together from nothingness, as if no wound had been dealt.

Aeron's jaw clenched, but he showed no hesitation, no flicker of frustration. His eyes narrowed, cold and calculating, as he circled the beast, his movements fluid and poised. The three-headed dog roared in frustration, as its claws scraped across the cobblestones, splintering stone and earth, and each of its heads lashed out in blind fury, meeting only empty air.

To the onlookers, he was a blur, a dark figure moving so swiftly he seemed to vanish and reappear at will, slipping through the monster's attacks like a wraith. He ducked and weaved, sidestepping the swipes of massive paws, leaning out of reach as jaws snapped shut mere inches from him. Each dodge was precise, calculated, and unfathomably fast. Not a single move was wasted.

Then, in a single heartbeat, Aeron spun, his scythe carving an arc of brilliant violet light as he sliced through the air. Both outer heads fell in unison, severed cleanly, their massive forms crumbling to the ground. The beast stumbled, its central head alone remaining to release a guttural, furious howl that reverberated through the city, a sound of rage and pain.

Everyone watching felt a chill as they observed the severed heads begin to reform—yet this time, something was different. The heads regenerated, but slower, the shadows sluggish as they weaved the creature back together.

Aeron stood, scythe at his side, eyes cold and unyielding as he watched the beast struggle to regain its form, the violet glow around him intensifying with every breath.

The three-headed dog, sensing the danger, let out a guttural snarl, each head rearing back. With a sudden, violent lunge, its central maw clamped down on a large, wooden trading cart, splintering the timber in its powerful jaws. With a furious twist of its neck, it hurled the massive cart toward Aeron, the air whistling as it barreled forward.

Aeron didn't flinch. In a movement as effortless as breathing, he sidestepped, his form blurring as he dodged the projectile, letting it soar past him.

Buta scream, raw and sharp and filled with pain and fear, made him turn.

The cart had crashed into Seraphina, striking her with brutal force. The sound shattered the last restraint within Aeron. His aura surged, a blinding purple light flaring around him as he let out a roar—a sound of pure, unrestrained fury, something primal and vengeful that reverberated through the city.

In an instant, he was upon the creature, moving with a speed that defied all logic. His scythe became a whirlwind, an extension of his fury as he struck again and again, each swing carving through the creature with such velocity the beast itself appeared blurred, struggling to even react to his onslaught. Every blow landed with the weight of his wrath, each strike faster and more devastating than the last. It was a brutal, relentless storm of attacks, his violet aura leaving trails of light in the air, the sheer force creating shockwaves that rippled outward.

In one final, blinding flash of purple light. Aeron's scythe arced through the air in a sweeping motion, cleaving through all three heads in a single, devastating blow.

The beast's bodies slumped, and slowly, each of the three heads fall, hitting the ground with a sickening thud. The monster's hulking form shuddered, and began to dissolve, its dark, oozing flesh dissipating into faint wisps of smoke, vanishing in the night air as though it was never there.

As the last remnants of the beast faded, Aeron was left hovering, his form suspended effortlessly ten, fifteen feet above the ground, his dark figure cloaked in an ethereal glow, the purple light still pulsing faintly around him, almost alive with his lingering rage.

Seraphina groaned, pain rippling through her as she pushed herself up, clutching her side. Splinters and debris from the shattered cart surrounded her, and her vision blurred for a moment as she steadied herself, her fingers gripping the jagged edge of the wood. She looked up, her eyes finding Aeron's dark, hovering figure, cloaked in a menacing violet glow that pulsed like a heartbeat.

"Aeron?" she called out, her voice wavering, almost questioning. There was a hesitation in her tone, an uncertainty as she studied him. Was this even Aeron? The thought lingered, her heart pounding with both fear and hope. Her mind raced, remembering the man she knew—the one who cared deeply, who fought with courage but always with restraint. Now, before her, stood something otherworldly, something fierce and terrifying.

She called his name again, louder, her voice echoing through the ruined street. "Aeron!"

As if the sound of her voice reached something deep within him, Aeron's form suddenly flickered. The violet aura dissipated, his figure losing its shadowed intensity. In an instant, his body transformed back to his usual self, the armor gone, the darkness vanishing as quickly as it had appeared.

And then he fell.

His body dropped from the sky, plummeting the ten feet to the ground below. Seraphina's heart clenched as he crashed into the earth, his form crumpling upon impact. She gasped, rushing forward, her own pain forgotten as she stumbled over debris to reach him, the sound of his fall still echoing in her mind. He laid still, his chest rising and falling shallowly, unconscious before her.

Seraphina knelt beside Aeron's still form, her hands trembling as she gently shook his shoulders. Tears blurred her vision, streaming down her cheeks as she called out to him, her voice broken with fear and desperation.

"Aeron, please, wake up," she whispered, her fingers brushing against his face, searching for any sign of life. Her heart pounded, each beat a painful reminder of the possibility that he might not open his eyes. She shook him again, her voice rising, "Aeron, come on! Don't do this to me!"

She bowed her head, her forehead resting against his chest, sobs wracking her body as she clutched him tightly. The fear, the tension, the horror of the night—all of it seemed to crash over her as she waited, hoping against hope that he'd respond.

Then, a soft, raspy chuckle stirred beneath her, and Aeron's voice broke through the silence. "Good..." he murmured, his voice barely above a whisper but carrying a familiar warmth. "Glad... you're not hurt too bad..."

Seraphina gasped, lifting her head to see his eyes slowly

opening, a faint, tired smile tugging at the corners of his lips. Relief flooded her face and a smile broke through her tears as she cupped his face, her hands shaking as she studied him, making sure he was really there.

"You absolute fool," she breathed, her voice wavering between laughter and tears. "You scared me half to death."

Aeron's hand moved slowly, brushing her cheek, his fingers rough but comforting. "Sorry," he whispered, his voice weak but steady. "Guess I… overdid it a bit."

Seraphina laughed, a small, shaky sound filled with both frustration and overwhelming relief. She pressed her forehead gently against his, closing her eyes as she let herself savor the moment, grateful beyond words that he was back and alive.

As Seraphina cradled Aeron, wiping away the remnants of her tears, hurried footsteps echoed down the street. Pinder appeared, his shirt only halfway buttoned, his boots on the wrong foot and hastily pulled on. His hair was tousled, and a faint blush colored his cheeks. He'd apparently come running straight from the blacksmith's quarters. He paused, taking in the scene, his eyes flickering between Seraphina's tear-streaked face and Aeron's barely-conscious form lying on the ground.

"By the gods," he breathed, quickly closing the distance between them, his usual humor subdued. "What … what happened? Is everything alright?"

Seraphina looked up, her face etched with a mixture of sorrow and exhaustion. She glanced back at Aeron, gathering herself, and then turned to Pinder, her voice trembling as she tried to explain. "It was … it was Koko. He—" She stopped, swallowing hard, struggling to keep her composure as she relived the horror. "The creature … it was a three-headed beast, bigger than anything we've faced. It tore through the lower city, and … Koko was there."

Pinder's face fell, and he reached out, resting a gentle hand on her shoulder. "Seraphina … I'm so sorry."

She nodded, her gaze falling, her fingers gripping Aeron's hand as if grounding herself. "Koko… he… he didn't make it. Aeron was with him in his final moments." Her voice broke, and she took a shaky breath, blinking back the tears that threatened to fall again.

Pinder's expression was heavy with grief, but he remained silent, his gaze flickering to Aeron's still figure.

"That wasn't even the worst of it," she continued, her voice barely a whisper. "When… when Koko died, something happened to Aeron. He… he changed, Pinder. It was like nothing I've ever seen." Her voice caught as she remembered, and she shook her head, her gaze distant. "He transformed—his entire body, his armor, everything about him. It was dark, like he became something else… something that felt like… like death itself."

Pinder's eyes widened, his hand slipping from her shoulder as he struggled to absorb what she was saying. "You're saying… that Aeron…"

"He fought that creature," she said, her voice trembling, her eyes distant with the memory. "He tore through it with a speed and power I didn't even know was possible. And every time he struck, it would regenerate, as if nothing could kill it. But Aeron didn't stop. His scythe glowed with this violet light, and he… he was relentless."

She glanced down at Aeron, a hint of sadness softening her expression. "In the end, he destroyed it, all three heads in a single strike. And then he just… he just hovered there, like something otherworldly." She looked back at Pinder, her eyes clouded with both awe and sorrow. "It was as if he wasn't Aeron anymore. I called out to him. I called his name, and… he came back."

Pinder was silent for a moment, absorbing her words, his gaze settling on Aeron with a newfound solemnity. "And now he's back to himself?"

Seraphina nodded, brushing a hand across Aeron's forehead, her touch gentle. "Yes. When he fell, it was like he was himself again." Her voice softened, a tear slipping down her cheek. "But we've lost so much tonight, Pinder. Koko's gone!"

Pinder reached out, giving her shoulder a comforting squeeze, his voice low and filled with empathy, "We'll get through this, Seraphina. Whatever's happened, whatever Aeron is going through, we'll be here for him. For each other." He looked at Aeron, a faint glint of determination in his eyes. "One way or another, we'll make sense of this."

The three of them sat in silence, bound by loss and the uncertainty that lay ahead, the faint glow of the city's distant fires cast shadows over the path that stretched before them.

As Seraphina, Pinder, and Aeron lingered in the aftermath, footsteps approached, heavy and purposeful. The commander of the city guard strode forward, his armor clinking with each step. He halted beside them, his expression somewhere between awe and wariness as he studies Aeron's unconscious form.

"That…" The commander's voice was low, almost reverent, as he glanced at Seraphina and Pinder. "That was unlike anything I've ever seen. It was as if a force beyond this world had taken hold of him."

He paused, shaking his head as if still trying to process what he had witnessed. "Aeron moved like a shadow, faster than any living thing. His strikes were precise and relentless. He faced that creature—no, he annihilated it, with a power that felt… impossible. It was like something out of a tale told by firelight, of gods and death incarnate."

Pinder exchanged a glance with Seraphina, both of them silent, feeling the weight of the commander's words. The commander sighed, his voice softening as he watched Aeron's still form.

"Quite frankly," he continued, "I would call it unbelievable if I hadn't seen it with my own eyes. I've led men in battle against beasts, bandits, and armies, but this? Aeron was something else entirely. And as much as I'd like to deny it, I can't." His gaze dropped, a hint of respect and fear mingling in his eyes.

The commander straightened, regaining his composure as he gestured to his men, who had been watching from a short distance, their expressions filled with awe and unease. "You," he said, pointing to a pair of guards, "take him to the medical garrison. Whatever power he summoned took its toll. Let him rest. He deserves as much."

The guards stepped forward, hesitating for a moment before gently lifting Aeron's weak form between them. As they carried him away, the commander looked back at Seraphina and Pinder, his expression thoughtful.

"Stay close," he advised. "Whatever Aeron's become, he's going to need all the support he can get, and so will we."

With a nod, he turned, following his men toward the medical garrison, leaving Seraphina and Pinder alone in the quiet aftermath of the night.

The morning sun cast a harsh, almost surreal light over the city, illuminating the smoldering remnants of the night's devastation. Thin tendrils of smoke rose from collapsed buildings and scorched rubble, their wispy trails drifting into the sky. Townspeople moved through the streets with somber faces, lifting broken beams, sweeping away ash, and gathering what little remained of their belongings. There was a quiet resolve in their movements as if the weight of what they'd survived hadn't fully settled yet.

Seraphina and Pinder made their way through the recovery efforts, the occasional murmur or glance in their direction hinting at the night's whispered stories. Stories of Aeron's unbelievable transformation and the monstrous creature that tore through the lower city. When they reached the entrance to the medical garrison, they were greeted by a city guard who allowed them inside.

The air inside the garrison was thick with the scent of healing herbs and smoldering incense, meant to cleanse the air and soothe the wounded. Beds lined the room, most filled with those injured during the attack, their faces drawn with exhaustion and pain. At the far end of the room, near a large window that let in a bright shaft of morning light, Mayor Godfrey stood, speaking in hushed tones with a few members of the city guard.

Noticing Seraphina and Pinder, the mayor turned, gesturing them forward. His face was lined with fatigue, but his look was sharp, carrying a mixture of relief and curiosity.

"Thank you for coming," he began, his voice steady but soft. "I know what happened was … harrowing, to say the least. I've summoned you here because there's much to discuss. After what transpired, there's been quite an… interest in Aeron. The people are shaken, and frankly, so am I." He paused, his gaze drifting to Aeron, lying on a bed nearby, his chest rising and falling with a slow, steady rhythm, a touch of disbelief in his expression. "I was briefed by the commander on what happened out there," he continued, his voice lowering. "It's difficult to wrap my head around, but the people are already talking. Some are afraid. Others think he might be a savior. Regardless, I need to understand exactly what he is."

Pinder shifted uncomfortably, glancing at Seraphina, his face was hard. He stepped forward, his tone sharp as he addressed the mayor. "With all due respect, Mayor, he's Aeron," he said, his voice carrying a rare edge. "The same Aeron who saved this city—twice now. The man who fought through hell last night, who lost his companion, and who's lying here unconscious after giving everything he had."

The mayor's expression shifted, a touch of surprise flickering across his face as he took in Pinder's words. Pinder didn't let up, his gaze steady and unyielding. "He's not some unknown force, not some legend. He's Aeron, our friend, and the man who risked everything for people who are already questioning him before he's even woken up. If anyone should be given a chance to explain, it's him."

A tense silence settled over the room as Pinder's words hung in the air, challenging and unapologetic. The mayor swallowed, his gaze softening as he looked back at Aeron's unconscious form, perhaps reminded that beneath the power and mystery, Aeron was still the person who stood beside them through it all.

Aeron stirred, his eyes fluttering open and taking in the familiar faces around him. Seraphina's face lit up with relief, and Pinder let out a deep breath, a small, knowing smile tugging at his lips. Mayor Godfrey stepped forward, his posture both respectful and reserved.

"Aeron," the mayor began, his voice gentle, "it's good to see you awake. We owe you more thanks than words can give." He hesitated, a somber expression crossing his face. "And... I want to offer my deepest condolences for your loss. Koko was a loyal companion to you and, after last night, something of a symbol to all of us."

Aeron nodded, a faint shadow of grief crossing his face at the mention of Koko. He slowly sat up, a quiet resolve in his eyes.

The mayor continued, his voice filled with sincerity. "To honor him, we've commissioned a statue to be placed in the town square. It's our hope that he'll be remembered here as he deserves, for his bravery and loyalty. After the cremation, we'd like to store his ashes within the statue, if... if that's alright with you."

Aeron's eyes softened, and he looked down for a moment, processing the gesture. He gave a slow, grateful nod. "I think... he'd like that," he replied quietly. "Thank you."

The mayor placed a hand over his heart, bowing his head respectfully. "It's the least we can do for him — and for you, Aeron. This town will remember what you've both done here."

The mayor took a step closer to Aeron, his expression filled with both curiosity and caution. "Aeron, forgive me, but do you remember what happened during the fight? The transformation you went through?"

Aeron's gaze drifted, his brow furrowing as he searched his memories. He took a deep breath, his voice low, as if he was reliving it even as he spoke, "I remember... so much pain. Losing Koko... it felt like something broke inside me, a weight I couldn't carry anymore. And then I remember the power."

He glanced at his hands, flexing his fingers slowly as if testing them, his voice steady but distant. "It was like I wasn't bound by the same limits. I could move faster, like time itself had stopped around me. My body didn't feel the same. I felt connected to everything—the air, the ground, like I was part of something larger, something unstoppable." His gaze hardened, his eyes meeting the mayor's with a quiet intensity. "I remember every moment of it, every strike. Until the creature was gone."

Aeron fell silent, glancing at Seraphina and Pinder, his expression softening. "I woke up in Seraphina's arms. And now I'm here."

The mayor's expression was contemplative, Aeron's words lingering in the air. He looked at Aeron with both awe and a trace of unease, clearly grappling with the mystery unraveling before them. But his expression softened with a mix of respect and sympathy. "Again, you have my condolences. Koko's memory will have a place here."

Aeron nodded, a faint sadness in his eyes as he met the mayor's gaze. "Thank you, Mayor. That means a lot."

The mayor hesitated, seeming to weigh his words before continuing. "I'll admit that last night was... difficult to understand. Whatever you became, whatever power you used to defeat that creature, was something beyond anything we've seen. If you learn anything about these mirages or about what that transformation means for you, please, let me know."

Aeron nodded, his expression steady. "I will, Mayor. If I find answers, I'll make sure you're among the first to know."

The mayor placed a hand over his heart, bowing his head in gratitude. "Thank you. Rest well, all of you. I'll leave you to recover." With a final respectful nod, he turned and stepped out of the room, leaving Aeron, Seraphina, and Pinder alone to contemplate the weight of what lay ahead.

The door creaked open, and Tate stepped in, his usual composed demeanor softened by a look of concern. He scanned the room, his eyes landing on Aeron with a mix of relief and curiosity.

"I just heard what happened," Tate said, his voice quiet, filled with a rare solemnity. "Are... are you alright?"

Aeron nodded, though his expression was distant, still processing everything. Seraphina exchanged a glance with Pinder, then turned to Tate, her voice low.

"Tate... Koko didn't make it," she said gently. "When the creature attacked, Koko was caught in the path. Aeron... he lost it, and that's when... when the transformation happened."

Tate's face fell, his eyes dropping as he absorbed the loss. "I see," he said quietly, his voice tinged with regret. "Koko was a bit heavy on the hoof, true, but a remarkable companion all the same. Memorable in ways few of us could ever be."

A faint, sad smile touched Aeron's lips, and he nodded in agreement, appreciating the small tribute. Tate stepped closer, his gaze shifting between Aeron and the others, clearly processing the news.

"So... this transformation," he said, his tone thoughtful, yet cautious. "Do you remember any of it, Aeron? What it felt like?"

Aeron took a deep breath, his voice steady but distant as he recalled the events. "I remember everything. The pain, the power... it felt like I wasn't myself, like I was something more, something tied to everything around me. Time felt different, like I was moving through it with no resistance. And then the creature was gone, and I was just... back."

Tate listened intently, his expression thoughtful, the wheels of his mind turning as he considered the implications. Finally, he met Aeron's gaze, his eyes filled with understanding. "Koko was a true friend. And from what I gather, he's the reason you could become what you needed to be. I'm sorry he's gone, but I think his spirit will be with us in ways we might not yet understand."

Tate cleared his throat, his expression shifting from sympathy to a more serious focus. "Aeron, Seraphina, Pinder, while you were recovering, there have been some developments at the temple," he began, glancing between each of them. "The scholars have made progress with the scroll. It's limited, but it's something. They're anxious to share what they've uncovered."

Aeron looked up, a flicker of curiosity and urgency crossing his face. "Do they think they're close to understanding it?"

Tate nodded, though he kept his tone measured. "They believe they've made sense of a few key passages. Enough to have a working theory, at least. I spoke with the head priest briefly. He suggested that tomorrow, once you've rested, we should all meet at the temple. He'll go over what they've found, though he emphasized it's still incomplete."

Seraphina rested a reassuring hand on Aeron's shoulder, glancing between him and Tate. "Then tomorrow, we'll be ready. Aeron, get your strength back tonight," she said softly, giving him a small, encouraging smile.

Tate nodded in agreement, his gaze steady. "We'll need you at your best. This might be the first real step toward understanding all of this." He placed a comforting hand on Aeron's arm. "Rest well."

As the early morning light filtered through the garrison's windows, the door swung open again, and the city commander strode in, flanked by a pair of guards carrying trays laden with food. Platters piled high with fresh bread, roasted meats, cheeses, and fruits were set on a nearby table, the scent filling the room and lifting the spirits of everyone present. The commander stepped forward, his expression solemn, yet warm as he surveyed Aeron and his companions.

Clearing his throat, he raised a goblet, gesturing for the others to join him. "Aeron, Seraphina, Pinder… I don't believe there are words for what you've done for this city. Twice now, we have faced dangers beyond anything our walls were built to withstand. And twice, you've answered the call when others would have faltered."

He looked at Aeron, his gaze steady, respect shining in his eyes. "Aeron, you've shown strength, resilience, and a spirit that goes far beyond mere bravery. When the creature tore through our city, it was you alone who stood against it, risking your life for people who may never understand the depths of what you sacrificed."

The commander paused, glancing at Seraphina and Pinder, his expression softening. "And to all of you—Seraphina, whose compassion and courage I have witnessed, and Pinder, who would charge into fire itself for his friends—I give my gratitude. You have shown what it means to stand together, even in the darkest of hours."

He raised his goblet higher, his voice lifting with a note of pride. "So today, we honor you. Not only as defenders of this city but as the heart of what holds us together. When others look to flee, you stand your ground. And as long as we have people like you among us, I know this city can endure anything."

The room was quiet for a beat, each word settling like a vow among them. Finally, the commander's voice lowers, becoming almost reverent. "To Aeron, to Seraphina, to Pinder, may you never know defeat, and may this city never forget your names."

He raised his goblet, his eyes meeting Aeron's as he said, "To our protectors."

The room joined him in a chorus of gratitude, lifting their

cups high, and for a moment, the weight of their losses and battles faded as they shared this tribute in honor of all they'd endured together.

Tate cleared his throat, a playful glint in his eyes. "Ah-hem," he said, casting a sideways glance around the room with an exaggerated look of feigned indignation. "So, what am I then? Just a common researcher?" He raised an eyebrow, a smirk playing on his lips.

A few chuckles rippled through the room, and Tate crossed his arms, leaning back with a mock-serious expression. "I mean, I might not have been the one directly saving the city last night, but let's not forget my noble contributions. After all, someone had to dig us out of that mess in the desert. And let's not overlook the small detail of my being elbow-deep in dusty scrolls, trying to make sense of these mirages."

Seraphina laughed, rolling her eyes. "Oh, we'd never forget, Tate. No one could replace our 'common researcher'."

Pinder raised his goblet, grinning. "To Tate—the bravest scholar this side of the temple, and a man willing to face deadly scrolls so we don't have to."

The room filled with laughter, and even the commander chuckled, nodding in Tate's direction. "To Tate, our common researcher," he added with a wink, "whose efforts might be quieter but no less essential."

Tate feigned a gracious bow, lifting his own cup with a look of satisfaction. "Thank you, thank you. I'll happily accept the title of 'the glue that holds you all together.'"

As the laughter and camaraderie died down, everyone gradually found their way out of the room, leaving Aeron and Seraphina alone. The quiet settled around them, a comforting contrast to the chaos and grief of the night before. They sat together in the soft morning light, the remnants of the feast on the table nearby, but their focus was solely on each other.

Seraphina shifted closer to Aeron, her gaze soft, a gentle

smile playing on her lips. "I thought I'd lost you last night," she murmured, her voice barely above a whisper. "You scared me more than I thought possible."

Aeron's hand reached for hers, his fingers intertwining with hers as he met her gaze. "I'm sorry, Seraphina," he said, his voice laced with sincerity and regret. "I never wanted to make you worry. But when Koko was gone, something inside me just… shattered. I think that's what unleashed… whatever that was."

Seraphina nodded, her thumb tracing circles over the back of his hand. "You're more than what you became last night, Aeron. You're still you. Who I've come to love. Not just the one who wields the power, or who fights monsters, but you."

Aeron's breath caught at her words, a warmth spreading through his chest as he realized the depth of what she was saying. He reached up, gently cupping her cheek, his thumb brushing a stray tear from her cheek. "Seraphina, you've been with me through everything. You keep me grounded, keep me human, in all the best ways. I don't know what I'd be without you."

She leaned into his touch, her eyes glistening with unshed tears, a faint smile on her lips. "I don't ever want to be anywhere else, Aeron. I love you."

He exhaled, a weightlifting from his heart as he finally spoke the words he'd held back for so long, "I love you too, Seraphina. More than anything."

Their gazes locked, the world fading away as they leaned toward each other, the warmth between them filling the quiet space. Slowly, Aeron tilted his head, and their lips met in a kiss, soft and tender at first, but deepening with their emotions. The kiss was filled with longing, relief, and a promise. A silent vow that whatever came next, they'd face it together.

When they finally pulled back, Seraphina rested her forehead against his, a soft smile lighting her face as they sat in the peace of the moment, knowing they'd found something to hold onto amidst the storm.

As the evening sun dipped low on the horizon, casting a warm, amber glow over the city, the people of Great Oaks worked tirelessly to rebuild what was lost. Shadows stretched long and thin across the cobbled streets, yet there was a renewed energy in the air, a shared determination to restore their home.

The city was a patchwork of activity; men and women of all ages moved with purpose, carrying wooden beams, loading rubble onto carts, and sweeping away the remnants of destruction. Where stone walls had crumbled, new ones were already taking shape. The broken stalls of the marketplace were being replaced, the scent of freshly cut wood mingling with the lingering traces of smoke from the fires that had ravaged the lower city. Children ran errands, carrying buckets of water for mixing mortar, their laughter lightening the somber mood as they weaved through clusters of workers.

Near the town square, Pinder and several other volunteers worked side-by-side, lifting broken carts, salvaging what they could from splintered wood, and reinforcing the makeshift barriers that had protected the city. Despite the grime on his face and the sweat-soaked tunic, Pinder's usual smirk was ever-present, encouraging the weary workers around him. He traded jokes, lightening the burden of their labor with his infectious humor, making even the youngest apprentices laugh despite the hard day.

Tate, meanwhile, moved between groups, directing efforts where he could, his mind always analyzing, planning, finding the most efficient way to make progress. His sleeves were rolled up and his hands dusty. He had traded his usual research for physical work, yet there was a glint of satisfaction in his eyes — a quiet pride in contributing to something tangible.

Seraphina was in the heart of it all, coordinating the efforts, checking on the wounded, offering words of encouragement. Her calm, steady presence brought reassurance to those around her, and her compassion shone through as she took a moment with each person she encountered, ensuring they know they weren't alone.

As the last rays of sunlight dipped below the horizon, lanterns flickered to life throughout Great Oaks, casting a warm glow over the bustling streets. The sounds of hammers and voices echoed into the night, blending with the quiet hum of the wind. Though the scars of the previous night's battle still marred the city, a quiet resilience filled the air, a determination shared by every soul that walked its streets.

Slowly, the city quieted as the workers finished their day, gathering their tools and sharing tired smiles, their collective effort breathing life back into Great Oaks. The citizens returned to their homes, some exchanging weary goodnights, others pausing for one last look at their hard-won progress, pride glinting in their eyes.

As the last of the workers faded into the night, the city stood calm under the starlit sky, its spirit unbroken. And somewhere within the walls, Aeron slept, unaware of the people who had come together in his absence, rebuilding not just the walls but the heart of their home, standing ready to face whatever came next.

Chapter 24: Shadows of Purgatory

Back in Purgatory, the realm existed in a perpetual, muted twilight—a place where time barely stirred, and the air carried a chill that seemed to seep into the bones. It was a place between worlds, designed to be neither welcoming nor cruel, but a vast, empty plane where souls lingered in waiting. The ground stretched as far as the eye could see in soft hues of gray, blending into a horizon that vanished into mist. Shadows hung heavy in the air, their forms shifting, twisting in the absence of light or warmth.

Amid this desolate expanse, eleven figures stood, cloaked in dark, ethereal robes, their expressions concealed by the faint hooded shadows of their attire. The other reapers, who once worked in silent harmony with Death itself, now gathered under the command of someone new. Their posture was tense, uncertain, as they shifted their weight and glanced at one another, sensing the gravity of the moment.

At their center stood Merripen, a figure now enveloped in an aura unlike any she had carried before. Her presence commanded the same chilling respect, yet bore a jagged edge—something incomplete, barely restrained. Her stance was firm, her gaze cold, as she readied herself to address her peers.

The air thickened as she raised her hand, calling for silence. Her voice, cold and unyielding, echoed across the twilight expanse, yet there was an edge of frustration barely hidden beneath her steely tone.

Merripen raised her head, her gaze cold and resolute as she addressed the gathering. Her voice cut through the quiet like a blade, sharp and unyielding. "Since I assumed Death's place, time has moved quickly. And, in my eyes, things are going well." A slight smirk played at the corner of her mouth as she continued, her tone tinged with satisfaction. "The more aggressive approach to reaping souls seems to be paying off. The cycle is moving faster, the souls are coming in droves, and Purgatory grows more populated by the day. Efficiency has replaced mercy, and as a result, the balance is shifting, finally tipping toward something stronger."

She let her words hang in the air, watching the other reapers with a keen, calculating gaze. Though her tone was confident, there was an edge beneath her words—a forceful reassurance, as if convincing herself as much as her audience.

As Merripen's words hung in the air, heavy with threat, one reaper finally gathered the courage to step forward—Edric, a seasoned reaper known for his unwavering adherence to the old ways. His eyes, shadowed beneath his hood, met Merripen's with a steady, calm defiance.

"Merripen," Edric began, his voice respectful yet firm, "I understand your desire to bring order, but forcing the cycle like this goes against everything Death once upheld. We were meant to guide souls with balance, not wield power with a clenched fist. Death's duty was to maintain equilibrium, not disrupt it."

Merripen's eyes narrowed, her patience visibly thinning.

Another reaper, Cale, nodded in agreement, glancing at Edric before speaking. "Edric's right," he said cautiously. "The pace you're setting is shifting things too far, too fast. It's as if something else is being forced through. If we don't consider the consequences, we may—"

"Enough!" Merripen's voice rand out, cutting Cale's words short. She stepped forward, her presence dark and menacing, as if the very shadows around her had thickened. Her gaze was sharp and unyielding, sweeping over both Edric and Cale.

"Things are going exactly as I have planned," she growled, her tone filled with a fury that silenced the room. "The balance, the cycle, the reaping—it's all in my control now. And if either of you, or anyone else here, dares to question my authority again, know that I will not hesitate to make an example of you."

The room fell silent, the tension palpable as Edric and Cale exchanged glances. Merripen's gaze held them all in check, daring any other to challenge her. For now, no one did.

As the tense silence settled around the gathering, a slow, deliberate clapping echoed from the shadows, and Conquest stepped forward, his expression twisted in a pleased smirk. His presence radiated an unsettling confidence, his eyes gleaming with a dangerous amusement as he addressed the room, then shifted his gaze directly to Merripen.

"Well said, Merripen," he purred, his tone smooth and laced with an almost mocking respect. "Finally, someone with the resolve to push beyond those archaic notions of 'balance.'" He cast a brief glance at Edric and Cale, shaking his head as if disappointed. "Why worry about some intangible 'order' when you can wield true power? The old ways were soft, too bound by restraint. But you, Merripen... you're breaking that mold."

Edric's jaw clenched, his fists tightening as he held his tongue.

Conquest stepped closer to Merripen, his voice dropping to a near-whisper that only she and a few others could hear. "Don't you see? This... aggression, this bold approach, it's exactly what Purgatory needs. A little chaos, a little shake-up. It's long overdue." He leaned in slightly, his voice soft and coaxing, his gaze holding a dark intensity. "You're not here to keep the peace, Merripen. You're here to wield Death's power as you see fit. Let the others tremble if they must. They'll understand in time that your way—our way—will bring about a new era." He grinned, as if savoring the discomfort around him. "After all, without a bit of chaos, we're just stagnant shadows in a world that's moved on."

Merripen's gaze flickered with a dark satisfaction as she listened to Conquest's words, and a faint, dangerous smile curved on her lips. She straightened, her eyes flashing as she looked at the gathered reapers. Conquest's endorsement strengthened her resolve, solidifying her decision as she reveled in the support of a fellow Horseman.

"Well, there you have it," she said, her tone dripping with finality. "Chaos brings change. And if you don't like the direction we're headed, then perhaps it's time you found your place in the new order." She glanced at Conquest, sharing a look of mutual understanding, knowing well the turmoil they were sowing—but neither of them cared.

A murmur rippled through the gathered reapers, their unease palpable as they exchanged wary glances. Merripen stood tall, her dark satisfaction mingling with the subtle thrill of wielding control, knowing she had Conquest's unwavering support. She looked over the reapers, daring any of them to speak up, to challenge her authority. None did, but the tension among them thickened, their silence tinged with doubt.

Conquest stepped up beside her, his presence an imposing shadow, and his smirk deepened. "What's wrong?" he taunted, his voice dripping with mock sympathy. "Are the old ways so ingrained that you can't see progress even when it's right in front of you?" He gestured toward Merripen with a sweeping motion. "This is what we were meant for. The endless cycle of predictable, mundane reaping is stale. It's time to bring power and purpose to our work."

Edric's voice, though tempered with caution, broke the silence. "Purpose is one thing, Conquest, but chaos for the sake of it? To force souls from their paths—"

"Paths?" Conquest interrupted, laughing bitterly. "There's no path, Edric. Only what we create, what we mold in our own image. And Merripen has the strength to make a new path—one that doesn't grovel to the whim of balance." He glanced at Merripen with a gleam of dark approval, his tone softening in a way that almost seemed conspiratorial. "Balance is a comfort for the weak. True power is a game-changer."

Merripen let his words resonate, savoring the looks of discomfort and suppressed anger among the reapers. She reveled in the fracture between herself and the others, a divide that cemented her control. "You've all had the privilege of watching Death rule as a passive force, watching the cycle spin predictably," she said, her voice echoing in the shadowed expanse. "But that was then. I am not Death. I am something new. I am force, I am fire, and I will take us into an era where we are feared, not just respected."

Her gaze locked onto Edric, whose quiet defiance persisted despite the evident danger. "You, and anyone else who doubts, will adapt," she said, her voice low and dangerous. "Or you will fall by the wayside."

Conquest's smirk widened, his satisfaction clear as he watched the brewing turmoil. "Are there any others who have 'reservations' about this new era? Or are we finally ready to accept Merripen's rightful place and get on with the business of real power?"

The other reapers glanced at each other, torn between the pull of duty and the grim realization of Merripen's authority. One by one, they bowed their heads, acknowledging her dominion even as unease lingered in their eyes. Conquest, ever the devil on her shoulder, watched with a smug satisfaction as the last of the dissent faded into reluctant submission.

Merripen's smile returned, dark and triumphant. She lifted her head high, feeling the weight of her authority settle more fully onto her shoulders. The power she wielded was unstable, imperfect, but it is hers, and she intended to wield it without restraint.

"Good," she murmured, a dangerous glint in her eyes. "Then let's proceed."

Edric, unable to hold back any longer, stepped forward, his usually calm demeanor shattered by a rare fire in his eyes. He looked directly at Merripen, his voice trembling not with fear, but with a rage that had been simmering beneath the surface.

"What you did to Aeron and to Death itself," he said, his voice thick with contempt, "was a betrayal of everything we stand for. You've twisted this mantle to serve your ego, not the balance we were sworn to protect. Death chose Aeron because he believed in compassion, in understanding the weight of every soul he reaped. But you—" he stepped closer, his finger raised accusingly, "you know nothing of that. You wield this power like a tyrant, to feed your own hunger for control."

Merripen's face hardened, her eyes narrowing as Edric's words hung in the air, laced with disdain.

"You tore Aeron away from his path," Edric continued, his voice breaking with emotion. "And you would defile Death's mantle to serve your lust for chaos. You've taken something sacred and twisted it, Merripen, and for what? To play conqueror? To leave chaos in your wake? You're not Death. You're a pretender, a desecrator of everything we've protected since time immemorial."

The room was thick with tension, the other reapers frozen, their expressions a mix of fear and admiration for Edric's bravery. But Merripen's face was cold, her gaze hardening with each word he uttered.

"Careful, Edric," she said, her voice low and dangerous. "You're walking a very thin line."

But Edric, unafraid, pressed on. "I would rather walk that line and fall than serve under a false Death like you. You've corrupted this realm, betrayed your own kin. If there is any justice left in this forsaken place, you will fall, Merripen."

The air grew colder, shadows twisting around Merripen as a

dark, malevolent aura gathered around her. Her expression shifted, a flicker of pure rage crossing her face as she raised her hand, the shadows coiling tightly around her fingers.

She stepped forward, her voice an icy whisper. "Then fall you shall, Edric."

In a swift, brutal motion, she swung her hand downward, and the shadows exploded from her fingertips, wrapping around Edric in a choking, inescapable grip. His form trembled as the darkness consumed him, twisting through his being like tendrils of smoke, ripping him apart from the inside. His eyes widened, his mouth opening in a silent scream as he began to fade, his very essence torn into nothingness.

The last trace of Edric vanished into the void, leaving only silence in his wake. Merripen lowered her hand, her gaze sweeping over the remaining ten reapers, who stared in horror, their expressions a mix of shock and submission. She let the silence linger, the weight of her power sinking into each of them.

"You see," she said, her voice cold and unwavering, "this is what happens to those who cannot accept the new order. Edric's defiance was his own undoing. Let it serve as a warning. I am Death now. Any one of you who questions my reign will meet the same fate."

The remaining reapers bowed their heads in submission, their spirits broken, knowing that any resistance would be met with the same merciless destruction. Merripen's gaze lingered on each of them, satisfaction glinting in her eyes as she turned to Conquest, who watched with an approving smirk.

The other ten reapers stood silently, shadows in the presence of Merripen's new reign, bound to a master they neither loved nor respected, yet too terrified to resist.

The reapers and Horsemen stood in silence as the ground beneath them trembled, a low, ominous rumbling that felt as if the very fabric of Purgatory was unraveling. Shadows swirled, coalescing into something larger, something ancient — a dark presence that dwarfed even the Four Horsemen. The void itself seemed to ripple, bending to the will of a colossal figure as Oblivion manifested, greater and more formidable than any had ever seen.

The air grew thick with a force that weighed heavily upon them all, pressing down with the unbearable authority of an entity beyond mortality. Oblivion's form was an ethereal, shifting darkness, woven with tendrils of shadow and power, and as it solidified, two piercing eyes open — cold, ancient, and filled with judgment.

For the first time in its existence, Oblivion spoke, its voice resonant, otherworldly, like countless voices layered in unison, filling every corner of Purgatory.

"Merripen."

The single word echoed, holding an accusation that cut through the air like a blade. Merripen stiffened, her expression wavering between defiance and apprehension as she stepped forward, her gaze narrowed but determined. Conquest, who had previously encouraged her every decision, now kept his head down, his face unreadable, avoiding Oblivion's gaze as if he feared being unmasked as the one who pushed Merripen down this path.

Oblivion's gaze burned through Merripen as it continue, each word filled with a gravity that shook the ground. "You have taken upon yourself powers and decisions that were not yours to wield. Your actions have left a scar upon this realm, an imbalance of Death's mantle that threatens not only Purgatory but the very balance you swore to protect."

Merripen's expression hardened, her jaw set as she straightened defiantly. "The old ways were weak, Oblivion. Too passive, too forgiving. Souls languished, the reaping was slow, and Death himself —" she practically spit the name, "clung to outdated notions of balance. I've brought efficiency, strength, and fear back to the mantle. The souls come faster, the power flows stronger. I have elevated Purgatory."

Oblivion's eyes darkened, narrowing as it leaned closer, its presence radiating an energy that seemed to distort reality itself. "Strength? Fear? You have twisted your purpose, corrupted the essence of your role. Purgatory was never meant to be ruled by terror, but by equilibrium. You have imposed chaos, violating the very foundation upon which you stand."

Merripen clenched her fists, her gaze unyielding. "I have done what needed to be done! Death's mantle needed authority, and I've wielded it without hesitation. We've grown stronger under my rule, and the cycle moves with purpose. The souls come willingly, drawn to the power of certainty and strength."

Oblivion's voice cut through her justification with chilling finality. "You sought power, Merripen, not balance. Your actions have brought instability to this realm and beyond. Purgatory is not your dominion to reshape as you see fit. The mantle of Death was forged to guide, to uphold harmony. Not to serve as a weapon for personal ambition."

Merripen's defiance faltered momentarily, but she quickly steeled herself. "And what of Death? He was weak, unfit. I did what he couldn't. His mantle is mine, and I won't apologize for using it to bring a new order."

Oblivion's form pulsed with restrained fury, the very air thickening with its ominous presence. It leaned closer, its gaze locking onto Merripen with an intensity that felt like the weight of countless ages pressing down upon her.

"Know this, Merripen," Oblivion intoned, its voice dropping to a quiet, foreboding tone that chilled the air around them. "If you continue down this path of corruption and chaos, you risk tearing apart the very fabric of existence itself. The balance you have shattered is not yours to rewrite. Purgatory is not your dominion to wield as you please. It is a force, a cycle that must be maintained."

A tremor ran through the ground, a faint, dark resonance that hinted at the magnitude of Oblivion's words. "What you call strength is merely a shadow of true power. And if you push this world—and the next—into an abyss of your own making, then know I will intervene. Not for your sake, but to save existence from the ruin you would bring upon it."

The final words echoed, each syllable a warning resounding through the gathered reapers and Horsemen. Merripen held her ground, though her expression faltered briefly, as the reality of Oblivion's threat pierced her resolve.

Oblivion's form loomed closer to Merripen, the weight of its presence pressing down like an invisible force. Its eyes pierced her with a cold, ancient wisdom, and then, in a voice layered with judgment and a hint of grim resignation, it said, "Your recklessness, Merripen, did not kill your adversary."

Merripen's smug defiance flickered, her expression shifting sharply, eyes widening in shock. The silence that followed was heavy, a heartbeat of realization sinking in, cracking her confidence.

Oblivion allowed the revelation to sink in before continuing, its tone unyielding and relentless, "Your actions against that reaper—your attack on Aeron—did something far more consequential. It tore open a rift, an unnatural tear in the barrier between Purgatory and the mortal realm, casting him to Earth."

Merripen stared, her face a mixture of confusion and horror as the truth settled upon her. The implications rippled through her mind, her earlier satisfaction now replaced by an icy dread.

"And now," Oblivion continued, its voice filling the void, "because of your transgression, Aeron—a reaper, a being meant only for this realm—exists on Earth. This imbalance has disrupted everything, destabilizing the very foundations of existence itself."

Oblivion's eyes narrowed, a glint of frustration—almost desperation—breaking through its otherwise unshakable calm. "I have tried, Merripen. I have attempted countless measures to restore him, to mend this rift, but all efforts have failed. He remains, anchored to Earth, while the balance deteriorates. Worse still, in his displacement, Aeron has unlocked his full potential, bearing powers no human should wield. He is becoming something beyond control, beyond prediction."

The words echoed, each one sinking into Merripen like lead, her face twisting as Oblivion's ominous prophecy unfolded before her.

Oblivion's gaze sharpened, its presence looming darker and more intense. "Understand this, Merripen: if I cannot correct this mistake you created, if Aeron's presence on Earth cannot be reversed, then the consequences are beyond anything you can fathom. The world, Purgatory, the Four Horsemen—everything—will collapse. Existence itself will unravel."

The final words resonated through Purgatory, hanging in the air like a dark omen. Oblivion's form pulsed with restrained fury, its eyes locked onto Merripen's now-stricken expression, the enormity of her actions crashing down upon her as the scene faded to silence, leaving only the weight of Oblivion's warning.

Merripen, still reeling from the gravity of Oblivion's words, struggled to regain her composure. Her voice trembled, a mixture of disbelief and frustration spilling forth as she met Oblivion's cold gaze, "But... how?" she demanded, her tone sharp and desperate. "How did he survive? Why hasn't he come for vengeance, if he's still alive?"

Oblivion regarded her, its expression unreadable. "He has no recollection of the events that brought him to Earth. The rift you created stripped him of his memories. In his current state, Aeron feels he belongs on Earth—rooted to the mortal realm as if it were always his home."

A pause followed, filled with a deafening silence, and Oblivion's next words settled heavily over Merripen, "To him, Purgatory and the life he led here are lost, hidden beyond his grasp.

He walks the Earth with no notion of what he truly is, or of the vengeance he could seek. Yet he grows in strength every day. And if he remembers what you've done, if his power is not contained, it will be the end of us all."

Merripen's face paled, her defiant resolve cracking as the full weight of Oblivion's warning pressed down upon her. She said nothing, her voice lost in the tension that lingered as the scene faded into the stillness of Purgatory, leaving her to face the consequences of the chaos she had wrought.

Oblivion's form began to recede, its towering presence gradually fading back into the shadows of Purgatory. But its voice lingered, each word etched into the minds of the reapers and the Four Horsemen like a dark omen, "I will continue to try and resolve the issue you have unleashed, Merripen, but know this: if I cannot correct the imbalance, if Aeron cannot be returned, then I will be forced to destroy all that exists. Every soul, every plane of existence, will be obliterated, to prevent the complete collapse of creation itself."

The last words reverberated through the silent expanse as Oblivion dissipated, leaving only the faintest whisper of darkness in its wake. For a moment, there was nothing but stillness, a silence so profound it felt as though Purgatory itself held its breath.

Finally, War, always bold and blunt, broke the silence, "Well, isn't that something," he said, his face pale, despite his bravado. "Our very existence on the line, and all because of a reaper's ambition."

Famine frowned, her usual quiet demeanor taking on a solemness. "It's more than just ambition. Merripen's actions have put all we know at risk, unraveling what was never meant to be touched. And if even Oblivion cannot contain this…" her voice trailed off, the unspoken consequences chilling the air.

Conquest stood rigid, a new edge of fear visible beneath his usual mask of cockiness. He glanced sidelong at Merripen, who remained silent, her expression fixed in a hardened scowl. She had never shown fear before, but Oblivion's warning had clearly unsettled her.

Conquest leaned toward her, his voice barely a whisper, but urgent. "Merripen, listen to me. You can't leave this to Oblivion. He's already failing. His efforts to bring Aeron back have only made him stronger. If you want to save your own existence, our existence, you'll need to act yourself."

Merripen's eyes flickered toward Conquest, her expression a mixture of anger and uncertainty. "And how exactly do you propose I do that, Conquest? Oblivion himself can barely mend the rift. What makes you think I could?"

Conquest glanced around, ensuring the others weren't listening too closely, and whispered, "You need to find a way to create a rift of your own, to reach Earth. If you can confront Aeron, eliminate him directly, there might still be a way to restore balance before it's too late."

A flicker of uncertainty crossed Merripen's face as she absorbed his words, her mind racing. "And if I do manage to get there… if I face him directly… what guarantee is there I won't tear existence apart in the process?"

Conquest clenched his jaw, his usual confidence faltering as he whispered back, "There's no guarantee. But if you do nothing, Oblivion will destroy everything regardless. We're out of options, Merripen."

Merripen's gaze hardened, a glint of cold resolve sharpening in her eyes, narrowing with a dangerous intensity that seemed to deepen the shadows around her. The dark resolve within her was as unyielding as iron, as if the very essence of her being had crystallized into a singular purpose. "Then I'll find a way," she murmured, her voice barely above a whisper, though it carried a weight that reverberated through the room. "If Aeron's presence threatens my power, my rule, then I'll end him myself."

Her words, spoken as much to herself as to those around her, seemed to hang in the thick, stifling air of Purgatory. There was a chill in her tone, a ruthlessness that silenced any remaining doubt among the reapers and Horsemen gathered. Each of them felt the words sink in, the unsettling realization of just how far Merripen was willing to go settling heavily upon them.

The Horsemen exchanged uneasy glances, their expressions a mixture of caution, fear, and, perhaps, the slightest trace of admiration. Yet, none of them moved closer to her. The quiet exchange of looks reflected the unspoken truth: Merripen had crossed a line, one that separated duty from domination, loyalty from fear. The weight of Oblivion's warning pressed down on them all, but for Merripen, it was fuel, igniting a fire of relentless ambition that left the others hesitant, wary of her, as though she had become something foreign, unknowable.

In the silence, the twilight of Purgatory seemed to darken, shadows stretching and deepening, casting elongated forms across the cold, gray landscape. The air itself felt heavier, oppressive, as though even Purgatory recoiled from the force of Merripen's will. There was no breeze, no stirring of life—only the looming, silent tension that filled every corner of this world, a reminder of the delicate balance she had already pushed to the brink.

A faint tremor rippled through the ground, subtle but undeniable, as if Purgatory itself sensed the precarious edge it now teetered upon. The vast, spectral landscape, once held in careful equilibrium, now felt strained, fraying at the seams as Merripen's ambition threatened to pull it apart. Shadows flickered along the edges of the reapers' forms, dimming their outlines, and the hollow void stretched like an expanse of barely contained darkness, its depth hinting at the abyss that laid in wait should balance completely shatter.

Conquest watched Merripen with a wary gaze, his once-confident demeanor slipping, a hint of fear betraying his own doubts. He shifted back, the slightest trace of regret shadowing his face, as though he realized, too late, the monster he helped to unleash. War clenched his fists, the usual bravado in his eyes clouded by something deeper, something raw and vulnerable as he wrestled with the knowledge of what this could mean for them all. Famine and Pestilence remained silent, but the unease in their posture spoke volumes, each of them keenly aware that the precipice they stood upon was no longer stable.

As Merripen turned away, her figure almost blending into the vast, oppressive twilight, the others held their silence, watching her as one might watch an approaching storm—powerful, unpredictable, and utterly untethered. Oblivion's warning and the depth of Merripen's ambition lingered like an impending cataclysm, casting shadows over what remains of their world, as if all of Purgatory stood in wait, bracing for the inevitable collapse she had set in motion.

Chapter 25: Enigma

Soft rays of early morning light filtered through the lingering haze of smoke and dust still clinging to the city streets from the recent chaos. The air was cool, carrying a freshness that contrasted starkly with the memory of the night before, as if the city itself was attempting to shake off the shadows that had so recently threatened it. Amidst the quiet resilience of the townsfolk beginning their routines, Seraphina, Pinder, and Tate gathered outside the medical garrison, each of them visibly weary, but driven by an urgent sense of purpose.

Seraphina was the first to arrive, her face still shadowed by worry despite the brief rest they managed to find. Her eyes scanned the entrance of the garrison, the structure imposing but warm in the morning light, with ivy crawling up its sturdy stone walls. The building was one of the city's oldest, a place where countless wounds had been tended and battles survived—a beacon of survival, even now. Seraphina clasped her hands as she took a steadying breath, readying herself for whatever news awaited them within.

A few moments later, Pinder appeared, his usual grin subdued, replaced by a look of quiet contemplation. His gaze shifted from Seraphina to the garrison door, his eyes carrying a weight rarely seen. He offered her a nod, standing close by, a silent show of solidarity. Tate arrived soon after, clutching a worn leather notebook and tucking a few stray notes into the pages with his characteristic precision. His expression was one of intense focus, his mind already spinning with questions and theories he hoped the temple scholars might answer.

The three exchanged brief nods, each of them feeling the gravity of what laid ahead. With a final glance among them, they stepped inside the garrison, the warm glow of torchlight guiding their steps as they moved through the wide, stone corridors. The scent of herbs and the faint tang of medicinal balms permeated the air, mingling with the quiet murmur of healers tending to patients in nearby rooms. The walls bore faded tapestries depicting past battles, reminders of the resilience that defined this city—a resilience they now hoped to draw upon as they faced what laid ahead.

At the end of the hall, they reached a door guarded by a sturdy figure—a soldier who nodded solemnly as they approached, recognizing them instantly. Without a word, he opened the door, gesturing for them to enter. Inside, they found Aeron propped up on a simple cot, his face still pale but his eyes sharper, more aware, than they'd seen since the battle. His posture was strong despite his recent ordeal, a quiet determination in his gaze as he looked up, meeting each of their eyes with a hint of gratitude and a weariness that ran deeper than any physical wound.

Seraphina stepped forward first, her expression softening as she reached out, taking his hand briefly. "Glad to see you're awake," she said, her voice barely above a whisper, a mixture of relief and concern evident in her tone.

Pinder and Tate joined her, each of them offering Aeron a nod, an unspoken acknowledgment of the bond they shared—one forged through battles, mysteries, and the looming unknown.

Aeron offered a faint smile, his voice still a bit hoarse but filled with warmth. "Good to see you all too," he said, his gaze lingering on each of them. "Thank you... for everything." His words carried a sincerity that underscored the depth of his gratitude, and for a moment, there was a stillness, a quiet acknowledgment of what they'd endured together.

After a few moments, Seraphina cleared her throat, glancing toward the doorway with a renewed sense of urgency. "The temple priests," she began, her tone steady, though her eyes flickered with apprehension. "They said they've managed to decipher some parts of the scroll. They're expecting us soon, to go over what they've found."

Aeron nodded, pushing himself up slowly with a determination that left no room for protest. Despite the evident strain, he rose, adjusting his cloak and nodding toward the door. "Then let's not keep them waiting," he replied, a quiet resolve in his voice. Whatever answers the temple held, he was ready to face them.

Together, the team left the garrison, stepping into the morning light that bathed the city in a soft, golden hue. The streets were bustling with townsfolk already hard at work, clearing debris, repairing damaged buildings, and setting up stalls in the market square. There was a sense of resilience in the air, a collective determination to rebuild and reclaim the city from the shadows that had threatened to consume it. The team moved through the streets, each of them feeling the weight of the task ahead, their footsteps steady as they made their way toward the temple looming at the far end of the square.

The temple itself was a towering structure, its ancient stone walls adorned with symbols of the Scholars of Grace, intricate carvings and inscriptions that told stories of knowledge, of faith, of mysteries that spanned generations. As they approached, the high, arched doors opened, a subtle invitation to those seeking wisdom within the hallowed halls. The atmosphere was reverent, almost otherworldly, as they stepped inside, the quiet echo of their footsteps amplified by the vaulted ceilings and vast expanse of polished stone.

Inside, the air was cool, filled with the faint scent of aged parchment, candle wax, and incense. Rows of towering shelves lined the walls, each filled with scrolls and books, ancient texts that seemed to carry countless secrets. Tall, narrow windows cast slender beams of light that danced across the marble floor, creating patterns of shadow and light that shifted as they moved deeper into the temple.

A young acolyte, dressed in simple robes, approached them with a respectful nod, his expression one of both excitement and caution. "The head priest is waiting for you in the inner sanctum," he said, his voice barely above a whisper. "He's eager to share what we've uncovered."

They followed the acolyte through a series of corridors, each one leading deeper into the heart of the temple. The walls were lined with faded tapestries, depictions of ancient battles, of beings that resembled the Horsemen and reapers, shrouded in shadows and mystery. The images seemed to flicker in the dim candlelight, as if alive with the secrets they held, and a quiet tension filled the air, a sense that they were walking into the depths of knowledge itself.

Finally, they reached a heavy wooden door, its surface carved with symbols that radiated a quiet power, a reminder of the sanctity of the knowledge contained within. The acolyte bowed, stepping aside as he opened the door, revealing a chamber lit by a series of flickering torches set into the stone walls. At the center of the room was a massive table, covered in scrolls, ancient maps, and an array of strange artifacts that glinted in the firelight.

The head priest, Aldric, stood at the far end of the table, his weathered face illuminated by the warm glow. His gaze was sharp, filled with a mixture of curiosity and somber understanding as he looked up, acknowledging their arrival.

"Thank you for coming," he said, sounding like someone who had spent a lifetime steeped in ancient knowledge. "We have much to discuss."

They gathered around the table, the atmosphere tense as Aldric began to speak, his hands moving with careful precision as he unfurled one of the scrolls. The parchment was aged, its edges frayed, the ink faded but still legible—a testament to the care with which it has been preserved. He gestured to a series of symbols, his fingers tracing the lines.

"The scrolls speak of a time long forgotten," Aldric began, his voice steady but filled with reverence. "A time when the realms of the living and the dead were in delicate balance, held together by forces we barely understand. There are mentions of Horsemen—beings tasked with upholding this balance. And of an entity known as Oblivion, a being forged to protect existence itself from falling into chaos."

A shiver ran through the group as they listened, the words carrying an eerie resonance with what they had recently witnessed. Seraphina leaned in, her expression intent.

"The scrolls are fragmented," he said, his brow furrowing as he gestured to sections where the ink had faded, the symbols barely visible. "But they speak of a moment, an instance when this balance was threatened. A soul meant to be taken was... left behind, unclaimed. And in the wake of this neglect, creatures began to appear—shadows born from the breach, beings that sought to correct what had been left undone."

He looked up, his eyes meeting Aeron's, a hint of recognition in his gaze. "These creatures, these... mirages... they are not random. They are drawn to imbalance, to entities that disrupt the natural order. And as for your recent... transformation," Aldric paused, his expression solemn, "we have no record of anything like it. It is an enigma even to us, something beyond the lore contained within these walls."

Aeron took a deep breath, absorbing the weight of Aldric's words, his mind racing as he struggled to piece together the fragments of his own past, of the power he had only recently begun to understand. "So, what am I?" he asked quietly, his voice filled with a mixture of fear and determination. "If even the temple has no answers, what does that make me?"

Aldric regarded him with a thoughtful expression, his gaze softened by an understanding born of years spent in pursuit of truth. "You are an enigma, Aeron," he said.

The quiet lingered, a thickening silence as each of them absorbed the magnitude of what had been revealed. The mystery of the mirages, the fragile balance between realms, and Aeron's own unknown nature—all of it seemed to hang suspended in the air, a puzzle with too many missing pieces.

With a scoff and an exaggerated shrug, Pinder broke the silence, looking between the priest and his companions with a raised brow. "Right, so… for those of us who didn't exactly attend the Scholar's Academy of Big Words, what does all that mean?" His tone was light, but there was an undercurrent of anxiety beneath his humor, a need for clarity in a situation that felt increasingly out of his depth.

Aldric's lips curved into a faint smile, though his eyes remained serious. "Very well," he said, folding his hands thoughtfully as he chose his words with care. "In simpler terms, the scrolls are incomplete, missing pieces, fragmented by time. But from what we have managed to decipher, here is what we know." His eyes rested on each of them in turn, as if to impress upon them the gravity of what he was about to reveal. "There are four powerful beings," he began slowly, his voice steady. "Four who uphold the balance of existence. They are not merely symbols or stories, but forces in their own right—Death, War, Famine, and Pestilence. Each one serves a purpose, holding dominion over an aspect of life and death, ensuring that no single force grows too powerful." His gaze drifted toward the flickering candlelight that casted shadows across the ancient walls, the symbols etched into the stone seeming to shift and move in the low light. "But if one of these beings fails in their duty, or worse, seeks to step beyond their bounds, if they act in a way that threatens this delicate balance ..." his voice trails off, his expression darkening.

Aldric took a slow breath, the solemnity of his tone filling the room with a palpable tension, "Then there exists a fifth being," he said, his voice barely above a whisper, that feels almost sacred. "Oblivion. This fifth being is neither life nor death, not aligned with any single force but bound to all of them. Oblivion exists solely to correct any imbalance, to prevent these four from turning their power against each other or against the very fabric of existence."

The words settled heavily, sinking into the silence that followed, as if the air itself grew denser with the realization of what they'd learned. Pinder's face paled slightly as he processed the gravity of it, his usual smirk replaced by a look of quiet contemplation. Seraphina's gaze was fixed on the priest, her eyes widening as the implications unfold, and Tate, ever the scholar, nodded slowly, his fingers absentmindedly tracing the edge of his notebook.

"Oblivion," Aldric continued, his tone reverent and almost fearful, "is not a force to be wielded or controlled. It is a presence, a power that exists beyond the comprehension of any mortal—or even immortal—being. It was created to act only in the most extreme of circumstances, to correct what should never be allowed to go astray."

The head priest's voice softened, as if he himself was in awe of the very concept he described. "And so, when one of these four beings—Death, War, Famine, or Pestilence—acts out of line, when their ambition clouds their duty, Oblivion intervenes. Its sole purpose is to restore balance, by any means necessary. It ensures that none of the Four become too powerful, that none of them disrupt the equilibrium that holds existence together."

He glanced at Aeron, his eyes filled with an unspoken question, as if the mystery of Aeron's transformation, the rise of the mirages, and the strange fate that has followed him may somehow tie into this ancient cosmic design.

"This is all we know," Aldric said, his voice low but unwavering. "The rest is shrouded in lost knowledge, buried in fragments scattered across the world, hidden from mortal eyes."

The weight of the revelations settled over the group like a heavy shroud. They absorbed the enormity of what had been laid before them—the forces that shaped their world, the mysteries still cloaked in shadow, and the unknown path that now lay ahead.

Pinder stared at Aldric, his expression a mixture of disbelief and frustration, hands on his hips as he tried to process the magnitude of what had been revealed. He let out a sharp, exasperated breath, his voice edged with the biting sarcasm that had become his way of coping with the incomprehensible. "So let me get this straight," he said, his tone heavy with irony. "This Oblivion—this all-powerful fixer of the universe—spits out these mirages to deal with imbalances? And we're supposed to just accept that? What in cosmic bullshit is the imbalance, then, and why the hell do we have to be the ones to solve it?"

He glanced around at his companions, his face painted with a mixture of annoyance and helpless bewilderment. "I mean, really, if these mirages are here to fix some celestial glitch, why are they tearing through villages, destroying our cities, and coming after us? Are we just supposed to sit back, watch them burn everything to the ground, and call that balance?"

The room fell into a stunned silence as his words echoed off the stone walls, each syllable laced with the kind of raw frustration that only Pinder could voice. He shook his head, his gaze sweeping over the flickering candlelight and ancient scrolls, as if searching for an answer among the dust and shadows. His voice dropped, the anger giving way to a softer, almost weary confusion, "Great Oaks... this place, these people... what have they done to cause an imbalance? What could possibly be so off-kilter in the grand scheme that the answer is to destroy it?"

His shoulders slumped slightly, the question pressing down on him as he looked toward Aldric, hoping for an answer that would make sense of it all. "If these mirages are the so-called 'fix' for whatever's broken, then are we supposed to just stand aside? Watch as they tear through the city, let them wipe out everything we've fought to protect, and just call it fate?" His tone was bitter, the fire in his eyes fading into something darker, a despair that simmered beneath his usual bravado. Pinder's hands balled into fists at his sides, his voice growing rough, almost pleading, "Because I don't see how letting them ravage this city and the people who live here, who've done nothing wrong, is a kind of balance worth keeping."

He stared hard at Aldric, a mixture of anger, confusion, and defiance in his gaze, as if daring the head priest to justify the cosmic forces at play. The silence stretched, thick and heavy.

Seraphina was quiet for a moment, her arms crossed, brow furrowed as she absorbed Pinder's words. A shadow of uncertainty crossed her face, and she glanced toward Aldric, then back to her friends, the question she'd been holding back now tugging at her lips. "I mean ... Pinder's right," she said, her voice soft but laced with a growing unease. "How could allowing an entire city to fall—to be destroyed by these... mirages— possibly fix anything?"

She looked around the room, her gaze lingering on the ancient scrolls and symbols lining the walls, each one a testament to ages of reverence and trust in the cosmic forces that governed their world. But now, doubt flickered in her eyes, a quiet rebellion against that trust. "What if these beings—Oblivion, the Horsemen, all of them—are wrong?"

The question hung in the air, heavy and unbidden, as if the room itself resisted the very idea. She shifted her weight, her fingers tightening on her arms as if bracing herself against the enormity of what she was suggesting. "What if they aren't wise and just, but vengeful? Fallible? What if they're willing to sacrifice entire cities, lives, everything we hold dear, just to preserve their idea of balance?"

A ripple of tension settled over the group, Seraphina's words casting a shadow over the faith that had seemed so absolute. Her voice was steady, but there was an edge of disillusionment that gave her question a sharpness, an almost accusatory tone. "Maybe this isn't about justice at all," she continued, her gaze darkening as she looked back at Aldric, as if searching for any sign of disagreement. "Maybe it's just about power."

The silence that followed was thick, laden with the weight of her words, as if they'd ventured into territory forbidden to mere mortals. Each of them stood motionless, grappling with the unsettling notion that the forces they thought were guiding them might not be as benevolent—or as infallible—as they'd once believed.

Tate, who had been listening intently, stepped forward, clearing his throat as he adjusted his glasses. His gaze was steady as he looked from Seraphina to Pinder, then to Aldric, a calm resolve settling over his usually sharp features. "Alright," he began, his voice even but filled with quiet conviction. "I understand the frustration, truly, but none of us can actually know the truth of these cosmic forces. These accounts, these ancient scrolls, they tell us only that there are powers in play, forces meant to keep each other in line. And when one of these forces steps out of bounds, when an imbalance is created, Oblivion attempts to correct it."

He glanced at Seraphina, sympathy in his gaze. "But instead of debating whether we let the city fall, or try to stop something we can't fully comprehend, maybe our best option is to focus on what we can do. We should turn our attention to investigating changes—any shifts, disruptions, events that could have set off whatever this imbalance is. Something, somewhere, must have triggered this reaction." A soft sigh escaped him as he shook his head. "Granted, that may be nearly impossible. We're mere mortals, and as Seraphina pointed out, we don't actually know if these powers are as purposeful or benevolent as we've always assumed." His eyes flickered with a brief uncertainty, acknowledging the weight of her skepticism. "Maybe the Four Powers did just get bored with eternity and decide to cause chaos for the fun of it. We can't say for sure they didn't." The faintest hint of a wry smile pulled at his lips. "But the truth is, we don't know what's going on up there, and we probably never will. What we can do is follow our own sense of balance, our own instincts about what's right. If these creatures are drawn to imbalance, then perhaps understanding the world around us — our world — will give us the answers we're looking for."

Tate's gaze shifted back to Aldric, his respect evident, then he looked to his companions, a quiet determination settling in his eyes. "We can't know for sure what's true or just, or what motivations the forces beyond us have. But what we can do is search, learn, and prepare. That's all we have, and maybe that will be enough."

As his words faded, a contemplative silence settled over the room, each of them absorbing the enormity of the task ahead, knowing that while they may be fumbling in the dark, they weren't entirely powerless.

A reassuring smile softened Aldric's otherwise grave expression. "You're right, Tate. And fortunately, we have more than just our own efforts to rely on. Here, within these walls, we hold the world's knowledge — or as close to it as any place on Earth. The temple holds vast archives, and the best minds we can summon." He straightened, a spark of determination in his eyes. "I've sent word across the lands to every scholar, every priest with expertise in ancient lore and cosmic mysteries, urging them to come at once. We'll have double the eyes and double the minds on this matter by tomorrow, all scouring our archives, seeking any reference, any forgotten clue that might help us understand what we're facing."

He gestured to the towering shelves around them, filled with scrolls and books that spanned centuries, millennia even. "With everyone's focus set on this task, I believe we will find something—some lost knowledge, some insight that has evaded us thus far. It may not be easy, and it may not be complete, but I have faith that we will find at least one piece of the puzzle to shed light on what is before us."

The words seemed to breathe new life into the room, a quiet hope sparking in each of them. The weight of uncertainty lifted, if only slightly, replaced by the resolve to press forward, to dig deeper, to search tirelessly until the shadows of doubt gave way to understanding.

A palpable sense of purpose filled the air, letting in a glimmer of hope. Seraphina, Pinder, and Tate exchanged glances, each nodding in quiet agreement as the enormity of their task became clearer. They may not understand the forces they were up against, but they now had a direction, a path through the unknown.

Seraphina stepped closer to Aldric, her gaze softening. "Thank you, truly. Knowing that we aren't alone in this, that there are others willing to put everything they know to the test… it makes a difference. More than you might realize."

Aldric met her gaze, his eyes filled with a warmth that spoke of years spent guiding others, of holding faith when others could not. "You're not alone, not in this or in any battle for balance," he replied gently. "Knowledge is power, yes, but it is also our duty, our guiding light. And this temple was built for times like these—for moments when the world tilts, and we need to right it."

Pinder let out a soft laugh, his usual humor returning. "Good to know all those dusty books might be worth something after all," he muttered, hands on his hips as he glanced at the shelves.

"Even if they do come with a bit of a wait."

Aldric chuckled softly, a rare sound that seemed to break the tension in the room. "Yes, patience will be required. Knowledge seldom reveals itself without it." His gaze swept over the group. "But by tomorrow, you'll see priests from all over the land arriving. Together, we will work tirelessly to unearth any scrap of wisdom, any hint of prophecy, and every piece of forgotten lore we possess. And with that, we will create the path forward."

Tate, always a pragmatic thinker, nodded with a quiet resolve. "We'll do our part here, and maybe... maybe that's all we can control," he said, though his words carried a sense of hope.

Aldric placed a steady hand on Tate's shoulder. "Indeed. Our own strength lies in how we face the unknown, how we come together in the darkness." He looked at each of them, his expression one of pride and unshakeable faith. "Now, go. Rest, gather your energy. Tomorrow, we embark on this journey together, and I have no doubt that, between us all, we will find the light."

Aldric turned back to his work, signaling that they're dismissed. One by one, they took a last look at the sprawling archives, the towering shelves, and the artifacts glinting in the candlelight. There was a silent understanding between them now — a pact formed not just of necessity but of purpose.

As they stepped out of the chamber, the weight of their mission settled over them once more, but this time it felt different, lighter, as if buoyed by the collective strength of the minds and hearts soon to be united in their cause. For the first time in a long while, there was a sense of direction, a glimpse of a way forward, however distant or uncertain.

And so, they left the temple with renewed resolve, each step echoing with the determination to protect their world and restore its balance, no matter the cost.

The inn's common room was warm, filled with the gentle hum of patrons winding down after a long day, the scent of roasted meats and fresh bread hanging in the air. Aeron,

Seraphina, Pinder, and Tate sat around a sturdy wooden table near the crackling hearth, tankards of ale in hand and plates of hearty food spread before them. The flickering light cast a comfortable glow over their faces, but their expressions were thoughtful, each of them lost in their own reflections as they mulled over the knowledge they'd just acquired.

Aeron took a sip from his ale, savoring the warmth as it slid down, grounding him. He set the tankard down, glancing at the others with a hint of a smile. "Hard to believe how far we've come, isn't it?" he mused, his tone contemplative. "Just a few weeks ago, I was just… existing on that farm, barely knowing who I was. And now we're facing mysteries and powers that seem larger than life."

Seraphina, seated next to him, nodded, her gaze distant as she traced the rim of her tankard. "I remember thinking life was so simple," she said softly. "I was a healer, and I thought that was my purpose. But now, I feel like I'm standing at the edge of something so much bigger than I ever imagined." She looked at Aeron, a gentle warmth in her eyes. "And I'm grateful I'm here with all of you."

Pinder chuckled, raising his tankard in a mock toast, though his grin was genuine. "Here's to bigger purposes and cosmic mysteries, I suppose. Though I could've done without the mirages trying to kill us every other day." He took a hearty gulp of his ale and leaned back, his gaze softening as he looked at his companions. "But if I'm honest, I'd probably be back in Tideheaven, dodging trouble and swiping the occasional purse if it weren't for you lot." He smirked, glancing at Tate. "Even you, scholar. Wouldn't have made it this far without your brainy nonsense."

Tate rolled his eyes, but there was a smile playing on his lips as he set his tankard down. "Brainy nonsense, indeed," he muttered, though there was a fondness in his tone. "Truth be told, I never thought I'd end up on the road with a farmer with strength and speed of 20 men, a healer with the soul of an adventurer, and a thief with a peculiar sense of honor. But here we are, sitting in an inn, discussing the mysteries of the cosmos over ale." His gaze drifting to the flickering fire. "It's strange, really. I spent years with my nose buried in books, studying things I thought were myths, trying to understand a world I believed was logical and predictable. But now, every day challenges everything I thought I knew. Forces beyond our understanding, ancient beings, and a fate that seems tied to all of us." He let out a soft laugh. "If I hadn't seen it all myself, I'd say it sounds like the ramblings of an overimaginative historian."

Aeron studied his tankard with a contemplative stare. "What Aldric said about Oblivion, about the balance… it's humbling, in a way. We're just pieces on a much larger board, but even the smallest piece has its part to play." He glanced up, a subtle determination in his eyes. "I don't know what lies ahead, but I know I'll keep fighting. If these forces are real… if there's truly a risk to our world, I'm not going to stand by and watch it fall apart."

A comfortable silence settled over them, each lost in thought as they absorbed the enormity of their journey, of the bonds they'd formed, and the challenges that lie ahead. Finally, Seraphina raised her tankard, her expression warm yet resolute. "To us," she said softly. "To the path we've chosen and the mysteries we'll face together."

They raised their tankards. The quiet clink of metal and wood was a small but powerful testament to the strength they found in each other. For a moment, they weren't adventurers facing cosmic forces or heroes destined to battle creatures from the unknown. They were simply friends, sharing a meal and a drink, bound together by a purpose greater than any one of them alone.

As the fire crackled, casting dancing shadows across their

faces, they found solace in each other's presence. The conversation drifted to stories of past escapades, laughter filling the room as they recalled the humorous mishaps and victories they'd shared.

Seraphina set down her tankard, offering a soft smile to the group as she rose from her seat. "I think I'll head over to the medical garrison," she said, glancing toward the door. "There were so many injuries after the attack… if I can offer any help to the wounded, it's the least I can do."

Tate pushed his chair back, nodding with his usual calmness. "I'll join you," he offered, already gathering his things. "I know a thing or two about patching up wounds, and if nothing else, I can help keep things organized."

Pinder leaned back in his chair, grinning as he raised his tankard in a mock toast. "Well, while you two saints go tend to the sick and injured, I think I'll go see if that lovely blacksmith has a different kind of healing in mind for the evening." He winked, an unmistakable gleam in his eye. "You know, a little hands-on therapy."

"Try not to get into too much trouble, Pinder," Seraphina teased, heading toward the door with Tate at her side.

Pinder laughed, shrugging. "No promises. But trouble does have a certain charm, doesn't it?"

With that, Seraphina and Tate headed out into the night, the inn door swinging shut behind them.

Pinder downed the rest of his ale, sending Aeron a parting grin. "Hold down the fort, Farm boy, I've got some personal business to attend to." With a playful salute, he sauntered off into the night, leaving Aeron alone at the table, the warm light of the inn casting quiet shadows across his face.

As the door swung shut again, Aeron found himself surrounded by the soft murmur of patrons and the crackling of the fire, left to his thoughts and the weight of the journey still ahead. His fingers traced the rim of his tankard, the remnants of ale warming his palm. The inn's lively murmur faded into a distant hum as he drifted inward, his gaze fixed somewhere beyond the flickering light of the hearth. Shadows danced along the walls, cast by the dim glow of lanterns and firelight, moving in silent rhythm to his quiet thoughts.

The weight of the past few days pressed on him, a relentless tide that ebbed and flowed, tugging at memories he couldn't fully grasp. Koko's absence felt like a wound, a hollow ache that sharpened with each flicker of light that reminded him of the warmth of his companion's eyes, the steady presence that had been by his side through every uncertain step since he woke up. The image of Koko's final breath lingered painfully, raw and sharp, as if the moment were branded onto his soul. A part of him ached to turn away from it, but he couldn't—not fully. The bond they shared ran deeper than he'd realized, and the loss cut in ways he wasn't prepared for.

He leaned back, eyes drifting to the rafters above, where the low beams caught the amber glow of the fire. There was a heaviness in his chest, a sensation he couldn't quite name, as if something far greater than grief was gnawing at him, something older and darker. It was as though the transformation he underwent, that surge of impossible power, left a lingering echo within him—a pulse, barely noticeable, but thrumming beneath his skin. It was unfamiliar, yet felt like it belonged, like a distant memory he should recognize but couldn't fully reach.

For a fleeting moment, he thought back to the scythe—the way it materialized in his hand, its dark, pulsing aura an extension of himself, a piece of him he hadn't known was missing until it returned. He remembered the sensation vividly, like slipping into a second skin, one that fit with terrifying ease. The power had felt boundless, a vast and roaring force that carried him effortlessly through the fight, each movement precise, as if time itself had bent to his will. The memory of it sent a shiver through him now—powerful, yes, but something about it was too consuming, too complete, as if he'd become something else entirely.

And then there was the knowledge shared by Aldric and the others at the temple. The ancient scrolls, the cryptic references to Oblivion, to the Four Powers meant to maintain balance, and the shadowy figure of Oblivion watching over them, a judge in the dark. The idea of these forces, of a cosmic struggle woven into the fabric of existence, left a strange taste in his mouth, both awe and unease mingling. He felt as though he'd stumbled into a play where the rules were written long ago, yet he had been cast in a role he didn't understand, an actor unaware of his own lines.

A faint draft stirred in the room, sending a flicker of cool air over his skin, grounding him for a moment. The warmth of the inn, the soft sounds of laughter from nearby tables, the smell of roasting meat—all of it contrasted sharply with the haunting memories he was confronting. He could feel a divide growing within him, one foot anchored in this earthly life of friends and inns, of quiet moments by the fire, while the other teetered on the edge of something unknown and dark, a chasm of power and duty he barely understood but couldn't ignore.

The flickering firelight drew his attention back, casting shadows over his face, and he wondered how much more he was willing to lose to uncover the truth. He didn't know what he had become, or why the scythe felt so… right. And in the back of his mind, a quiet question stirred, one that lingered each night as he closed his eyes.

What am I?

The question felt heavier tonight, pressing down with an intensity that demanded an answer. Yet, there was no one here to answer it—only the fire, the silence, and the weight of all that had happened. His hand tightened around his tankard, his jaw set, as if bracing himself against the unknown path he was destined to follow.

Aeron closed his eyes, letting the warmth of the fire seep into him, grounding him as he sat alone in the inn, bound between the life he lived and the shadows of the one calling to him from the darkness.

Aeron sat alone, the warmth of the inn's fire lulling him into a soft, quiet haze. The hum of patrons faded to a distant murmur as his eyelids grew heavy, the events of the past days weighing on him like a cloak made of shadows. Before he realized it, sleep pulled him under, and his mind drifted somewhere darker, somewhere unknown.

In an instant, he was no longer seated at the inn's table. He stood in the heart of the town square, yet it was different—eerily still, as if frozen in time. The buildings were shrouded in a thick, rolling mist, their forms distorted and warped, casting ominous shapes against the darkened sky. The usual warmth of the town is gone, replaced by a cold that bites to the bone.

A low hum rose from the ground beneath him, vibrating through the cobblestones like the thrumming pulse of a heartbeat. Aeron glanced down and noticed cracks beginning to splinter outward, fissures that glowed faintly with a sickly, unnatural light. The ground shuddered, as if the town itself was alive, writhing in agony.

Then, from the center of the square, the ground split open with a violent crack, and a rift tore itself into existence. It's a churning mass of shadows and pulsing light, each wave of energy surging outward, casting the entire town in a harsh, otherworldly glow. The portal's edges flickered, raw and jagged, like wounds torn through the very fabric of reality.

Aeron tried to move, to turn away, but he found himself rooted to the spot, watching helplessly as the rift widened, its swirling depths revealing glimpses of something ... watching him. Shapes shifted within the darkness—shadowy figures with eyes that gleamed faintly, almost expectantly, like predators biding their time. He felt a pull, a call from the other side, and a wave of dread swept over him, deeper than anything he'd known.

The air thickened, pressing down on him, and he heard it— a voice, low and haunting, barely more than a whisper but laced with an urgency that made his heart pound. "Prepare yourself. The door you thought closed is opening."

The words echoed in his mind, reverberating with an intensity that felt almost physical, as though each syllable pressed against him, demanding he listen, demanding he understand. The voice faded, but its presence lingered, heavy and cold, like a hand resting on his shoulder, unseen but undeniable.

In the vision, the portal pulsed again, a deep, visceral throb, and for a brief moment, he thought he could see a familiar figure—a tall, cloaked form, standing in the depths of the rift, watching him with eyes that burned with cold, unfeeling intent. The presence was overwhelming, suffocating, filling him with a raw, primal fear that twisted in his stomach. Every instinct screamed at him to run, to fight, to do anything but stand still.

Then, just as quickly as it began, the vision shattered, and Aeron jolted awake, his body tensed, his breath ragged. The inn's fire flickered steadily, casting soft light over the familiar room, yet the shadows seemed to cling to the walls a little longer, a little deeper than before. The voice's final words lingered in his mind like an echo: The door you thought closed is opening.

For a moment, he sat in silence, his heart pounding as he looked around the empty inn, half-expecting to see shadows creeping closer, reaching out. But all was still. The only sounds were the crackle of the fire and the faint murmur of distant patrons. Yet he knew, with a bone-deep certainty, that something was coming for him, something that wouldn't stop until it founds him.

Time slipped by unnoticed, the hours melting into one another as Aeron remained lost in the shadows of his thoughts, the vision lingering like a cold weight pressing on his chest. The inn filled and empties again, the fire dimmed, and by the time he registered the soft click of the door opening, darkness had fallen beyond the windows.

Seraphina stepped into the room, her expression shifting to one of mild exasperation as she took in Aeron's unchanged position. She crossed her arms, a small smirk tugged at her lips. "Have you even moved an inch since I left?" she teased, her voice warm, pulling him from the depths of his mind.

He shook himself slightly, blinking as though he was seeing her for the first time in hours. "I guess I lost track of time," he admitted, trying to manage a faint smile.

Seraphina stepped closer, softening as she tilted her head to study him. "You look like you've been through another battle," she said, brushing a hand over his shoulder. Her gaze searched his face, lingering on the shadows beneath his eyes, as if sensing the weight of something he hadn't yet spoken.

After a beat, she offered him a gentle smile. "Come on," she said, her tone light but laced with a quiet insistence. "Let me help you get cleaned up. You could use it." Her hand rested on his shoulder, her touch both grounding and comforting.

Aeron nodded, letting her lead him, the vision's haunting echo lingering in his mind, yet softened somehow by her presence.

As the warm water surrounded them, steam rising in soft wisps, Aeron leaned back, feeling the tension slowly melt from his body. Seraphina sat close, her fingers gently tracing lines over his shoulders and arms, washing away the grime of the day and, he hoped, some of the weariness settled in his bones.

For a moment, there was only the sound of water lapping softly against the basin and the gentle flicker of candlelight casting warm shadows over the walls. The intimacy of the moment offered a rare comfort, and he found himself wanting to share his thoughts, the lingering dread that the vision left behind.

"I had a strange dream, or maybe a vision," he began, his voice low, almost as if speaking too loudly would bring it back in full force. "It felt more real than a dream, though. It was like I was standing there, in the town square, watching something tear through reality."

Seraphina paused, her hand on his shoulder. "What did you see?"

He drew in a breath, the memory of the vision sharp and vivid. "There was a rift, right in the heart of the square, as if the ground had been ripped apart. And there was something on the other side. Shadows, figures I couldn't make out, and a terrible power pulsing from it." He glanced at her, the intensity of the memory flickering in his gaze. "Then, I heard a voice—quiet, but unmistakable. It warned me, said that something was coming, a door closed was about to be opened."

A shadow of worry crossed her face, but she remained steady, absorbing his words. "Do you think it was a warning, or a threat?"

"I don't know," Aeron admitted, his brow furrowing. "It could have been either. But whatever it was, it felt inevitable, like something that's been waiting a long time and now it's finally reaching across." His eyes met hers. "It didn't feel like a dream, Seraphina. It felt like a message."

She searched his face, then brushed a gentle hand over his cheek. "If something is coming, then we'll face it together. Whatever it is, you're not alone in this."

Aeron nodded, her words grounding him, bringing a sense of calm in the face of the unknown. In the warmth of her touch and the soft glow of the candlelight, the shadows seemed to retreat, if only for a moment, leaving him with the certainty that, whatever came, he wouldn't be alone.

In the quiet warmth of the room, surrounded by soft candlelight and the gentle ripples of water, Aeron reached out, pulling Seraphina closer, his hand tracing the curve of her back with reverence. Her skin was warm beneath his fingertips, smooth and inviting, and he felt a spark of connection, a closeness he'd never felt so deeply until that moment. She leaned into his touch, her own hands resting lightly on his chest, feeling the steady beat of his heart beneath her palms.

Their eyes met, and an unspoken understanding lingered between them—a need, a longing, and a love that had been growing steadily amidst the trials they'd faced together. Seraphina's gaze was soft yet intent, her breath quickened as she leaned closer, her face just inches from his. He brushed a stray lock of hair from her cheek, his fingers lingering, tracing the line of her jaw with tenderness. Her lips parted slightly, and he could feel the warmth of her breath mingling with his, drawing him in, tempting him to close the distance.

Slowly, he tilted his head, and their lips met in a gentle, lingering kiss that built with each passing second, deepening as their hands found each other, fingers interlocking. Each breathless exchange was a testament to the love and trust they had built. The world beyond those walls faded away, leaving only the warmth of each other's embrace.

They moved together in unspoken harmony, each touch and caress a silent promise, a vow that transcended words. Aeron's hand trailed over her shoulders, down her arms, savoring the feeling of her skin against his, every touch igniting a fire within him that he'd almost forgotten could burn so brightly. Seraphina responded in kind, her fingers weaving through his hair, pulling him closer as their breaths quickened, the space between them disappearing as they became lost in each other.

The water rippled around them, their movements gentle yet fervent, creating a rhythm all their own. They pulled each other closer, exploring and savoring every inch, every whispered sigh and shiver of anticipation. Their love, once built on quiet moments and shared battles, now expressed itself in the fierce, passionate connection they shared, each touch a reminder of the trust and devotion they held for one another.

As the candles flickered, they gave in to the passion, letting it flow freely, binding them together in a way that words alone could never capture. The moment became their refuge, their sanctuary, and in each other's arms, they found solace, strength, and a love that felt as boundless as the stars.

When at last they laid together, hearts still racing and breaths mingling in the warmth of the room, there was a sense of peace, of wholeness, as if they'd shared something sacred that no one else could ever understand. In the quiet that followed, they simply held each other, content and bound by love and unbreakable trust.

As the night settled deeper around them, Aeron and Seraphina laid entwined, their breaths slowing, matching each other in a quiet rhythm that spoke of comfort and closeness. The warmth of the room faded into a soft glow, the flickering candles casting gentle shadows over their resting forms.

Seraphina nestled closer, her head resting against Aeron's shoulder, her hand still entwined with his, fingers laced together as if to anchor them in that fleeting, peaceful moment. Aeron let out a deep breath, his gaze softened as he watched her in the quiet of the night, feeling a profound sense of calm settle over him, more comforting than anything he'd felt in a long time.

As sleep slowly overtook them, their faces relaxed, breaths growing slow and even. Wrapped in each other's embrace, they drifted off into a deep, restful slumber, undisturbed and tranquil, the weight of their love holding them steady, even as the world beyond their door continued to stir.

For tonight, there was no worry, no lingering fear—only peace, as they found rest together, hearts and souls bound in the stillness of the night.

Chapter 26: Wrath and Revelation

The morning sun spilled through the windows of the inn, casting a soft glow over the table where Aeron, Seraphina, Pinder, and Tate gathered for breakfast. The usual sounds of city life—vendors calling out, children running through the streets, and townsfolk chatting—were strangely absent, leaving only an uneasy quiet hanging in the air.

Pinder glanced around, his brow furrowing. "Is it just me, or is it too quiet out there? Even at dawn, this city isn't usually so still."

Seraphina nodded, setting down her mug of tea. "You're right. Normally, you'd hear the merchants setting up or the chatter from the markets by now."

Tate, ever curious, peeked out the window. His eyes narrowed as he took in the scene below. "Look there," he said, pointing. "The temple doors are wide open. And... are those people outside with scrolls?"

The team exchanged a puzzled look before rising and heading out into the unusually quiet streets. As they approached the temple, the reason for the quiet became clear. The steps leading up to the temple were crowded with people, all deep in study, poring over stacks of ancient scrolls, books, and parchments. Some were kneeling in clusters, sharing notes, while others read in silence, their faces drawn with intense concentration.

Aeron's gaze swept over the crowd, recognizing not just priests and scholars but townsfolk of every kind—the local blacksmith leaning over a heavy tome, fingers tracing faded text; the Mayor himself seated on a low step, cross-legged with a scroll unfurled across his lap; the commander and a handful of guards standing nearby, their usual stoic expressions softened as they conversed quietly over their own stacks of texts. It was as if the entire city had gathered, each person doing their part to uncover something crucial.

"This is incredible," Seraphina said, her voice tinged with awe. "They're all here, all volunteering to help. Every single one of them."

Pinder chuckled softly, though there was a reverence in his tone. "Never thought I'd see the commander reading a scroll. Or a blacksmith, for that matter."

A young priest noticed them standing nearby and approached, his face earnest. "Everyone is helping," he explained, motioning to the gathered people. "The head priest called upon the city to aid us, and they came. They're combing through every piece of history we have, trying to find anything that might explain the creatures or what might be causing this imbalance."

Tate looked over at Aeron, his expression contemplative. "It seems the weight of this situation has reached everyone. Even those who don't fully understand it are willing to help."

Aeron nodded, his chest swelling with a mixture of pride and gratitude for the people who had come together. He stepped forward, moving among the townsfolk, nodding to familiar faces, each occupied with their own piece of the mystery.

The air was thick with quiet determination, a unified focus that transcended personal roles or past conflicts. From the blacksmith to the Mayor, every single person was absorbed in the pursuit of knowledge, digging through ancient lore and forgotten histories, each one hoping to uncover the secrets of the rifts and mirages, the fragments of a truth that would help them face whatever was coming.

The team moved through the crowd gathered on the temple steps, making their way into the vast hall where rows of tables and stacks of scrolls had been set up. Inside, the scene was just as intense as outside—people poring over ancient texts, scribbling notes, and exchanging insights in low voices.

At the center of it all, they spotted Aldric, the head priest, moving between groups, offering guidance and helping to organize the chaos. When he caught sight of Aeron and his companions, a warm smile broke through his usually serious demeanor. He walked over, looking both exhausted and energized.

"Aeron, Seraphina, Pinder, Tate—welcome," Aldric said, inclining his head respectfully. "I'm glad you're here. As you can see, it's all hands on deck." He gestured to the groups of townsfolk and scholars, his pride evident. "The city has shown a remarkable willingness to help. We're gaining so much information at such a rapid pace, it's honestly more than I expected."

Seraphina smiled, glancing around the bustling temple. "It's incredible, Aldric. I don't think I've ever seen so many people united like this."

Aldric's expression grew more serious. "I must admit, as quickly as we're moving, we still haven't uncovered anything new about the creatures or the cause of the imbalance. It's as if we're searching for answers that aren't even in our realm of understanding." He sighed, rubbing a hand over his forehead. "But we're not giving up. Every set of eyes brings us closer."

Pinder crossed his arms, leaning casually against a nearby column. "So, we're still playing a waiting game then?"

"For now, yes," Aldric said, glancing over the many open scrolls and books scattered across the tables. "But with this many people combing through everything we have, I'm hopeful that something will emerge—some missing piece that can help us understand what we're truly up against."

Aeron looked around the temple, taking in the scene, feeling the weight of the responsibility he bore, yet also reassured by the unity surrounding him. "Thank you, Aldric. For everything. Knowing everyone is working toward this makes a difference."

Aldric met his gaze with a respectful nod. "We all have a stake in this, Aeron. Rest assured, if there is an answer, we will find it."

Aldric gestured toward a set of tables stacked high with scrolls and books, many already unfurled and partially read. "Take whatever catches your eye," he said, glancing at Aeron and his team. "We can use every set of hands to get through as much as possible."

Each member moved toward a different corner of the hall, diving into the sea of texts with determination.

Aeron headed for a stack of old, leather-bound books piled near a tall, ornate window. He picked up a volume, the faded cover barely revealing its title. Carefully, he opened it, reading the faded script, his mind combing through passages of ancient lore and tales of cosmic beings. Every word seemed to draw him deeper into the possibility that somewhere within these pages lay a hint about his past—about who or what he might truly be.

Seraphina wandered to a table where several loose scrolls were spread out, organized by symbols and rough sketches of various creatures. She started with one depicting an eerie image of a three-headed beast similar to the one Aeron fought, her brow furrowing as she tried to decipher the accompanying text. Beside her, a priest offered to translate a few symbols, and they worked together, their quiet voices blending as they discussed theories about mirages and other strange entities described in the writings.

Pinder strolled toward a corner stacked with parchments featuring old battle tactics and ancient weapon lore. Not exactly a traditional approach to understanding cosmic balance, but he was hoping to find anything about powerful weapons or defenses against supernatural beings.

Grumbling under his breath, he scanned page after page, occasionally tossing a wry comment over his shoulder to anyone nearby who seemed remotely interested. "If these cosmic beings think we're just going to roll over..." he muttered, more to himself than anyone else.

Tate, ever the researcher, found himself in front of a table covered with religious texts and scrolls marked with ancient runes. His fingers itched with excitement as he picked up a worn parchment, noting the strange symbols and diagrammed connections between cosmic entities and reapers. He read each line carefully, deciphering the links and relationships described, trying to understand the delicate balance the texts hinted at. Every now and then, he jotted down notes, his brow furrowed with concentration as he pieced together fragments of information.

The hours passed quietly, each of them fully immersed in the texts before them. The temple hummed with the sound of pages turning, hushed whispers, and the scratch of quills on parchment. Though progress felt slow, there was an unspoken sense of unity—of hope—that bound them all together as they search for answers in the ancient words of those who came before them.

The quiet hum of activity filled the temple as everyone remained focused on their research. Pages turned, quills scratched, and whispers passed between townsfolk and priests alike as they delved into their studies. Suddenly, Pinder's voice cut through the noise, loud and abrupt.

"Oi! Aeron, Seraphina!" he called, causing several heads to turn. "Can you two explain again what exactly Aeron looked like during his... you know, that transformation?"

Aeron and Seraphina exchanged a curious glance before Seraphina spoke up, her voice steady, "It was... intense. He wore dark, skeletal armor that looked like bone but seemed made of something stronger, something... otherworldly. His face was hidden beneath a hood, and a sort of purple aura radiated from him. He didn't look like himself at all. He was a figure of pure power, a shadow."

Pinder listened intently, then nodded with a gleam of excitement in his eyes. "That's it—that's exactly what I needed!" With a triumphant cry, he grabbed a scroll he'd been studying and sprinted over to the nearest table, where Aldric, Aeron, and Tate were gathered. He slammed the scroll down in front of them, a grin stretching across his face.

"Look at this!" he exclaimed, his finger tracing the image sketched on the parchment. "I don't know what these words mean, but this picture—it's exactly what you described. It's you, Aeron. Or… it's your other self."

Aeron leaned in, his gaze sharpening as he studied the sketch. The image showed a figure in dark, skeletal armor, wielding a scythe and surrounded by an aura reminiscent of Aeron's transformation. But what captured his attention even more was the wall—a massive, imposing barrier drawn between the figure and a scene on the other side, depicting what appeared to be a lush, vibrant world. The wall was marked with symbols, its height and thickness exaggerated, as if meant to be an impossible boundary.

Aldric, standing beside him, furrowed his brow as he inspected the image. "The barrier," he said, glancing at the depiction of Earth—or what they assumed was Earth—on the other side. "This seems to suggest that this being cannot pass through it."

Tate, ever observant, leaned closer. "It's almost as if the figure is bound to one side, unable to reach the other. The wall looks solid, unbreakable. But Aeron, you're here. You crossed it."

A realization dawned on Aeron, his heart pounding as he pieced it together. "What if this isn't just a figure, some ancient legend? What if… this is me? What if I'm not supposed to be here at all?"

Seraphina's eyes widened. "Are you saying... Oblivion isn't tearing the world apart for cosmic balance, or to punish us, but to get you back behind that wall?"

A silence fell over the group as the gravity of her words sank in. The mirages, the attacks, the relentless chaos—it wasn't about Earth, or the people suffering. It was about Aeron.

Pinder smacked the table, still brimming with excitement. "That's exactly it! This whole mess, all of it. It's about you being on the wrong side of that wall."

Tate stroke his chin thoughtfully, studying the scroll. "But then, if Oblivion's trying to bring you back, why hasn't it succeeded? Why can't it just... force you across?"

Aeron shook his head slowly. "Maybe it's the scythe, or the powers I've inherited. Or maybe something about this world itself is keeping me anchored. I don't know. But if this is true, then Oblivion won't stop until it's either brought me back, or destroyed everything in its path."

Aldric looked at Aeron with newfound respect and a touch of sadness. "You're an enigma, Aeron. A soul caught between realms, bearing powers that defy nature. But whatever the reason, you've crossed a boundary no one else could. And perhaps it's a choice you must eventually face, whether to stay or to go."

The weight of Aldric's words settled over them as each one processed the revelation in their own way, their perspectives forever changed. The stakes became clearer, and the path ahead, though uncertain, now held a deeper purpose for each of them.

The ground beneath the temple trembled, subtle at first, then with an intensity that no one in Great Oaks had ever felt. Scrolls and books tumbled from tables, spilling across the floor, as a low, ominous rumble filled the air. The walls shuddered, cracks snaking along the ancient stone as the very foundation of the temple began to shake. People cried out, clutching onto whatever they could find, as the world itself seemed to heave in protest, as if something deep within was tearing itself apart.

Outside, a thunderous roar rippled through the streets, echoing off buildings and reverberating across the city. The ground bucked and heaved in great waves, splitting cobblestones and tearing through the earth as trees swayed violently, their roots exposed. It was as if the city was a ship caught in an unyielding storm, the very world pitching and groaning under something unimaginable. Dust and rubble filled the air, blurring vision and muffling sound, and a faint metallic scent—sharp and foreboding—drifted through the atmosphere, as if signaling the arrival of something unnatural.

The rumbling intensified, each quake a heartbeat of the world breaking beneath them, until it felt like reality itself was fraying. Shadows flickered and distorted, bending in strange, impossible angles as the sky above began to twist and swirl with ominous clouds, dark and thick, rolling over each other like waves of ink. It was a terror beyond understanding, a nightmare come alive, and those who once held hope now clutched it desperately, knowing that whatever was happening was beyond anything they had ever known.

Suddenly, a guard stumbled through the temple's doors, his face pale, his breath coming in short, ragged gasps. He braced himself against a column, his eyes wide with horror. "Something… something has happened in the town center," he managed, struggling to form the words. He pointed weakly, as if reliving the sight. "A… a rip… in the sky. It's like… like a black curtain, torn open. It's pulsing with energy."

Aeron exchanged a tense, knowing look with Seraphina, dread creeping into his veins. He remembered the vision—its dark warnings echoing in his mind, the swirling void opening over the town.

"I saw this," he murmured, his voice barely above a whisper. "I had a vision of this exact thing."

Aldric's gaze sharpened, the gravity of Aeron's words settling heavily over him. "Then this was foretold," he said, his voice steadier than the trembling earth. "If you saw it, then it's not just a disturbance. It's a warning."

Aeron turned to Aldric and the Mayor, his voice firm despite the terror pulsing through him. "You have to get everyone out of town. Whatever that is… it's not safe for anyone to stay here. Evacuate everyone—immediately."

The Mayor nodded, his face pale but resolute. He looked at Aldric, who called out to the guards scattered through the temple, barking orders to begin the evacuation. People scrambled, priests and townsfolk alike rushing to help as the temple continued to shudder, the air thick with fear and tension.

Aeron's heart raced as he watched them move, each footstep echoing with urgency. The ground trembled beneath his feet, and he took one last, steadying breath, steeling himself for whatever waited beyond that dark rift in the sky.

Aeron, Seraphina, Aldric, Pinder, and Tate made their way through the trembling streets, weaving past townsfolk running in the opposite direction, their faces stricken with fear. The closer they got to the center of town, the more intense the tremors grew, rattling the earth beneath them as if the world itself was struggling to hold together.

As they rounded the final corner, the sight before them brought them to a halt.

Hovering just above the ground in the town square was a massive, gaping rift, a portal of utter darkness, like a tear ripped through the fabric of reality itself. The edges of the rift shimmered and undulated, an unnatural boundary where their world met an abyss devoid of all light. It hovered ominously, three to four feet above the cobblestones, casting an eerie glow as the dark energy pulsed with a slow, relentless rhythm, like a heartbeat in the void.

The air around it was thick and oppressive, charged with a silent hum that prickled their skin, as if the rift itself exuded a dark, sentient power. Within its depths, there was no texture, no form—only a vast, empty darkness that seemed to swallow everything, a place where even shadows disappeared into nothingness.

Seraphina shivered, her gaze locked on the portal. "It's like looking into the end of everything. There's nothing beyond it. Just emptiness."

Pinder shifted uneasily, his usual bravado tempered by the sheer terror of the sight. "I've seen plenty of dark corners in my time, but this… this isn't just dark. It's like it's waiting for something. Or someone."

Tate took a hesitant step closer, his eyes filled with awe and dread. "A void… an absolute void. If that's what's on the other side, then it's not a place meant for us."

Aeron felt a strange, familiar pull deep within his chest, a tug that seemed to resonate with the rift, as if it called to some buried part of him. His hand instinctively moved to the handle of his scythe, its weight grounding him even as the unknown beckoned.

"This wasn't just a portal," he said, eyes narrowing as he studied the swirling darkness. "It's a doorway between worlds, and it shouldn't be here."

The rift pulsed once more, the energy crackling in the air like silent thunder, and a faint, cold wind drifted from its depths, chilling them to the bone.

From within the swirling void of the portal, a shape began to emerge. At first, it was just the sharp, unmistakable curve of a scythe's blade, slicing through the darkness as if heralding something far worse. The metal gleamed with an unnatural light, an ethereal silver that caught every hint of darkness around it, amplifying the void rather than reflecting any of the dim surroundings.

Slowly, the rest of the figure followed—a tall, imposing form cloaked in robes so black they seemed woven from the night itself. Her armor glistened in jagged, obsidian hues, each piece crafted to resemble sharp, skeletal features, with intricate, spiked patterns etched into every surface. Shadows clung to her like living extensions, shifting and coiling around her form, giving her an aura of endless depth, a figure whose darkness went beyond mere absence of light.

Her face was shrouded by a hood, revealing only piercing eyes that glowed with a cold, merciless gleam, a shade somewhere between violet and deathly blue. They were intense, predatory, and wholly devoid of empathy—a gaze that had seen eons pass and held no kindness for the world before her. Her lips curled into a subtle, knowing smirk, as if the sight of Aeron and his companions was less a surprise and more a long-expected inevitability.

Her skin, what little of it was visible, appeared as pale as bone, contrasting sharply against the blackness surrounding her. Wisps of dark energy drifted from her form, like smoke rising from a long-dead flame, twisting around her fingers and trailing from the tips of her gauntlets.

As she fully emerged from the rift, she hovered above the ground, defying gravity as easily as she commanded death. Five or six feet up, she floated with a regal, terrifying grace, her scythe resting effortlessly in her grip. It was a weapon more akin to an extension of herself than a mere tool, the blade curved and wicked, humming with a faint, dark energy that mirrored the shadows swirling around her.

Merripen's presence alone sent a chill through the air, a quiet, deadly warning of the power she commanded. She regarded Aeron and his companions with a look of contemptuous amusement, her head tilting slightly as if already weighing their worth—and finding them wanting.

She said nothing, but her stance spoke volumes. This was no chance encounter. She had crossed the boundary between worlds for a reason, and her cold, unyielding gaze is fixed squarely on Aeron.

Merripen's gaze locked onto Aeron, her eyes gleaming with dark amusement as she began, her voice cold and dripping with a mock gentleness that did nothing to soften its razor edges. "So, you truly have no recollection of how you ended up here?" She let the question hang in the air, savoring the silence before she continued, "Allow me to fill in the gaps, then. Consider it a generous gesture from Death herself." She raised a hand, gesturing to herself with a cruel smirk. "Yes, I am Death, Aeron. And you, well, you are the thorn that never should have existed."
She shifted, floating slightly closer, her voice carrying a chilling clarity. "The tale, as you may not remember, is quite simple. I, Merripen, had earned my rightful place as Death's successor. I completed every trial, passed every test. I stood ready to ascend, to take on the mantle, to lead and guide the reapers as is my right. But then you appeared." Her smile vanished, replaced by a look of disdain. "You, a jealous reaper, saw fit to attack me, to stop my ascension. I had already proven myself; I was chosen. And yet, you—breaking the most sacred rule of our kind, the rule that forbid reapers from engaging in combat with one another—dared to strike at me, to deny me my birthright. Your insubordination, your insolence, tore through the very fabric of existence." She narrowed her eyes, her voice now sharp as steel, "That's why you ended up here. When we clashed, your actions broke the natural laws that bind our world. The rift you created hurled you into this mortal plane—a punishment, perhaps, or simply an accident. Either way, you were cast out, and I assumed the mantle I had rightfully earned."

Merripen paused, sweeping her scythe in an almost theatrical arc, the blade catching the eerie light around her as if drawing all shadows toward it. "Since then, I have led a flawless world, free from the disorder you so recklessly brought upon us. I am the balance that keeps death itself in harmony. But it seems... that balance is threatened, yet again."

Her eyes darkened as she leaned in closer, her voice dropping to a whisper that somehow still filled the square. "You see, Oblivion contacted me. Apparently, despite my perfect rule, there remains one problem. You, Aeron. It seems Oblivion—the great and terrible force that ensures our cosmic balance—is unable to handle you alone. You are a disruption, a thorn that Oblivion, in all its power, cannot pluck. It begged for my intervention, requesting I bring you back, that I clean up the mess it cannot handle."

She straightened, her expression hardening as she regarded him with a mixture of pity and contempt. "So here I am, come to return you to where you belong, to end this little charade you've created here on Earth. Because, Aeron, this world was never meant for you."

The dark portal behind her pulsed ominously, casting twisted shadows over the square, as Merripen hovered in silence, waiting for his response, her scythe gleaming in the foreboding gloom.

As Merripen's words settled over them, a stunned silence filled the square. Aeron's companions stared at her, expressions etched with disbelief and anger.

Seraphina was the first to find her voice, her eyes wide and fierce. "Jealous? A thing?" She stepped forward to face Merripen, her voice trembling with indignation. "How dare you? Aeron has done nothing but risk his life for others since the moment he woke up in this world. He's fought creatures, saved people, and protected towns that have nothing to do with your so-called mantle of Death. How can you stand there, claiming he's some... some petty, envious monster?"

Pinder, usually the first to break tension with humor, found no trace of it now. His face was tight with anger as he pointed a finger toward Merripen. "Jealous? I've seen Aeron face down mirages and shadows, things most of us could barely stand to look at, let alone fight. He's saved us all, countless times. Does that sound like the actions of someone driven by petty envy?"

Tate stepped forward, his brow furrowed as he regarded Merripen with a measured, almost academic curiosity that quickly turned to disdain. "I don't know what kind of twisted world you're running beyond that portal," he said, his voice laced with sarcasm, "but here on Earth, Aeron has been a force of good. The very idea that he's capable of 'jealous rage' is as absurd as it is insulting."

Merripen's eyes flickered from one to the other, an unreadable expression settling over her face, but the arguments didn't seem to faze her.

Aldric, who had been silently absorbing her words, finally spoke up, his voice calm but unyielding, "I don't know the dynamics of your world or the expectations of this role you call Death," he said, looking her squarely in the eye, "but the Aeron we know is a protector, a guardian. He's defended our people, our towns, without hesitation or expectation. If he's some supposed villain in your realm, then something is deeply wrong with your understanding of character."

Seraphina nodded, her voice rising as she addressed Merripen again, "Do you know what it means to give everything for others? To risk your life for people you barely know, with nothing to gain? Because that's who Aeron is. He's saved me, saved all of us, over and over. And you're telling us he's some jealous, scheming reaper?"

Merripen's face remained impassive, but there was a flicker of something cold in her gaze—a spark of irritation, perhaps, as she surveyed their loyalty and disbelief.

Pinder stepped forward again, refusing to back down. "Let's be clear here. Whatever happened in that world of yours, whatever mistakes or rivalries you think Aeron's guilty of, we don't see them here. Here, he's been a hero. Here, he's been the only one who stood between us and the darkness that's been trying to tear our lives apart. So tell me—how does that fit into your little story?"

Tate raised a hand, his voice sharper than usual, "You claim to know him as some malicious creature, but we know him as the one person we can trust. The one who's protected us every step of the way. So forgive us if we don't just blindly accept your version of things."

The team stood together, defiant and unyielding, each of them staring down Merripen with a mixture of loyalty and fury. The air was thick with tension, as if the very world around them held its breath, waiting for her response. Merripen watched them, her expression dark and unreadable, her eyes narrowing as if measuring the depth of their devotion to Aeron.

Merripen's lips twisted into a sneer, and a low, contemptuous laugh escaped her, cold and mocking. She cast her gaze over Aeron's companions, her eyes gleaming with a dark, almost feverish amusement.

"You think I care what a handful of mortal insects think?" she asked, her voice dripping with disdain, echoing through the square like the tolling of a death knell. "Your opinions, your little displays of loyalty... they are meaningless. Fleeting. I have watched kingdoms rise and fall. I have seen empires crumble to dust and souls cling desperately to life only to slip into the oblivion they feared. Compared to the eternity I command, you are nothing more than sparks in a dark, unfeeling cosmos—brief, inconsequential, and so very easy to extinguish."

Her gaze sharpened, and she leaned forward, her voice dropping to a cold, chilling whisper, "You have no idea who or what stands before you. I am Death itself, and in my hands lies the power over every breath, every heartbeat, every fragile flicker of life. I don't just witness the end; I decide it. I am the balance that holds the cosmos in place, the blade that cuts through existence itself. Your precious Aeron," —she spat his name with venom, "stands in defiance of that balance. And you fools dare to think you understand the depths of his betrayal?"

Merripen's grip tightened on her scythe, her knuckles white against the cold, black metal. "What I did to achieve my place as Death is beyond your comprehension. I endured, I proved my-self worthy, I was chosen. And then he," her eyes flashed with anger as she gestured toward Aeron, "had the audacity to dis-rupt everything. To question my right. A lesser being like him… to attack me, to break our laws… it's laughable. Unforgivable."

She glanced back at Aeron, her lips curving into a cruel smile, one that held no warmth, only malice. "The fact that you clung to this world, wrapped in your newfound admiration and love from mortals, doesn't change the truth. You are nothing more than a stray dog that defied its master, one that should have been put down long ago."

Turning her attention back to Aeron's companions, her voice grew louder, ringing with deadly conviction. "And yet here you all are, standing in my way, defending a traitor as if your words, your loyalty, hold any power over me. I am not here to convince you, nor am I interested in your naive, sentimental understand-ing of him. You cannot sway me with tales of heroism and kind-ness. These are illusions you mortals cling to in a desperate at-tempt to find meaning in your fleeting lives. They mean nothing to me, to the eternal balance I uphold."

She raised her scythe, its edge gleaming with dark energy that seemed to draw in the very light around it. "I am here for one purpose: to correct the blasphemous stain Aeron has left upon existence. He either returns with me to face the conse-quences of his actions, or he dies here and now, his soul oblite-rated into nonexistence. I do not care which path he chooses, nor do I care if you stand in my way."

A sinister smile spread across her face, and she regarded each of them with a look of amusement mixed with contempt. "Inter-fere, if you must. Let your precious hero choose his fate. But un-derstand this, mortals—you are nothing to me. I could end each of you with a flick of my wrist, snuffing out your lives as easily as a candle in the wind. And once you're gone, the world will continue, unbothered by the memory of your short, insignificant lives."

She floated a few feet higher, her presence growing even darker, her scythe arcing in the air like a blade of judgment hanging over them all. "So go ahead, cling to your loyalty, your misplaced trust in a traitor. But remember, I am Death, and I do not bargain, I do not forgive, and I certainly do not care."

Merripen hovered in silence, the dark energy from her form pulsing outward like a heartbeat, filling the air with a cold, oppressive weight that threatened to crush every soul present. The message was clear: she had come for Aeron, and nothing, neither loyalty nor love nor mortal defiance, would stand in her way.

Aeron took a steady step forward, meeting Merripen's cold, piercing gaze, his expression calm but filled with a deep sadness. His voice cut through the heavy silence, steady and sincere.

"You're right about one thing. I don't remember who I am or how I came to be here," he said, his tone even, almost gentle, but carrying a weight that resonated through the square. "But I don't have to remember to understand one thing about you. I can feel it—your hatred for me. It's not just some facade; it's real, pure, and deep. And if your hatred runs this deep, if it's fueled by something so raw… then there can only be one explanation." Aeron's gaze didn't waver, his words cutting through the tension like a blade, "You hate me because, somewhere in your heart, you truly believe I wronged you. I can see that. But I also know that the person I am now, the person I've become here on Earth—he wouldn't do the things you say. I wouldn't betray, wouldn't break the laws you cling to so fiercely." He let his words hang in the air, the weight of them seeming to deepen the shadows around them. "If you feel I've wronged you… then maybe the problem isn't with me, and maybe it isn't with this world. Maybe the issue you're trying to fix doesn't lie with me at all."

A quiet, profound silence filled the square, as Aeron's words settled over Merripen, her form silhouetted against the pulsing darkness of the portal behind her.

Merripen's face contorted with fury, her eyes blazing with a hatred that seemed to darken the very sky. Suddenly, she threw her head back and screamed, a sound so powerful, so primal, it reverberated like thunder, echoing across the heavens. The very earth beneath their feet trembled, and for a brief, terrifying moment, even the people miles away in Tideheaven heard the piercing cry as if she stood among them.

"Enough!" her voice boomed, laced with a divine wrath that chilled the blood of all who heard it. "I'm tired of this foolishness! If you will not return, then die here with your mortal friends!"

Merripen became a streak of dark lightning, a bolt of pure, furious energy hurtling directly toward Aeron. Her speed was incomprehensible, the air crackling with raw, dark power as she tore across the distance in an instant. Her form blurred, an embodiment of pure, vengeful intent, her scythe raised to deliver a blow that promised death.

The others barely registered her movement, their minds unable to process her swiftness. In the blink of an eye, Merripen's scythe arced down, aimed to cleave Aeron's head from his shoulders. The world seemed to hold its breath, the space between life and death so thin it could shatter with a single stroke.

But in that split second, before her blade could strike, Aeron's scythe rose instinctively, an unseen force guiding his hand. Steel met steel with a blinding flash, the clash of their weapons sending a shockwave that rippled through the square, throwing dust and debris outward in a ring.

Everyone around them stood frozen, eyes wide, hearts pounding, unable to comprehend what they'd just witnessed.

The air crackled, heavy with the aftermath of the violent impact, as Aeron and Merripen stood locked in place, his scythe holding hers at bay, the force of his instinctual defense rippled outward, leaving a stunned silence in its wake.

Merripen's eyes narrowed, her voice dripping with venomous disbelief. "So, you're fast now?" she sneered, circling him, her gaze flickering between Aeron and his scythe with a mixture of contempt and confusion. "That doesn't make any sense. I know you have your scythe, but you shouldn't be human and reaper at the same time. This is unheard of."

Aeron, sensing the briefest opening, leapt back, putting space between them, his feet barely touching the ground as he moved. He held his scythe steady, his grip firm and instinctive, his gaze fixed on Merripen as he searched her expression, trying to piece together the fractured memories she claimed belong to him.

Merripen's stance was unyielding, her eyes flashing with anger and something deeper—an unease she couldn't fully mask.

With a snarl, Merripen lunged at Aeron again, her scythe a blur of dark metal as she rained down an onslaught of attacks, each strike faster and more brutal than the last. It was like the beginning of their clash in Purgatory, when she'd tried to claim the mantle of Death, and he had narrowly evaded her fury. But now, with even greater precision, Aeron anticipated her every move, his instincts guiding him as though he danced this dance a thousand times before.

She swung her scythe in wide, furious arcs, each blow slicing through the air with a sharp, whistling sound. Aeron side-stepped one swing, leaning just out of reach as her blade carved through the space where his head had been only a split second before. Dust and gravel scattered underfoot as her weapon struck the ground, splintering the stone beneath with raw power.

He pivoted, bringing his own scythe up to parry her next blow, the clash of their weapons rang out like thunder. Sparks fly from the impact, illuminating the twisted shadows cast by the dark portal hovering above them. Merripen's movements were wild yet controlled, a blend of rage and deadly precision, but Aeron's body flowed as if he was moving with the currents of a silent river. Each strike she threw, he deflected effortlessly, his scythe seeming to anticipate her every maneuver.

Around them, the townspeople watched in awe and terror, the sheer power of their clash shaking the very ground. Market stalls were overturned, goods scattered across the square as the force of each impact sent shockwaves through the space. Walls cracked, windows shattered, and debris littered the cobblestone streets, evidence of the sheer fury embedded in each of Merripen's strikes.

Aeron dodged another vicious swipe, bending back as her scythe arced over his chest, missing him by mere inches. He rolled to the side, using the momentum to come up in a crouch, his eyes locked onto her, unwavering. Merripen snarled in frustration, launching herself forward again, her blade coming down with relentless force. But he parried and sidestepped, moving fluidly, each motion a reminder of the grace and precision he once held as a reaper.

"Stop. Dodging!" she growled, her anger intensifying as her attacks grew more ferocious. But for every strike she threw, Aeron was there, slipping out of reach, his scythe meeting hers in brief flashes of steel, deflecting, countering, moving as if their duel was a memory etched into his bones.

The square, once vibrant with life, was now shattered around them, littered with broken stone and dust swirling in the air. The dark portal loomed above, casting an eerie glow over the scene, framing their battle in a surreal, otherworldly light. To the onlookers, it was like watching gods clash, each move otherworldly, each dodge and parry an impossible feat of skill and speed.

But even as Merripen pressed forward with fury, Aeron's expression remained calm, focused—a stark contrast to her rage. It was as though he was in a trance, guided by instincts he never fully understood, his movements fluid and confident as he matched her blow for blow, his body reacting with a power he was only beginning to grasp.

Merripen swung her scythe in a powerful arc, and Aeron, focused on avoiding the lethal blade, sidestepped—only to find himself caught off guard by the scythe's hilt as Merripen twisted her weapon at the last second. With a fierce, brutal motion, she drove the blunt end straight into his chest.

As Merripen's hilt slammed into Aeron's chest, the force of the blow was cataclysmic. His body rocketed backward, slicing through the air with a speed that defied comprehension. He connected with the stone wall, the impact sending a deafening crack through the square, a sound like a mountain fracturing in half.

The wall buckled beneath the force, stones crumbling and mortar exploding in a cloud of dust and debris that filled the air, shrouding everything in a haze. Loose stones rained down, skittering across the ground with the sharp, grating sound of rock grinding against rock. A massive, gaping indentation was left in the wall, cracked and splintered where Aeron's form collided, the devastation radiating in jagged, splintered lines.

Aeron's body slumped within the broken recess, his head tilted, his eyes closed, his form motionless amid the settling debris. Dust swirled around him in thick plumes, blanketing the ground like ash after a fire. The square fell into a heavy silence, broken only by the faint sound of stones still tumbling from the fractured wall, each clattering echo magnifying the eerie stillness.

Merripen stood amidst the wreckage, her chest heaving, eyes locked on Aeron's still form. She lifted her head slowly, taking in the aftermath of her attack, a cruel, grim satisfaction settling on her face as she drew in a deep breath, savoring the silence that settled over the battlefield. Each fallen stone and cracked surface in the square was a testament to her unyielding power.

Merripen turned slowly, her gaze sweeping over the mortals gathered around the square, a twisted smile creeping across her face. "Your hero," she sneered, her voice dripping with disdain, "lies defeated by my power—the power of Death itself." She allowed the words to sink in, savoring the palpable fear in their wide-eyed faces. "I don't usually meddle in the useless affairs of humankind, but I can see that the loss of dear, pure-hearted Aeron will haunt you." She chuckled darkly, her eyes narrowing with cruel amusement. "So, out of the kindness of my heart, I'll do you a favor. I'll end your existence now and save you from all that sorrow."

Her gaze locked onto Seraphina, who stood frozen, a single tear tracing down her cheek as she stared at Aeron's lifeless form, her voice breaking as she called out to him. Merripen's smile sharpened, her eyes gleaming with malice. In an instant, her body shifted, and she bolted across the square with inhuman speed, a streak of dark energy, her gaze fixed like a predator on Seraphina.

The distance between them closed in a heartbeat, a final, terrifying blur of shadow and intent.

Just as Merripen closed in on Seraphina, her scythe poised to strike, a flicker of movement—a blur—caught her attention. In that split-second, she had no time to react before an explosion of force erupted between her and her target. The blast radiated like a storm unleashed, a shockwave so powerful that even Death herself was hurled back, her body rocketing across the square, crashing into the cobblestone as the ground trembled beneath the impact.

Dust billowed, swirling in thick, churning clouds that filled the air, obscuring everything in a murky haze. The townspeople shielded their faces from the gusts, eyes wide with shock, as Merripen regained her footing at the edge of the square, a look of stunned disbelief on her face. Slowly, the dust settled, the debris drifting to the ground in a near-silence that hung heavy over the square.

There, standing before Seraphina, was Aeron—no longer the farmer they'd known, but transformed, his presence filling the space with an undeniable, commanding power. Clad in dark, skeletal armor that gleamed like obsidian under the dim light, his form exuded an aura of otherworldly strength. The armor clung to him like it was forged from shadow, intricately designed to resemble the bones of some ancient being, yet made of a metal so dark it seemed to absorb the light around it.

His face, concealed beneath a hood, was shadowed, his eyes invisible, save for a faint, fierce glow that hinted at a power beyond mortal understanding. A torn, ghostly cape flowed from his shoulders, billowing as if stirred by an unseen wind, giving him an air of silent authority, of unyielding resolve. In his grip, his scythe pulsed with a purple aura, the blade gleaming with an edge so sharp it seemed to cut the very air around it.

Aeron's expression was different—no longer hesitant or conflicted, but calm and assured, a quiet confidence radiating from him as he stood like a sentinel, unyielding and immovable. There's a look of pure resolve etched onto his face, one that spoke of both strength and an understanding of his purpose. He held his scythe steady, the dark energy of his transformation swirling around him, a testament to the depth of power he now commanded.

Merripen's gaze locked on him, a flicker of fear breaking through her mask of disdain as she processed what just happened. The townspeople stared, breathless, as the tension in the air crackled like thunder, every eye fixed on the figure standing guard over his mortal friends.

Aeron's stance was unwavering, his presence a shielded between Merripen and those he swore to protect.

Aeron stood tall, his voice resonating with a clarity that

seemed to echo across the square, reverberating with the weight of his newfound memories. He fixed Merripen with an intense gaze, a quiet power beneath his words as he spoke.

"I was never unconscious, Merripen," he began, his tone steady yet brimming with authority. "When your strike landed, it shattered something within me, awakened the floodgates of memories that had been sealed, locked away. I remember everything now, every piece of who I am… who we were."

He took a slow, purposeful step forward, his scythe held low but steady, his eyes fixed unflinchingly on Merripen. "I stood beside you during the trials, treating you as an equal, as family, alongside the other ten reapers. I saw you as a sister, someone bound by purpose, by duty. I trusted you with that purpose, just as I trusted every other soul chosen by Death." His gaze darkened as a flash of sorrow crossed his face. "Death didn't choose me to ascend out of favoritism or some arbitrary decision. It was the cycle, Merripen. The mantle was meant to pass, as it always has, to the one Death deemed ready. When Death chose me, it was not a slight against you. It was simply the natural order of things, the way it has always been."

His voice softened, though the edge of grief remained. "But you… your jealousy, your need to seize what was never yours, clouded your judgment. You put the entire balance of existence at risk for a selfish hunger for power. And now, the cost of that choice has rippled through every plane, every thread of reality. Your actions have unleashed something far darker and far more destructive than you could have ever imagined."

Aeron's voice strengthened, laced with a resolute certainty. "I now know why Oblivion has been after me. Neither of us was ever meant to walk this plane, Merripen. We were chosen to serve in silence, in shadows, unseen by mortal eyes, bringing souls from one existence to the next. We were never meant to interfere in the lives of the living, to cross into the worlds of men. The reapers were never meant to be gods among mortals. We are custodians, not conquerors."

He stepped forward, closer to her, his voice unwavering. "This realm wasn't ours to shape, to rule, or to destroy. We have duties, ancient and sacred. And the moment we violated those duties, Oblivion awoke, seeing us as nothing more than a cosmic error, a fracture in the balance."

He leveled his gaze at her, an intensity radiating from him that seemed to pierce through the shadows she wielded. "And yet, here you are, clinging to your anger, clinging to a power that was never yours to wield. If you cannot see the path of destruction you've set in motion, then you are blinder than any mortal."

The quiet fury in his voice settled into something more profound, more certain. "If you are determined to stay and force this world to suffer for your ambition, then I will stand against you. For the sake of these mortals—for the sake of the balance we were sworn to protect."

As he finished, silence fell over the square, a weight settling in the air as the gravity of his words lingered. Everything had come to light—the truth, the betrayal, the tragic error that led to this moment. And now, with his purpose clear, Aeron was ready to face whatever darkness his former sister brought.

Merripen let out a bitter, mocking laugh, her voice laced with venom. "So what if you remember everything, Aeron?" she sneered, her eyes gleaming with dark satisfaction. "Do you think that changes anything? I am Death now. I'm the one who holds the power over life and death."

She took a step forward, her form radiating a fierce, chilling energy. "You speak of balance, of duty, of purpose," she continued, her tone dripping with disdain. "But all of that is beneath me now. I've transcended those petty chains. I no longer answer to rules or codes. I am Death incarnate, and I wield the power to decide who lives and who suffers an eternity in shadow."

Her gaze shifted to the mortals behind Aeron, lingering on

each face with a cold, calculating smile. "And your precious humans," she whispered, her voice soft and sinister, "will not escape my wrath. Out of spite, I will bring them to heel. I'll strip them of their souls and make them reapers under my command, bound to me for eternity."

She savored the words, her eyes glinting with malevolent delight. "They will serve me, Aeron, as shadows, slaves, for all time. And every moment they exist, they will remember that they were once cherished by you—a foolish protector who couldn't save them from their fate."

She leaned closer, her voice a twisted echo of triumph. "I will not only defeat you, I will dismantle everything you hold dear. And as you watch them suffer, helpless and chained, you will know it is all because of you. Because you dared to challenge me. Because you dared to stand in the way of my rightful power."

Merripen's words hung in the air, sharp and seething with bitterness, her ambition laid bare as she stood before him, her gaze locked with his, defiant and unwavering.

Aeron was firm, unwavering, a newfound confidence radiating from him as he met Merripen's eyes. His voice was calm, filled with a quiet power, each word cutting through the venom in her threats, "You can scoff all you want, Merripen," he began, his tone steady, almost compassionate, "but there's something you can't deny, even with all your bluster and hatred. I was chosen by Death, handpicked to carry on the mantle. You took that role by force, twisted it to fit your own ambition, but you were never meant for it. That throne you've tried to seize was never yours."

Aeron took a step closer, his voice low but piercing. "No matter how you forced yourself into this role, you never fully gained all the power that true Death holds. And you know it, don't you?" His words struck with undeniable certainty. "I can sense it, Merripen. The power you wield is fractured, incomplete."

He paused, allowing his words to settle over her, watching doubt flicker across her face, her composure breaking for just a moment.

"Deep down, you feel it, too," he continued, his gaze piercing, his voice carrying an almost sad understanding. "There was a hollowness inside you, an emptiness you couldn't quite fill, no matter how hard you try. You know that as much as you want to rule as Death, you are not, and will never be, complete." Aeron's expression softened. "That ache you feel, that shadow gnawing at the edges of your soul—it's the truth. You know you're just a pretender, clinging to something you can never truly hold. And that's why you hate me, isn't it? Because deep down, you know I was meant for this. And no matter how much power you try to wield, you'll never be whole."

The air between them grew heavy, Merripen's fierce façade wavering as Aeron's words found their mark, his truth stripping away the bravado, leaving the reality she tried so hard to ignore laid bare. The silence stretched, thick with the weight of everything unspoken.

Merripen's scream ripped through the air, a visceral, furious sound that seemed to tear at the very fabric of reality. The windows of the temple and nearby buildings shattered, sending shards of glass raining down like deadly rain. The people in the square brave enough to stay, fell to their knees, clutching their ears in agony, as the sheer force of her rage crashed over them.

"You don't know anything about me!" she screamed, her voice filled with a venomous hate that reverberated through the stone walls and echoed into the night.

Without hesitation, Merripen lunged forward, her scythe a flash of dark, jagged metal as she swung it down with deadly precision. Aeron met her strike with his own scythe, and the blades collided in a burst of power—purple and yellow auras erupting on impact, the clash lighting up the square in a blinding explosion. Sparks flew, and the force of their collision sent shockwaves outward, rattling the ground beneath them and creating cracks that spread like spiderwebs across the stone.

Merripen spun, striking at Aeron's side. Her blade caught him, slicing through his dark armor, and a thin line of glowing energy bled from the wound. Aeron grit his teeth, barely acknowledging the pain, and retaliated with a fierce upward slash. His scythe cut through the air, the purple aura trailing behind like a comet, and grazed Merripen's shoulder, tearing through her own armor and sending a spray of yellow light into the air.

They moved with inhuman speed, a blur of shadows and light as they danced around each other, each blow delivered with lethal intent. Merripen's movements were wild, fueled by anger and desperation, each swing of her scythe a testament to her raw fury. Aeron, by contrast, was measured, every strike calculated, his movements grounded in a deep understanding of his power, yet infused with the emotion of someone fighting for both his past and his future.

Merripen thrust her hand forward, and a wave of blinding yellow energy surged toward Aeron like a tidal wave. He braced himself, holding his scythe before him as the energy crashed into him, pushing him back, his feet skid across the ground. But he quickly countered, channeling his own aura—a deep, rich purple that pulsed with an ancient power—and hurled it forward in a fierce arc, the wave slicing through Merripen's energy and crashing into her chest.

She stumbled, but quickly regained her balance, her eyes blazing with renewed fury. With a snarl, she leaped into the air, her form twisting gracefully as she brought her scythe down in a vicious strike. Aeron sidestepped, the blade narrowly missing him, and retaliated with a powerful upward swing that connected with her side. Merripen was thrown back, landing hard against the cobblestone, but she quickly sprung to her feet, her scythe flashing as she charged once more.

They clashed again, scythe against scythe, the impact of their blows sending bursts of purple and yellow light exploding like fireworks. The ground trembled with each collision, and the air was thick with the energy they released, a storm of power and raw emotion swirling around them. Their faces were mere inches apart, each filled with an intensity that reflected the stakes of this battle.

Merripen snarled, thrusting her shoulder into Aeron and knocking him back, then followed up with a series of rapid, brutal strikes. Aeron blocked and dodged, but one strike slipped through, her scythe slicing across his forearm. He grunted, feeling the sting, but he channeled the pain into his next strike, swinging his scythe in a wide arc that caught Merripen across the chest, leaving a glowing line that pulsed with purple energy.

They separated, breathing heavily, the aura around each of them flickering like flames in a storm. Merripen's eyes were wild, her rage fueling her movements, while Aeron's gaze was steady, his determination burning as fiercely as her fury.

With a roar, Merripen summoned her energy, her aura flaring up around her in a blazing, golden light. She raised her scythe high, and the air around her seemed to bend and crackle with her power. Aeron matched her, his purple aura intensifying, casting deep shadows across his face. They charged each other, their war cries echoing through the square, two forces of nature colliding with everything they had, their scythes poised to strike as they closed the distance in a final, explosive clash.

The world held its breath as they surged forward, locked in a deadly, fateful collision, their powers blazing like twin stars on the brink of collapse.

Chapter 27: The Price of Balance

In the center of the shattered square, purple and yellow auras collided in a blinding cascade of light, swirling in furious waves that rippled outward. The ground quaked beneath the sheer force of their impending impact, stones cracking and debris lifting into the air, caught in the electric energy of the two combatants. Each step forward was a declaration, a clash not merely of power, but of destinies intertwining, each fighting for supremacy in a world that seemed to hold its breath, teetering on the edge of ruin.

The townspeople stood frozen, a silent circle around the battlefield. Faces were etched with a mix of horror and hope, breaths held tight as their eyes darted between Aeron and Merripen. Seraphina gripped Pinder's arm, her knuckles white, unable to tear her gaze from Aeron. She knew him not only as the quiet, determined man who walked with them but also as a force far beyond human, a being caught between realms. And yet, he was still hers, still bound by the love they shared, even if only for a fleeting moment in this mortal world.

Pinder watched, his jaw clenched, knowing all too well that this battle held the fate of not only their lives but the very balance of the cosmos. He felt an uncharacteristic lump in his throat, a rare moment of vulnerability for a man who lived with humor and swagger. But now, even he stood humbled, feeling the weight of something ancient and unbreakable, as if witnessing the turning of history itself.

Tate, usually a figure of calm intellect, stood in silent awe, his sharp mind grasping the enormity of this moment. Every theory, every piece of knowledge he'd uncovered about the cosmos, barely scratched the surface of the truth now unfolding before him. This was power in its rawest form, a collision between two titans, one of whom he had come to consider a friend.

The aura surrounding Aeron glowed with a deep, unearthly purple, a shade that seemed to pull in all light, an embodiment of every soul he had guided, every path he had crossed. It was vast and encompassing, a power woven from a responsibility he could now feel to his very core. Opposite him, Merripen's yellow energy pulsed like the scorching sun, a blinding, wrathful force driven by ambition, tainted with jealousy, yet forged from the same ancient power as Aeron's. The two auras seemed to twist and coil around each other, each trying to consume, to overpower.

And in that moment, everyone, whether mortal or divine, understood that the fate of both realms rested on the outcome of this clash.

Time itself seemed to hold its breath. The world faded away, and Aeron found himself in a strange pocket of silence. He hovered mid-air, locked in the surreal moment with Merripen, her fierce, blazing yellow aura frozen in place before him. Her scythe was poised, her eyes filled with unyielding resolve, yet neither of them moved. The roar of their auras, the crackling energy and war-torn world around them—all of it fell silent, like the calm at the eye of the storm.

In the stillness, Aeron's thoughts drifted. Memories flowed through him, vivid and unfiltered, each one a heartbeat in the strange silence.

He thought first of Koko. His companion in quiet moments, the steadfast friend who had been with him through fields and forests, carrying supplies without complaint. Aeron remembered the softness of Koko's coat, the warmth in his gaze, the way his eyes would light up at the sight of apples. The scene of Koko's final breath lingered in Aeron's mind, a moment of gentle peace amidst chaos—a life lost because of the path Aeron had unwittingly carved. Koko had been more than a mule; he was family, a steady presence in a world filled with shadows and violence. And now, his memory served as a reminder of all Aeron had to lose, and all he had left to protect.

His thoughts shift, almost instinctively, to Seraphina. Her face came to him like a soft glow amidst the darkness, her touch, her laughter, the warmth in her eyes when she looked at him. She had been there from the beginning, tending to his wounds when he first awoke, offering him compassion and kindness even when he was a stranger. He recalled their journey together—the quiet moments by the fire, the whispered conversations, and the nights they had shared in rare moments of peace. The love they found with each other had grounded him, anchoring him in a world he barely understood, a reminder that there was beauty and solace even amidst chaos. Her love had shown him that he was more than a weapon, more than a tool of fate. With her, he had become someone worth saving, someone who could belong.

He remembered Pinder, and the shared laughs, the jokes thrown across countless miles. Pinder, had been the ever-resilient spirit, the one to lighten the mood with his wit and bravado, who had become a friend without hesitation. Pinder had stood by him, had fought alongside him, had shared in this journey with an unbreakable loyalty. He thought of Pinder's smirk, his half-grumbled jests, his loyalty disguised as casual banter but more steadfast than stone. Through Pinder's friendship, Aeron had found the joy in camaraderie, the value of companionship. There had been light, even in the heaviest of moments.

Each memory unfurled in perfect clarity: the quiet villages, the desperate battles, the laughter shared, the lives lost. The journey up Mount Limbo with Seraphina by his side, the stolen glances and whispered promises. The journey to Tideheaven, the people they'd met, the knowledge they'd gained, and the sacrifices they'd been forced to make. The lessons etched into his soul—the moments that had shaped him.

And as Aeron floated in that moment, Merripen before him, he felt a surge of realization. This was the life he had fought to live, a life he had found by accident and came to cherish with every fiber of his being. He'd tasted love, felt the weight of friendship, and discovered the beauty of bonds that transcended purpose and duty. All of this—the love, the loyalty, the memories—they were part of him now. They were why he was fighting and standing firm against the darkness.

He gazed at Merripen, her frozen expression filled with hate, ambition, and a cold determination. And in that timeless moment, he understood. Her ambition had led her down a path he couldn't follow, a path she was willing to destroy everything to maintain. She hadn't known the quiet joys, the sacrifices, or the warmth he'd felt in this world. Her power had become a cage, locking her in a world of rage and isolation.

But Aeron had tasted freedom, he had found love, he had built a life worth cherishing. And now, he knew with every beat of his heart that this battle wasn't merely a power clash. It was the final defense of everything he had come to hold dear.

In the stillness, Aeron steeled himself, a profound calm settling over him. He may have to leave this world, but he would do so not as the weapon Merripen accused him of being, but as a man who had loved, lost, and found meaning. He would fight for the life he had cherished, for the love that had grounded him, for the friendships that had sustained him.

As time resumed its relentless march, Aeron's instincts took over. He twisted his body, narrowly avoiding Merripen's strike, her scythe slicing through the air inches from him. In one fluid, instinctual motion, he arced his own scythe, unpredictable yet precise, as if guided by an unseen force. There was a split-second of silence, a pause where even the air seemed to hold its breath.

Time halted once more, freezing them both mid-motion. Aeron hovered, his scythe embedded deeply within Merripen's chest, its edge piercing through her very essence. The blade was silent, almost reverent, as if sensing the gravity of the moment. Merripen's expression was frozen in shock, eyes wide as she looked down at the weapon lodged within her. She had yet to comprehend the truth—she didn't yet realize she was dead.

Aeron breathed deeply, his heart heavy with sorrow. He leaned forward, his voice barely a whisper, soft and filled with a regret that only one who had truly loved could feel. "I'm sorry, my sister," he murmured, the words catching in his throat. "I'm sorry you went astray. I'm sorry you never got to feel the things I have felt, the joys, the connections. I'm sorry it had to end this way."

A single tear formed in Merripen's eye, trembling on the edge before it began its descent down her cheek. For the briefest moment, her fierce, unyielding expression softened, a hint of vulnerability slipping through as she absorbed the weight of his words. She looked at him, as if realizing what could have been, what she lost by letting ambition and envy consume her.

The tear faded into nothingness, evaporating as it slid down her face, dissolving into the very air, just as her form began to fragment. Her image flickered, breaking apart like wisps of smoke caught in a gentle breeze. The golden light of her aura dimmed, piece by piece drifting away, her once-powerful figure fading into the void, leaving nothing but silence in her wake.

As the last remnants of her being dissipated, Aeron stood alone, his scythe hanging in the empty space where she once was. The battlefield quieted, the echoes of their clash settling, as if the world itself was mourning the loss of a soul that had gone too far astray.

The air around Aeron thickened, charged with an other-worldly energy as Merripen's last remnants dissolved into nothingness. The battlefield fell into a profound silence, as if every force in the universe had turned its gaze toward him, waiting, holding its breath. The weight of what he had done settled over him, a moment heavy with fate, and in that silence, he felt it pull, the shift in the very fabric of his being.

A dark aura began to swirl around him, spiraling upward in wisps of shadow and smoke, gathering strength and density as it coiled around his form. This wasn't the aura he once wielded. There was something infinitely older and more potent in its presence, something woven from the very essence of life and death. It pressed into him, sinking beneath his skin, reaching deep into his core, claiming every cell, every part of him, with a force that felt as if it could tear him apart. Yet, instead of breaking, he felt himself expanding, as if he was becoming something far larger, far more ancient than he ever was.

The scythe in his hand pulsed, merging with him, becoming an extension of his own will, his own soul. Its metal grew colder, darker, transforming into an ethereal weapon that hummed with silent authority. The weight of it was both heavy and light, as if it was bound to him by more than physical force—by a purpose, by an ancient duty that went beyond understanding.

A hood materialized, a shroud of midnight black settling over his head. Beneath it, shadows gathered, cloaking his face in a darkness so profound that even light couldn't pierce it. His armor shifted, fusing with the bones of his body, reshaping itself into something timeless and haunting, a seamless extension of death's own design. The metal gleamed with a dull luster, dark and impenetrable, like the void itself.

Power surged through him, filling him with a presence so vast he felt as though he could see every soul in existence, every flicker of life and death across all realms. He sensed the ebb and flow of mortality, the fragile line each soul walked, the whisper of their final moments. With each pulse of energy, knowledge floods his mind—ancient knowledge, truths about existence, life, and the delicate balance he now embodied. It felt like centuries of wisdom, countless lifetimes, all coursing through him, settling into place as though they were always part of him, waiting to be unlocked.

He stood taller, his form imposing, exuding an aura of inevitability. His eyes, hidden in the depths of the hood, burned with a faint, otherworldly light—purple, a testament to the power he wielded, but tinged with a coldness that spoke to his new role. He was no longer simply Aeron. He was the bridge between worlds, the hand that guided souls to the beyond. He was Death.

In the midst of his transformation, there was a moment of profound clarity, a stillness within him. He felt at peace, a strange, quiet acceptance. This was what he was always meant to become—the culmination of every struggle, every sacrifice.

As Aeron stood in his new form, an embodiment of Death itself, he heard Seraphina's voice calling out to him. There was a tremor in her tone, a desperate hope woven with fear, as if she was reaching out, searching for the Aeron she knew beneath this dark, powerful figure before her. He turned slowly, his gaze falling upon her and his companions—Seraphina, Pinder, Tate, each with faces etched with a mixture of awe, confusion, and grief.

"Aeron?" Seraphina's voice was soft, almost pleading. She stepped forward, her eyes searching, seeking assurance that he was still there, that the man she loved wasn't lost in this ascension.

Aeron's voice was calm, filled with a new depth, yet it held the warmth and familiarity they'd come to know, "I'm still here, Seraphina," he said, and though his words carried the weight of his transformation, there was a gentleness to them, a thread of the man he was. "All of you have given me strength, purpose beyond what I could have ever imagined. But... I now understand what I must do."

He looked over each of them, his gaze lingering as he addressed them all. "The imbalance that had plagued this world, that summoned Oblivion's wrath, it was because of me. Because I was here ... where I never should have been."

Tate's face, usually thoughtful, was marked by a deep sorrow as he realized the weight of Aeron's words. Pinder, uncharacteristically silent, clenches his fists, struggling to process the inevitability before him. Aeron felt their emotions, their pain, as keenly as his own, yet he knew this was the only path left.

"Oblivion will not stop until the imbalance is corrected," Aeron continued, his voice steady, resolute. "The only way to restore balance, to ensure this world is safe, is for me to return to Purgatory. To fulfill the role I was meant to take."

He took a long, final look at each of them, memories flooding his mind—moments of laughter, of friendship, of battles fought, each memory a testament to the bond they shared. "You have been more than companions. You've been my family. And though I go now, know that I carry each of you with me."

Aeron's gaze fell upon Seraphina, his heart tightening. He took a slow breath, preparing for the final farewell, the one that would be the hardest to give.

Seraphina's composure shattered, tears spilling down her cheeks as she stepped forward, reaching for Aeron. "Please," she sobbed, her voice breaking, "don't leave me here. Take me with you to Purgatory, or wherever you must go. I can't ... I can't lose you."

Aeron's gaze softened, his otherworldly form radiating an unexpected warmth as he looked at her. His eyes, shadowed within his hood, held a depth of understanding that went beyond any mortal wisdom. He gently shook his head, stepping forward to hold her hands, his touch surprisingly human, grounding.

"Seraphina," he said quietly, his voice steady but tender, "your journey here isn't over. There is still so much you're meant to do, so much left for you to experience in this world." He lifted one hand, brushing a tear from her cheek. "One day, our paths will cross again. I promise. When it is time for you to find peace, we will meet again."

He glanced down for the briefest moment, a subtle look lingering on her abdomen before his gaze returned to her face. It was a fleeting gesture, so brief that she barely registered it, yet something within her stirred—a faint, unexplainable warmth. She didn't fully understand it, but some part of her felt a new purpose, a continuation of their bond, as if a piece of him would always be with her.

Her tears continued to fall as she realized he couldn't stay. Seraphina's shoulders sagged, her grief overwhelming as she nodded, a quiet acceptance settling.

"I'll wait for you," she whispered, clinging to his promise.

Aeron leaned forward, pressing a gentle, final kiss to her forehead. "Goodbye, Seraphina," he murmured, his voice filled with a love that reached beyond life and death.

Pinder, who had been watching with reddened eyes, stepped forward, wrapping an arm around Seraphina as she struggled to stand. His own voice choked with emotion, but he forced a smirk, calling out, "You think you're making us cry, Aeron? Ha! We're just allergic to all this sentimental nonsense."

He lifted a hand in a farewell salute, his humor masking the ache in his heart. "Safe travels, you glorified, beet farmer!"

Aeron smiled one last time, then turned toward the portal. Without a second glance, he stepped forward, his form dissolving into the darkness, merging with the shadows of Purgatory as the portal shuddered and collapsed around him, closing the doorway between worlds.

The silence settled, deep and heavy, until their eyes fell on the ground beneath where the portal had been. Aeron's human body lay motionless, seemingly untouched by his transformation, a final echo of his mortal self left behind.

Seraphina, held up by Pinder's arm, stared at the body, a mixture of grief and bittersweet understanding flooding her heart.

Seraphina gasped as Aeron's body stirred, a faint movement that sent a jolt of shock through the group. For a breathless moment, hope flared within each of them, a spark against the darkness of their loss. Seraphina rushed forward, tears streaking down her cheeks, her hands trembling as she cradled his face, her voice a broken whisper.

"Aeron? Aeron, please. Is it really you?" she choked out, her heart pounding as she searched his eyes.

But as his eyelids fluttered open, a different light filled them—confused, soft, and unfamiliar. He blinked, looking around in bewilderment. "Seraphina? Where am I?" His gaze shifted to the faces around him, each one full of astonishment, their hope fading into something deeper, more resigned. "Who… who are all these people? And … why does my farm look like a city?"

Silence fell, heavy and profound, as realization set in. This wasn't Aeron. Not anymore. The spirit they knew, the fierce reaper who had fought by their sides, loved and protected them, was gone. This was Roland, the farmer Aeron had once inhabited, awoken in his own body, unaware of the journey it had taken without him.

Seraphina's hands dropped, her fingers brushing his cheek one last time as the weight of the truth settled over her heart. Her tears fell quietly now, no longer with the hope of reunion but with a profound acceptance of what had passed.

Pinder, unable to look at her grief-stricken face, shifted his gaze to the ground, a silent farewell lingering in his eyes. Tate took a step back, his shoulders slumped, understanding that this was the price of balance—the price of letting go.

They each took in the quiet farmer before them, a man who knew nothing of their shared battles or the bond that had formed between them and Aeron. With heavy hearts, they understood that Aeron, the reaper, the hero, had returned to the realm he was meant to guard. The man they loved, the friend they fought beside, was truly gone.

And as Roland stared at them in confusion, the bittersweet knowledge filled the silence—a life restored, and a life lost. They knew it was the way things had to be, yet the ache of his absence weighed on each of them, leaving an empty place in their hearts where Aeron's memory would forever remain.

Aeron stepped into the shadowed vastness of Purgatory, his presence now commanding, cloaked in the quiet, intense power of Death itself. Before him stood the Throne of the Reapers, a dark monolith towering above the endless void. Its ancient stone gleamed faintly, marked by the eternal weight of those who had come before, each one carrying the responsibilities that now rested upon him. The throne was his, a testament to the role he must uphold, an anchor in the chaos of existence.

Around him, ten reapers stood in silent vigil, their expressions a mixture of respect and acceptance as they acknowledged him as their equal and leader. No longer an outsider or an heir. Beyond them, the other three Horsemen of the Apocalypse— War, Famine, and Conquest—watched him with a newfound envy and reverence, seeing in him a strength they had not foreseen. Aeron felt the weight of their gaze, the recognition that he was now among them, bound by duty but transformed by his own journey.

He took in the somber assembly, the endless expanse of Purgatory, and the throne that loomed like a reminder of everything he'd lost and gained. The reality of his transformation, of the sacrifices he had made and the humanity he had left behind, settled over him, deeper than any wound. He was Death, but he was also Aeron, and the paradox of his existence weighed heavily on his soul.

Just as the silence began to press around him, a sound broke through—a soft, familiar rhythm echoing in the darkness, a flopping, steady clip of hooves on the shadowed ground. Aeron's heart stirred, the echo of a life left behind mingling with the reverence of his new realm. He turned, and there, emerging from the shadows with a gentle determination, was Koko.

The loyal mule stepped forward, his coat darker now, his form as powerful and ethereal as the realm he now inhabited. His eyes held a quiet intelligence, a peace that spoke of an eternal bond, one that transcended life and death. In the realm of shadows, he was transformed—a glorious, noble creature, a dark steed befitting the realm of Death itself.

Aeron's gaze softened, and he moved toward Koko, reaching out to place a hand on his loyal companion's neck. In Koko's steady, unwavering presence, he felt the faint warmth of all he fought for, the remnants of the life he left behind. Even in death, Koko had chosen to stand beside him, the two of them bound by loyalty and friendship.

In that silent moment, Aeron understood that, for all the power and responsibility he now bore, he wasn't alone. He had his companions in this realm, and with Koko by his side, he found a small, quiet solace amidst the vast responsibilities ahead.

As he stood before his throne, surrounded by the reapers, the Horsemen, and his steadfast companion, Aeron accepted the profound balance he had become, knowing that together they would face whatever laid beyond.

ABOUT THE AUTHOR

Kevin M. Broadway, known in online gaming as "Noisi", hails from the small town of Robeline in Natchitoches Parish, Louisiana. Growing up with a love for the outdoors, hunting, fishing, and camping, he built his life around hard work and resilience. From early days washing dishes in a local restaurant to managing them, Kevin always pushed forward, eventually exploring a range of jobs from corrections to factory work with cranes and forklifts, cable installation, and even the oil fields of Wyoming.

After returning to Louisiana, he resumed work in corrections and ultimately graduated from the police academy at 33. Now a patrol deputy with the Sheriff's Department, Kevin is pursuing his career goal of becoming a K9 deputy. His downtime involves gaming, collecting vintage Pokémon cards, and heading outdoors for a bit of hunting and fishing. As a proud father of two boys and a self-described "loving, yet asshole of a husband," Kevin never saw himself writing a book. Yet, a story he'd carried in his mind for years kept calling, and he finally decided to see where it might lead. His life goal? To someday own a house on the lake where he can balance the demands of work with the tranquility of nature.

Liked this book?
Please leave a review!

Reviews are important to authors and publishers.
Please take a moment to leave a review on Amazon and/or Goodreads.

They help authors sell more books.

20-25 reviews and Amazon includes the book in the "Also Bought" and
"You Might Like" lists.
50-70 reviews and Amazon highlights the book in spotlight positions and in
its newsletter.

Thank you!